The Strangest LOVE

Where the curse ends ...
{Inspired by Real Life Experiences}

Melanie Calhoun

authorHOUSE®

AuthorHouse™
1663 Liberty Drive
Bloomington, IN 47403
www.authorhouse.com
Phone: 1 (800) 839-8640

Published by AuthorHouse   09/14/2015

ISBN: 978-1-5049-3369-8 (sc)
ISBN: 978-1-5049-3368-1 (e)

Contents

Author's-Brief Bio

In the city of Detroit during what many refer to as the era of the "crack epidemic" during the early 1980s, where the beautiful sounds of music no longer danced around Motown, and the fancy cars no longer ran this city's motor, a royal entity was produced. Melanie "GODmadeQueen" was born. Not to what many would view as a normal life, but far more abnormal. She was taken away from her natural birth parents at three months old, and placed in an orphanage until she was adopted. That's when her life of tragedies began. Not having any one to trust, she turned to writing. She believes this is her gift not only to others, but a therapeutic gift to herself.

"As a child, I began to write. I didn't recognize what it was, considering so many ignored me. But in kindergarten, my teacher told me, "Melanie, this is beautiful poetry." Since then, my best friend was a pen, my home girl was a book, and I gave them beautiful sceneries and

catchy hooks. I realized it's a gift. I am a Writer in addition to being a Poet" -**GODmadeQueen.**

Writing has always been my passion. Being an inspirational author has always been my dream. I entered the Detroit Public Schools creative writing contest and won 1st place for several consecutive years beginning in 1st grade. I also won 1st place in the Women's Writing Contest while attending Detroit Job Corp. I love creating inspirational, educational, page-turning, and entertaining novels such as *The Strangest Love* expanding from bits and pieces of my own personal experiences to inspire generations. In addition to being a writer, I am also a motivational speaker, and a Publish Poet with a Spoken Word CD titled "My Words, My Life- Inner desire to inspire" sold everywhere music is sold on-line.

- Melanie 'GODmadeQueen' Calhoun

Introduction

    Staring at the aqua blue river of Detroit, I crave to be those waves. I would like for my life to flow through opportunity and space, receiving the energy to transfer this pain. If I could build up enough courage and strength to tell him this sick affair is over, I don't know how he would react. How did it get this deep? How did it get this far?

Chapter 1

I often sat alone reminiscing and reflecting on my childhood. The feelings of desperately needing and desiring to be loved always penetrated my thoughts. *Mama neglected me. I blame it on Mama. Yeah, it's Mama's fault.* Now that I think about it, I can remember as far back as when I was about five years old. Mama opened the door to a closet of knives, spears, bows, and arrows—sharp enough for my tiny heart to search for a wound suppressor.

Reminiscing …

Mama and I lived in the Brewster Projects. Many say it's the starting point for African Americans who were receiving low incomes. Mama was rarely home. Every day she would get dressed in short skirts, black fishnet stockings, and her red Ronald McDonald lipstick. She would kiss me on my cheek and inform me she was going to work. She always said, "Victoria, Mama's using what she got to get all the things she wants. When you get a little older, Mama will teach you too."

I didn't know then exactly what Mama meant by that. She often made sure I stayed with Mama Jackson, my best friend Latoya's mom.

But sometimes Mama would ask Uncle Stanley—whom we called "Stan" for short—to watch me as well. The majority of the time, Uncle Stan volunteered to keep me.

Staying with Uncle Stan was never a problem for me until the day he tickled me in a way that changed my entire perception of him. On this one particular day, I heard Mama asking Uncle Stan if he would watch me again. I stood near the top of the stairs as I tuned my ears in to their conversation:

"Stan, I need you to watch Victoria again."

"Tammy, you know I love Victoria. You know how good ole Uncle Stan loves the kids."

I stood at the top of the stairs smiling. I knew Uncle Stan loved me, because he was always so nice to me. He wore a lot of flashy jewelry and nice, fancy clothes. When I walked through the projects with Latoya and her brother Romeo, I overheard Romeo and his friends saying how they wanted to be just like Stan when they grew up. Though I was a little girl, I knew Uncle Stan had something a lot of people wanted. That further led me to believe he was in a position of power, especially when he pulled his car up in the projects.

Everyone ran after his shiny, cherry-red-and-black, drop-top 1964 Ford Galaxy 500 as if he were driving the ice cream truck. Having someone who everyone admired loving me, made me feel important.

"Victoria, Mama's got to go to work. Your Uncle Stan is down here. I'll see you later on," she yelled. "Stan, you're a sick bastard. I hate you!" she screamed before slamming the door shut behind her.

That's something Mama did regularly. She would often curse Stan out when she was the one who left me. At that time, I couldn't understand why Mama cursed at Stan and told him how much she hated him. I didn't see any reason at all to hate him, especially since I spent the majority of my days with him. Even though Mama never spent a lot of time with me, I valued every moment when she did. I wished there was some way I could have convinced her to love me, but I couldn't do it. I often had dreams about my efforts in trying to gain her love, but apparently they were rejected.

I actually remember one particular day, in the early 1990's, as if it were yesterday …

Mama Didn't Love Me Anymore

I sat in the backseat of Uncle Jared's station wagon holding my bag, staring out the window and admiring how the trees ran away from us. I knew there was a chance I was not going back to Mama's house. She kept telling Uncle Jared she was going to '*get rid of the problem*'. I overheard them arguing about Stan being at the house every day and leaving my baby sister Jasmine at his mama's house all the time.

I didn't see Jasmine much after Mama no longer carried her in her belly. I saw Jasmine a few times when Mama first came home from the hospital. For some reason, Uncle Jared's mother told Mama she didn't want Jasmine anywhere near Stan. I wish I was old enough to understand what was going on then, but my little brain could not process much at that time.

"This is the house right here, Jared," Mama said as she pointed to a big, pretty house with a lot of flowers. "Stop the freakin' car, dammit. You're passing it!" Mama yelled.

Uncle Jared stopped the car, and Mama opened the door. She got out and lifted the latch on the side of the passenger seat.

"Okay, Victoria, get your bag and come on. Hurry, child! I don't know what is wrong with you. You move so damn slow. Bring your ass on now," Mama said as she pulled my hand, dragging me from the backseat.

"Listen here, Victoria," she said as tears rolled down her caramel cheeks, "Mama is so sorry, but I can't give you everything you need right now. I'm doing the best I know how to do. I know you don't understand it right now, but trust me, Victoria. I know you living here with your uncle is the best thing for you right now. Plus you know how much he loves you," she explained while attempting to smile as she wiped her tears. "Motherhood doesn't come with a handbook and instructions, you know. When you get older and have your own kids, you will understand. My mother did me this way, and this is the only way I know. Your uncle gone get you enrolled in school and will make sure you have food every day. And, guess what?"

"What, Mama?" I asked while wiping the tears falling from my eyes.

"You don't have to worry about them damn roaches crawling in your bed, and you're gonna have lights. Plus you can meet you some new friends and sleep without hearing all those gunshots. Look at the grass and flowers." She pointed to all the different houses, including Uncle Stan's. "You got yourself flowers and thangs; we don't have this type of stuff in the projects. You mind your manners, and listen to what your uncle tells you—you hear? I'll call and check on you sometime. I love you. Now jump back there and give your baby sister a kiss."

She lifted her seat up again, and I leaned over and kissed Jasmine, who was sitting in her car seat. "I love you, Jasmine," I whispered in her ear.

"All right, go on now." Mama shooed me away while turning her head. I assume it was to hide her tears. I don't know why Mama didn't seem to love me. She said she did, but I felt as if she didn't, or else she would not have left me.

I remember standing on the curb, staring at Mama with a face full of tears and wondering when I would ever see her again. Jasmine's daddy honked the horn, and pulled off.

I guess Uncle Stan was expecting me, because he walked outside and grabbed my grocery bag containing a twenty-five-cent bag of Doritos, a twenty-five-cent juice, and a bag of ramen noodles as I held on to my Raggedy Ann doll. He picked me up and carried me to my room. Christine—my uncle's fiancée—stood in the doorway with her arms folded, hugging herself as she dried the tears falling from her eyes.

Uncle Stan took me to my room. He had it fixed up very nice. It was painted pink with pink sheets, blankets, big pillows with stuffed animals, and teddy bears sat on the bed. I had my little pink television sitting on my pink and white dresser. There were stars and little moons on the ceiling that glowed in the dark. He opened my closet. I had brand new clothes. My drawers were filled with panties, t-shirts, and pajamas. I had a closet full of brand-new shoes, and all types of toys.

Christine walked into the room smiling. "You like?" she asked. "Your uncle let me decorate it nice for you. I figured since I don't have any kids of my own, I could get my practice out on you. I always wanted a room like this." She leaned down on her knees, wiping away my tears. She hugged me tight and said, "Victoria, your uncle must really love you."

I smiled and looked at Uncle Stan. "Yeah, I guess he does, huh?"

Stan came into my room and closed the door. He whispered in my ear, "Victoria, remember what I told you. Never tell anyone about the way we play. We only have each other. Never tell anybody our personal business."

He informed me if I told anyone about the way we played, people would get mad, jealous and they would try to separate us. That's something I refused to let happen. I knew I would never tell our secret. Besides, if I did and Uncle Stan and I separated, I didn't have anywhere else to go. Mama Jackson already has three kids; therefore, living with her was not an option. Besides, having a bond with a female other than my own mother was hard for me to do. I love Mama Jackson as if she were my own mom, but she's Toya's mom, not mine. My mother left me.

When Mama left me, my entire attitude changed. My thoughts about everything changed, including my feelings for my Uncle Stan. I somehow threw out the disgusting feeling I had when he touched me out the window. He was all I had left in the world. I remember that day so clearly. I guess the day Mama left me was the day I realized Uncle Stan was all I had and he truly loved me.

Stan explained he had to go to court so he could become my legal guardian and obtain full custody of me. He told me in order for us to stay together he had to have a girlfriend or a wife. He said his engagement to Christine was for us as a family. He needed to appear as a *'perfect father figure'* in the eyes of the system. Uncle Stan informed me living in the State of Michigan, the legal system of Child Welfare would not allow a single man to obtain custody of a young girl; there had to be an adult female residing in the home.

Bye Christine!

The court awarded Uncle Stan full custody and made the adoption finalized. About two years after the adoption was final he broke it off with Christine. I sat in my room listening as they argued back and forth.

"Christine, I need you to leave!" Uncle Stan yelled. "Take your broke ass back to the projects! You are not getting a free ride here. I asked you to go to school or at least clean up around here- cook or something, but No! You instead sit around the house on your lazy ass chit chatting on the phone with them broke, lonely ass girlfriends of yours. Call and tell them to come get you since y'all so damn close! It doesn't make any since every day I get home from work Victoria has not been fed nor has the house been cleaned. I told you to make sure she is taken care of!" he yelled.

"You treat her better than me. You always want me to cater to Victoria. Why is she so special? Her Mother left her besides she aint yo kid no way!" She cried and yelled.

As soon as she said that, I heard a big clap. I cracked my door open and stuck my head out just enough to see what was going on. I noticed Christine lying on the floor. I guess Uncle Stan had done slapped the taste out her mouth. Sad to say, but I had no sympathy for her. She had no right discussing my mother and her leaving me at all. I sat there wiping the tears from my eyes because Christine's comment was like 100% Isopropyl to a severely scraped knee.

I sat in my room listening to all the yelling back and forth. I hate when people argue and I most definitely hate when people cry, but listening to Christine cry brought a smile to my face. I'm not sure if it was because she was experiencing the same pain I felt when she brought up my mom or if it was just that she was becoming a bit of nuisance.

I listened to her crying and begging Uncle Stan to give her another chance. I admit Christine was gorgeous; nice slim figure, long natural hair, pretty brown complexion, but Stan was right- she was lazy. I usually had to wait until he got off work to get some food when I got home from school. He said I was his princess and he was definitely not buying that.

I stood up and walked outside my bedroom door. I could not help but to notice Christine resembling a child as she sat on the floor kicking her legs and pouting like a baby, throwing a tantrum. From the looks of her actions someone would assume she was my age at the time, but even I did not throw tantrums such as her.

When Christine's friends came to pick her up she looked at me and rolled her eyes while I smiled at her thinking, *yeah take your lazy butt on with your girls. This is my Uncles house!* I thought to myself.

Throughout the duration of the two and a half years I had been living with Stan and Christine, I learned a great deal in school. I actually loved my school. I loved my class and my teachers.

My Teacher Mrs. Kittles said I had a special talent which is the gift of poetry. She entered my Poem titled "Butterflies" in a poetry contest and I won first place. Stan often reminded me of how smart I was. He has always explained to me I was "ahead of my time" just as my teachers did. Though, I never knew what either of them meant at that time.

Stan was very impressed with me maintaining all A's and all 1's in citizenship. When he visited my school my teachers would often tell him, "Whatever you are doing to this child, you are raising her right. You are doing an excellent job."

Hearing those comments made him quite proud of me at least that's what he tells me. He loved to see and hear about me behaving myself and minded my manners. I knew it must have made him happy considering he would reward me with shopping sprees and trips to the hair salon.

When Stan was nice to me and kept his hands to himself, it made me feel good. I honestly believed that's what our love should have been about, but soon did he change. I guess I would say he went back to his old ways about two or three months after Christine left. For some odd reason, he felt it necessary to remind me when I turned twelve he was really going to show me how much he loved me.

The inner cry of a butterfly craving to fly speculated my deepest emotions. The words that exited the lips of Stan imitated whistles of a birds call. His constant repetition of reminders, describing a day and age where him showing his unclaimed love to me anticipated around the curves of my cocoon were heard, but ignored. Wishing and hoping that day would never come was like wishing and hoping I would never need oxygen in order to breathe. It seemed somewhat impossible.

By this time, I had already reached my tender age of nine while my once known as rose buds were now occupying a 32b. I was expected to grow a lot more; at least that's what the Doctor said. So much for the embryo cocoon with no formation, I basically had wings- at least I was wearing them.

On the day I crossed over to my "woman hood" I thought something was wrong with me. I was scared to tell Stan, but when I told him, he asked me to have a seat as he began talking, "Victoria you have now reached puberty which is a normal process for a girl your age. What you're experiencing is most commonly known as a menstrual period and you'll begin to have them every month. So, now you'll need to write down today's date and look to expect this same thing every month around this time."

I sat there staring at him wondering how he could possibly know what I was experiencing as a girl. He obviously picked up on the expression my face refused to hide when he stated, "I guess you're wondering how I know all this huh?" He then began to explain he knew more than average about women and the way the female body operates because he grew up in a house with all females, with my mom being amongst those particular females who also included my grandmother and my Aunt Jessie. Plus, he said he had a lot of different girlfriends and he also read a lot of books on the study of the female body. He almost often referenced a lot from Aunt Jesse as he admired her a great deal.

I remember when I turned twelve years old, Stan threw me a party at Aunt Jessie's house. She had 7 kids and at that time she was pregnant. I thought to myself *wow Auntie, how many are you going to have?* She has long wavy hair sort of like mine. My hair flows like water waves considering it was almost down to the middle of my back. Stan had been taking me to the hair salon since I moved in with him because he said he did not know how to do hair and I knew Christine didn't either because her hair was looking a hot mess the majority of the time.

My best friend Toy and I were going to the same hair salon. We actually went the day of my party and got our hair dyed with golden blond streaks. Once we left the salon she ended up staying over for my birthday party. Mama Jackson sent me a blue jean DKNY jean and matching jacket set with the matching blue jean DKNY shoes.

At twelve years old, I wore a size twelve shirt and pants, but full body suites were my preference. The rest of my gifts received were: a full body guess jumpsuit, four pair of guess jeans, four guess tops, two pair of k-Swiss, a pair of Jordan's and a small guess jean purse. I liked guess more than Polo and Tommy Hilfiger at that time besides, Stan said *Hilfiger didn't want black people to wear his clothes*, whatever that meant.

The gifts I received at my birthday party had me stepping in middle school looking extra nice. I was actually supposed to be in the seventh grade, but since my mom was "cracked out and prostituting" as Stan says, she didn't get me registered on time. It didn't matter because I guess Stan and Mama Jackson's nice taste in clothing and shoes allowed me to set the fashion trends and standards at my middle school. So of course, my level of being behind was neither an issue nor discussion when everything I wore cost more than half of my classmates parents rent.

My first year in middle school, the sixth grade and I was the bomb. Yes, I was that deal. So many eighth grade boys wanted my phone number and the eighth grade girls hated it. Many of the eighth grade females had little organizations, clicks, and gangs as they call it. I was the talk of the eight graders. The fact I was a middle school freshman had nothing to do with it. I had everything all the girls my age and older wanted, but simply did not have.

I had the long wavy hair with blond streaks, big gold hoop earrings, top of the line clothing and shoes, nice body which included my 38C breast which seemed as if they were never going to stop growing, not to mention a very pretty face. It seemed as if I was the only one who did not have a face full of pimples. All of the things I possessed- brought or simply genetics got me in a conflict I preferred not to be associated with.

My entire character intimidated a group of eight grade females who jumped on me. They walked up to me and started swinging. As they were punching me, I heard a few of them saying I thought I was better than everybody. As I fought them back I could not help, but to think about the fact that I never made that statement. I never thought I was better than anyone. I guess that's how they felt about me. They envied my outer appearance and assumed because I stayed to myself, not to mention I had the latest name brand attire on the market that I thought I was better than them.

Getting beat up was not sitting well with me. I was by myself so I had to fight back. As a matter of fact, I let them have it. I don't know where all my aggression came from, but I beat at least three of them up pretty badly. I was scared to be quite honest. I guess it's true when they say someone who is scared will tear your behind up. I didn't show I was scared, but I was that's no lie. The security guard broke up the fight and took us to the principal's office.

As we were sitting in the principal's office I looked at the girls, "now was all that called for? Now y'all are bleeding because of jealousy." I guess seeing blood on their faces knowing that it was not mine gave me time to gloat. Tracey, who I guess was the "leader" of their gang yelled, "Shut up before I call my big sister to come shoot you!"

With no hesitation I replied, "Oh you little jealous tricks, my Uncle is part of a mafia and you will be dead before you can get your sister on the phone."

Mrs. Wiggins who was the principal at that time came in after she had the secretary call our parents. Mrs. Wiggins called me in her office. "So, what's the problem Victoria? I haven't had any trouble out of you since you been here. Why are you fighting?" she asked.

"I was standing outside when that group of females" as I pointed at each one of them, "walked over to me and began to hit me. The only reaction that came to mind was to defend myself and that's exactly what I did. I believe they mentioned I thought I was better than everybody or something like that." I replied.

"Well Victoria, do you think you are better than everyone else? I see you with all your designer clothes, with your long pretty hair and I never see you associating with any of your peers. Victoria, do you think you're better than everyone else?"

That question that eased from her lips triggered the frown that raised my left eyebrow. I sat there with my legs crossed in my turquoise, orange and blue Prada blouse and matching jeans and jacket; with my turquoise and white Air Jordan's. "First of all Mrs. Wiggins, I am a student and just because I carry myself in a way young ladies should and I wear some of the finer clothes does not make me feel like I am any different or any better than anyone else" I responded.

She tilted her glasses with the long knock off pearl string connected to them that went around the back of her neck, as her eyes stared directly at me. "Ms. Campbell, just so you know, I will have to suspend you for three days."

I looked out Mrs. Wiggin's office window and noticed Stan pulling up. He had gotten rid of his shiny cherry red and black drop top 1964 Ford Galaxie and gotten himself a drop top 1989 Jaguar XJS Convertible, candy apple red with red leather seats, red black tint on the windows with two big red and black cloth material dice hanging over his rear view mirror.

Stan loves his old school cars. Every guy we rode past loved his cars also. He entered and won second place in the 2001 Detroit Dream Cruise. I actually had no idea where Uncle Stan worked, but I did know whatever he did he made a lot of money. People still admire him just as much now as they always have. When I told those girls about Stan being in a mafia I was making it up, but I figured maybe it could have been true. He had so many guy friends and they were all riding in nice cars and dressed in nice fancy clothes.

One thing I can truly say about Stan is he has never been caught looking like he's *having a bad day*. He looked exceptionally well when he entered Mrs. Wiggin's office. Those gang of females most definitely understood why I looked the way I do. They all sat there staring at him as if he was a celebrity. I must admit, Stan was looking very fly in his black and grey Armani suit.

Once Stan entered the office, he spoke to Mrs. Wiggins as he sat in the seat next to me. He then asked me what happened. I told him how those girls jumped me and assumed I thought I was better than everyone because of the way I dress and carry myself. I then explained to him how Mrs. Wiggins confronted me about the same issue and questioned if I thought I was better than everyone. I guess that question triggered the both of us because as soon as I told him that, he raised his eyebrow just as I had, sat up in his seat and leaned over to Mrs. Wiggin's desk. "Let me get this straight, you questioned my niece, asking her if she thought she was better than others because of the way she carries herself and the way she dresses? Victoria is a child and that is not a question you should have asked her anyway." He stated.

Mrs. Wiggins cleared her throat "According to Victoria, she is not a little girl, she is a young lady" was her only response.

I could tell Mrs. Wiggins comment triggered a nerve in Stan because his veins began to pop out of his forehead when he replied, "School is supposed to be a place where learning takes place and by you being the Principal, I would think that you should enforce and teach them instead of focusing on fashion. That's the problem with these schools now! You all are so busy being envious and judging of the kids based on their appearances, you all cannot focus on teaching them! Mrs. Wiggins you do not have to worry about Victoria anymore. I will be removing her from this unprofessional school any way." He stood up and grabbed my hand. "Oh and by the way Mrs. Wiggins, you'll be hearing from my attorney. You better get your act together or this will be another one of Detroit Public Schools that will be closing."

As we walked out her office, I noticed her sitting there with her mouth wide open. It was apparent that she felt very stupid. I also glanced at the girls who jumped me thinking of how I couldn't wait to tell my best friend Toy and our little click up in the Brewster's Projects. I wanted to catch them alone, hopefully one by one and make them feel the pain. That's something Toy and I were known for; winning any fights we were faced with.

I am so thankful Stan let me continue spending the night over Toy's house after Mama basically abandoned me. Toy and I are like sisters. We have beaten a few girls down before. Even though, Mama Jackson moved and Toy and I both lived in better neighborhoods, all our friends were still left behind in the projects so we continued hanging out there. Toy knows everything about me, all of my secrets, except me and Stan's closeness.

He can't be serious!

After returning home from my school, I went in my room, and changed into my lounging around the house clothing.

"Victoria!" Stan yelled.

"Yes" I responded.

"Come in here for a minute." He requested.

I walked in the room, and out of nowhere Stan grabbed me. My heart began beating rapidly because I was totally taken by surprise. "You remember what I promised you, right?"

I stood there puzzled not exactly sure what he promised me, but for some reason the way he startled me with that unwanted kiss, I figured it had something to do with his perception that I am now a butterfly with full-fledged wings. I was definitely hoping that was not it.

I smiled and replied, "not exactly, but what is it?"

"Here" he said as he handed me a CJS Pharmacy bag. "Take that in the bathroom, read the directions and do what it says. Take a good clean shower and come back out here." He insisted.

I took the bag in the bathroom as he instructed with the look and thought of curiosity overwhelming me. I took out the box and it read *Summers Clean feminine cleansing douche.* I sat on the toilet contemplating on how I could escape this new and improved way of Stan confessing his *love* to me.

"How is it going in there?" Stan yelled through the door.

"Fine, I'll be done in a few" I replied.

I walked out and at that moment, everything seemed to change right before my very eyes. As I began to realize the shadow afloat was just an inner image of a vision to be free I could not fulfill; I was then awakened. I woke up inside the body of the innocent girl who screamed and cried for help, but was never heard. As I laid there crying, begging for a rescue- I viewed the look in Stan's eyes that resembled flames fueled by laughter.

His fire piercing energy somehow transplanted into me. My cry for help transformed into a plea for him to never leave me. Tears began to fall from my eyes, because this feeling caught me by surprise. He made loud noises that now sounded like music to my ears. I began to feed off his actions. When I realized I could not help me, I decided to help him. The liquid produced by my vision organs suddenly dried away. There was no sense in wasting bodily fluids that provided no merit. I had no idea what I was saying when I agreed to love him always and forever, but I knew it was something that I had to do because he told me to. Every command he gave became a task that I felt I had to complete.

"Always remember, Your Mother abandoned you and so did your Father, I am all you have. Guys may pretend to love you, but they don't. They don't want you! They will not love you and will most definitely never do anything for you like I do. Do you hear me!!" he screamed.

I took another shower in hopes of being able to scrub away what was happening and the unexplainable feeling that all of a sudden come over me. The feelings were not cleansable and the unlocked entrance to a once sacred treasure no longer had a seal.

"Come here Victoria" Stan requested.

I walked in the room and stood in front of him. "Sit down, I'm sure you know that I don't bite by now" he smiled. I sat down on the bed next to him. "I know that this all might seem a little strange to you. Don't let it be. This is 'love' Victoria. When you love someone you want to make them happy. The love we have is unique. I meant every word I said, you are mine now."

We watched movies for the remainder of that night. The next morning I was awakened by him unexpectedly. I woke up in the reality that yesterday was not a dream. I looked at him staring at me. Once he noticed that he awakened me, he stood up and began tying his tie. "Good morning beautiful."

I rubbed my eyes and replied "Good Morning."

"I have to go to work. I made you breakfast. You can sit around and relax; when I get to work I'll begin looking for you another school. I think I am going to place you in a private school" he said.

I admit I was happy at the fact that I would be going to a better school, but the curiosity of wanting to know exactly where Stan worked and what he did was jogging my mind. That was my first time being home while Stan got ready for work. Stan grabbed his guns and put one in his gun strap under his arm and he placed one in a holster around his ankle. Curiosity urged me to finally ask him. "Stan, where do you work? What exactly do you do?"

He dabbed on a bit of cologne around his neck and replied, "I work for the government. I'm in the FBI, it's a higher rank than regular police."

Stan asked me to keep it a secret because he was working undercover. He then began to explain that he and his team played the role of a big drug mafia to bring down a notorious drug dealer by the name of "Money Mike." He also explained that in his line of work he was risking his life daily which is why confidentiality was extremely important.

I stayed home all day watching television and cleaning up; I had to make sure the house was clean after Stan went to work. He hated a dirty house. I picked that up a long time ago when he would curse Christine out for not keeping the house spotless.

As I walked around the house making sure everything was neat and organized, I tried recapturing everything that happened the day before. I sat on the edge of a twig awaiting flight. The butterfly I craved to be in the poem I wrote in Mrs. Kittles class, did not seem as free as the one I imagined. I became a woman in less than an hour. Even though being a woman is what Stan proclaimed I was, I didn't notice the change. Unless being a woman meant that I had to free the belief that loving me did not mean penetrating me and having a desire for my mother's nourishment instead of nature's wild life being my nest, defined my crossover.

My acidic thoughts of this nectar soul being betrayed were interrupted when the phone rang. I glanced at the caller id and recognized it was my girl Toy. "Hey girl, why aren't you at school?" I answered

"We had a half a day, but that's not important. "Girl, guess what happened?"

Not in the mood for the guessing games," Just tell me Toy." I replied.

"Well, you know Sean the one who likes you, he's in the hospital. He just got shot."

"Oh my goodness Toy, What happened?"

"He supposedly got raided today and he tried to shoot at the cops, so the cops shot him in the leg."

Hearing that tragic news triggered my mental process into thinking if I had mentioned anything about Sean to Stan? I quickly transferred my thoughts to Stan wondering if he did actually have something to do with it and if so, was he ok. I remained calm as I began expressing my concern. "Dang Toy, that's messed up." My heart began racing faster by the second. I wanted to go see Sean, but at that time, you had to be at least sixteen to go without a parent. Asking Stan was definitely out of the question. I heard the sound of keys dangling. I looked at the clock and noticed it was only 3pm. I panicked. "Hey Toy, stay by the phone, I'll call you right back." I hung up the phone and acted as if I was watching T.V.

Stan walked in looking a bit different by his clothing. It was obvious he changed his clothes. When he removed his jacket, I noticed he was wearing a blue long sleeve shirt with gold letters on it that spelled out FBI. He walked over to the coffee table and sat his key's down. "Hey baby, come here and give me a hug." he requested.

The constant racing of my heart never ceased. I tried not to express any emotions as if something was wrong. I stood up and hugged him. "Hey, you're home a little early; how was work?" I asked.

"It was work, I almost got shot on the job today" he replied as he sat on the sofa pulling my arm forcing me to sit on his lap as if I was still that five year old girl he read books to.

I sat there with my arm around his shoulder appearing to be concerned and comforting, though being disgusted and feeling uncomfortable was becoming a bit evident. I forced my eyebrows to remain relaxed as I viewed the beast that sat before me.

Realizing that Stan was connected to Sean's shooting was vivid. Suddenly my memory began working overtime to service my predictions. I began to remember two or three months prior to the date at hand, I shared with Stan the fact that I liked Sean and I explained to him I thought Sean or maybe his friends were dealing drugs. That was actually when Stan appeared to be someone who cared about *his niece*. Sizing up that situation allowed me to realize that it was all a plot to obtain information from me for his personal gratification. While I sat there analyzing Stan, my thoughts were focused on Sean.

Sean was nineteen, about 5'11, 165lbs. He had an earring in his ear, mocha chocolate skin tone, with an expensive taste in clothing such as mine, plus he had an old school cutlass sitting on twenty two inch rims. Sean was an urban, street thug, type of guy who smoked cigarettes and drank beer. Even though I didn't smoke or drink at the time, watching him do it seemed cool. We often went to the movies when I spent the night over Toy's house. Since Romeo and Sean are friends, I was able to see him every time I spent the night over there. I had deep feelings for him. We related well and our communication was on point. As I sat there reminiscing on the good times that Sean and I shared as well as hoping he was going to be okay, I couldn't help but feel responsible. I should have never shared his personal business with Stan in the first place.

"I wish I could stay here and lay on these big jugs, instead of trying to hunt down the bad guy's every day." Stan expressed as he laid his head upon my breast.

"Hmm" I sighed aloud without realizing it.

"What do you mean 'hmm'? Are you implying that my job is not hard? I have to protect and serve this entire city and some parts of the United States every day in hopes that I don't get killed." He explained.

I remained in silence. My non responsive actions caused Stan to remain silent as well. He deeply exhaled and then grabbed my legs gently and swung them off of him as he stood up. He walked in the kitchen and grabbed a beer from the refrigerator. He walked over to the blinking light flashing from the caller id box. "Oh I see your friend Toya called, what did she want?"

I knew I had to think of something quick. "She called to see how I was doing and if I wanted to spend the night this weekend. I told her I had to check with you first. So how about it, can I?" I asked.

He turned the brown beer bottle up and took a nice swallow while letting out a loud belch without saying excuse me. "Yeah, you can spend the night, but you better not be around any knuckle head boys or I'm going to get you." He replied. I smiled and ran up to him and planted a kiss on his cheek.

I went in my room and called Toy to inform her that I was spending the night over her house. Mama Jackson said that I did not have to ask if I could stay the night at her house because she considered me as one of her own children. I packed my overnight bag then Stan dropped me off.

I walked up to the door and rang the doorbell. Romeo walked to the door "Oh, it's you" he said with no excitement as he walked away with his head down. I glanced back at Stan signaling him that I was entering in the house so he could pull off, but I guess the sight of Romeo answering the door made him sit outside in his car for a while. I tried paying no attention to Stan and focused on Romeo's unusual body gestures and upsetting look upon his face.

"Dang Romeo, what's wrong with you?" I asked as I closed the door behind me.

"On some real shit Victoria, I'm not in the mood for yo shit today. We got some snitches on the loose" he said as he paced back and forth in his black Nike socks on Mama Jackson's plush cream carpet.

"What happened?" I asked, as if I didn't already get the 411 from Toy anyway.

"The Fed's hit Sean's spot today and I know somebody snitched because he's a low key cat and he hasn't been dealing with any new clientele. They shot my homie" Romeo said as he tried to catch the tear that dripped from his eye. "When I find out who snitched I'm going to make sure they get stitched real good" he threatened while punching his hand with his fist.

"Oh my goodness Romeo, that's messed up. What's the feds anyway?" I asked.

"The FBI" he replied.

"Oh that's straight foul, so how is he doing?" I inquired as my heart continued racing. I tried hard to appear uninformed as I possibly could. I did not want to risk losing my friends because I ran off at the mouth.

"He tight! We soldiers! It aint shit! He gone be alright" he replied as if he was trying to convince himself of those very words.

"I'm sorry to hear that Romeo. If and when you go down to the hospital, please tell him I said I hope he gets better. Is Toy upstairs in her room?"

"Yeah, her big mouth ass up there" he replied with anger.

Shocked by his response, I headed up the stairs. When I got near Toy's bedroom I heard sniffling as if she was crying. I softly knocked on her door as I was entering. Toy was lying in her bed face down in her pillow. I sat on her bed next to her, rubbed her back and asked, "Toy, what's wrong?"

She sat up with a face full of tears and her eyes blood shot red. The words *Victoria, do not panic* ran across my mind. "Oh my goodness boo" I said expressing my concern as I placed my arms around her. "Toy, what's wrong?"

She wiped the nasal mucus that drained down and landed at the top of her lip. "Romeo smacked me because he thinks I snitched on Sean. He assumed because I'm dating Robert, whose parents are both cops that I told them. I didn't tell you Victoria, but Sean and I got into a minor argument regarding him making a transaction in front of the house. I saw him accepting money for a bag of weed. I told him it was very disrespectful to do that in front of Mama's house like that. We argued, but after I spoke my peace I dropped it. I never mentioned anything to Robert about Sean. I am not a snitch Victoria, I swear."

The feeling of guilt rested upon me. I tried not to express any emotional feelings because I was a second and a half away from crying along with her and breaking down. *It was me Toy, It was me* is what I forbade to exit my lips. Though my actions showed were distinctly separate. "Girl, don't pay Romeo no mind. He is mad right now and due to the fact that they are refusing to accept full responsibility that they got caught slipping, the only thing he could do was take it out on you- that's all. Romeo knows good and well that you would not do anything like that. I think the best thing to do is to stay clear of his path. Let him figure it out. It usually takes time for the guilty to come to the realization that blaming it on others is not the correct thing to do. So girl stop all that crying and let it fly" I replied as I felt a cool tingle transpire throughout my body.

"You're right girl, let me get up. I'm just tripping on the fact that my own brother flipped on me like that."

"Yeah girl, it's just that you were the only one in his face at the time, he was angry not to excuse it, but he knows in his heart that you did not snitch on him. Get on up girl." I explained as I handed her the box of Kleenex from her night stand.

As my hollow muscular director of plasma- rapidly played drums in my chest, it seemed to have skipped a beat as I tried joking with her. I would not, could not and realized that I should not confess to Toy that I was the one who was responsible. Stan tricked me into thinking he was actually concerned about my personal life outside of him. Toy is my sister, my best friend and my ace boom. I would never in a million years risk losing her friendship and our sister bond. Even though Toy is two years older than I am and we have different mothers and fathers, it has never changed the closeness of our relationship. Mama Jackson made sure of it.

Mama Jackson had a great helping hand in raising me. She never treated me any different from the way she treats her own children.

Mama Jackson explained to me that she watched me daily ever since I was six months old. She always told me "despite the fact that your mom is not with you I cannot replace her, but I can and will be the best mother I can be to you." I love her for that. Toy and Romeo never treated me any different either. They treated me just like their baby sister. I am thankful for that and I am also grateful that Stan never stopped allowing me to visit with Mama Jackson.

Being at Mama Jackson's placed me in the character for which I belonged. I was not forced to be a woman. In fact, Mama Jackson always encouraged Toy and I to act our age and never try to grow up too soon. She explained that being a child is beautiful because the only responsibility we had was to go to school, get good grades and keep our rooms cleaned. "Once you become adults real life will kick in. Sometimes we will make decision that may be bad ones, but it's never too late to correct them. That's why I get up and go to school every day so I can provide a better future for my children" she often explained.

When Mama Jackson finished nursing school she and Mr. Jackson, Romeo and Toy's dad moved their family out of the projects. Even though Mama Jackson and Mr. Jackson were separated, he never forgot about his family. They forced themselves to live in the same house for the sake of their kids, but once Mr. Jackson became a lawyer he and Mama Jackson divorced and went their own separate ways.

The divorce was a tough situation for both Romeo and Toya to accept. Toy and Romeo cried almost every day. I cried with them even though I never had a close relationship with Mr. Jackson because when I was at Mama Jackson's house he was never there. Mama Jackson was very sad also. She always told me and Toya that *money changes people*. She was the one who taught me to never think that I was any better than anyone else because nothing would prevent us from being in others who were less fortunate than ourselves situations. "Never forget where you come from girls, and never forget those who help guide you towards your future" she often told us.

Though we were taught that and I accepted that, Stan told me different just as Mr. Jackson taught Toy. We were both told that we were princesses and we are better than everyone else. It was something about the sincerity in Mama Jackson's voice that allowed those egotistical beliefs that Stan fed me to be over powered.

Now Toy on the other hand, you can't tell her that she's not better than the other females we know, that's like telling her that she can't have oxygen to breathe. Even though Toy is a bit narcissistic, it's not her fault because I often find myself trying to fight the fact that I often think I am better and placing judgment on others as well. It's kind of hard not to feel that we are better than others when the men in our lives stressed that to us daily and not to mention the fact- that's the way a lot of people treated us.

All of the boys we came in contact with seemed as if they worshiped us and the females within our age group envied us and still do for that matter. A lot of people say that Toy and I resembled one another a great deal. We told everyone that we were sisters anyway; so hearing how much we looked alike was nothing new to us. Though there is one thing that people were often shocked to hear- the reality that I was only twelve years old.

I assumed it was because the formation of the proportionately structured outer representation of the inner rose bud had blossomed prematurely. No one could see the broken bits and pieces of a shattered garden full of fallen thorns. *They focused on the fine colors and detailed aligned depiction of the masterpiece* instead of the pain from within the artist's creation that defined the true existence.

I guess I would transfer the credit for my misrepresentation to Stan. He was the reason that people believed that I was "ahead of my time"; some called it being mature and well developed. Some people who knew my Mom said I was her splitting image and others blamed it on the chemicals that are placed in food.

My breast had reached a 38D. They were bigger than the majority of the females at my middle school and half of the females in high school. My hips had spread so wide and my behind was so huge I was barely squeezing in a size twelve. Toy was about my size also, the only difference between our body figures was Toy lacked the heavy back pain bosoms.

My figure attracted unwanted attention from men Stan's age. They would ride on the side of Toy and I, asking us if we wanted to have some adult fun. Of course that disgusted Toy and I both. They reminded me of what I already had to face at home. There was absolutely nothing fun about it.

I wanted to share my secret regarding Stan and I with Toy because it was simply beginning to be too much for me, but Stan mentioned that I could not. Plus, I was too embarrassed at that point. Just as revealing to Toy that Stan was an FBI agent was a secret that I could not disclose. As far as everyone knows, he's a manager at a corporate office. That's exactly how I left it. Besides, I had just found out myself that Stan was FBI. He disguises his true being by depicting a character of a mighty protector of life's entity, captivating the considerable field of herbal essence while destruction unfolds behind closed doors. I find it very interesting how a garden of colorful flowers makes the outside of a house appear to be a home and how those colorful organisms mistakenly cover the *dying rose.*

Chapter 2

Six years later ... ...

As my pedals began to shed, my roots were growing stronger. It seemed like the past five years this rose died. However, due to the strength of my roots, the rose continuously grows back. In every growth beauty becomes evident and the strength of my pedals last much longer. The solid ground where my existence is cultivated allows me to occupy tainted soil unwillingly. Every day as I lean towards the sun to provide me with energy to grow, I realize it does not come easy, especially when there's a beast feeding off of the beauty of my pedals and there is absolutely nothing I can do about it.

Unfortunately, the fact that I am the legal age limit to vote has not caused Stan to change at all. I often find myself daydreaming of how beautiful my life would be if Stan was no longer a part of it. I am usually awakened to the harsh reality of him still using his unwanted key to enter inside my treasure box without my consent, as well as controlling my every move.

Stan has gotten very possessive. The more my beauty inside and out becomes evident to myself and others, he gets more and more jealous. His convincing me that I am not going to be beautiful and loved by another male has changed. While he constantly reminds me, he is the only one who will ever love me; I began to notice that statement is invalid. I admit I still love him, but not in the way that he wants me to. I realize that loving me is actually not so bad.

The mirror image reflection of this once broken and lost girl, who once hated me, now looks at me and smiles. As I smile gracefully from the inside out, using the strength that the sun provides every day as fuel to embrace the crystalline molasses of the beating of my four chamber valve organ, I realized that I am beautiful and not only through Stan's eyes. My new found love thinks I'm beautiful and he also loves me for me.

For some peculiar reason, the love that Chuck shows me and expresses to me seems like the right type of love. Initially, when I began noticing these feelings I have for Chuck developing I backed away. I remembered what Stan told me as it relates to when someone loves me, allowing them to enter inside of me was the best love that I could ever give or receive.

I explained to Chuck as my feelings grew stronger that *I felt we should remain friends because I was not ready and did not want him to enter inside of me. I could not hold back my tears* when Chuck explained, "Victoria, just because I am in love with you does not mean that I am trying to have sex with you or enter inside of you there" as he pointed towards my lower abdomen and then placed his hand on my heart "I want to enter in here. When someone truly loves you, it doesn't mean they want to get you in the bed with your clothes off and legs open. Love, real true love is so much more than that. It's about spending time, having fun, getting to know one another and exploring this world that God created together."

After he shared that with me, I knew I wanted to be with him for the rest of my life. *I can't imagine my life without him.* To my new found love of the image in the mirror, I owe some of it to him. Meeting Charles "Chuck" Matthews brought a light in my life that I never knew existed. Being around him makes me feel like the teenager that I am and not the woman that Stan forces me to be. I can be myself around him and sometimes I feel like the butterfly I always dreamed of being; - free and beautiful.

When we met in the ninth grade, I knew right then that I wanted to be around him all the time. It's actually kind of funny because I never thought that he would be interested in someone like me. As I was in the cafeteria playing spades with Toy, Michelle and Lisa, he walked over to our table, sat down and said "Me and Victoria got next."

I looked around the table and sarcastically asked, "Is there someone else here named Victoria?"

He put his arm around me and replied "You know God couldn't have put two of you here for the men to go crazy over. Instead he just put you, with yo sexy self."

I sat there staring at him trying my best to refrain from being frost bitten by all of the ice he was wearing around his neck and wrist. I did exactly like Mama Jackson taught Toy and I. *"Never show your true emotions girls. Never let anyone take you out of your Diva shoes. Your Diva shoes are a representation of your character. A trend setter sets limits. Be mesmerized by nothing"* she often reminded us.

I followed her advice as I kept my Diva shoes firmly planted giving a slight blush expressing to him that I was not impressed. "Well … what's your name again?" I asked as if I didn't already know it.

He smiled, "oh ok, you got jokes. It's Charles, but everybody calls me Chuck, baby" as he smiled making my insides tingle with that buffed chest, those sexy eyes and pearly white teeth.

"Oh ok Chuck Baby, my girls and I just started and since I never lose, I will let you pick another partner that will like to lose with you."

He leaned over and whispered in my ear, "I'm digging your style lil Mama. Yeah, I'm digging you."

I smiled as I glanced down at my attire. I had on my lime green guess jeans, lime green guess purse, lime green and white button up with my caramel breast sitting up, looking extra juicy. Oh for sure baby! And to top it off - I also had on my special made lime green and white Air Jordan's, with my platinum chain that has the big V charm with diamond chips glistening.

Stan made sure that I kept up with the latest, hottest clothes, shoes and jewelry. Sometimes I often think that Stan might believe that he owes me that because I never asked to be a part of his sick, perverted, ideal version of love.

I assume Chuck noticed that I was confirming my appearance because he leaned over and whispered, "You are sexy as hell, and aint no need in checking. You're wearing my favorite color anyway. Plus I like the fact that you're not stuck up when you have every reason to be. Yeah, I got to have you."

One of my Diva shoe's almost slipped off, but it was quickly tightened when he said "You might as well ride out with me because you will definitely look like a winner on my arm."

I whispered back in his ear, "Oops boo- I'm already a winner baby, so be easy ok and I might add a little finesse to your style."

"Oh yeah, I like you," he said as he smiled from ear to ear staring back at me while walking back to his table.

Once he walked away from the table, I knew that I was going to get some type of reactions from my girls. Not even seconds after I was thinking that, Lisa said "Ooh girl, you pulling Chuck; oh boy! You doing it big girl."

I blushed and replied, "Well, you know" in a laughing, boastful type of way. I instantly became the center of attention. I glanced at the six eyeballs that were glued on me. "What are you guys looking at? I didn't think he would like someone like me."

"Someone like you; Girl Please" Michelle replied.

Toy joined and said, "Victoria, come on and stop fronting. You know as well as everyone else that you are extremely pretty, with long natural hair, an awesome body, everything you wear is top of the line and you keep it real. You are not conceited like these other broads that walk around here looking like medusa. Plus you're my baby sister so why would he not want you? Girl, I don't know where you get off acting like you not all of that when you hang around me. I thought for sure I would have rubbed off on you by now."

I didn't need helium to make my head swollen, because my girls were doing a great job. They boosted my esteem to a totally different level. I couldn't stop blushing.

Michelle and Lisa became real cool with me and Toy, though our friendship never went outside of school. Toy and I are a little skeptical and particular about whom we choose to hang out with in the "real world." We were friends at school and that's as far as it went because

Toy and I did not trust a lot of females because they could smile in your face, but will stab you in the back when you are not looking. Besides, I had too much on my plate to consider new female friends; the only friend I was interested in getting to know was my baby Chuck.

Once Chuck and I began dating, we instantly became "High School Sweethearts." Everybody knows about Victoria and Chuck. Last year we were selected first place as the *couple's most likely to succeed* and *the cutest couple*. The couple *most likely to succeed* vote is something only time can predict, but the *cutest couple* selection is right on the money because we definitely are, if I should say so myself. I must admit, I didn't think Chuck was cute when I found out he smoked weed. Stan explained to me that weed was an illegal drug and it can cause addiction and it will also cause a person to go to jail. I was a little disappointed until Chuck explained that he was not addicted and it did not control his life.

Stan's tactic of preventing me from getting involved in smoking weed no longer provided fear. Once Chuck explained to me that he was not addicted and he could quit at any time, I started smoking it also. I tried it once before when Romeo and Toy were smoking, but I couldn't handle it then. Plus, I was terrified of what Stan would do if he found out.

The aroma left behind from weed is very strong and I did not realize how strong it was until I went home after spending the weekend at Toy's. Stan smelled it in my clothes, my hair and in my overnight bag. He was super furious when he found out. He forbade me from spending the night over Toy's for two whole months because he assumed that Romeo was the reason I smoked. Little did he know; I was hanging out with Chuck and the weed smoke came from being with him. Stan said I was weak minded and stupid because I allowed someone to influence me with drugs after he told me how bad they were. Since Chuck was smoking it, I assumed it to be ok. Plus, Toy and almost everyone we know smokes it every day. I often analyze the reasons for me engaging in the usage of marijuana. The notion subjecting me to be a *product of my environment* weighed in heavily. Though the fact that Chuck had a great influence on me weighed equally.

His influence on me is not limited to inhaling and exhaling green leaves. He uplifts me in *every way* imaginable. He loves to read and listen to my poetry. He often refers to me as a little Maya Angelou. I often believe he is being a bit too modest because Maya Angelou and I are no comparison. I can only dream of reaching that nectar of knowledge that she possess. I do accept it as a compliment because of the admiration I have for her.

The compliments that Chuck continuously showers me with, seem to be endless and I love it. Chuck treats me like a Queen because that's what he tells me *I am*. He's so good to me. He has already taken me on trips to Chicago, New York, Miami, Atlanta, Kentucky and Canada. He says that he wants me to see the beauty of life and all it has to offer.

When we went to Miami three months ago, Chuck proposed to me. My heart pounded as if that little energizer bunny was inside of me pounding against my chest. I said yes with no hesitation. I also explained to him how much I would love to be his wife. Though, I didn't know anything about being a wife or a good woman for that matter. He explained that he did not know what it was to be a husband, but *as long as God directed his path,* he could teach the both of us.

Chuck told me that I was appearing to be diffident when I had absolutely no reason to be. I wanted to say, '*Chuck, only if you knew what I go through behind the walls of what's supposed to be my home,*' but I couldn't. I cannot and will not risk losing him by sharing my secret that Stan has forced me to keep with him. I wish I could take the remote and point it at Stan and press power so he could disappear. I would change his channel in a heartbeat. Oh how I wish it were that simple. I want this whole Stan situation to be completely over. I told Chuck that Stan is very mean and over protective so showing up at my house would not be a good thing to do. I didn't want to risk something bad happening to him because Stan has the power to make it happen.

Every boy that Stan thought I might have been interested in, he threatened. And due to the fact that he is an undercover FBI agent, he uses his cop friends to scare them off so his cover will not be blown. I'm beginning to get frustrated because I do love Stan, but not in the way that he thinks I should. He is smothering me and it's beyond irritating. On top of that, he is now starting to act as if he wants to ground me. He has been trying very hard to understand why I seem so preoccupied when I return from school. I try extremely hard not to leave any evidence that will lead him to discovering Chuck. I often find myself wanting to break down and tell Chuck everything. I don't want him to think that I am a pervert or some type of freak. I wish I could explain to Chuck that the relationship that I have with Stan is not by choice, it's by force.

I've been watching talk shows such as Oprah and The Steve Wilko's and they have guys like Stan on their show all the time. I learned that a grown man having a sexual relationship with a child is called *molestation* and if they are members of the same family it's called *incest*.

I knew there was something about the whole relationship that did not seem right and it definitely did not and does not feel right. I wish I could have called their show to get some type of help, but I'm too embarrassed to tell anybody. I'm eighteen years old and I feel like I've been in this relationship far too long. It just seems like there's nothing I can do.

Even though I listen to the psychologist as they try explaining when these types of things happen that it is not my fault, I still feel like I should've known better. I feel so stupid listening to Stan tell me that when someone loves me I should let them do basically whatever they want to with me. I'm so glad Chuck has shown me differently; that's exactly why keeping me and Chuck's relationship from Stan is so important. I don't think I will ever mentioned Chuck to Stan because I know he would trip out, especially with the way that he has been acting lately.

These last couple of months, Stan has turned into this very cruel and wicked, overly jealous, unrecognizable being. He is in love with me and I don't know why. I wish I knew how to make him fall out of love with me, but it seems nearly impossible. It has gotten to the point where he shows up at Toy's house when I am over for the weekend, just to make sure that I'm there. Mama Jackson and Toy has been covering for me pretty well. Toy said he started out calling, but after she continued telling him that I was in the bathroom that's when he decided to stop by.

When I was in Miami, Toy called me and told me that he was knocking on her door so hard that she was afraid to answer it, so she didn't. Even though she did not answer, Stan still accused me of being out with another guy. He was correct, but that was beside the point. Chuck is not just another guy, he is my fiancé. Stan tried telling me that Toy answered the door and told him that I was not there. I knew that was

Chapter 3

Back to reality

As I stare at this aqua blue Detroit River, I crave to be the waves that I've been starring at as I reflected on the past of where this crazy and strange unfortunate love affair began. I guess for Stan its love, but for me, I consider it as the thin line between love and hate. I know that I should hate him with all my might, but I love him at the same time. I don't know how that can be possible. How can you hate someone you are supposed to love and love someone you should hate? I wish I could figure it out, but it's harder than trigonometry with no graphing calculator. I know that I am going to try as hard as I can to get myself out of this situation because I cannot keep living these secret lives between someone that I love to hate and someone that I would hate not to love.

Chuck provides the beat to my heart. The only thing that I require is that I remain his one and only desire, as he continues giving all of his love to me. He is the sun that shines on me adding that extra glow within my soul, he makes me feel whole. That shattered girl I used to be has been glued back together with no flaws, just from the simple thought of him. I've sat here for the last past three hours staring at him and the waves of the river and I still cannot understand how in his sleep he delivers kinetic over flow of energy to my neurotransmitters as I quiver desirably.

"Baby what's wrong?" Chuck asked as he awakened to me drying the tear from my eye.

"Nothing's wrong, I just got a little lost in thought. I'm fine, how was your nap" I asked.

"Baby, those waves will cause you to think deeply and in my case they put me right to sleep. I know that you just said nothing is wrong, but I sense differently. You look frustrated and worried. Victoria, what's wrong?"

"Ok to be honest Chuck, I am a little worried about the S.A.T.'s. I have to study that's all. I really want to get into a great college."

"Well it's Friday Vicky, relax. The S.A.T's are not until at least two weeks from now. Hopefully, this weekend we can have some fun so I can help you relieve that stress. Victoria, don't worry about it, everything is going to be ok. I mean it. Everything Victoria! You hear me?"

I didn't like the fact that I had to lie to him, but I have to keep this secret affair, simply that *a secret*. I grabbed his hand and squeezed it gently, "I know baby, I know. I'm cool boo. Can you drop me off at Toy's house?"

"Yeah you know I can. I love you girl."

I looked over at Chuck and replied, "I love you too."

I love my fiancé, I really do. That is exactly why I need to figure out how to get out of this situation with Stan. I am past the legal limit of surfeit if there is one.

Today is the day! When I get home I am going to march right in Stan's room and read him his rights. He has to accept them. I am tired of this! I'm sure he will understand. How long does he think this sick affair is going to go on? I guess he figured that I would be so dumb that I would actually believe that he was the only person who would take interest in me. The sad fact is -I did for a moment until I was introduced to reality by Chuck. That's why I love him so much.

We pulled up at Toy's. Chuck turned my face around to him and kissed me with his thick juicy lips.

"I love you baby and I hope that I can see you tonight."

"Yeah babe, I do to" I smiled as I got out of his car.

I went in the house and spoke to Mama Jackson and Stephen's dad. It's kind of weird that I am not the baby anymore. Mama Jackson got married three years ago and then she gave birth to little Stevie. Little Stevie's cool as a little brother and Romeo's cool to be my big brother even though he acts whey younger than Toy and I.

Speaking of Toy, she just ran down stairs as if she is in a hurry to drop me off. My mind and my thoughts are so foggy right now, clouded with breaking it off with Stan; I didn't even bother teasing Toy about how fast she ran down those stairs. I'm sure Toy has a hot date or something anyway because she is looking quite fly. I have so much on my mind that it feels like it is about to explode.

This entire secret affair with Stan had me bugged out for the last couple of months and I know Toy has noticed it. She tells me all the time that I have been appearing to be frustrated and acting strange the last couple of months. I never told her about Stan either. Telling Toy the reason I've been acting strange and frustrated is due to *the man that everyone knows as my Uncle will not let me sleep in peace without Trying to touch me and multiple unwanted ways* - would not be a good excuse. I know if everyone else is noticing how much this is bothering me, I know Stan notices it as well.

If he loves me like he says he does, my feelings should be very important to him. I have to put an end to this nonsense right now! My mind is so preoccupied with the way I would like to break the news to Stan; I have not heard a thing Toy's been babbling about since we got in the car. I heard sounds of her voice, but I was not listening.

"I hope you get your head out of the clouds and bounce back Victoria, because you've really been tripping lately" Toy said as she dropped me off in front of this house filled with darkness.

Every time I arrive in front of this house I dread entering. As I approached the front door I took a deep breath because I have no clue of what the end results will be after I explain to him that I want completely out of this whole ordeal. My hearts beating fast, but I refuse to reverse my decision. I have to keep it real with him. I wish my Mom would have gotten herself together and came back to rescue me. I wish she was here with me right now. I miss her so much.

I glanced up at the sun that is slowly snuggling away in the cotton resembled clouds and took a deep breath. I have now gained strength to stick the key in the lock and open the door.

Stan is in his room watching TV, which is good because I have time to go in my room and prepare my speech. I entered my bedroom and put my book bag away. I am not sure why I carried it any way considering the fact that I did not go to school because today was our senior picnic. I actually enjoyed myself today. It has allowed me time to reflect on my past and gain will power to make this decision. I might be a bit naïve, but I am expecting Stan to completely understand why I am making this decision and permit my request.

Repetitious respirations have now caused rapid contractions throughout my ventricles while my right and left atriums competed against one another. My adrenaline raced as I continued to exhale preparing for a positive response from Stan. I looked in the mirror, fixed my hair and sprayed on some of my pear Victoria Secret so Stan would not smell marijuana on me. I do not need to add coal to the forest fire that's already difficult to snuff out.

I entered the room where Stan is sitting in his leather recliner wearing his boxer's and wife beater t-shirt. That's a funny name for the T-shirt he's wearing right now. I hope he doesn't get that angry to the point where he'll hit me. Plus, I am not his wife anyway; I am his niece so that's exactly how he should treat me. I walked over to him and sat on the edge of the bed so that we are facing one another. I grabbed the remote and put the TV on mute.

"Hey Stan, can we talk for a minute?" I asked as my hands trembled in nervousness.

He took a sip of his Budweiser and sat the can on the table, "Sure, what do you want to talk about" he responded as he adjusted his posture.

"Well it's like this" *as I took in another deep breath trying to control the rapid beating of my heart.* "I want to date guys my own age. I just want you to be my Uncle. I don't want you to treat me like I'm your girlfriend. I don't want to do any of the physical things we've done in the past. I prefer if we remained as family should be."

He leaned forward as he appeared to rise out of his chair. He looked at me as if I just cursed at him or something. He frowned and raised his eyebrow the way he always does when he is angry.

"Ok, let me get this straight. You don't want me to sleep with you anymore and you want to be with another guy who is around your age. So basically, you are seeking my support and you want me to be your Uncle and behave the way family should. Am I correct?" He asked calmly.

Wow, he is taking this quite nicely. I am overwhelmed and ecstatic at Stan's response. Even though this is the reaction I was hoping for; over the course of the years I have known Stan I did not expect him to respond so calmly and so understanding especially judging his facial expression.

"Yes Stan, that's what I want. I just want it to be over! "I replied as I smiled.

"What the hell do you mean? I made you! If it wasn't for me, you would probably be dead or in the streets somewhere with your crack headed Mama!" he replied as he jumped to his feet in defense.

I immediately stood up and walked towards the living room trying to think of a response, but the only response I could think of was to defend my mother. "Don't talk about my mother like that. Besides, she is your sister! You could have helped her if you wanted to."

He remained silent. The statement I made obviously struck a dose of reality.

"That whore is not my sister! My mom adopted her homeless ass. I tried to help her a long time ago. She continuously stole my money and smoked it up. I did her a favor since I could not help her I decided to help you! I brought you into my house making sure you were comfortable. I made sure you had a real bed to sleep in instead of that dirty ole pissy mattress. I buy you all the finer things that life has to offer. Everything I do, I do it for you!" He shouted.

His lips were moving, but for some reason I heard nothing else. I stood here trying to register everything exiting from his mouth, but the only thing that kept repeating in my head was "not my sister." As I am standing here lost and confused I interrupted him.

"What do you mean Mama is not your sister? Are you trying to tell me that we are not biologically related?" I asked.

"Correct! My mom adopted her when she was a teenager" he shouted.

That's a relief that this affair cannot be classified as incest, but manipulation and molestation is still a big factor. Stan is too old and besides the fact, biological or not we are still related in the eyes of the system. *Just because we are not biologically related does not make it right or acceptable. Neither does it change my thoughts. I want to be with Chuck and I want this relationship to be over, that's the bottom line!* I stood here staring at him as he went on and on.

"I brought you everything you have, you never want for anything. Why do you want our love to be over? What is his name? I'll kill him!"

"Stan, there is no one else! I simply do not want to engage in this strange affair with you anymore! I want you to be my Uncle like you are supposed to be. This is getting played out! I don't want this, I never wanted this! I hate the type of love that you have for me and expect me to have for you" I yelled, trying to control the tears that are blocking my vision as I began backing away from him.

As I backed away from him I ended up closer to the window which allowed the sun light to beam in from the blinds. The reflected sunlight added glare from my diamond. I looked at my hand and noticed I had on the ring that Chuck gave me. I tried to hide it before Stan could see it, but from the look in his eyes he spotted the glare also.

"Wait a minute! Let me see your finger" he commanded as he grabbed my hand. "You know this is your engagement finger right? And this looks like an engagement ring!" he screamed.

No shit, Sherlock! I thought to myself before I responded. "It's not an engagement ring Stan. It's just a friendship ring."

"Take it off and give it back to whatever boy you got it from!"

"I can't and I won't! I'll be nineteen soon. Therefore, I'm grown and I do not need your permission or approval on anything that I choose to do in my life!"

The rainbow colored stars began to fade away after his heavy handed smack seemed to erase my memory. He grabbed my hair and began dragging me into his room. The state of shock that I'm in has stimulated my eyes to pour out tears in response to Stan's actions. "Stan, I'm sorry. Please, stop. Stan, Please!" I begged.

Pangs of jabs influenced the arrival of the little girl who once shadowed afloat of this familiar destruction. Circular boards of flesh I have now become as pointed missiles are closely thrown at me. The more I try to grow, the more he stunts me. I envy the air that I breathe due to the fact that it comes and goes as it please.

"Stop Stan, please I can't breathe" I cried.

"Shut up tramp! You used me for everything I got; now you're yelling stop! I thought you loved me! Vickie, why don't you love me anymore?" he asked as tears fell from his eyes.

I am trying to decipher the meaning and reason for his tears. I am the one hurting physically and mentally. Why is he crying? Maybe I am wrong. It must be something that I possess that attracts him to me. Maybe it's not his fault. Even though that acidic liquid is dripping from his eyes, it has not directed him to cease this unwanted abuse. I refuse to believe that this is not a beast before my very eyes.

"You belong to me! Do you understand me! "Now go clean yourself up!" he yelled.

I staggered into the bathroom trying to keep myself standing as I tried to bear such agonizing pain. Stan has never hit me before. He attempted once before, but he never did. I locked the bathroom door and instantly fell to the floor. Holding myself up is something that seems close to impossible right now.

I finally regained some strength to turn on the shower. I am sitting in this tub allowing this hot water to rain abundantly over my entire body. My tears began to mix with the water that's providing no soothing to this open sore also known as my existence, while I am trying to piece together what just happened and why? I still cannot believe how Stan just flipped out on me like that. He never did this before. He threatened me in the past saying that he would hurt me if I ever tried to disrespect him. I promised that I would never do anything to disrespect him or hurt him in any way. I assume when you make a verbal commitment to someone no matter who it is and what the commitment is regarding, there is no rescinding.

As I am fighting this excruciating pain, I'm trying to captivate my strength. I am finally able to stand. I reached for the towel and began to scrub. I'm trying to scrub away the pointless thorns covering this rose lacking pedals. If my thorns were thick enough they might have been able to protect me. Once again, they failed.

How can one man be so cruel and evil when he claims that he loves me? *This is the strangest love!* Love that causes mental, physical and emotional pain is more than strange; it is out of the ordinary to the highest power. He is yelling my name right now as if he has lost the mind that I don't think he has ever had. I don't know what I am going to do at this point.

Leaving does not appear to be an option and having my body actually classified as mine seems too far of a distance. If I imitate the image I yearn to be, my life might be a little bit easier. I always wanted to be an actress so I figured this would be an awesome time for me to get in some practice. I dried off and slipped on my night gown. Here goes.

I walked back in the room over to him where he is sitting in his recliner smoking a black and mild. *I had no idea he smoked. I smelt it before, but he said it was his boys.* "Stan, I want to apologize for being disrespectful especially since you have done so much for me. I disrespected you as a person and I am sorry. Thank you Stan for everything, please forgive me" as I began to fall to my knees trying to control these tears falling from my eyes. *I better make it to Hollywood for sure.* I cannot believe I almost believed this crap I just fed him. I am forcing myself to sit here on my knees pretending to be more than humble when the plot of figuring out how to escape this evil being is the original thought occupying my mind.

He smiled and took another puff from his cigar. "Get up and come over here" he commanded, while grabbing my arm. "I want you to know that I did not mean to be so mean and it will not happen again. The fact of thinking about another man being with you makes me crazy. I truly love you Victoria. You are my light and my sunshine. Every day I wake up and go to work risking my life with the possibility of being killed is all for you. I fight the bad guys so I can make this world safer for you as well as afford to keep you in the best clothes, shoes and jewelry that money can buy. Making you happy and pleasing you, provides me with an indescribable feeling. It is something about you that is hard to define. I know you remember when your mother left you on the curb in front of my house. She knew how much I loved you. That is the reason why she brought you over to me. I told her that I would provide you with everything you needed. Victoria, I proposed to Christine and put up with her drama for three and a half years just because I wanted to make sure you were always safe. I had to do that in order to meet the expectations and requirements to be the best possible guardian in the eyes of the system" he explained.

While I am sitting here listening to this nonsense I can't help but think *yeah you sure fooled the heck out of the system. FBI my ass Stan; protecting people from the bad guys? You are the bad guy! They need to lock your insane ass up immediately!* If I did not realize that this man has lost all of his marbles, I realize it now. I have to get away from him before he kills me.

Escaping this dungeon of darkness is now my number one priority. The sun was shining brightly before I entered this house today. He is sitting here actually looking like he is apologetic for what he has done. His tears are not fooling me.

"Stan, you hurt me badly tonight. You almost killed me Stan. How can you attempt to cease life of someone you claim to truly love? You are the only man who has shown me the type of love that you do" I replied. *Wow, I'm getting good at this.* I have to tell him what he wants to hear or he might beat me again. I cannot allow myself to believe that this is love. I just can't. This love is too painful. I hate how much he loves me.

"I'm sorry Victoria. I promise I was not trying to hurt you again. Do you want to watch movies? Are you hungry? What can I do to make you feel better?" he asked.

"I think if I go over to Toy's for the weekend so she could help me study for my S.A.T's would make me feel a whole lot better. Can I go? Please" I begged.

Oh shoot, he looks like he's buying it. He took a sip of his beer. "Yeah, I guess you can go over there. I will be checking up on you so don't try anything slick. I know Romeo likes to have his friends over, so you better not be in any of their faces. Don't try to play me Victoria. Remember I am 38 years old; I am familiar with all the games. Y'all youngsters just repeating what I done when I was y'all age" He replied jokingly.

When you were my age you probably did not have anyone telling you that you had to sleep with them or else you would die. You lived your life as a teenager! I wish you would allow me to live mine, I thought as I stared at him desiring to say it aloud.

"Play you Stan, yeah right! Not after tonight. You will never have to worry about that again. I was just unsure if you still loved me like you used to. It seemed like you have been acting funny lately, but you showed me that you still love me. Thank you" I replied before I kissed him on the cheek. "I'm going to my room to pack my overnight bag" I said as I left his room.

Precipitation of oversized ice cubes seemed to melt away as the pedals of this rose began to dry. I guess the sun is out again. It seems a little brighter even though it is almost 9 p.m. As I gargled with my Listerine I chuckled. That was an excellent performance I put on with Stan. I had to get the script right on the first try or else he would have believed that I was not sincere. I can't wait until me and Chuck get married, I won't have to live here anymore.

I know if I tell Chuck he would help me get away, but then again I am not sure if he would be able to handle this preposterous secret that I have been keeping from him. I am not absolutely certain that our love alone will aide him in understanding my position in this illicit relationship. I know my baby loves me. As a matter of fact let me check my phone because I know that he has called me by now.

Just as I expected, he has called me eight times. I know he has called Toy also. I guess he considers her as my personal voice mail. Let me call her so she can come pick me up anyway. Hmm, I wonder what is taking her so long to answer my call.

"Hello!" she finally answered.

"It's about time."

"Girl, where you been?" Toy asked. "Chuck said he has been chirping you all day..."

"All day Toy? I just left him about three hours ago. If he calls you again before you get here tell him that I could not find my charger."

"Is that your way of asking? You might want to check your tone boo. Don't snap on me because your Uncle is getting on your nerves."

"I know Toy, my bad. So are you on your way?"

"Yeah Girl, I'm on my way. Cheer the heck up ok. Oh yeah, you want me to call the house phone right?"

"You know the drill" I replied.

The phone is ringing. Stan usually always answers. That is a part of our plan. Toy calls and asks am I still going to be able to spend the night. Stan replies "yes" before he brings me the phone blah, blah, blah. We have been pulling this same routine every weekend for the past two years. Stan never tells Toy or Mama Jackson no when it regards me spending the night. Toy usually gets here in twenty minutes or less the way she drives.

Toy got her car on her sixteenth birthday which was almost five years ago. Mr. Jackson brought her a 2000 cherry red grand prix. Romeo recently added some twelve's and a new amplifier since he uses her car the majority of the time because he wrecked his. Mr. Jackson brought Romeo a Ford Mustang. I think that car was too fast for Romeo anyway. Not only that, he was drinking and driving so he ran into a tree. Mama Jackson said that she was glad that it was a tree instead of a person. Toy makes sure before she hands over the keys that Romeo has not been drinking. I think he learned his lesson because he had broken his arm and Mama and Mr. Jackson forbade him to drive for the first two years after his accident. Toy does not drink and drive, but she sure does drive fast.

I see Toy's car turning the corner now. I grabbed my Louis Vuitton knapsack and headed out the door as quickly as possible.

"See you later Stan. Toy just pulled up" I yelled.

"Not so fast! Come here aren't you forgetting something?" He asked.

I walked in the room, "what did I forget?"

"Don't play dumb. You know you forgot to give me a kiss."

Nausea seemed to inhabit my abdomen. Regurgitating all over Stan would be the high light of my day, but I held back my disgusted feeling of him and kissed him on his cheek. He smacked me on my butt as I walked away. Yuck! I hate him touching me. Now I probably smell like the cigar he's smoking.

I reached in my purse to spray myself with my pear Victoria Secret body spray, and popped in a Listerine strip so Toy would not have any funny suspicion. I guess I am overly paranoid, but if this secret gets out I don't know what I would do. This is a secret that I am too embarrassed to share and I might just have to carry it to my grave which I hope is not soon.

"Hey Toy, pop the trunk for me."

I sat my knapsack in her trunk. I always try my best to over pack because Chuck likes to surprise me by taking me out of town. I like to be a little more prepared now. As I sat in the car I looked up at the house and noticed Stan staring out the blinds. He is so nosey.

"Toy, hurry up and pull off please" I insisted. "Girl, my Uncle be tripping all the time like he wants to put a sista on punishment now. I guess he's getting old because he is always cranky. He trips on every little thing I do. I told him I am eighteen years old now and I will be moving out and making my own decisions. Shit, I'm getting tired of arguing with his old ass. I can't wait to get out of his house" I uttered.

This sounded real good if it were true. I wish I could say that to him without waking up from a ten second coma. I have been hoping and wishing that I could tell Toy about our relationship, but I know Toy. She would judge me without a doubt. I know her too well now and plus I was watching Oprah with her once when she had people who were engaged in the type of relationship I'm in with Stan. Toy said that the female was stupid because she should have told someone. She went on and on about how the teenager on Oprah's show probably wanted it just as much as the molester did because she never told anyone. When she makes those types of comments I remain silent. I guess Toy's response to situations like mine is the reason that I believe Chuck will leave me. That is exactly why I cannot tell anyone. Like I said, Victoria's got this secret and I'm riding it to me grave.

Toy turned the radio off and looked at me.

"Victoria, you will be graduating soon; have you figured out what you want to do with your life? What are your plans? I hear you talking about leaving your Uncle's house, but how do you plan on doing that? Have you really thought about it" she asked.

Wow! These questions hit me hard. I never actually thought about it that much. I know I want to do something with my life as well as leave Stan's house, but I never figured out how. I feel completely foolish because a plan is something that I do not have right now. I guess I do need one. I sat here slouched back in my seat rubbing my finger across my chin. "You know Toy, I never thought about it like that. I know that I want to go to college. As far as my career goals, I have been thinking of doing something with my poetry. I want to write novels like Terry McMillan and my role model Dr. Maya Angelou."

"Oh, now that's what's up." Toy responded as she nodded her head agreeing.

"I feel that Vickie. You most definitely should do something with your poetry because you are a natural. Writing Novels is not a bad idea either because books are in. I know Mama would be your biggest fan plus I love to read also. Just as long as you do something with your life and don't let your talent go to waste. I just got through talking to Rob and he was telling me how his sister will be graduating with her Master's in Business Administration next year and she is only twenty-five. Rob will be receiving his bachelors in Criminal Justice in two years. He keeps asking me when I am going to go to college and do something with my life. Plus you know Stephen has been on my head telling me about how rough it is out here being African American with no education. On top of that, we're females. Girl it's a wrap, the odds are already against us. Romeo tells me how he applies for different jobs and when he goes in the interviews, those white folks look at him and tell him right on the spot that they have already filled the position. Stephen said that Romeo needs to cut his braids and they may give him a better shot. Cornrows and earrings are not a great look when applying for position in Corporate America. I want to do something too, but I don't know what right now. It seems like everyone around me is doing something positive with their life and then they turn their noses up at me. I know I smoke a lot of weed and spend a lot of money, but that's me. My daddy has not told me to do anything nor has Mama. Neither one of them is pressuring me to go to school or get a job anyway. Stephen on the other hand is totally different. I guess since he is my step father and a professor at University at Detroit he feels obligated to encourage me to do something with my life, but Victoria I feel like this -"

I sat here listening to Toy and at the same time I am beginning to realize where she is getting all of this from. I know she could not have possibly come up with this revelation on her own. I was trying to figure out what made Toy suddenly become interested in my education and goals. I thought she didn't care about anyone, but herself. I can understand why she does not know what she wants to do with her own life. I always thought Toy was going to be a professional shopper or something because she loves to shop. She did graduate with honors, but since she didn't go straight to college I didn't think she cared. I guess now that Stephen and Robert has been in her ear she felt it necessary to blow smoke in mine. I glanced over and looked at Toy's lips steadily moving, but I somehow tuned her out because I have my baby on the brain. I reached in my purse and grabbed my Nextel.

"I hear you girl, but hold on one second," I lied. I have not heard anything she just said. I sent an alert to Chuck.

"Hey baby, I thought you forgot about me" he immediately responded as if he was sitting there staring at the phone waiting on my call.

"Forget about you? Never in a million years. So where are you" I asked.

"Waiting on your sexy ass; I've been calling you all day."

"I know you have, baby. My battery was dead and then you know how my Uncle be tripping."

"Yeah Toy told me. What's the deal with your Uncle anyway?"

"Chuck, honestly I don't know. He's always talking about how he does not want me out hanging around in the streets especially being around guys who would try to hurt me and things like that."

"Damn, your Uncle sounds like he wants to be your man instead of your Uncle!" He laughed.

I checked my top for blood to make sure it was not ruined from the sharp stab by that comment. I kept it Diva and laughed it off. "You are so silly boy, where you at?

"I'm on Jefferson. Do you feel like riding out with your man right quick?"

"Stop asking silly questions. You know I want to ride out with you"

"Ok. Cool. That's what's up. I am going to pull in at the Marriott Hotel, tell Toy to drop you off up here."

I glanced at Toy and she shook her head yes because she heard our entire conversation over the speaker phone.

"She heard you bay, I'm on my way" I chirped.

"Ok boo. I'll see you in a minute," he chirped back.

"Thanks Toy. If my Uncle calls you just tell him that I am with your mom and we went somewhere. Make up something and if that doesn't work stop answering his calls."

"Ok, but you know how crazy your Uncle acts when he can't get in contact with you especially if we are not together."

"Yeah I know Toy, but at this point, to be quite honest- I don't care what he thinks or does. I am going to be with my baby and that's all I really care about right now."

"I hear you girl" Toy replied as if she now understands the way I am feeling.

"Chuck, we just pulled up to the hotel, where are you?" I chirped.

"I'm in this black Lexus with the black tinted windows." He responded.

Toy pulled up to the Lexus. "Oh yeah, y'all doing it like that?"

"Y'all?" I questioned. "Girl you must mean Chuck's doing it like that. We just arrived at the same time. I do not have a car that's why I am riding with you." I said sarcastically. "But you know my baby; he likes to do it real big boo." I stated as I stood outside of the car.

"Alright girl, be careful."

"I will as soon as you pop the trunk."

"Oh girl my bad! You know a sista smoke." Toy responded

"I know boo." I replied as I grabbed my bag. "Thanks Toy, I'll call you."

"Alright girl, have fun for me" she yelled while driving off.

Chapter 4

Road Trip

My lips greeted Chuck's when I entered his car. My heart began to tingle as a cool sensation stimulated my veins. I have a type of love for this boy like I never had for anyone before. It is a … I know I want to spend the rest of my life making this man happy, type of love.

"And Hello to you too my beautiful Queen" Chuck replied, as he removed the remains of my lip gloss from around his lips. "You are looking top dollar, better than a super model sexy ma."

"Well baby … you know I stay dressed to impress … - you. You're looking real sexy yourself, as usual."

"You always look good anyway. That's what attracted me to you from the very beginning. You dress like a lady, sophisticated with mad sex appeal" He said while winking his eye at me.

Yeah, I am looking good, I thought to myself as I glanced in the side view mirror to confirm the accuracy of his compliment. Yeah, my baby is right on the money. I do look good if I shall say so myself. I decided to wear my turquoise and black Parasuco jeans with my black Parasuco tube top with the small turquoise patches.

Turquoise and lime green are my favorite colors. They're Chucks' also. We have so much in common; I know we have to be meant to be. I glanced down at my black six inch Kenneth Cole boots as I placed my Nextel in my matching purse. I pulled down the sun visor to reapply my strawberry lip gloss. I noticed how the different shine glared from different parts of my upper body.

The diamond chips in my gold Cartier earrings, the diamond dipped V charm on my gold necklace and my diamond tennis bracelet that Stan brought me for my sixteenth birthday is sparkling real nicely. Plus my 10 karat diamond engagement ring that Stan insisted that I give back to Chuck is adding extra shine. I try hard not to get caught up in material things, but it's hard not to when I've had it basically all of my life. I am addicted to looking good and staying fly. I not only look good for myself, I make sure that I am especially looking my best for Chuck.

"Here boo, blaze up" Chuck insisted as he passed me the blunt.

I lit it and with smoke blowing out my nose I asked, "Bay, where are we going?"

"We're going to Indiana right quick to drop off this package."

"Everything is legit right" I asked. Sorry boo I had to ask that question.

I don't have a problem riding with my baby, but I know that he does something that's most likely illegal. I told Chuck not to share with me what he does to get all of the money that he has. I don't want to know anything. Even though I have made the assumption that he distributes narcotics. He has to. I don't know any nineteen year old young black men living in the City of Detroit with the type of finances that Chuck has who is not a street pharmacist. Though Chuck never mentions to me what he does, I am pretty sure he knows that I am very intelligent and very far from stupid plus we live in the dirty D one of the largest dough boy capitals.

Chuck looked at me and replied "Of course baby. I have my license and full coverage on this rental."

"Oh yeah, I meant to ask you why aren't you driving your car anyway, not that I'm complaining." I guess that was a silly question to ask judging from the look on his face.

"Baby come on now, you know my car is hot. I think I am one of a very tiny percentage of young African American males who owns a lime green candy coated caprice sitting on 24inch rims. When the police see my car, they know it's me. They are ready to catch me slipping."

I felt stupid for asking so I just sat back and handed him the blunt, "Yeah you're right."

Chuck and I have been together for almost four years and we don't know much about one another as far as our family and personal issues are involved. We never question each other about things like that. We spend time together and have built our relationship strictly on us and what we do together and things that we physically learn from one another with our own eyes. He knows that my mom left me when I was little and he also knows that I live with Stan. He has also met Mama Jackson, but that's about it. It's not much that I can share with him anyway. Now in Chuck's case he talks about him living with his Uncle and that's about it. I have never been to his house nor have I met any of his family.

I never asked Chuck much about his parents and the reason for him living with his Uncle because I don't want him asking me questions regarding Stan. He already insulted me earlier today with the comment he made about Stan wanting me. I guess that hurt as bad as it did because it's true. My Uncle does want to be my man and let him tell it, he is my man. I have heard people say if the truth hurts say ouch. *OUCH!!!!! Chuck!!!* It's fine though because he does not know that he hurt my feelings. After what happened today, I better find out as much as I can about the man that I know that I want to marry. Today I noticed no matter how much you think you know someone you really don't know them. I am never one to ask a lot of questions, but when I smoke it changes my entire character and I don't like it.

When I smoke I begin to think about so many different things. I honestly don't like to smoke and I cannot explain why I continue to do it. It seems like my mind begins to get cluttered and my thoughts appear to be a bit foggy. I am very nervous at this point because I am not sure if I go ahead and ask Chuck about his family and his personal life, if he will begin to question me about mine. The responses that I may give while I am under the influence of marijuana may get me in a lot of trouble. All I have is the truth anyway. I have to ask him.

"Chuck, I have been curious to know where your mom and dad are. Tell me about your family. I love you for you, but I still want to know things about you. I know that you told me that you live with your Uncle, but you never told me why."

"I never told you because you never asked. I have been wondering when you were going to ask. I was beginning to think that you didn't care about your future husband." He replied as he leaned over to kiss me keeping his eye on the road.

"Chuck, I try not to ask you a lot of questions. I learned that a quiet person is a wise person, but I realized that this is important. I want to know baby. I love you." I replied as I sat here trying to control the rapid beat of my heart. The weed that I smoke does not change the way that I feel about him at all. I just seem to ask silly questions often and I prefer not to be insulted by Chuck because he is good for doing so. That's another reason that I hate smoking, it minimizes my intelligence sometimes and I despise that.

"Victoria, my life has not been all that great, but I am still here by the grace of GOD." Chuck replied as he hit the off button on the stereo.

"When I was ten, my mom killed my brother who was sixteen at the time. Sometimes my mom would have these spells and blink out and start beating on my brother. My brother looks exactly like our dad. I assume my brother reminded her of my dad which was obviously not a good thing. My dad used to beat my mom badly. He also raped her several times after they separated. My dad had become addicted to heroin. He sniffed it a lot and that's how he lost his job with the Detroit Police Department. He was a Police Sergeant who used his power with the law to put my mom in jail by making false statements against her. My mom explained that he often lied and accused her of physically attacking him. Momma said that daddy usually accused her of cheating because of the beauty she possessed."

I sat here listening and thinking of how his dad sounds awfully familiar. "Excuse me Chuck, How did your parents meet and what did your mom do as far as a career" I interrupted.

"They met in college. My mom graduated from Wayne State University with her Bachelors in Social Work. She became a Social Worker for the Child Welfare System about three years before she had me. My mom was real nice, Victoria. She received so many awards for being selected as the "Most Inspirational Life Changing Social Worker of the Year." Momma told me and Detrick that she caught my dad cheating with one of her girlfriends and she had a suspicion that he might have been using drugs. When my dad was fired from the Police Department, Mama explained that her accusations were then validated. I guess my daddy felt like everything was my mom's fault because he started beating her every day. Momma tried to continue going to work, but when my dad broke her jaw and blackened her eye she stopped going. She turned into an alcoholic and changed completely."

"I apologize boo, I don't mean to keep interrupting you, but how did you feel watching your dad beat on your mom like that" I asked.

"I hated it. I loved my mom and dad equally. I just wanted them to get along. What made me extremely angry was the day when I walked in on my dad raping my mom. At that time I did not know what he was doing to her, but I knew that it was not right because Momma was screaming and fighting him. I could not do anything about it. My dad looked up at me and noticed how I was staring at him. He immediately jumped up and went in the bathroom. I noticed he was in there for a long time so I decided to walk in and see what he was doing. When I entered the bathroom I saw my dad sitting on the toilet, with his eyes rolled into the back of his head with white foam around his mouth. I glanced down at his arm and noticed he had some type of elastic band tied around it with a needle hanging out. I remember standing in the doorway with tears rolling down my eyes. I couldn't move. It seemed as if I didn't hear anything or see anything, but my dad sitting there looking like some type of monster. My mom saw me standing there so she walked over to me. Momma had her usual drink in her hand. I guess that was her way of numbing the pain. What's the matter with you boy, you look like you seen a ghost momma said as she walked towards me. She walked over to me and looked in the bathroom. When she looked in the bathroom her whiskey and bologna smelling vomit showered the both of us. The only thing I remembered after that was watching the ambulance carry my dad out zipped up in a black body bag."

"Where was your brother" I asked as I wiped my tears.

"Detrick was at football practice. He was the starting Quarter back for Southfield High School." Chuck replied as he wiped his finger across his eye. I assume it was to catch his tear.

Though, Chuck showed no emotion at all. I know that sharing this with me is hurtful. I get teary eyed when I think about the day Mama left me so I know losing a dad and a brother that will not be returning is even more painful, which reminds me …

"Chuck, how did your Mom kill your brother? I understand if you don't want to continue talking about it. You don't have to tell me anymore if you don't want to."

"No baby it's cool. God is good and he has surely brought me from a mighty long way, those days are behind me now. I get a little sad when I think about it, but what can I do to change the past. Nothing, I can take it and learn from it. The day my mom killed my brother it seemed like a sudden cloud of darkness covered our house. It all started when my mom asked Detrick to take out the trash. He asked her could I do it because he needed to finish studying. Momma yelled at him and told him that he better do as she said or she was going to get angry. Detrick told Momma that he did not care anything about her getting angry. I noticed the change in my brother after our dad died. He never said anything, but I know he blamed her for our father's death because of the way that he started disrespecting her. After Momma told Detrick to get up and do as she said he jumped in her face and said he didn't have to do anything that she said. He then told her if our dad was there that she would be taking out the trash herself. I guess that last statement Detrick made triggered something in my mom. I knew that she had already been drinking because that's what she did every single day. Momma took her glass and broke it over Detrick's head and then she ran to the kitchen and grabbed a big butcher knife and ran back and stabbed my brother fifteen times in his chest. The ambulance came and took my brother out in one of the same bags that my daddy was taken out in. Shortly after, the police took my mom out in handcuffs."

"Is that when you moved in with your Uncle?"

"No actually I went to a foster home first. I went to live with Justine. She had become my foster mom. Justine is the nicest person I have ever met, besides you." Chuck stated as he grabbed my hand and kissed it gently.

"I truly feel blessed to have met Justine. She took me to Church with her every Sunday. I joined the junior deacon's board after I accepted Jesus as my personal savior. Justine died from cancer when I was fifteen. I had no clue she was sick. She was pretty good at keeping her emotions locked in as well as disguising the way she actually felt. She was very good at keeping secrets. I had no clue that she had a son who basically disowned her because he was gay. Plus, her ex-husband left her and married her best friend. When she died I found out a lot of things about Justine that she never told me. I guess she was sent in my life for a reason. She helped me realize that dark clouds are meant to be moved and life is not always what it seems. No matter all of the things Justine went through in her life she made sure she credited God for everything. She told me that she saw the story on the news regarding my family. She said God personally put it on her heart to make it a priority that she received custody of me. As I look back she did exactly as God instructed her to do. Justine told me right before she took her last breath to make sure whatever life throws at me to make sure that I lean on God and trust in him no matter what I go through. She told me to remember that people will fail me every single time, but God will never fail me. No matter what I do in life God will never turn his back on me. She also explained to me that she knew her time had come and it was time for her to go home and get some rest.

"Oh my, Chuck, she seems like she was a very nice lady. I wish I could have met her."

"I know, but let me finish telling you Victoria." He insisted. "Justine made sure she kept in contact with my Aunt Lynn who is my mom's sister. Aunt Lynn loves God just as much as Justine did. After Justine died Aunt Lynn explained that she contacted my dad's brother 'Uncle Martin' who everyone calls 'Uncle Bud'. She explained to me that he said he was willing to take me in since he had his own place and no kids. I moved in with him and that's where I have lived for the last three and a half years. When I moved in with him, I instantly became a man. The reality of street life was introduced to me and surviving in them was and still is my daily goal. I know you never wanted to know what I did out here in the streets, but I know you know. I am positive that you are already up on it. My Uncle introduced me to this dangerous game of life and death, titled "the dope game." He told me that in order to live in his house I had to provide something and school books weren't going to cut it. He handed me a sandwich bag with a cream colored rock. He showed me how to chop it up and sell it. The money's been so good, quitting and getting an average job seems like it will be hard to do. Trust me Victoria, your man has a plan and God is going to take care of me."

Chuck looked over at me as sincere as he possibly could with a slight tear in his eye, "Victoria, I'm serious. I don't plan on staying in this my whole life. I'm trying to save enough money so I can go to college without paying for it sixty years from now. I want to get out the game ma. I'm tired of selling crack to my own people. Trust me, I know it's not right, but I pray that God gives a brother like me a minute to get it together. I refuse to be a statistic out here getting locked up in this crooked system for distributing this bulshit to my own people. I know that this dope shit is what's destroying our city. As a matter of fact, it's destroying cities all over the world, especially in our Black Community. You know what Vickie?" he asked.

"What baby?" I responded.

"Sometimes I think if the idiots's who created this dope shit didn't give it to dude's like me so we could make money, what would we do in order to live good and comfortable without living with rats and roaches and shit like that. I try to convince myself that it's all temporary. It's easy for people to judge us and talk about the situation while they're standing on the outside looking in. I just try to be as careful as I can be. You know it's messed up that we didn't even make these drugs, but somehow they ended up in our neighborhoods. A nigga will get more time selling drugs then they will for damn near blowing up a nation. This whole American dream concept seems a bit more like a nightmare. I try not to let it bring me down. That's why I keep my faith in God and continue praying for the sun to shine my way." Chuck said as he glanced up at the sky.

The struggle of a young black man has never saturated my thoughts until now. I watched it in movies, heard people talking about it, but I never heard it from the horse's mouth so to speak. I can't believe my baby has been through all this. I knew Chuck was intelligent and I trust his decision in the way he is choosing to live his life right now. Long as he sees a better future, I definitely stand behind him. Mama Jackson always told me that it's better to wake up and chase a dream instead of sleep your life away. As these tears roll down my cheeks my heart is beating fast.

"Chuck, I just want to let you know that I love you and I have your back no matter what you decide to do. I am sorry about your family baby. I can be your family if you want me to."

He glanced over at me while keeping his eyes on the road. He noticed the tears running from my eyes. He briefly looked at me again and handed me a Kleenex from the armrest. "What you mean if I want you to. You know I want you to. Don't cry for me, ma. There's no need to tear up those sexy eyes, I'm straight. What don't kill a real Man only makes him stronger, you feel me boo" he replied.

For some reason I think that I am about to ask Chuck a stupid question. I know that I should know the answer to it, but I don't. I remember my fifth grade teacher Mrs. Kelley told me that the only stupid questions are the ones that I don't ask. Remembering that phrase assisted me in setting the fact that I might be embarrassed behind me.

Who's GOD?

"Chuck, you know how you keep saying God I know it might seem silly, but who is that?

I felt a huge insult headed my way as he sat there doing a double take.

"Victoria, please tell me that you are joking. You don't know who gave his only begotten son, that whosoever believeth in him should not parish, but have everlasting life?" he questioned.

"No Chuck, I don't know that's why I am asking you now" I replied sarcastically. I am trying to refrain from getting upset at the way he's looking at me as if I am stupid or dumb for not knowing. Even though that's exactly how I feel about myself, don't make me feel even worse by letting me know you feel the same way. Mama Jackson talks about God and so does Chuck. I never asked anyone to explain it to me because it seemed like everyone already knew. I guess this is where the stupid question that was not asked applies. I am asking now. That should be good enough. That's the only thing that upsets me with Chuck. He always seems to treat me like I am stupid or lacking intellect because I don't know everything he thinks I should know.

"I am so sorry baby" he stated as he kissed my hand. I assume he felt my frustration from the silent treatment I gave.

"Everybody does not know who God is. I guess that is why God allowed you to ask me so that I can tell you. Besides, I would have never known if it had not been for Justine. She made sure that I knew who God was before she died. I can understand why you may not know him. God was never a subject of discussion in my household when I was growing up. That's why all of those tragedies occurred simply because no one in my house knew him. Victoria, God is how we became; he created us in his own image. He gave his son Jesus to die on the cross for all of our sins."

"Really" I responded with great interest.

"Baby, you have to love God. I pray every day when I am out here in these streets that the Lord watches over me."

"Does it work?" I asked.

"I'm here aint I?" He replied with a smile.

"Chuck, can you teach me how to pray?"

He pointed to the glove box.

"Baby girl, look in that glove box. There is a small green book in there. That's my pocket bible. Look in the front of it and find where it says 'prayer'. I don't want to steer you wrong at all so I think it might be best if you read for yourself and if you have any questions ask me. That's basically the Book of Life. When we pray it's our way of communicating to God and when we read its God's way of talking back to us." Chuck explained.

I reached in the glove box and grabbed it. I opened it and as I began to read through the first pages it describes where to find help when you feel a certain way. There are also scriptures that tell you what you are going through and how to solve them. I glanced at the cover that reads, "New Testament: Psalms Proverbs." I flipped back to the first page. The first word I noticed was, Afraid: psalms 34:4. I turned to "Psalm 34." I assumed that under that 34, I would go to where it had a number 4. I began to read:

"I sought the Lord, and he heard me, and delivered me from all my fears."

The only fear that I have right now that is really bothering me is Stan. Especially after what happened today; I realized that leaving Stan is my biggest fear. He already threatened me. I know that Stan is capable of killing me. What makes me any different than the people he kills on the job? I watched a show on television that said once a person kills the first time, killing a second or third will be a piece of cake. In my case, I could be Stan's one hundredth victim. I believe Stan would actually kill me if I did leave him for Chuck or if I left him for anyone for that matter. He has already threatened guys who he suspected that might have had interest in me. As I sat here thinking about what I fear the most I continued reading and learned that God will take away all of my fears. I flipped back to the first page to look up how to pray and the closest word I could find is *prayer.*

The first Scripture was *Luke 11:1-13.* I began to read:

"Now it came to pass, as He was praying in a certain place, when He ceased, that one of His disciples said to Him, "Lord, teach us to pray, as John also taught his disciples." "So He said to them, "When you pray, say:

Our Father in heaven,
Hallowed be your name.
Your kingdom come.
Your will be done
On earth as it is in heaven.
Give us day by day our daily bread.
And forgive us our sins,
For we also forgive everyone who is indebted to us.
And do not lead us into temptation,
But deliver us from the evil one"

I kept reading on and I got to a part where it read: *"ask and it should be given to you, who ever ask shall receive. If you seek you shall find."*

I feel more than encouraged. Recognizing the fact that Chuck said this is God's way of talking to us, I feel so honored that he has spoken to me. I sat back in my seat and began to stare at the dark sky. I wonder is heaven up in the sky behind the clouds somewhere.

"Victoria, are you ok? Are you going to answer that?"

"Huh? What?" Oh he's talking about my cell phone. I grabbed my cell from my purse. I glanced at my caller Id. Oh its Toy. *As if anyone else has the number.* I thought to myself.

"What's up girl?"

"Hey Victoria, your Uncle just called. He said that he needs you to call him right away."

"Ok Toy, Where did you tell him I was?"

"I told him that you were in the shower."

"Ok cool. Click over and call him on a three way so it looks like I am calling from your house." I insisted. I am taking a major risk by calling him on the three-way like this. He has never said anything to disclose our secret before, so I hope this is one of those times. The phone rang twice when Toy clicked back over.

"Yeah" he answered.

"Hey Uncle, you called me?"

"Yeah, I was sitting here thinking about what happened earlier today. I wanted to call and apologize once again. If I hurt you in any way I really am sorry. I don't know if you understand that I love you that much. I don't want to see you get hurt out here in these streets by these guys who only go after you because of the way you look and dress. These young boys don't mean you any good Victoria. That's all I have been trying to explain to you."

"Uncle Stan, I totally understand your view point. I love you to. Well Uncle Stan, Toy and I are about to finish studying so I guess I will talk to you on Sunday."

"Ok Vickie, don't study too hard. Talk to you later. I think I am going to go over to my mother's for a while."

"Ok, tell granny I said hello." I said.

"I will. Bye" he hung up.

I felt a big relief because he kept it family oriented. "Thanks Toy."

"Where y'all at" she asked.

"We are on the highway heading to Indiana."

"Alright, y'all be careful out there."

"I will. Thanks again, you know you my girl. I love you Toy."

"I love you too," she reiterated before hanging up.

"Victoria, my love, are you okay?" Chuck asked.

"Yes baby I'm fine. I drifted off after I read a few of the scriptures from the bible." I replied as I turned to face him. "Chuck, how do you know if there is a heaven?"

Chuck gripped the steering wheel with his left hand and used his right hand to tilt his navy blue Detroit fitted cap as he scratched the top of his head.

"Well bay, I just trust in God that there has got to be a better place than the one we are in right now. I am going to take you to Church with me one Sunday and I will introduce you to my pastor, he can explain it ten times better than I can." He replied.

The cold tingly sensation that I often feel when I am with Chuck has just ran free throughout my body. As I quiver from these chills, I am instantly heated as I stare into his beautiful brown eyes. I can only see them for a second because Chuck likes to keep his eyes on the road. As I am sitting here holding his hand, I feel so protected.

"Baby, we will be alright trust me. Your future husband is going to make sure that you are taken care of" Chuck assured. I assume that he felt my kinetic energy as he assured our relationship, making me feel safe and secure just as he always does.

"Chuck, I have to use the rest room."

"Okay I got you" he replied as he put on his right blinker and merged in the right lane. As he switched lanes, he stated, "I have to use the bathroom also, but I was gone ride it out for a couple more miles, but it's all good."

Chuck exited the highway and pulled into a Mobil Gas station. The sign above us before we exited stated that we were one exit away from the "Ohio Turnpike." We are not quite out of Michigan yet, though it seemed like we have been riding forever.

"Oh, I better fill up since we're here" Chuck stated as he pulled up at the pump. "Do you have to go right now" he asked.

"I can hold it for a few minutes, why what's up boo?"

"Let me put the gas in right quick. I don't want you going in there without me."

He took his Mobile gas card out and placed it in the pump and began pumping his gas. He looked at me and then looked at the pump. "Bay, you see this?" he asked.

"See what?" I replied looking and feeling confused.

"This gas is $3.12 a gallon. This is freaking ridiculous."

I stood here still confused because I never thought anything about gas prices because it does not apply to me. I don't have a car yet and by the way Toy, Chuck and even Stan complains about the price of gas, I'm not sure if I want to.

"See this" Chuck pointed at the $3.12 above 87. "Victoria, remember when I was telling you earlier about the American Dream becoming an American Nightmare, this explains a little bit about that. Remember when we were watching Kat Williams?"

"Yes" I chuckled.

"Remember when he made that joke saying that *"we shouldn't be at the gas station making life decisions"* this is the truth right her. We're getting pimped at the pumps." Chuck laughed.

I stood here watching Chuck cheering himself up, but at the same time, *is that an inside joke or something*, I thought to myself, because I do not see the amusement. Chuck obviously noticed that I was still confused.

He continued chuckling "Oh babe, you probably don't understand. If you had to pay your hard earned money for gas in your own car you would probably get it." He said.

Right ... I thought to myself. Yeah, I guess I might need to figure that one out on my own. I mean he is really tickled. While Chuck is providing himself with jokes that only he finds funny, I began to review my surroundings.

As I look around, I am beginning to notice that I do not see any other black people out here besides me and Chuck. It's very quiet out here. Now that I think about it, there are not a lot of White people living in Detroit. I grasped on to Chucks arm. I know that White people do not like African Americans; at least that's what I learned in my Black History Class and from some of my friends.

My hollow muscular organ is rapidly beating through my chest. I don't feel comfortable out here. They are staring at me and Chuck like we are some type of criminals. I don't like the looks they're giving us. I never understood what it is about our skin that poses a threat to them. It might have something to do with the fact that every time we turn on the news it's one of us exploited. I know it's the weed that might have me paranoid. All the effects that I get from weed doesn't feel good. Though I have noticed it makes me think about things and notice things that I probably would have never noticed or paid any attention to.

"Baby, you are fine. Trust me. I will not let anything happen to you." Chuck replied. He felt the tightness of the hold I had on his arm because he put his hand on my hand "Victoria, relax boo" he said as he loosened my grip. We headed towards the front door of the gas station.

As Chuck reached for the door, the man on his way out held the door for us. "How are y'all folks doing tonight?" he asked.

"Great sir, Thank you" Chuck replied.

What in the world – That's different. He was actually one of the White men who I perceived to be staring at Chuck and me strange. I looked back and watched him get in his truck. The opinion I had already drafted in my mind was just erased when he spoke and kept going. Everybody was greeting and smiling at us. My perception has changed. They don't appear to be as dangerous as I thought. My friend Lisa at school is white and most of Stan's guy friends who come over to the house are white, but I never considered them to be the average white person because they grew up with us. Actually I never paid much attention to the color of their skin anyway. I feel a bit more at ease now that I notice people are still going on about their business.

Chuck felt my sense of relief. He looked at me and smiled. "See I told you. You have to trust me. Your man has your back for real. I would never put you in any danger like that ma." He stated as he released my hand in front of the ladies restroom. "I'll meet you here when you finish" he said.

I entered the restroom and released what seems to be at least a gallon of fluids. I looked in my purse, pulled out my Summers Eve cleansing cloth and wiped myself. Mama Jackson told me that keeping my own wipes is a necessity. She explained how being a female comes with extra sensitivities especially when it comes to using public restrooms. She also said it's healthier for me to use wipes because my butt is so big. I have to give my mom the credit for that. I flushed the toilet and walked out the stall.

"Hi there, how are you?"

"I feel about ten pounds lighter, so I guess you can say that's great right?" I smiled.

"Well you have yourself a great day young lady. Well I guess you can say night now. I drive those big trucks from sun up to sun down. I'm sure you can see how this old lady often gets confused." She responded with laughter as she exited the restroom.

Hmm, it seems like everyone is so happy and friendly. I often expect for someone to change or at least play the role of the perceived characters I assumed them to be, but it's not at all like that.

I washed my hands with my own personal soap that Mama Jackson also told me to keep with me at all times. I guess since she is a registered nurse she feels obligated to inform Toy and I on being sanitary. I am actually thankful for that. I stared at my nice round apple bottom as I dried my hands under the automatic dryer. I fixed my hair and then took out my strawberry Bath and Body Works lip gloss. One of Toy friends works there. Once she introduced Toy to the lip gloss, of course she told me. Ever since Bath and Body Works lip gloss and I made a connection, it's been love at first use. I have them in every flavor. Even though Bath and Body works sold me on the lip gloss I couldn't betray Victoria's secret body fragrance.

I sprayed on my pear Victoria Secret's and rubbed on the hand lotion. Now I am good to go. Remaining the Diva that I am and the Queen that Chuck fell in love with is hard work. I know Chuck is probably wondering what is taking me so long, but I'm sure when he sees me it is more than worth the wait. I turned around to see if my booty was still looking plump and juicy then I plumped my breast and now I am ready to exit the restroom. Let me go out here and put an end to my fiancés miserable wait.

Oohhh I love him!!!!

Whoa! Chuck startled me. "Hey boo" I said appearing not to be as startled as I really am. Wow he caught me off guard. "What is this" I questioned the three roses he held in his hand.

"Here baby. This is a rose for your heart, a rose for your soul and a rose for your spirit. Victoria, I love you. You are different from all the other females I have ever met. I feel so blessed to have you in my life. I can't wait until we get married. I want you to be Mrs. Victoria Matthews. You are an example of a Queen. You are a woman that I often dreamed of and prayed for. Every time I think about you I know that God loves me. He gave you to me and I am so thankful."

Oh my goodness. I cannot help these tears that are rapidly flowing freely from my eyes. He's wiping my tears. I stood here feeling like the roses that I hold and the rose that I always feel I am. It's ok now for me to lack thorns. My stem is smooth without supplying pain. My pedals feel strong as I am leaning to my sunshine.

The light Chuck possesses has brightly giving out rays of sunlight like I have never seen before. He has tapped into my spirit and placed a glow there. As I stood here allowing the eucalyptus of his words sooth my pores as my love begins to grow.

"Chuck, you are rare and distinct from all the rest. I never knew there was such a thing as Real Love until I met you. Many people try to explain what love is, but their perceptions have been proven invalid. I often dreamed about being able to love and be loved unconditionally by someone. With you, I love you more than that. You provide smooth, gentle, rhythmatic contractions to the ventricles and atriums of my existence. You expose me to different parts of life that I never knew existed. You provide me with security. I feel so safe when I am with you, protected when I am in your arms. When I am away from you sometimes I can't eat, I can't sleep, and often times I find it difficult to breathe when I am not with you. I love you Charles Matthews. I am not sure if I know exactly how to be a Queen, but I know that I will do everything in my power to make it right. I love you so much. Thank you for loving me" I replied as I laid my head on his chest and compared our heart beats.

The rhythms are identical. I have received this same identical cool chill throughout my body for the last couple of months since our relationship has been growing stronger and stronger. I often get this same chill when I am happy or when I say certain things. It's one of the best feelings I have ever felt. I love this man so much, though I am not quite sure if my definition of love is absolutely correct, but from what I can convey I like everything about him. I want to protect him from all of his pain. I want to be by his side till the day I die and I hope it won't be soon. Chuck mentioned that God hears our thoughts; I really hope he hears this.

"Dear God,

If you can really hear my thoughts, please show me your presence; please let me know that you are real. God, I am open to all new things. I hope you are real and you actually are listening to me. I know other people talk to you, but I never knew that I could. God, I need you now. In Jesus name I pray that you are real."

Chuck said that I had to ask everything in Jesus name because in order to get to God I must go through his son Jesus.

"Baby, I could stand here and hold you forever, but right now we have to go." Chuck said as he lifted my head from his chest.

"Ooh Chuck can we get something to eat from that Churches Chicken right quick? My high is gone, but I still have the munchies boo. I'm hungry." I replied.

We walked over to this Churches that's connected to this gas station. Chuck placed our order. He knows me oh so well. He ordered a 4 piece white with a large order of jalapeno poppers, biscuits, mashed potatoes with a coke and a fruit punch. After we received our order, we got in the car and headed on our way. Chuck said that we didn't have enough time to eat in side. I fed my baby his food and I ate mine as well. Now I'm developing the usual symptoms of somnolence. It usually occurs right after I eat.

I don't know how Chuck is feeling right now, but I know when I get full I am on my way to sleep. I realized that I had dozed off when I felt Chuck shaking my leg. "Baby you sleep?" he asked.

I don't know what was keeping me from providing that sarcasms that he usually has when I ask a silly question. *You just shook me to wake me up, but you are asking me if I am sleep. Well, I'm not anymore* I thought to myself.

"No, I'm up baby. I was just thinking about something, what's up?" I asked.

"I thought you left me hanging. You were so quiet" he responded as he reached and turned the radio on. "Isn't this your song, ma" he asked while turning it up.

"You know it baby." I smiled.

"♫♪Pretty brown eyes ... ... you know ... I see girl. It's a disguise the way you treat me; the way you treat me. You keep holding on ... To your thoughts of rejection, if you're with me I'm secured ... ... Listen to love ... ... your heart is pounding with desire ... ... waiting to be unleashed. Quit breaking my heart ♫♪

I sat here listening to my baby butcher Mint Condition's song as my insides began to tingle all over again. At the same time he's turning me on. I love this song. I love him. He kept glancing over at me, keeping his eyes on the road as he was singing this song, melting my heart.

Chuck's cell phone started ringing. He looked at his phone, "Oh this is my man's I'm supposed to be meeting up with. Turn that down some, ma." He said as he pointed to the radio.

Of course I turned it down, as a matter of fact let me turn it off. I'm too nosy for my own good.

"What up doe" Chuck answered.

"Change in plans dawg!" I heard the guy yell through Chuck's phone. "The Feds just hit my spot. Where you at homie?" he asked.

"I just left Toledo, Ohio about thirty minutes ago. I'm getting ready to jump on Interstate-94. Tone, are you straight? Is everything cool? What do you want me to do? Do you want me to continue coming or what? What's happening?" Chuck asked.

"Yeah, it's a couple snitches on the loose, but my partners already on the job. Keep on coming. When you get near you will see me. I want you to meet me on I-94 right before the South End exit. Don't exit the freeway. I will meet you on the freeway because shit is real hot around here" he yelled.

As I'm sitting here listening to Tone yell through the phone my stomach has started bubbling. Nervousness is scratching the inside of my belly. *Please don't go, it's a set-up,* is what the little voice in my head continued repeating. I am not sure where the voice is coming from, but it's one that I refuse to ignore. I tried convincing myself that it might be the weed playing tricks on me until I just had a premonition of flashing lights and handcuffs being accessories to me and Chuck's attire.

"Ok, dawg be cool. I'll be there in about maybe four more hours. I will call and let you know when I'm close." Chuck stated.

Tone hung up without saying bye or anything. I noticed the look of confusion on Chucks face. He looks like he is worried. I sat here and remained quiet about the voices and the premonitions. I don't want Chuck to think that I am crazy or trying to jinx him or anything. Most of the times I get premonitions that are about minor things. The sad thing is when I get them; I never pay attention to them. They usually play out the way that I see them and when they do, I usually say déjà vu. Mama Jackson explained that my mom shared with her that she often had them. She said Mama told her that my grandmother got them all the time. I wish I knew how they reacted to them. I can't ignore this premonition, it seems so real.

I have been sitting here for the last three and a half hours contemplating the issue of telling him. We are getting closer to Gary, Indiana. The sign just read *Gary Indiana 20 miles.* I grabbed Chuck's hand.

"Baby, I was not trying to be nosy, but I overheard your boy saying that his spot got hit by the Feds."

"Yeah, what you getting at ma," He asked as he glanced at me with great interest.

My heart continued pounding as I tried to block out the previsions of us being separated by the criminal justice system.

"Well baby, I don't think you should go. My reason being is simply because it was his spot. Nine times out of ten that could possibly mean that they are probably watching him or looking for him. I really don't think you should go right now. At least not tonight, it sounds too risky, plus I have this gut feeling."

"Baby, this is a quick 42g's. I need to make this money! Don't you like for your man to keep you fly? This is not just for me Victoria; I'm doing this for us. Everything will be fine, you're just paranoid" he replied.

"Honey, I understand that. Thank you for keeping me in mind when you make your decisions in doing what you do, but right now Chuck, I need you to consider my feelings. I do not feel right about this. If you love me and value my thoughts and concerns, you'd listen to me this one time, please." I begged.

I can't tell him that I just received a premonition that we are going to jail if we continue on this journey tonight. Mentioning that my Uncle is the Feds does not seem like a great decision either. The odds are against us. I wouldn't put it past Stan if he received a tip that I was on my way to Indiana. I don't trust Stan, especially the crock about him going to see grandma because they don't get along at all. I haven't seen her in almost ten years. Everything that's bothering me right now has a connection to Stan. I am paranoid with all reason to be. This is my first time attempting to change my vision of the future and Chuck is not listening to me.

"Victoria, calm down. We will be alright." Chuck said.

I am getting very agitated. He said that he loves me, but he is disregarding my feelings. This is hurting like hell right now. "Chuck, I am serious. Why won't you listen to me" I screamed.

"Whoa lil Mama, you don't need to yell at me. Let that be your last time raising your voice at me! Now what do you suggest that we do since you seem to know it all right now."

"First of all Chuck, I did not mean to yell at you and second of all, I don't think I know it all. I am simply telling you that I do not feel right being in this car with you while you are going to meet a guy who just told you that his spot was hit by the feds. Not to mention he informed you that shit was hot, I believe those were his word. I am getting angry because you are thinking about the money. What good is the money going to do either one of us if we are locked up" I replied.

"Victoria, I understand that. Now again I am asking you, what do you suggest that we do?"

"I think we should go to a hotel. You can call your boy and tell him that you caught a flat and you can't get a tow truck until morning. That sounds good to me. How does that sound to you?"

"You know what little Mama" he said as he began merging in the right lane. "One thing Justine told me was when I got a good woman who cared about me enough to inform me when she had a bad gut feeling about something, I better listen. She said it was like female intuition or something. Baby, I'm sorry I tried to argue with you and disregard your feelings. I am going to come up at the next hotel sign I see. Plus, I'm tired of driving anyway" he explained.

The smile on my face is my expression of relief. Though, I am still paranoid. Let me call Toy right quick. She needs to call Stan for me. If he does not answer then I know he has something to do with this situation in Indiana. I reached in my purse and grabbed my cell.

Hmm … I wonder why Toy is not answering her cell. It is only 12:15 a.m. Toy does not go to sleep this early. I called again, still no answer. I have the bubble guts. Oh my goodness, I can't stop all of these different thoughts that are invading my mind. Where could Toy be, I wonder did Stan go over her house. Is he standing in front of her? Come on Toy, pick up the phone. Damn it! I keep getting her voice mail. Let me try one more time.

"Vickie, what's up" Toy answered appearing to be out of breath.

"Dang Toy what took you so long?"

"Girl, I was washing my hair, why what's the problem?"

"Nothing, did my Uncle call?"

"No! Is he supposed to?"

"No he's not. I'm just checking in. Toy, can you call him for me right quick. Please" I asked sounding as if I'm not in the mood for games.

She clicked over and called him.

"*Hey baby*" he answered.

No the heck he didn't! He just pissed me off. Maybe I'm over reacting. All I want to know is *why the hell you answered the phone like that,* I thought to myself. Let me stay in my Diva shoes and keep it moving.

"Hi Uncle Stan, what are you doing?"

"Nothing, I'm still at my mother's house, why? What are you doing?" he asked sounding as if he knew something.

"Nothing much, just kicking it. Toy and I just came back from the movies. I decided to call and check on you before I went to sleep."

"Oh, I'm okay I think I'm going to head home and go to sleep too, because I'm a little tired and I have to get a haircut tomorrow" he said.

"Alright then, don't let me hold you up. I will see you Sunday. Toy and I have a lot of plans for tomorrow so I may be busy all day."

"Ok Victoria, remember what I said about them knuckle headed boys. Love you and see you Sunday." He hung up.

"Hello, hello" Toy repeated. She clicked over and then clicked back. "Hello" she repeated again.

"Hey Toy, I'm here. I just wanted to make sure that he actually hung up." I feel so much better and so relieved. "Thanks Toy, I will talk to you tomorrow ok."

"Girl bye, Robert is on his way to pick me up. I have to finish freshening up. I need to get me some girl. Shoot a sista is horny than a mutha. Love you boo" she replied.

"TMI, Toy" I laughed. *That was too much info*, I thought "Thanks again boo. I will call you tomorrow." I said before I hung up.

"Victoria, are you ok?" Chuck asked.

"Yeah baby, I'm fine. I was just checking with my Uncle. Why do you ask?"

He looked over at me again with that double take look he gives as if I have done something or said something wrong.

"You asked me about my family earlier; it's my turn to ask you. Baby, why is your Uncle so hard on you, seriously." He asked.

This is the question I knew would possibly come up. I inhaled deeply and exhaled slowly.

"Too be honest Chuck, sometimes I have no clue why my Uncle is very strict on me. I have questioned him also about the same matter. He has told me that he does not want me to end up like my mom. My mom is on drugs and she is a prostitute, at least that's what he tells me. My mom dropped me off on the curb in front of his house when I was five. He tells me daily, how he doesn't want me to grow up to be like her. The only thing is he degrades my mom. I understand that my mom might have done and still does things that are not morally right, but at the same time she's my mom and no matter what I still love her. Don't get me wrong, I sort of understand where he is coming from. He says that my mom caused everyone a lot of heartaches, money and pain. It all started over some guy which is probably my father. I guess he's trying to make sure that I don't make the same mistake."

"Oh ok I feel that." He replied.

I'm feeling that story too, especially if it were all true. The crack head and prostitution part is what he told me about, but not her losing her mind over some guy. *Seriously Chuck, can you handle the truth? The real honest truth is my Uncle is hard on me because he is in love with me. He does not want another male near me. That's the real reason why that dummy is so hard on me! He does not want anyone near me. That's why that bastard is so hard on me Chuck!!!!"* I screamed in my mind! If it came to the point where I felt it totally necessary to share that with Chuck, I don't think that's the perfect way to do it.

Ooh I like this Hotel. I had my sixteenth birthday party here at the Hilton. Chuck pulled up to the door and hopped out.

"I'll be right back" he informed me as he shut the driver's side door behind him. When I was at the Hilton in Auburn Hills a year and a half ago, I had an all-girls sleep over while Stan had a security guard outside of my room to make sure there were no boys. I didn't want to tell Chuck that's where my party was because he couldn't come. Being here with him now will make up for it. I am very excited, but my Diva shoes will remain on. Ooh, I hear little whispers of one of my favorite songs coming through the speakers.

Ooh now this is my song. I turned up the radio~ it's my girl Sade. What perfect timing. "♫♪ this –is- no -ordinary love, no ordinary love♫♪." I love Sade. I feel so relieved and so relaxed. Look at my baby. He is so sexy. Now Sade you never lied because this love we have, this is no ordinary love.

"I hope this Hotel is good enough for you. Let me know because I will find us another one." Chuck said as he drove to the other side of the hotel.

"Stop playing with me." I replied as I rolled my eyes at him.

Chapter 5

Tempo Slow Baby ... ...

I've been to the Hilton before, but not in a honey moon suite. At least that's what it looks like. The heart shape bed, with the red velvet blanket, heart shaped pillows, and the big red heart shaped Jacuzzi tub can't even begin to describe this thing that's beating on the inside of my chest. Oh -this is cute. The small refrigerator is filled with champagne, strawberries, whip cream, and little bottles of water. *How freaky,* I thought. I'm so amazed and mesmerized by this room, it is so beautiful.

"This is nice isn't it" Chuck asked as he laid across the bed.

I know I said that my Diva shoes would remain on; yeah- that's what I said, but I just kicked those shoes so far across the room and ran to him. "Oh Chuck, it's gorgeous. I know it must be expensive."

He sat up and folded his arms behind his head while lying on his back.

"There is nothing too expensive for my baby." He replied.

I smiled as I provided him with a little tongue wrestling.

"Ooh baby you must be feeling this huh? You act like you love me or something." He said with his hands around my waist. I began kissing and licking on his neck spelling out *I love you* with my tongue.

"I do, Chuck, I really do. You are so sweet to me. What have I done to deserve such a love?"

"Just for being Victoria, You deserve the world. You do me good too baby, so stop all that. I'm your man. I don't need you buying me expensive gifts and doing things like that for me to show me you love me. All I want you to do is continue being you. Tonight when you yelled at me telling me not to go meet up with Tone you showed me that you truly love me. You got your man back and I love it. That's the type of love I need. Just show me you got my back and continue loving me and whatever you want, I promise I will give it to you because you deserve it all. Sometimes I often wonder how I got so lucky. If the world had a lot of real females like you little Mama, real dude's wouldn't have time to fight and hate on each other. We would be too busy in love. Why fight when you can lay up under all of this" he replied as he put both of his strong hands firmly on each of my booty cheeks and squeezed them firmly.

Eruptions and over flows of this emotional roller coaster have given me strength to hold on. The muscle contraction of my inner love maker is stirring up juices ready for release. Ooh I want to give him all of me.

"Chuck, I'm going to take me a warm bath real quick."

"Ok baby, don't take too long. I have a sweet tooth" he replied.

He grabbed the remote and turned on the T.V. I smiled and grabbed my bag as I headed to the bathroom. I turned around and walked back over and kissed Chuck dead smack on the lips and then headed back to the bathroom. "I'll be right back" I said as I smiled and closed the door behind me.

This bathroom is gorgeous and very spacious. I unpacked my knapsack after I rinsed out the tub and started my bubble bath. The last time I came to the Hilton I used this La Source Serenity Bath bubble baths and soaps. I don't remember breaking out from it. My skin is very sensitive; I will break out in hives if someone blows on me incorrectly. I better use my strawberries and cream Victoria Secret shower gel just in case. Mama Jackson said it does not matter if the products I use are expensive or not because my skin will still break out. I must have gotten this sensitive skin from my mom. Though, I don't know anything about my dad or what's hereditary on his side. Oh well, I'm not going to worry about it tonight. I just want to relax and be free.

I sat here soaking in this hot bath while it's smelling like a room full of strawberries. I made sure that I cleaned my treasure gem extra good after trimming it neatly. I'm glad I remembered to bring my Sweet Romance Summers Eve douche. Chuck said he has a sweet tooth and I'm sure he wants me to fulfill it. It's not my fault if he gets himself a couple of cavity's tonight.

I'm done here. *You can't get any cleaner than this.* I let the water out and turned on the shower to rinse the access hair down the drain after I picked the majority up with tissue. I don't want Chuck to think that his future wifey does not know how to clean. That's one thing Stan and Mama Jackson taught me how to do. Stan basically taught me so I can keep the house clean for him. Mama Jackson taught me to clean for myself as well as my future husband when that time came.

Now is the time. Chuck will be my husband and I am going to do everything in my power to make him happy and keep him satisfied. I sprayed on my strawberry Victoria Secret body splash and massaged in the hand lotion especially on the area where I just shaved. I knew this red sheer matching bra and thong set would come in handy. As I viewed the reflection of this Diva's image, I think I'm doing this set some justice. I should have been one of their models. I look sexy and feel amazing. I am going to let Chuck have me tonight. Ooh I look so sexy in red. I don't know if I love Victoria Secret as much as I do because it describes my life to the T or if it's just because I love the fragrances and lingerie that they distribute. *I think it's a little bit of both,* I thought as I brushed my hair.

My hair looks so pretty and wavy when it's wet. *Damn I look good!* I thought as I viewed the reflection in the mirror. I have to make sure that tonight goes perfect. I'm ready to get intimate with Chuck tonight. My baby has been waiting long enough. It's been three and a half years already. He has respected the fact that I didn't want to sleep with him until I was ready. To be honest, I thought that Stan could find out some kind of way that someone else's key was used to enter my secret temple. Chuck does not need a key because the door is unlocked. Stan didn't actually have a key, he used forcible entry. It's painful just thinking about it. I am so thankful that Chuck has provided healing to these open wounds, that's why I have to share my love with him. I want him to be able to access the inner me. I love him that much. He deserves every ounce of love that I am about to put on him. I dropped down and did a few squats so I can stretch my legs.

I want to be as flexible as I can be. Let me show him why I am his Queen. *Uh oh, uh oh, uh oh,* I sang as I did the Beyonce dance. *Go get him Girl!* I cheered the image in the mirror.

Chuck is sitting at the table rolling up a blunt in his boxers. Hmm, I guess I do look as good as I feel judging the way Chuck is staring at me. He dropped the weed and is now sitting there with his mouth wide open as if he is mesmerized by this beauty that stands before him.

"Um, you're staring at me like I look good or something. You like what you see" I asked in a flirtatious manner. Do you like what you see or something boy?" I teased.

Silence allows me to captivate his response. "*♪♪I got you so hypnotized the way my body's moving round and round. Watch this booty keep bouncing and bouncing up and down ♪♪,*" I teased him as I sang Plies and Akon's song while making my booty bounce up and down. He's still marked by the absence of sound as his eyes sized up my thighs. His silence broke once he walked over and picked me up.

"Damn ma, that red sure looks good on you. Ooh you smell so good. Baby you look sexy as hell, that is no lie and I damn sure can't deny ... I'm feeling you. Ooh, look what you did." He said as he took my hand and put it on his enormous, seems like a foot long love maker.

Ooh baby, take me, have me, and love me I moaned quietly. My body is invaded with warm chills while my 44DD's are sitting up nice and plump. *♪All I want to do is- say yes♪,* I harmonized Floetry's song in my mind once Chucked began kissing my neck and massaging my shoulders. His actions appear to be of a young child, hungry for its mothers nursing. As he slowly laid my back up against the heart shape pillows, I became excited by the assumption of what he would do next.

His tongue decelerated once he arrived at my freshly pedicured toes. Licking and sucking on each digit while massaging my heels. He released my toes from his mouth and began chasing his tongue that led him on a journey.

Stars and bright lights are the unforeseen images visualized underneath my eye protectors. Underestimating the owner of the thick muscular tissue coated with hot saliva rapidly creating currents of warm air through the entrance of my soul has now depreciated its power. "OH Chuck, I love you" I screamed.

"Shh, don't scream now. I told you I had a sweet tooth." he replied.

Ooh he's fulfilling his sweet tooth tonight, I thought. "Oh my goodness Chuck, what are you doing to me!!!!" I asked. I should have known I was not going to receive a response.

The magnitudes regarding the nectar of my juices are beginning to rupture. The vine which is my spine that supplies the fruit is so divine. My roots are organic; separate and distinct. The intense pleasurable sensations draining from my brain is causing me not to think. Poetic notions have become my primary source of expression. Trying to regain any parts of my brain would be helpful right about now.

"Oh I bet you think you are Mr. Big shot now huh?" I asked. *As soon as I gain just a little bit of my strength it's on,* I thought to myself. Oh he's so arrogant. How dare he lie there on his back with his arms behind his neck smiling at me? He knows he was wrong for that.

Now that I have gained some strength and captivated my thoughts, it's my turn. Chuck's smiling from ear to ear, "Ooh Victoria, you clowning for this one girl. Why you doing Daddy like this?" he asked while grasping the roots of my wavy threadlike structures. As Chuck's grip on my hair is getting tighter I have come to the realization that he's now dominating my performance. My capabilities to manipulate my insufficient oxygen intake without volition have now become inadequate.

"Baby, what the … Um, um get up." He demanded. *Did I do something wrong* I thought. I looked at Chuck with a confused expression.

"Don't look at me like that, you know what I want. Yep, I know you're a smart girl. Get up here!" he commanded. "Don't worry, I got you. I just need you to hold on because it's going to be a bumpy ride. You can have your seat, but make sure you sit down slowly. I must inform you before you get on this ride; you might experience a couple of speed bumps that will require you to rock back and forward. Once you get familiar with this ride, I guarantee you will enjoy it. Are you ready?" he asked.

I might not be big enough for this ride, I thought as I sat down. Even though I never rode anywhere before, I have been forced to take a trip. Though the trip I was forced to take was a short walk next door compared to this hundred mile journey I'm taking now. I'm almost positive Chuck will assume I never left the house.

"Damn, I love you girl!" Chuck yelled.

Chuck seems like he's holding on to dear life once I began to accelerate.

"Let me show you how your fiancé gets down." He said.

He has turned this sybaritic experience into a satisfaction competition or is this just love? Back breaking, deep diving; boy what are you searching for? I never knew there was a pleasure to pain. He's digging deep as if he's trying to unclog my drain. Obviously that is his intentions.

"Victoria, I want you to be my wife. I want you to be mines forever."

"Charles, I want to be your wife. I love you."

The sound of Chuck deeply exhaling is like music to my ears. His smile and silence clearly describes his vivid satisfaction. "Oh my God, you are the best baby" he proclaimed as he rolled onto the bed and began staring into my eyes. "We didn't get a chance to use the strawberries and whip cream," he chuckled.

My heart is still tingling on the inside, "I think we did well without it." I said as a frisson of warmth shot through me. I glanced over at Chuck to view that he was fast asleep.

Chapter 6

"♪ This is why I'm hot ♪ this is why I'm hot♪ this is why, this is why, this is why I'm hot ♪" Ooh my phone startled me. Why is Toy calling me this early? It's 7:25a.m.

"Hey girl what's up?" I answered.

"Girl, why is your Uncle over here ringing the doorbell like he's crazy?" Toy asked.

From the sound of her voice Toy was obviously still sleeping as well. This question attacked me as a thief in the night. I wasn't expecting this. What could Stan possibly want at 7: am?

"What?" I asked in hopes of buying sometime for a response.

"Yes Victoria, what am I supposed to do?"

I can tell that Toys is frustrated. I know how she feels. Stan woke her up and now she's waking me up and I hope Chuck doesn't wake up. Chuck and I just fell asleep about three hours ago. *Come on Victoria think*. I thought to myself. "Is Romeo there?" I asked while I am trying to piece together a plan.

"Yeah, he's here. He just told me your Uncle is at the door." Toy replied before yarning.

"Ok Toy look, this is what I want you to do. Tell Romeo to tell him that we left a few minutes ago to go jog at the Martin Luther King Jr. track." I insisted as if I came up with a master plan.

"Alright girl, hold on. I'm going to sit this phone down and have Romeo pick up the one by the front door so you can hear them ok, hold on."

I heard her sit the phone down and I heard the other phone being picked up. A few seconds later I heard the door opening through the phone. I pressed my ear up to the phone so I could understand and hear exactly what he was saying.

"Hi Mr. Campbell, What's up?" Romeo asked.

"Go wake Victoria up and tell her to come here for a second."

"They just left a few minutes ago. They went jogging up at the King track.

"You're lying; they spent the night over some nigga's house didn't they?" Stan asked.

Oh my goodness. I can tell that Stan's mad because he said "nigga." He forbade me to use that word. He said people changed the "er" and added an "a" as if it's ok now. Though he's right about that, everybody I know refers to their selves as that. I even heard Chuck refer to himself as a "nigga" on more than several occasions.

"Why, what's wrong? I can call Toya on her cell phone if you want me to." Romeo suggested.

"No, don't worry about it. Just give her this for me. Thanks"

"No problem" Romeo said. I heard the door close and the phone being hung up.

"You there Victoria" Toy asked.

"Yeah, I'm here" I replied as my heart beat went into triple overtime.

"Here, give this to Victoria. I would appreciate it if you and Victoria get y'all shit together. I don't appreciate being woke up at 7 in the morning behind some shit that you and Victoria into. Y'all lucky Mama and Big Stevie still at work cause Mama would curse both of y'all out. Shit, I was in the hot tub with Tyra Banks sexy ass. Shit!"

"Girl, you heard Romeo didn't you?"

"Yeah, Toy I heard him. Tell Romeo he doesn't have anything to worry about because he's definitely not getting any type of play from

Tyra" I laughed. "No, but seriously tell Ro- Ro I apologize about that. So Toy, what did my Uncle give me?"

"As far as I can see it's an envelope."

"Ok, Now that we got that part out the way, do you think you could tell me what's inside of the envelope?"

"Chic, I know you are not getting smart because my brother's right, I was in the middle of getting a complete body massage by Morris Chestnut" she giggled. "It looks like a note and five one hundred dollar bills."

"Alright, c'mon and read the note so you and your brother can get back to dreaming." I chuckled. "For real Toy, I love you boo."

"I love you to with your smart mouth ass. Ok this is the note:
'Vickie,

I had to go to Indiana for my job, an emergency came up. Here is some money, because I know you and your girl are probably going to the mall. I will call you soon as I get there.

P.S. Remember what I said and I love you.'

Dang girl, your Uncle loves you." Toy said after she read me the letter.

"I know girl, go ahead and spend what you need out that money ok. Thanks for having my back Toy. Oh yeah make sure you give Romeo fifty bucks and tell him I said thanks. I love you for real." I know that offering Toy money would get her little attitude about being woken up repaired quickly.

"Thanks girl and you better hurry up and get back." Toy replied. I can tell from Toy's tone in her voice that her attitude has readjusted instantly especially since the money is involved. You can smack Toy dead in the mouth and she will be your best friend immediately after if you offer her cash. Cash means shopping for Toy. That girl is addicted to material.

"Ok, I think we might be coming back tonight. I'll let you know in a few. Go ahead and finish having your unrealistic, never gone happen, wet dream" I laughed.

I assume that Toy did not find my sarcastic comment funny since she just hung up in my face. I expected that. I hope I was not too loud because I don't want to wake Chuck. Darn, it's too late. He just rolled over and grabbed me by the waist.

"Good morning ma, is everything alright?" he asked.

I know I must love him and he has definitely got to love me because I know both of our breaths are kicking. I snuggled in his arms trying to bury my face in his chest to avoid this awful morning breath that Chuck has.

"Yes, everything is cool. That was Toya. She said that my Uncle stopped by and left me a note telling me that he is on his way to Indiana"

Chuck pulled away from me with a strange look in his eyes. "Why is he coming to Indiana?"

"I don't know baby, I think Toy said the note mention something about it being business" I replied. I'm also trying to figure out why Chuck just gave me that look.

"What time is it?" he asked.

I looked at the clock on my cell "its 7:45" I replied.

Ooh I love his body, I thought as I'm watching Chuck walk to the bathroom. I heard him gargling, so that reminded me to jump up and grabbed a Listerine strip from my purse. As a matter of fact I need two. Ooh wee these things are strong. Chuck came walking out the bathroom with his long one eye mini me swinging from side to side. He walked over to the table and grabbed his Nextel from the charger.

"Damn 22 missed calls" he said while walking towards the bed. He sat on the edge of the bed and began scrolling through his calls.

"Oh shit, I forgot to call Tone back last night" he remembered. Chuck put the phone on speaker once he dialed his number.

******************The call******************

"A dude … Where the hell you at?" Tone asked without saying hello or anything.

"A, what's good?" Chuck replied as if he is not in the mood.

"Aint nothing good; you tried to set me up homie?"

"Tone, what are you talking about?"

"I've been sitting up here on the freeway with all this cash waiting on you. I told you the Fed's raided my spot last night. You told me you were going to be here four hours after we talked. I been calling you all night and all morning!" He screamed.

"I'm on my way right now." Chuck replied as he quickly began putting on his boxers while directing me to get our things together. "My bad I didn't call you, but where are you now? I can meet you right now." Chuck insisted.

"Where the heck do you think I'm at? I'm still parked on the freeway where I told you I would be waiting on you. Now you call me once the police surround me. That's a real foul move right there my dude. That's exactly why I don't deal with new cats. That's messed up homie you done set me up and I was helping you out. That's why a brotha can't come up because of foul dude's like you who always got some shit in the game."

"First off homie, you need to calm down. I aint no snitch and the reason I didn't meet you is because me and my girl caught a flat so we stopped at the hotel. My bad, I forgot to call you. Now that's my fault, but all that other crap about me snitching, that's for the bird's guy. Straight up!"

"Yo girl! Yo girl! You mean to tell me you up there chilling with some Bitch, instead of out here getting dis money! See that's …"

"Don't disrespect my wifey dawg, that's on some real shit." Chuck cut him off. "Situations happen, plus I told you I was going to call you when I got near the exit. You went and parked your dumb ass on the freeway. That's your fault, not mine."

"You on some real chic ish right now. I'm sitting here on this freeway surrounded with all of these news cameras in my face. I refuse to go back to jail. They won't be taking me alive today."

"So what you saying homie?"

"Just what it sounds like, I'm not going back to jail dawg" He replied.

Chuck stood up flipping through the channels with the remote in one hand and his cell in the other. He stopped the channel at CNT World News.

"Once again we have a breaking story in Gary, Indiana regarding a barricaded African American Male who police says is suspected of drug possession and illegal firearms. The suspect's name is Anthony

Knuckles; police are asking if anyone who has close ties with the suspect could give them a call. They need help in trying to get the suspect out of his vehicle alive. Officers on the scene note that the suspect is making suicidal gestures. I-94 eastbound and south bound near exit 25 is blocked off. Officers are suggesting that everyone in the area find alternate routes. Back to you Steve."

"Wait, I just received word that he appears to be on his cell phone." Steve said as he pressed his finger on the earpiece in his ear. "Authorities are trying to tap into the cell. Stay tuned as we await that connection." Steve informed.

I have never seen anything like this in my life. I mean I have watched the news and heard about things happening such as this, but to be able to watch it in great detail is … *What the?* Oh so this is the emergency that Stan had to attend. Why is Stan on T.V.? I am so glad Chuck does not know what he looks like. Oh my goodness. *Stay cool Victoria, Chuck does not know that's your Uncle,* I thought to myself.

"Taking your life is not the solution. You can at least live to see your son" I overheard Chuck say as he paced back and forth. "Tone, suicide is your first class ticket to hell because God will not forgive you for that."

I focused my attention to Steve the news reporter as the words Chuck stated were broadcasted on the bottom of the television screen. "Authorities have received entrance into the suspect's conversation. Let's take a listen." Steve suggested.

"Oh so you Mr. Preacher man now huh? You ain't no different from me. We just another group of ignorant niggas trying to keep our heads above water." Tone replied.

"Tone, trust me, it's not that bad. You're right I am no different from you. If I can make it, I know you can. You just have to find something that you are good at. I know it's still hard for us, but we have whey more opportunities now. I don't plan on living my life this way forever. Every day I set high goals and dare myself to reach them."

"That shit you talking sound good, but everybody don't see it like you. The way I see it, this world we living in is fucked up. When a brother like me is out here trying to get a legit nine to five the doors are basically slammed in my face. So of course I got to turn the streets for survival. I got bills, my kids got to eat. This racism shit makes me feel like I am less of man. No matter how hard a nigga try, this is still fucked up. First they fly the drugs over here, give it to a starving nigga like me who they know gone make it happen. After we make this fast money, they take it from us and then lock us up in cages after we done made them rich. There we go- slaved again. I'm not going back to jail dawg and that's it."

"Tone, do you know that everything you're saying is playing on the news? Chuck asked.

"Oh yeah? Get the fuck out of here! The white man done came up with some more new shit huh? Well I guess I am a star after all, but remember that you don't have to be like me. I just ran into a dead end man. I'll just go to hell and make the best of it. This world we living in is hell right now anyway, it can't get no worse than this."

"I'm telling you for real, killing yourself is not going to solve anything. If Martin Luther King Jr., Malcolm X, and all the other Black heroes killed themselves we wouldn't have half of the opportunities that we do now. Look how things have changed. We have a Black Man running for President of the United States of America, that right there alone lets me know that God is able and I can do anything that I set my mind too. You're just in a tough situation right now Tone, things can change. You never know what can happen. At least you will still be alive to see. God works in mysterious ways, I'm telling you. Don't do it.!" Chuck explained.

"Fuck that!" Tone screamed.

"Looks like we lost him" Steve stated.

"Is he still on the phone, Chuck" I asked.

"Nah baby, he hung up." Chuck replied.

Chuck sat on the bed next to me. We sat here staring at the TV.

"I'm not sure what has happened. It appears that he has disconnected the call." The reporter stated.

As the cameras capture Tone's green impala from a different angle they were able to zoom in on him. He has a gun up to his head. There was a small flash of light that glared from the inside of Tone's car. Chuck glanced at me and then stared back at the T.V. I am assuming that the both of us are sitting here wondering what just happened. The FBI ran up to the car and opened the driver side door. The officer put his gun in his holster. He instructed the other officers to lower their weapons before he placed his hands on his head as if he was disappointed. I don't know where Stan disappeared to. I could have sworn that was him. I know it was. I'm not crazy.

"Oh my, what a terrible tragedy. You have seen it live on CNT. Again the Suspects name is Anthony Knuckles who has ended his life today after police had suspicion that he was in possession of illegal fire arms and illegal drugs."

I ran to the bathroom. Tears and Vomit has become my facial disguise. As I am head into the toilet bowl, I can't help but think that this is possibly my fault. After cleaning myself up I exited the restroom.

Chuck is still sitting on the bed with his mouth open with a look of confusion occupying his face. I feel so bad. *This is all my fault*, I thought. Those stupid premonitions. The cop cars and flashing lights I saw was at nighttime. I have never had a premonition that was not one hundred percent accurate. *Maybe it's because I tried to prevent the outcome of the future.*

I walked over and sat next to Chuck. I inhaled deeply and exhaled in nervousness. "Excuse me Charles; do you think that this is my fault?" I asked.

He looked at me and used his finger to capture the tear that's falling from my eye. "Of course not. I know you're smarter than that. You should know that's not your fault. You got your man back, I already told you that. If I wouldn't have listened to you, that would be us trapped on the freeway. Victoria, I didn't know that guy like that. I met him through this other dude I deal with. I have dealt with him once before, but he came to Detroit then. This is my first time traveling to him. That's why I told you last night; this is a dangerous business. Everyday my life is on the line. We're all trying to survive in the devils game. That's why I've been praying for a change." Chuck replied.

I feel a little better about him not being mad, but it's eating at me because I know Stan has something to do with it. "I'm sorry any way baby." I said. I wonder who the other person that introduced them is. "Chuck, does the dude you met Tone through go by the name Money Mike?"

"Yeah," Chuck replied as he instantly stood up. "How did you know that?"

"I just figured every drug dealer knows each other."

Damn Victoria, how in the heck am I going to get myself out of this one. Some things are better left un-said, I thought. By the angry, defensive look that Chuck has on his face I think I might need to come up with a better answer than that one. This is not a good look. He's rubbing his chin as if he's thinking extremely hard while staring at me like I just said something totally wrong. *Did I say something wrong?* I thought.

"Victoria, shit's not adding up. I was just thinking, remember you said your Uncle had an emergency in Indiana with his job, is your Uncle the Feds?"

"Yes, I replied without giving it any thought.

"So you're trying to set me up!!" He yelled almost vibrating the roof.

"No, Chuck. I would never do that. I love you! I screamed. "I didn't tell you because I didn't want you to treat me any different. If I told you at the very beginning that my Uncle was FBI, would you have continued to date me? Hell No! So of course, I didn't tell you. I didn't want to risk that chance of not having you in my life and I don't want to risk it now. I knew if I told you that he was the Fed's, you would not have opened up to me. Chuck, that's my Uncles occupation, not mines. Besides, no one knows what my Uncle does except for you now."

"Are you sure Victoria?"

"Yes baby, why would I risk losing the sunshine in my life? You are my joy and my smile. I love you more than anything in this world. We are a team. If I have to fight my Uncle off to keep him from consuming your identity, so be it. He knows that I am engaged, but I never told him your name. He flipped out when I told him. If arguing with him and fighting with him daily to prove our love is what I have to do, I guess I have to do what I have to do. You feel me.

"Victoria, you know my world revolves around you. Please baby, don't hurt me." Chuck begged before he gently kissed my lips.

"Just because you know what my Uncle does now, does not mean you are going to start acting funny towards me right?" I asked.

"Stop playing" he replied.

"What's weird though Chuck is when I heard Tone saying that his spot was raided by the Fed's I figured it had something to do with my Uncle, but when I called him and he appeared to be at my grandmother's I didn't think any more about it. I knew when you mentioned Tone knew a dude you dealt with that it had to be Money Mike, especially since my Uncle was just on the news. He has an inside connection with that guy. Uncle Stan said they tried to arrest him on several occasions, but every time they try to lock him up he gets out the same day. He has been dealing with that guy over five years now. My Uncle is a crooked cop if you ask me." I explained.

"He probably is. It seems like all cops are crooked now a days. They're hustlers to. They just wear a uniform that legalizes theirs. We have to get out of here, ma. I have forty thousand dollars' worth of dope in my tires."

"What," I yelled. "Damn boo, I know I might not know much about the dope game, but I know that sounds almost like a life sentence."

"Now you see what I'm talking about; Life or death ma. Just get dressed, we got to go." Chuck yelled.

I noticed Chuck taking his battery out of his phone.

"Bay, why are you taking your phone apart" I asked.

"I'm sure the Feds have put a trace on my cell by now. If it's not powered on my location is undetectable. At least that's what my Uncle's girlfriend who's a Sergeant told him." He replied as he grabbed his bag.

"Come on Vickie, we gotta go!"

I got my things together and checked the bathroom. We have everything from as far as I could see. "Hold on Chuck let me grab the weed" I suggested once I spotted it still sitting on the table.

"Forget that weed, Victoria let's get the hell out of here!" he yelled as we swiftly walked to the car. He didn't return the key or anything. We got in the car and left.

We have about four hours to ride on these tires. Chuck says we need to get back to Detroit so he can get those drugs out of them. Catching a flat tire would not be a good look right about now. If I had known I would not have told him to use the flat tire excuse. Chuck should have known better than that. Oh yeah that's right, Chuck knows how to pray and I'm sure he is talking to God right now. *I really hope he is,* I thought. I am not looking forward to seeing Stan. I wonder if he knows that I was out of town. I'm sure Toy would have told me. I haven't smoked any weed today and I am already paranoid. I don't have any reason to be afraid. I think everything is going to be ok. *This reminds me,* I thought as I reached in the glove box for the small Bible I began reading yesterday.

Wow, this is perfect. *"Needing God's protection"*; Psalm *27:1*-6 it read. I have to see what the scriptures say about that. Psalm's 27: verse 1, here it is.

"The Lord is my light and my salvation; whom shall I fear? The Lord is the strength of my life; of whom shall I be afraid?" I read.

Since Chuck said that the Bible is God's way of talking to me I would presume from reading that verse up to verse six that God is telling me that I should not be afraid of anything or anyone, but him. I have to read the 6th verse again. *"And now my head shall be lifted up above my enemies all around me; therefore I will offer sacrifice of joy in his tabernacle. I will sing yes, I will sing praises unto the Lord."* After reading this verse a second time, my assumptions seem to be pretty accurate. Believing that God will protect me and keep me from my enemies does not seem that difficult, as far as the belief, but determining who my enemies are is where it seems to be confusing.

Determining if Stan is actually considered to be my enemy is what drafts up controversy in my mind. I am not sure if Stan is my enemy because he took care of me and he still takes care of me. *God, I know you will help me figure it out.*

"♪ Jesus loves me … oh yes he does ♪ for the Bible tells me so ♪" I hummed to myself. I remember when I was in the grocery store once; there was a lady behind me singing that song. It's weird in a good way how I know what she meant now. Plus, Whitney Houston sang it in one of my favorite movies, *The Bodyguard.* I'm not a bad person. I do believe that I am worthy of Jesus loving me. Chuck said he loves everybody, so I know he has to love me.

"Victoria! Victoria! Chuck yelled. "Lil Mama, you be dazed when you start reading the bible don't you?"

"Yeah I do huh?"

"It has the same effect on me too. I didn't mean to disturb you I just want to know if you're hungry."

I rubbed my stomach and smiled, "Yes I am."

I always thought the sun is what provided my source of energy. God created the Sun and this entire world, I never knew that. The fact that I learned that any type of flowers, roses or plants does not need food they only need the sun and water to survive made me feel that way. I am not denying the fact that I am a beautiful rose, it's just the source of my existence was not defined correctly. This world is so beautiful, I feel so foolish not knowing that God is the reason behind it all, or perhaps I should the one who created it all. It's still new to me now; all I can do is take it one day at a time.

Ooh I love this place. They have the best chocolate chip pancakes. Wow this line is extremely long. I hope that Chuck has patience and decides to wait. There is a Denny's next door, but I don't like their pancakes. If he didn't pull up to this International House of Pancakes, I wouldn't have my mouth tuned up for their chocolate chip pancakes. Good- the line is moving quickly. Chuck doesn't look like he's ready to leave, but he does look like he is stressing about something. I guess these last 24 hours would be enough to make anyone think and stress. I know I sure don't have a problem with it. I have other fish to fry. I need to get away from Stan. I want to marry Chuck. It's so much about him that I love, it makes me want to be around him and it's something that I would love to experience every single day.

"Hello, welcome to IHOP, how many is with you?" the hostess asked. *How many does it look like? It's probably only a handful of Black folks in here anyway,* I thought.

"Two" Chuck replied as if he was thinking the same thing.

"Smoking or none?" she asked.

"None smoking please." I replied.

"Hello, my name is Jennifer. I will be your waitress today. Are you ready to order?"

I ordered my usual chocolate chip pancakes, sausage links, bacon, scrambled eggs with cheese and a hot chocolate. Chuck ordered, steak well done with buttermilk pancakes, with his eggs over easy. I don't understand why people eat their eggs that way. It looks very distasteful.

"Baby, why do you eat your eggs over easy?"

"Justine used to make them for me that way. I have been eating them that way for almost five years. I like scrambled to, but I prefer to have an over easy egg every once in a while." Chuck replied.

I smiled at him, shaking my head. "I don't like them. They look raw" Oh my goodness, what did I say now? Chuck is giving me the, *I just asked a stupid question or I just said something stupid and he's about to tell me* look.

"Have you ever had over easy eggs Victoria?"

"No, I just told you that I don't like them." I replied. Judging by the way he just sat up and leaned over the table towards me, *I know he is not about to hit me.*

"Listen to me Victoria, and listen to me good. As long as God permits us to be together and you are a representation of me, I don't ever want to hear you making an ignorant comment like that again! How do you know that you don't like something if you have never tried it? You are my Queen, so watch what you say. You never know if you try them you just might like them. Don't judge a book by its cover, do you hear me! I don't care if it's a person, cat, dog, or something simple as a freaking egg. Use your brain and think before you speak! Do you understand me?"

"Yes" I replied. *Damn, somebody woke up on the wrong side of the bed.* I can't believe he's tripping like this. I must admit, I want to jump across this table and rock his world because he just turned me completely on. He's been getting a little bossy lately and I actually like it. That's a grown man move right there. I guess he is right, though. I actually understand what he means. As I think about it, I did judge those white folks at the gas station last night because of what I heard. I thought that they were going to attack us when all they did was be nice to us. He looks so sexy especially when those little veins pop out of his forehead. He's sending all type of chills throughout my body. Even though he just checked the crap out of me, I'm still not interested in trying those raw looking eggs.

"So how are you feeling so far, what a day huh?" I asked. I decided to change the subject since he's a little touchy about eggs this morning.

"First off Little Mama, I apologize for snapping at you just a second ago, but I need you to listen to your man ok. Judging a book by its cover is something that I cannot stand and I refuse to tolerate it, especially from a woman that I am planning to marry. That's what's wrong with the world today. We judge the outside instead of embracing what's on the inside. Now the answer to your question, yes it has been a day. Welcome to my side of life that you don't see when I am out and about trying to take care of business. I wanted you to go with me so you would know exactly what I do and see what I go through. We are getting married and I don't want us keeping any secrets." He replied.

Victoria is all about secrets unfortunately, I thought. I wish I could tell him the truth, but I don't think now is a good time. "I never seen anything like that today in my entire life" I said as I tried changing subjects again.

"Yeah I know. I can't believe how Tone just blew his head off like that. No matter how much shit I been through, giving up is not an option. I'm not going to sit here and front like I never thought about it because I have, but that's as far as it went, just a thought. The devil will attack your mind like that and make you think that there is no other way around hard times in life. Yeah he's good at making the situation appear to be more than one person can bear. Suicide is the easy way out with a burning cost. I rather struggle than get shit handed down to me anyway. It helps me to appreciate my accomplishments. Street life is the devils playground. He knows that people like us are vulnerable because we are in the game trying to succeed. He makes everything look so easy when you do it his way. Not to mention the fast material rewards he gives. I've come to realize that things like that don't matter. The expensive things that I buy for myself and the things I buy for you don't mean a thing. It's a price to pay for all of it. Everything that looks good does not mean it's good for you. We gone be straight though Victoria" he said as he grabbed my hands and kissed them.

"We're going to be straight for real. Once your man's get accepted into college, things are going to change. We might have to down grade for a minute, but it's all going to work out. Don't be slipping on me because yo man has a plan for real." He said with a smile. "Now I have to figure out how I am going to get rid of this dope." He said as his smile instantly turned into a frown and a look of confusion once again.

Chuck turned his head and began staring out the window. My baby looks so sad. I can tell my baby is beginning to get frustrated. He keeps talking about him not wanting to sell drugs. I know he has a plan. I am going to stand by his side and support him no matter what. The fact that he keeps talking about God is enough for me to understand that he must have a good relationship with Him despite his temporary occupation. I got my baby's back.

"Baby I don't know what to tell you, all I can say is be careful ok. I stand behind you one hundred percent. Everything will work out."

He looked at me as if he is trying to be strong. It seems like his eyes are beginning to tear up. I know Chuck is a strong man. He will get out of this.

"I know baby, I know" he responded as he looked out the window again deeply exhaling.

"♪This is why I'm hot ♪ this is why I'm hot♪, this is why, this is why, this is why I'm hot♪." My phone startled me. I need to change this ring tone or just put my phone on vibrate. No one but Toy and Chuck has my cell number anyway. I know Stan would take it if he found out I had this cell. Chuck brought us matching Nextel Blackberry's. He said he needs direct connect to his Queen. I'm not mad at him.

"♪This is why I'm hot ♪ this is why I'm hot♪, this is why, this is why, this is why I'm hot♪." *"What does she want?"* I asked loudly to myself. I sent her to voicemail, but obviously it's important.

"Hey girl what's up?" I answered.

"Nothing; I'm just checking on you. What you doing?" Toy asked.

"I'm at IHOP with my baby."

"I know you ordered your favorite chocolate chip pancakes, didn't you?"

"You know it!" I replied. It makes me mad sometimes because Toy knows me so darn well. Sometimes I think she knows me more than I know myself. That's my sister though, and I love her to death.

"Toy, I will be at your house today, so please be there."

"Ok girl, just call me soon as y'all hit the D ok."

"Alright Toy, our food is here so I will talk to you in a few."

The steam rising from both of our plates the waitress is holding, gives me the impression that they just took everything off of the grill.

"Excuse me, you had the chocolate chip pancakes right?" Jennifer asked me.

"Yes, ma'am" I replied.

"Here's your steak sir" she said while sitting Chuck's plate in front of him. "Do you guys need anything else?"

Chuck glanced at his food and then he looked at the condiments at the end of the table and replied, "No we're good, thank you."

"Ok, y'all enjoy your meals." She said as she walked away from the table.

"Baby wait, I'm going to go wash my hands and then you can go after me or whichever way you want to do it" I said. He opened his hands and shrugged his shoulders telling me to go ahead and go first. I went and washed my hands and came back out. He went and washed his.

I sat here waiting on him to come back. I wouldn't dare start eating my food without waiting on him. Mama Jackson taught me that. She is actually the mother I always wanted. She has taught me so much. I am so thankful. Oh here comes Chuck now.

He sat down at the table. "That's what I'm talking about, if you weren't down for me, you would have eaten your food while I was in the restroom. I love you girl" he reached over the table and kissed me with his juicy lips. He grabbed my hand and bowed his head as I did the same.

"Heavenly Father, we thank you for this food that we are about to receive to help strengthen our bodies and nourish our health. Please take anything harmful and dangerous away, in your son Jesus name we pray, Amen"

"Amen."

There's that tingly feeling again. It gives me chills throughout my body. We began eating. I knew we were a lot alike because when we both eat; we don't talk too much unless we are not that hungry. I came up for air when the waitress asked … … "Is everything okay?"

"Yes everything is great. Can I have some more ice water please?" I asked.

"Can I please have a refill on my lemonade as well?" Chuck recommended.

"You sure can sweetie" she replied to the both of us.

I'm beginning to notice every time Chuck and I go on an 'out of town' vacation people seem to be a little more polite. The majority of the waitresses I have had in Detroit seem to be very rude, but then again, I have run into some nice ones as well. I think everybody has their days. Some people can be so rude; it's hard to return the attitude because they're in charge of fixing my food. I learned that a long time ago from Stan and Toy. Once Toy cursed our waitress out so badly that when she received her food, there was hair and little pieces of paper in it. That experience has definitely taught me how to bite my tongue.

I'm not sure where this is coming from, but the urge to have my mother is coming into existence. I wonder where she is and if she ever thinks about me. Before she pretty much abandoned me, she told me that she didn't know how to be a mom, but she chose to keep Jasmine. That has always bothered me, but it's ok. I wish I could see her again. It's been almost twelve years. Chuck can always tell when I am thinking about something. He stopped chewing and asked, "Baby what's wrong? What's on your mind?"

"Actually, I was just thinking about my mom. I've been wondering what she's up to, how she's doing and does she miss me."

Chuck grabbed my hand, kissed it and replied "I am sure she does. What's your mom's name by the way?"

"Her name is Tamara." This look that Chuck is giving me now is one that I have not seen before. It does sort of resemble a look as if my mom's name sounds familiar to him.

"I know you are not talking about light skin Tamara with long hair, with the big ole booty, are you? Do you know if they call her short cakes?" he asked.

"I'm not sure, but it sounds like her description. Why? Do you know her or something?"

"Damn bay I feel bad," he said with a slight grin on his face, "but your mom is one of my biggest customers, at least she used to be. Now that I think about it you do look just like her, well you use to before she … well you know."

This facial expression of disgust is very vivid on my face and I really hope Chuck is noticing this. *Now how in the world are you going to sit here and tell me something like this and then what the heck are you grinning for? There is nothing funny about anything you just said*, I sat here thinking to myself as I began to stare at him with cut throat eyes. It's cool though. I guess he's just "keeping it real" with me. I took a hard swallow. "Oh yeah, so do you see her frequently?" I asked.

"Not as much as I used to. She used to live up in one of my spots back in the day" he replied.

I'm sitting here contemplating if I should take this glass and break it over his head. I know doing that will not solve anything. It's not his fault. My mom has been on drugs since Chuck and I both were kids. "Oh is that right?" I asked. "Chuck, please explain to me what do you think my proper reaction should be after you've just confessed to me that you have been serving my mother dope? I really would like to know how I am supposed to sit here continuing a conversation with you after you just confessed something like that. I mean, really Chuck?"

"Victoria, please don't get upset with me. I am just keeping it real with you. I am not holding secrets from you. I am your family now. I love you. I would never do anything to hurt you. I apologize if I hurt you ok. It's just that, I'm shocked that you said her, because she is so cool. I never looked at her like I did all of the other people I served drugs too. Your mom is different. She is so pretty, but she is starting to allow those drugs to destroy her look. I stopped selling to her about a year ago. I'm not into lying to you. If you don't want the truth than don't ask me anything ok. I feel like we're family Victoria. You are my family boo. I wouldn't do anything to hurt you and I put that on my life." He said as he grabbed my hand and kissed it. "So Vickie, Do you forgive me?"

Ooh he is so lucky I love his filthy boxers. Damn I love him. I know he doesn't mean any harm. How can I resist those big sexy, glossy brown eyes and that pearly white smile? "You know I do" I responded with a smile. "I'm sorry Chuck, I didn't mean to snap. It's just that I was thinking about my mom abandoning me like that and the only thing you could share with me is you know my mom because you use to sell drugs to her. I think I was a bit overwhelmed that you would actually tell me something like that." I explained.

"I really apologize about that. I am almost afraid to ask you what your dad's name is because I hope I don't know him at all. So what is your dad's name?"

"I hope you don't know him either, but his name is Carlos."

"Please don't tell me, ole fruity as Carlos" he laughed.

I snatched my hand away from him. "Damn, so what- you know him too!" He cleared his smile when he noticed the tears falling from my eyes.

"Damn lil Mama, that's messed up. I'm so sorry about your situation."

"Don't be- because I'm not," I said as I began rolling my eyes.

"So I guess we both got some jacked up parents huh? I know it's that damn crack that hit the streets of Detroit in the eighties. I've been reading about that shit. They say if you don't want black people to know something, put it in a book. My Mama told me that, a long time ago before she began to lose her mind. Justine told me that also. She said if I don't read anything, but the front page of the newspaper as long as I read something. So I try to read every book I can. The white folks who are responsible for putting that shit in our city recognize how it's been destroying it every day in rapid flow, and these stupid casinos' are not making it any better. It's funny how they have billions of dollars to build casinos, but they don't have enough money to keep the rehabilitation centers and homeless shelters open so the less fortunate can have a place to stay and these starving kids would have food to eat. It all reverts to living in this American Nightmare. The President is sending food to other countries when we have people starving right here in the States. I hope that this Black Man running for President gets in. I really think that he can help change some things. He knows what it feels like to be poor and he knows what it feels like to be rich. I just pray that when he does get in office that God protects him. God can fix anything Victoria, I know he can. He can fix this world and turn the tables around." Chuck explained.

"I guess so." I replied as I took a sip of my hot chocolate. He's staring at me with those big sexy brown eyes. I think he knows that he is the flame to my heart that's forcing it to melt.

"If we have kids Victoria, I really hope they don't turn out like our parents." He smiled.

"Aint that the truth" I agreed. "Do you see my mom and dad all the time?"

"I have not seen your mom much lately, but I often see Carlos up at the liquor store up on Mt. Elliot and Mack with a tight ass dress and a blonde wig. He's been on that same corner for years."

"Chuck, I have never met my dad. My Uncle Stan told me that's who my dad is. So I really don't know if that's him because my Mom has never mentioned anything about him." The tears that fall from my eyes are tears of pain and embarrassment. My mom does not love me and I do not know who my father is. I feel so incomplete. Even though I know that Chuck loves me, I still have an empty void in my heart.

Oh they look so beautiful. I wish I had that type of love, I thought as I looked at the family sitting across from me and Chuck. They seem like the perfect family. They resemble a reduce version of the Cosby's because there is a mother, father, son and daughter. They really look beautiful and they seem so happy.

I sat here staring at them interacting. The little boy said, "Daddy, Mommy keeps picking with me." The Father looked at the mother jokingly and said "You better stop mom. Stop picking with our son, he can't handle it," now they are all laughing. It's creating this warm tingly sensation on the inside.

I exchanged the faces on that mother and father with mine and Chuck's. I really wonder what it would be like if Chuck and I were to have children. I think we would make good parents considering the fact that we both want better and came from bad.

My day dream was interrupted by the waitress bringing the bill. Chuck looked at his wrist attempting to look at the time, "I forgot I broke my watch, I got to get me another one soon" he said as he looked at the time on his Blackberry. He then reached in his pocket and took out his wallet.

"Come on bay, we have to get back" he said as he paid the bill leaving the waitress a ten dollar tip.

"Thank you, have a Blessed day" she said with a smile as we were walking out the door.

Soon as Chuck merged on the freeway, I am beginning to realize that I am in doze off mode again. Every time I eat, this seems to happen. This time I think that I must consider the fact that Chuck and I did not sleep long. This day has been very interesting. Ooh this is another one of my old school joints from Mary J. Blige. I turned up the radio. The words are so deep; she puts feeling in her songs and adds her life to them. I respect that about her.

"♪ No- more- pain, no more pain, no more pain♪ no more games-messing with my mind, no more drama in my life♪ I -don't- know -only God knows where the story ends -for me, no more pain, no more drama in my life, no more tears no more crying every night ♪" I sang.

"That's your jam huh little Mama?" Chuck asked.

"Yeah" I replied. I began staring up in the sky. It seems like my outlook on life has changed drastically in the last 24 hours. I always sang this song, but I am really beginning to understand the meaning. It's amazing how songs helps describes the way I really feel. *Only God knows where the story- ends- for me,* I hummed to myself. I'm just going to take it one day at a time.

"Ooh now here's another one of my jams, "Soulful Moaning."

"Oh I like this cut right here" Chuck said.

"Chuck, do you know who sings this song?"

"Yeah, I'm pretty sure it's this group called Dale. I really like this song" he said as he turned the radio up to the maximum volume.

"♪ Ooh you just give me one of those feelings that I can't even explain. Soulful Moaning makes you want to scream, but you don't want to scream you just want to ... oh yeah♪" Chuck repeated the words of the song as he licked his lips and winked at me.

This guy is too much. The bass in this song is providing vibration to my back from this seat. This song is real ole school right here. It's so sensual. *I bet you there were a lot of babies made off of this song.* I feel so relaxed right now. The sun is shining even brighter now that my fiancé seems happy again. His smile just brightened up my day. The thoughts of meeting with my counselor are now preoccupying my mind.

I have to meet with her on Monday. I hope she didn't notice that I wasn't in class at all last week. Well, Chuck and I showed up around lunch time, but that's about it. It was Chuck's idea for us to ditch school anyway because it was Meap testing for the juniors and then Friday was our "Senior Picnic" at Belle Isle. So it was really no reason to go. I can't wait until I graduate. Maybe Chuck and I can get an apartment or something because I really want to leave Stan's house. Maybe, we can both attend Wayne State University. I know that's the school Chuck really wants to attend especially since his mom is a part of their Alumni. The question Toy asked me yesterday is really beginning to make since.

I really should think about my plans because graduation is less than three months away. I have read a lot of psychology books and it seems to intrigue my attention. I think I might go ahead and major in psychology because I need to do research on Stan's behavior. It is completely abnormal and I am almost positive there is a distinct reason behind it.

Though, I am considering psychology, the fact that I love to write cannot be hidden. Like Toy said, I should not allow my talent to go to waste. I won first place in every writing contest that I have entered. I love reading and writing poetry, I am also considering exposing my unfortunate affair with Stan by writing a book. I would like to help others who maybe experiencing the same abuse that I have. I'm so confused. Maybe Mrs. Thomas will be able to help me sort out some of my issues on Monday. I am really looking forward to our appointment.

Mrs. Thomas has been trying to help me stay on the right path. Actually, school is all I have; it's that places where I feel important especially, when I get good grades. Even though the work seems too easy, I still complete it. But hey I'm gifted, what I can say. I glanced over at Chuck. He looks like he's still thinking, which is only natural. I know he is trying to figure out what he's going to do to get rid of his drugs. Despite his drug dealing occupation, I am very proud of him.

Chuck has improved tremendously since we first met. He was supposed to graduate last year, but he was held back the same year I met him. He was a sophomore then. School did not appear to be his number one priority, the streets were. I have never seen him in school much until lunch time. He made sure he was there on time. He said he made it to lunch on time because he knew it was my lunch hour. Though, I know that his gambling; playing spades and shooting dice had a little something to do with it also. Once we started dating I'm sure everyone noticed that he was in school every day and on time. I am so proud of him. He is very smart and extremely intelligent; I think he just needed a reason to find school interesting again.

He often informs me that I am behind the reason that he chose to continue pursuing his education. I don't know how I did it but, I'm glad I was able to help. I was two years behind myself until I was double promoted, now I'm only one year behind just as he is. I guess I can credit Stan for getting me in school.

Wow, we are almost home. The sign read: *Detroit 22 miles. Yes! I can't wait to get back.* Besides the extremely high crime rate, I really do love my city. I guess it's because it is my birth place and everyone I know lives there. Out of all the different States that Chuck has taken me to, I have never seen a place like Detroit. It seem like all the other places I have been to especially down south, a lot of people seem like they are a little behind. No matter how beautiful all the other places are, the people seem false like. We are a tad bit crazy, but that's just how we were raised. We were raised on "keeping it real." Being phony is a no- no and will most likely get you a trip to the hospital or perhaps a first class ticket to your casket if need be. I'm getting older now; I think that it is time for a change. Maybe Chuck and I can find a college out-of-state. Even though I might go to and out-of- State College, it does not exclude the fact that I love my city. It's Saturday so I know it's jumping, plus the weather has been nice lately. I wonder what Toy and I are going to do today. Which reminds me, let me call her.

"What up doe chica; where you at?" she answered,

"Ok Toy, you are a little bit too hype right now. What's going on?" I asked.

"Oh my bad; you know it's Saturday and your girl done already started drinking. It's 80 degrees outside in the middle of March so please believe that dudes are wilding out. I'm listening to my girl "Kelly Rowland and my home boy Snoop Dog; I'm feeling this song right here girl. What you say Kelly? ♪ Rock yo timb's- sag yo jeans- ice yo grill- it's all good with me♪ ... so ghetto♪" Toy sung.

"Toy, who did you say sings that song" I interrupted.

"Kelly Rowland, you know ole girl from Destiny's Child"

"Exactly! Please let Kelly sing her own song. Please and thank you boo boo!" I laughed.

"Forget you! See that's why you get on my nerves. I'm on my way to get my nails and toes done anyway. Thanks again girl for the loot, I only borrowed $250."

Only $250! I thought to myself. *Damn, if somebody offers you something don't get carried away.* I am not going to trip because I told her to use what she wanted. I'm glad she thought enough of me to leave me half of my own money. I am so glad that I'm not broke because I would be straight pissed. Toy's my girl, more like sister, so it's cool. She obviously needs it. Even though she said "borrowed" I know I will not be seeing a dime of it. I don't understand why she continues using that word in her vocabulary.

"Oh that's cool girl" I replied as I tried to play off my actual feelings. "So what are we doing today?"

"Well you should already know that Belle Isle is definitely going to be off the chain. Girl, these guys done went in storage and brought out the real Tonka toys. I mean it's all types of candy coated paint jobs, spinning rims, with TV's galore. You know once these fools get a little heat, they got to wild out. Please believe I will be wilding out right along with them. Where y'all at? Oh yeah, tell your fiancé I said what up doe."

"Chuck, Toy said Hi."

Chuck gripped his steering wheel and glanced at me throwing up the peace sign. "Tell her I said what up doe"

"Toy, Chuck said what up. We're close. Chuck, how long you think we got? Oh that's it? Girl he said we will be back in about 2 hours max. I will call you soon as we get in the D"

"Cool. I know you hitting the mall with me right?"

"That's just like asking me if I need oxygen to breathe. Of course the answer is yes."

"That's what's up. Well hit me up when y'all get here. I'll holla" Toy replied before she hung up.

"Bay, Toy said them fools are already wilding out."

"That's what's up, I already know" he replied with the look of disinterest. "You know I have to flip these tires real quick. I've been sitting over here trying to piece together some type of plan, but I'm drawing blanks. I don't know how I am going to do it, but I have to do it."

"I think you can do it. As a matter of fact I know you can do it baby, even if you have to split it up some kind of way."

"Victoria, look over in that CD case and hand me that purple CD."

I reached in the slot on the door and began looking through what seems to be at least 150 CD's. I am so pleased to see that Chuck has the 'real CD's' and not the 'bootlegs'. Though, this purple CD must be a mixed CD of some sort because there is no name or cover, it just has Hip Hop Mixes written in permanent marker. "Do you want me to put this CD in sweetie?"

"Yeah Ma, Thanks" he replied.

"Oh snap! Straight up, Chuck. What you know about that?"

"♪ I'm a- Cheddar Boy baby- that's- fo -sho ♪." Chuck is really feeling this song.

"That's them Eastside Chedda Boyz right there baby. This before yo time right here ma" he laughed.

I attempted to change it to the next one, but from what I can see Chuck obviously likes this song. I like it too. I listen to our Detroit artist because they have at least tried that hard to get in the studio and record an album, the least I can do is support them. This must be my baby's anthem or something. I sat here watching my baby jamming to this cut. He reached over to change the track.

"Oh Snap Chuck, Now you going down my neck of the woods. You don't know nothing about this right here baby, let me school you right quick … ♪ When we dropped with that first Rock Bottom you ate it up ♪ What the …" As soon as I got into my jam, he changed it.

"Yeah bae, I feel you, but check it … ♪ It's two Tone in here, we got a saying in the D, it's called 'What up Doe' you know what I'm saying. In Atlanta they say 'what's happening', in H-Town they say 'what it do', I want to welcome y'all to Detroit where we say 'what up doe', so when you hear this song I want you to say 'what up', what up doe, 'what up', what up doe♪

Chuck is really getting it in with this CD. I just sat here grooving. This bass is banging in my back. I love Hip Hop especially the kind that makes me feel the struggle. Oh this is my song right here. It's fairly new, but every time I hear this song it reminds me of my mom. I guess because Jeezy is explaining through his song that his mom was on drugs and then Keyshia Cole shared with the world how her mom used to be on drugs, is what made this song so touching. These two are an awesome combination. I'm happy to see the change in their mom's; I just hope soon enough my mom will change also. Until then I'll do like their song says and keep "Dreaming." "♪Dreaming♪ Dreaming♪ I know it's been hard, but we made it baby ♪."

I have realized that everybody who sings and raps have a talent. They do it from their experiences. As I wiped the tears from my eyes I began to look in the sky again. When my mom does decide to give up drugs and come back looking for me, I'll be waiting on her. That will be a dream coming true.

I read and listen to a lot of opinions about how people say that Hip Hop is the reason for the evil in the world and it's simply not true. What I have learned from listening to rappers and singers of the Hip Hop community is that they tell their autobiography through song. Unfortunately, some of it has been negative because they were allowed to record through their painful times in life, which can also be fortunate because from my psychology magazines, it stated that sharing your story with others can be very therapeutic. This song right here tells me a lot. I know that if others who had parents strung out on drugs made it, I know I can.

The truth of the matter is a lot of people look at the way that I dress along with the beauty that I possess without recognizing that my outer appearance is simply a cover up. Just like Chuck, I had no idea that my baby had been through all the things that he has been through because on the outside he looks dressed up and he appears to have been raised in a great home and environment. I would have never known that his mom killed his brother right in front of him and he watched his dead father get carried out in a body bag. I would have never known that. Wow, it's interesting how I just came up with this epiphany even though I think this might qualify under the judging a book by its cover analogy that Chuck scalded me about earlier at breakfast.

Life's experiences are often not easy to handle. I learned that just by watching the episode with Tone today. He obviously couldn't take the things that he was going through because he chose to end it today. The sad part is he has kids left behind who knows that his father was a quitter. It's not like he quit a spades game or something petty like that, he decided to quit the ultimate game; life.

Life is a gamble, it's hard and it's also beautiful. I am so happy that Chuck came into my life because I never seen life as being as important as it is now. I felt that because Stan abused my body that I would never be good for nothing, but whatever he made me out to be. Things are actually starting to make a lot of since now. If God has all the power like Chuck said, I know he must have something better in mind for me.

Whoa! Yes, ten more miles to Detroit; I can't wait. I said quietly. I glanced over at Chuck I noticed he's been a little quiet.

"Hey Chuck, you ok baby?"

"Yeah I'm cool boo."

"I see you over there day dreaming."

"Bay, I can't daydream and drive at the same time. That's you over there super quiet." He replied with a smile.

"What's on your mind?"

"Nothing much; just thinking about what Tone did, man that shit was ill for real."

"Oh well, life goes on huh baby?"

"Yeah it does."

"So what are you going to do when we get home?"

"Well first I have to find out how I am going to flip this dope, after that I'm hoping I can see you again."

"That sounds good to me." I replied

Chapter 7

Back in Detroit; Yes!!!!

"Victoria! Victoria! Wake up ma!"

"Huh? What? Oh we're here already." I replied while wiping the slight sleep from my eyes. Wow, how did I fall asleep like that so quickly? I knew it was going to happen. I've been fighting my sleep because I wanted to make sure my baby didn't get in any trouble. Thank God we have made it. Let me call Toy.

"Hello" Toy answered.

"Hey Toy, we just made it in. Where do you want me to meet you at?"

"I'll meet you at that hotel where I dropped you off at because I am on my way over my Auntie's house in the King homes. How far are you away?"

"We're on I-94 crossing Telegraph. Chuck said it should be about 30-35 minutes."

"Call me before you come up on Jefferson. By the way, your Uncle called about five times. I didn't answer it because I was getting my nails done. You probably better call him."

"I will, soon as I get back."

"Ok girl, Bye."

"So what are you and your girl planning on doing today?" Chucked asked before he licked his sexy, juicy lips.

That's a good question, I thought to myself. "Bay I don't know maybe, go to the Isle or something. I know Toy wants me to go to the mall with her."

"Do you need some money, baby?"

"Nah boo, she said my Uncle dropped some off for me before he went out of town. I'm cool, Thanks for asking. Baby you are so thoughtful. You missed out on your money and you still offering to help me, I love you."

"Toy, we are almost at Jefferson. We're on 75 passing Mack Ave." I said when Toy answered.

"Ok, I am on my way now." She replied.

Downtown is off the chain. Toy was right. It's real hot out here. This weather is a trip. It was just snowing two weeks ago, now it's 80 degrees in the middle of the winter. This is very unusual. "Ok bay, there's Toy right there." I said as I pointed to Toy's car pulling up in the Hotel parking lot.

Chuck pulled up on the side of her. He got out and grabbed my bag and put it in Toy's car and then we kissed for about five minutes. I grabbed his face gently. "Baby, please be careful, please baby, be careful okay. You do what you do, flip that shit, do it easy and smart baby ok." I said.

"I hear you ma, he smiled confidently. "You know yo man got this."

"Alright you two, didn't y'all spend enough time together already?" Toy yelled out the window.

Chuck opened up Toy's passenger door for me. Once I sat down and fastened my seat belt, Chuck bent down and said "alright Toy, you be safe with my baby and don't be having her around a bunch of dude's ok."

"Yeah, whatever! I don't make it a habit in destroying love. You be safe alright!"

"You too!" Chuck replied before he kissed my lips. He got in his car and pulled off.

"So how was your little trip?" Toy asked.

"It was nice, but this morning was disturbing."

"Why? What happened?"

"Tell me why did the guy Chuck was supposed to meet last night blow his head off this morning?" I rhetorically asked.

"Are you talking about Anthony?"

"Yes, how you know that?"

"That's my cousin's, best friends, baby's daddy. Girl, that was crazy. I heard they had it broadcasting all across the airwaves. I didn't get a chance to see it, because my cousin didn't tell me until after it happened. When I got off the phone with you this morning I went back to sleep anyway. That was messed up, but girl don't let that bother you. That man knew what he was doing. It's Saturday, it's hot and it's a beautiful day. Life goes on baby sis. Sit back and chill."

I guess you're right, I thought. I glanced at Toy which reminded me that I should put on my sunglasses also since she's rocking her red Dolce & Gabbana's. I slouched back in the seat and pulled out my Palladium Juicy Couture's. Toy let back her sun roof and turned on the radio. "Uh oh Toy, put some bass in that. This is the cut right here." I said.

"♪*Boy you ... got me feeling so good ... you take ... all the pain away from me ... ... without ... ... you around I couldn't be ... and I know you fell in love with me, ... my love is ... so good -that wouldn't be without you bay♪ couldn't see being without you bay♪*" Toy and I harmonized until DJ Couzin interrupted.

"Thanks for tuning into your favorite station for Hip Hop and R & B, FM 98 WJMC. Spinning on the ones and two's. Detroit's favorite DJ ... DJ Couzin. Real talk Detroit, who watched the news this morning regarding the young man in Gary, Indiana? I don't think they should have showed him blowing his brains out on national television. The whole situation was devastating, very sad. I can't say that I disagree with the way he felt in regards to this racial discrimination, but at the same time killing your self is not the solution. We have to fight for our rights and not with violence. We were already created as Kings, but that's another story and I'm trying to keep my job. Ya heard me? Our prayers go out to the family as well as to those who listened in on it. Big ups to the young brotha encouraging him that was real talk my brotha. Now back to the jump off party going down tonight 18 & up at St. Andrews, ladies free before 11p.m so be there!"

"Oh yeah Toy, we got to hit that bad boy." I said.

"Girl- bye! You're not ready for a club."

"I really want to go out tonight Toy. I don't know why, but I feel real good right about now, *Not to mention DJ Couzin makes it sound like it's going to be off the hook.*"

"That's what's up. So have you figured out what you're going to do for graduation?" Toy asked.

"I don't know Toy. I haven't given it much thought. My graduation gift to myself would be to move out of my Uncle's house. I was thinking about asking Chuck if he wanted to get an apartment or something. I have to fill out some applications Monday when I go back to school. I'm meeting with Mrs. Thomas on Monday. She said she'll help me with filling out all of the applications to the colleges I should apply to."

"Ok that's good. Mrs. Thomas is a sweet person. I like her. She tried helping me with deciding on colleges, but I wasn't feeling more school at that time, but now that everybody's drilling me, I have to do something. Are you still thinking about being a writer or are you still interested in doing the psychology thang?" she asked.

"I was thinking about that today, Toy. I'm considering trying both, but I'm leaning more towards being a writer. You know writing is my passion, that's where my heart is. I want to write books that people can relate to. I want people to really feel the passion in my writing. I guess I want to keep people encouraged you know." I replied.

"I know you can do it, Victoria. You have to believe in yourself, have faith, and stay committed. The most important step is, believing in you. Once you believe in your own dreams along with believing in yourself all things are possible. It's funny how when we were little, Mama always told us 'It's better to wake up and chase a dream then to spend your entire life asleep', makes a great deal of sense now. I never knew what she was saying until now."

"It's ironic how you just said that because I was just about to ask you have you decided on what you're going to do with your life? I mean like, what's your goals? Your passions? What do you want to be?"

"Well, I put in an application at Oakland Community College and I got accepted. I start in the fall."

"Congratulations Toy. So what are you planning to major in, shopping or fashion, because you got both of them down packed" I laughed. "You know I'm just kidding girl."

"Ha, ha, very funny" Toy replied as she rolled her eyes. "I was thinking about being a lawyer like my dad or maybe a registered nurse like my mom. But, to be honest Victoria, don't laugh ok" Toy said.

"I won't" I replied.

"Do you promise Victoria? You can give me your opinion, but don't laugh."

"I promise girl, come on tell me."

"I was in the beauty supply store today and I realized that we don't have any Black owned beauty supplies. Who would be better at knowing what we need for our hair than us. These Chinese people are getting rich from us. I'm thinking about majoring in business so I can open up my own Beauty Supply. I'm going to name it Latoya's. So what do you think?" she asked.

"Toy, I am a little upset that you would think that I would find something like that funny. That's a great idea Toy! Now let me throw your words of wisdom back at you. As long as you believe in yourself, have faith and stay committed you can do it. Yeah Toy, I really believe you can do it. You already have the shopping and fashion expertise; you can use that to your advantage. You know what you like and what's hot. Yeah Toy, I like that idea." I smiled.

"♪*Lost without you- can't help myself*♪ *how does it feel*♪," my phone rang.

"Excuse me Toy."

"Hello" I answered

"Hey lil Mama, what you doing?" Chuck asked.

"Chilling, still riding around. Toy and I are discussing our career goals, why? What's up with you?"

"Nothing much; I just called to tell you that I got rid of that package. Now I am on my way to drop off this rental."

"That's good news baby. I'm glad it all worked out. Toy and I were just listening to DJ Cousin on WJMC; he was talking about a big party jumping off downtown at St. Andrews. We're thinking about going. You going?" I asked.

"Yeah, me and my fella's might role up in there or we might go to the River Rock. Now the River Rock is usually banging. So that's what's up. Your man is about to go get super fresh and clean."

"Yeah me too; I will see you later then boo."

"Ok, I love you." He said.

"I love you too." I replied.

Toy looked at me and stuck her finger in her mouth as if she wanted to make herself regurgitate. "You two are a trip. Y'all need to hurry up and get married for real!"

I smiled. "Girl you are so silly. I can't wait until we get married either. Chuck said that the River Rock is the club that's usually banging on Saturday's so we might have to hit that one up" I suggested.

"Oh yeah, I've been there a couple of times. It's usually off the chain. Yeah we can go there tonight

Oh this is my shit" Toy yelled as she turned her speakers up. Every time she turns them up someone's car alarm is activated. Thanks to Romeo for installing his twelve's and his amplifier in her trunk. I feel so good right now. I'm high on life. Toy and I must have been thinking the same thing. We looked at each other. ♪*Welcome to the Good Life*♪ *he probably think he could- but- but- I don't think he should*♪ *Welcome to the Good Life*♪" Toy and I laughed after singing our favorite part of Kanye West and T-Pain's song. Toy changed the station.

Here's a song I only heard a few times before, but it was one of the best songs I have ever heard by an artist name Kem. I read that he was homeless for a little while before he became famous, plus he's from Detroit. *Dreams are meant to come true*, I thought to myself. "♪ *I can't tell it, how we make this thing fly- I really thought we'd work it out -after all this time,* ♪"

"Sorry boo, I know that's your song, but you're the only one in love right now. Yeah, I'm hating." Toy said after she changed the station. "Now this is what I'm talking about. This is smooth right here. You can sing this without being in love" Toy said as she began singing. I joined in with her.

"♪*Ooo- Ooo- Ooo- Oooooo*♪ *Grove with you*♪ *uh, uh, uh, uhhh* ♪" We burst out laughing. We totally butchered 'Groove with You' by the Isley Brother's. *Why are we pulling up at Toy's house,* I thought.

"Toy, I thought we were going in the mall."

"We are; I just need to grab my charger." She said while getting out the car.

After Toy walked in the house I felt a mustache and a kiss on my neck. I looked around ... oh my goodness it's Stan. I instantly remembered Toy said I should call him. I tried to act as if I am happy to see him while controlling the beat of my heart that's pounding extremely hard right now.

"Hey, what are you doing here? I thought you were out of town."

"I was, but I just flew back in. The case I was working on was cut a little short." Stan replied.

"Stan, now you know you cannot be kissing me like that in public."

"I know, I know, I was riding past and I saw you and Toy pulling up. Did she tell you I called? I was checking to see if you got that money I left. You know I don't trust that brother of hers."

"Yes Stan, I received it. Thank you. We're on our way to the mall as soon as Toy grabs her charger."

"Oh ok. So what do you two have planned for the night" he asked.

"We are supposed to go to some club." I replied.

"And how do you plan on doing that? You're not 21 yet."

"I know that Stan. We're going to an eighteen and up club."

"You know I miss you. Why don't you come back home tonight?" he suggested.

"No Stan, I will be home tomorrow. Come on; let me hang out with my girl. I'm there at the house every day." I wined. "I've only been gone for a day and a half."

Thank God! Toy's walking towards the car. I was wondering what was taking her so long.

"Hi, Mr. Campbell"

"Hello Latoya. How are you?" Stan asked.

"I'm good. Victoria and I are on our way to the mall" she replied.

"Ok don't y'all be getting in any trouble" he said while giving me the look as if that comment was mainly directed towards me. "Y'all have a good time. Vick, I will see tomorrow"

"Ok Uncle Stan, I'll see you later." I smiled as if I'm really looking forward to it.

As I watched him pull off, Toy tapped me. "What the hell is he doing here? I though he went out of town."

"He said he went, but when he got there, they no longer needed him.

"I forgot your Uncle got that long bread." She replied.

"Yeah girl, I guess."

"He is looking kind of good girl. Would you mind if I was your new Aunty? Toy asked jokingly.

"Girl, please. Let your niece hold a couple bucks" I replied. *Girl, you can think he looks good if you want to. Don't let that cover up fool you,* I thought to myself. That guy is a real live beast if you ask me. Why did he have to attempt in ruining my day. Yuck! He really disgusts me.

"Which mall are we going to?" I asked.

"I was thinking about Eastland. Is that cool with you?" Toy asked.

"I don't care. You're driving, not me" I replied.

Chapter 8

Time to Shop

We pulled up at the mall. Eastland is the hood mall anyway so I'm not shocked at these females. These chics' are crazy. That's all you have to do for the City of Detroit. Give us a little bit of heat and sunlight, clothes are coming off, cars are coming out of hibernation and it's on and popping. Miami style all day. I know it's been in the high 70's and low 80's this whole entire week, but it's the middle of March for goodness sake. Everybody should know by now that this is straight up pneumonia weather. These chicks have on booty shorts, bikini tops with those hood rat sandals that have the flower on the top.

I guess I call them hood rat sandals because every rat in the hood has a pair. The sad part is they have them in every color. I saw them in the beauty supply for five dollars. All they need is 30 bucks and they can own all six colors. I pay more for my lip gloss, but hey to each its own. I'm just tripping on the fact that they have they're booty cheeks hanging out and are basically naked in the middle of winter. I know I wear shirts that reveal my 44DD's because it's hard to cover them up unless I'm wearing a turtle neck, but I don't have all of my body showing. It lacks taste and it looks cheap and trashy.

"Girl Bye!" Toy laughed as this female who walked in front of us with red, purple, orange and green hair with one red and one orange hood rat sandal. "Who's in the mood though, Victoria" Toy said loud enough for the girl to hear us.

I try not to feed into Toy's comments because I know we will end up getting into a fight with somebody. I tried to act like I was not paying attention to Toy when the girl stared at us. I know that girl don't want to see Toy and I anyway, but I try to prevent conflicts before they start.

"Toy, you think I should get some air force ones or should we sandal it out to night?"

She looked at me as if I just asked her to wear those hood rat sandals. "Girl, don't play with me. You know I just got my toes done, we're definitely doing sandals."

I looked down at my toes and replied, "Yeah you're right. I just got my pedicure done Thursday." My French tip toes are also fairly new. Are we going to Macy's or JC Penny's" I asked.

"One of my home girls put me up on this little store called Simply Fashionable, they have some cute clothes and they're not expensive" Toy replied.

What, I thought. That's a shocker. I would have never believed Toy just said that if I didn't hear it with my own ears. I guess Toy is changing. "What, Ms. Diva saving bread? That's what's up." I replied. She looked at me and smiled.

We went in Simply Fashionable. I haven't been in the store two minutes yet and I already see an outfit that I like. Oh, that lady looks like she works here. "Excuse me, do you work here?" I asked. She pointed at her name tag. *Oh ok, I guess she's a mute or deaf or something.* I began speaking to her trying to emphasize the words I was saying and giving more hand movement.

"Hi, I- was- hoping- that you could tell- me -where that outfit in the window is located. The –outfit- on -the manikin" I said while I pointed at the manikin.

"First of all, I'm not deaf I heard you the first time and second of all, they didn't make those outfits in your size. The plus size section is in the back"

Oh no she didn't! I thought as I stared at her with disgust. Damn! Why she have to say it like that! Just because she's a skinny broad that looks like she has never eaten. I am a size fourteen and I am damn sure sexy, these 44DD's are putting me over the top any way. I think she is simply evil. *If you don't like your job, quit!* I mumbled under my breath. I mean for real though. I decided not to entertain her statement, but of course Toy's not buying it.

Toy's standing here staring at this girl like she's about to cut her. I grabbed Toys arm. "Please Toy, don't even trip. She's not worth it. Let's just look back here and see if they have something that I like." I suggested.

"Nah, I'm good V. She lucky I just got my nails done because I would slap the shit out of her, but you right she aint worth it." Toy said loud enough for the girl to hear her as she walked to the back of the store with me. Toy was obviously offended as well because Toy and I both wear a size 32 in the waist, but she's in a juniors top because her breast are not big like mine.

"Ooh this is cute, Toy" I said as I held this blue jean dress, with the matching sandals that tie up around my calves. "Toy, I'm going to try this on." I informed her before I entered the fitting room.

Oh my goodness, this is sexy, I thought as I viewed my reflection. Let me get Toy's opinion since she is the fashion expert. I walked out the fitting room.

"Toy, what do you think?" I asked.

"Take all of it up to the register because that is definitely you!" she replied.

I thought so too. These shoes are gorgeous especially for them to be so cheap. The 4inch wedge heel makes my calf look super sexy. I've always been complemented on my sexy legs. I don't really like to brag on myself at all, I simply state the facts. I learned that if I don't feel good about myself, nobody else will.

Mama Jackson always told Toy and I that by us being thick females the way we are, that we have to make sure we look our best. She said that people will often treat us the way they see us treat ourselves. She said, "It does not matter what size we are. The way you carry your self is the most important." I think that's why Toy and I are the way we are. Mama Jackson made sure Toy's and I hygiene was always at A+ standard. "There's nothing like being a big girl with an awful odor" she often said. I always make sure that I look good and smell exceptionally well. So does Toy. I try my best not to act like I am any better than anyone else just as Mama Jackson taught, but Toy on the other hand, she's working on it.

Toy is a nice person, please don't get me wrong. It's just that Toy's father explains to her all the time that there is no other female better than her. Basically the same things that Stan taught me, but Stan's behavior has helped me to realize that Mama Jackson's advice is a whole lot more embracive.

As much as I embrace Mama Jackson's great teachings about twenty percent of Stan's is displayed in some of my behavior. To be quiet honest, I really feel like this is a low budget store and I feel that I am too good to allow this cheap material to occupy my body, but since Toy thinks it's ok, I'll rock it out. Besides, I do make this outfit look sexy.

"Victoria! Victoria!" Toy screamed.

"What? Why are you screaming?"

"Girl, I been calling you for the longest. You have to stop daydreaming so much. Give her your money!" she shouted.

"Oh, I apologize."

"Girl, I know how you feel, I day dream too. It's like a sense of relief, like a semi break from the world, but your total is $62.56." The sales clerk said.

"Oh ok, that's not bad at all." I gave her $65.

"She smiled as she placed money in my hand. "$2.44 is your change. Thanks for shopping at Simply Fashionable. Have a great day!"

"Thank you" I said, not really realizing this is the same girl who was extremely rude when I came in. She obviously didn't recognize it was me. It's definitely obvious Toy's not paying attention either because Toy's smiling as well as communicating with her. I guess her job must be stressful.

I often thought about applying for a job, but I really don't have to. If Chuck and I get an apartment I will get a job then. I consider the things Stan buys me and the cash that he gives me as my paycheck. He owes me that for violating my body, manipulating my mind and keeping me in disgust mode every second that he's in my presence. I overheard Toy's friends say that if a man sleeps with you he should be more than willing to pay for it. I don't feel like that about this situation especially with Stan. I would prefer that he didn't stay on the same block as I, let alone the same house. That's just the way Toy's home girls think anyway.

Toy kept in contact with her friends from the Brewster Projects. Toy's other female friends are straight up street girls. They're always talking about how they're all about getting money. Every time I see them they're always quoting "Closed legs don't get fed" from the movie Players Club. It's evident that they are some type of hookers or something. The sad part about it is I think they sleep around with hundreds of men for a happy meal. I can count on two fingers, who have entered my secret garden. Unfortunately, one of them used forcible entry and the other just entered yesterday. Everything I own is top of the line. I guess that's just the hood in those chicks.

They have lived in the Brewster's since we were little. Those are Toy's friend's not mine. I don't like to be around females who constantly hates on everything you do and everything you wear especially those who don't see any type of future. That's why I'm happy to see that Toy has changed her outlook on life. I guess her step-dad continuously drilling her is actually helping. I don't like associating with individuals who don't appear to be growing. Plus, I'm not good with hanging around a lot of females anyway. Anytime it's a large group of project bound females, something dramatic is guaranteed to jump off. Don't let it be a group of females who chase their dreams mixed in with a crowd of females who's sleeping their entire life away that's when a lot of shit tends to pop off and that's not my style. Even though I vibe off haters, these chic's right here eat, sleep and breath hate. Toy informed me that I'm usually the topic of discussion.

They told Toy they think that I'm bougie. I choose not to hang with them because their hood rats period. Toy said they don't like me because I think I'm better than them, but that's not the case. I'm thankful that I don't have to live in the projects anymore. I think that's where my mom got hooked on those drugs. The projects are like the starting point for many Black families. I'm glad my mom decided to move me out of the projects anyway. Even though I don't have to live there anymore, I don't think that I am any better than those who do.

Toy tapped me. "Come on, girl lets go." She said.

"Oh ok, you're finally ready" I said sarcastically.

I can't believe how Toy just stood at the register constantly changing her mind on that fake ass costume jewelry. Yeah, this chic is really changing. If somebody would have brought her some imitation jewelry like the kind she just purchased she would have gone ballistic. What's confusing me the most is how she just brought two imitation tennis bracelets? I want to put her in her place, but maybe I shouldn't. I guess this a side of Toy I have never seen. I was in a daze anyway. I find myself drifting off a lot. I like thinking about things instead of standing around allowing my brain to rest. Even though I day dream, that does not mean that I am not paying attention to my surroundings. Like now for instance; I wish I would have walked past these watches that are forty percent off.

"Wait a minute Toy; let me look at these watches right quick."

Oh now this is nice. Chuck will like this. "Excuse me sir is this watch forty percent off also" I asked.

"Yes and we also have buy one get one for a dollar." He replied.

"Buy one get one for a dollar" I repeated.

"Yes ma'am" he said.

"Which watch do you recommend I should get for my fiancé, he's nineteen with style?" I asked.

"This watch here is a popular one that I sell to young men regularly" he said as he pointed to the Kenneth Cole Section. "You're in luck, I have one more left. This is a sleek and stylish updated version of this retro- styled stainless steel design. As you can see it has the large day and date display. It has an adjustable 8 inch length accompanied with the Croco-patterned brown leather strap. It's usually $160.00, but with the discounted rate you can get it for only $95. If you are interested in the buy one get one for a dollar sale you can select either one of those watches there" he said as he pointed to the $50 Kenneth Cole Watches.

I purchased both of them. I know my baby said he needed another watch. I hope he likes it.

"Toy, do you think Chuck will like this" I asked.

"Girl yes, that's sharp right there. I see you have another one. Who is that one for?" she asked.

"My Uncle; You know his birthday is next month. Since it was only $1, I figure what the heck you know." *I shouldn't have brought Stan anything. If he continues tripping, I'll just give it to Chuck,* I thought to myself.

"Do you think I should get Robert one?"

"Did you two get back together" I asked.

"No we're not back together, but he is my friend. Robert acts too childish sometimes and then he wants to tell me that I need to do something with my life. I'm straight on being in a relationship with him. As a matter of fact, I'm not getting him anything."

"Girl, y'all probably will end up getting back together. If it's not Rob it will be Reggie."

"Victoria, you know that Reggie is my male best friend. Our relationship is strictly platonic."

"Right- and Chuck and I are enemies." I replied.

"I'm serious. We are strictly friends and that's it" she said.

"Toy, friends don't sleep together, but homie lover friends do."

"Girl, I told you that was only twice and that's only because we were gone off that Grey Goose."

"Yeah, ok" I replied while staring at Toy as I twisted my lips indicating that I don't believe her.

While we were on our way back to the car, we spotted the girl who Toy made fun of on our way in the mall. She's giving us the look like she might be feeling like a frog. I really wish she would leap over here. I wish she would try me. *I dare you,* I thought while staring at her.

"Victoria, can you explain to me what in the hell is that colorful bobble head chic staring at. I wish she would run up, she gone mess around and get done up." Toy expressed. It's no question that she felt the same animosity I'm feeling coming from the opposite end of the parking lot.

"Do you see something you like" Toy yelled.

"Ugh Toy" I said. As I watched the girl rapidly licking her tongue out at Toy.

"Sorry boo, I don't swing that way" Toy yelled as we got in the car.

"Ooh Toy, that girl wants you. She looks like she wants to taste your cookie. You better make sure she doesn't follow us. She might turn out to be your stalker" I laughed.

"I wish a bitch would. I'm strictly dickly" Toy replied as she turned on eight mile.

"Girl, Ole boy is trying to get at you." I said.

Toy rolled down her window, gripped her steering wheel and leaned back as if she's a dude. I guess she's trying to act hard for these guys. Those 24 inch spinners sure do look nice on that old school impala. The driver looked over at me smiling.

"Ooh, I want to talk to the passenger." He said showing his entire top row of teeth.

"Sorry boo, I'm already taken." I replied.

"Is that the same for you driver?" the guy on the passenger side asked.

Toy looked at me smiling, and then she looked at him and replied "No."

I'm sitting here listening to him trying to get his Mack on.

"Oh ok, so what are you about to get into?" he asked.

"Well, me and my girl is about to go get dressed, and then probably hit the Isle for a minute" Toy replied.

"Get dressed? Damn, y'all already look good." He replied as the driver agreed.

I glanced over at them again. They look just as good. They're both looking mad sexy and iced out, but I'm happy with my fiancé so I'm definitely going to pass. I glanced at them again and noticed the passenger has his cell phone in his hand. I can't classify him as a scrub because he looks like he might have his own car also especially since he's straight blinging. His cell phone is not cheap either. I know for a fact that had to run him at least five hundred dollars. I know Toy's picking up on that too because she never talks to guys in the passenger seat. The majority of the time I can tell by the passenger's appearance if he would be labeled as a scrub.

"What's your name boo?" he asked.

"Latoya."

"Can I call you?"

"I'll call you. What's your number?

"313-282-2222, you gone call me right." He asked Toy acting pressed.

"Yeah, I'll call you in a few." Toy replied

"Alright ma, make sure you do that with your sexy ass." He said.

"Passenger, you sure you don't want my number? I can make it worth your wild" the driver asked.

"I'm faithful to my husband" I replied as I flashed my 10kt diamond.

"I guess he got the picture" Toy said in response to him burning rubber as he pulled off.

When we got back to the house, Romeo and his boys were at the kitchen table smoking a blunt. I'm sure Romeo must know my reason for staring at him as if he has lost the little brain that he has. "Y'all smoking in the house Romeo, Mama is going to be pissed" I said.

He stood up, walked over towards me, blew his smoke in my face and said, "I got this lil sis. Mama and Big Steve went to Las Vegas for the weekend and Little Steven went to his granny house. So we got the place to ourselves."

Toy looked as if it just came to her mind. "Oh yeah, I forgot Mama was leaving today."

"Yeah- so get at yo boy." Romeo said as he popped his collar.

Toy pushed him up against his head and ran.

As we headed towards Toy's room I said, "Toy, I forgot Mama was going out of town."

"Girl yeah, you know her and Steven's Anniversary is next Monday."

"Oh yeah that's right. Girl how long has it been?" I asked.

"It will be six years on Monday. It's amazing how it seems like time's just flying by." Toy replied.

"Yes, it seems like we were just little girls making mud pies in the projects. I'm so happy for Mama. They seem like they are so happy together. I hope that's how Chuck and I marriage is and I hope we stay married forever."

"You will, you two are meant to be together" Toy said as she grabbed her clothes. "I'm going to use the bathroom downstairs. Hurry up and get dressed, all this love talk is making me sick. I need to get out of here so I can find me a husband too."

I took my shower; fixed my hair and now I'm wearing the mess out of this dress. Yeah, Chuck needs to come to the same club that we go to because I think I'm going to need protection.

"Victoria, let's go!" Toy yelled up the stairs.

Chapter 9

Belle Isle

It's still nice out here. This weather is scaring me. I have never known for it to be this hot in the middle of March and when I glanced at the news when I was getting dressed, the weather man said it's supposed to be in the 80's up until next week and then it's supposed to drop back down to the low 30's. That's how I know this is straight up killer weather, but I might as well enjoy it while it last.

I took a peak at myself in the side view mirror. I must admit I'm looking hot. Toy is too. She decided to get the orange and blue jean skirt and jacket set. It's real fly. Especially with her orange Marc Jacob open toe sandals. I knew Toy was going to try and out do me. That's probably why she encouraged me to get these cheap ass $35 shoes. Toy's shoes cost almost $500 alone. We have the same ones accept mine are black on black. That's ok though. I am not in a competition with her besides I'm sure my ring cost more than everything she has on.

I am so glad that Toy decided not to wear those imitation tennis bracelets. I might have made a mistake and broke them on purpose. I don't like it when people wear stuff that's imitating a genuine product. I feel that if it's imitating something, wearing it is an absolute fashion disaster and Toy knows that. We are looking good though despite my inside fashion price evaluation.

"That's what's up Toy, you remember the CD." I said when I heard our song beating through the speakers. We were listening to it earlier, but DJ Couzin cut it off. She has it bumping real loud, her twelve's are kicking hard, plus she just got her car washed today too. All eyes are on us.

"♪Boy you -feel me with so much joy♪ you give -whatever it is I need♪ ... Toy and I are basically butchering Ashanti's song.

This is me and Toy's favorite song. I actually love her entire CD. Even though it's old, it still bumps. Toy and I are finally getting on Belle Isle. It seems like we've been stuck in traffic on the bridge for the longest. I can tell Toy's heading to the strip.

The strip is similar to a fashion show. Everybody who is somebody hangs out here. It's also a car show. The entire dough boy's come out here and floss. Detroit has a lot of dough boy's I must admit. They can get a little wild out here also because it's a lot of young immature boys with more money than they can handle, especially the ones driving the cars with the butterfly doors. I can already tell the strip is packed because it's bumper to bumper traffic. It's nice right now. Toy and I are just cruising with the music blasting. Everybody's looking so good.

"Where you at?" Chuck burst through my chirp. *Dang he scared the crap out of me.* It seems like he burst in at the right time, right when the song went off.

I hit pause on Toy's CD player and replied "I'm on Belle Isle."

"I know, turn your head over this way." He said.

I turned my head to the right because I was already looking to my left where those hood rats are dancing. I don't have anything against females; I don't know why every female I see is a rat to me. I do categorize these chicks that I don't know. I guess that's another classification of "judging a book by its cover" that Chuck was talking about earlier.

"OOH look at my baby. Toy, pull up over there." I requested.

We pulled up next to him and parked. I got out and hugged Chuck.

"Damn baby you're looking good." I whispered in his ear.

"How are you going to take the words right out of my mouth like that?" He said before kissing me with these big sexy juicy lips.

Um, baby, I moaned to myself. He makes me weak at the knees.

"I don't know, I guess great minds think alike huh." I asked after removing the lip gloss from his lips that was taken from mine.

Chuck is drinking some Grey Goose Vodka and Cranberry juice. He offered me a sip. Ooh it's strong, this is my first time drinking.

"I didn't know you drink." I said to Chuck.

"That's because I'm trying to kick these bad habits." He replied.

My insides are beginning to feel like I just drank something hot. It was cool as I swallowed, but as its beginning to settle in my stomach it feels like it's on fire. I drank some more hoping that it would settle the flames roaring inside my belly. It actually tastes pretty good now and the heat is starting to go away. "Here baby" Chuck said as he handed me my own drink.

"Toy, do you want a drink?" he asked.

"Now you know I want a drink" she replied.

I'm not sure if I'm supposed to drink this like its juice because that's how it's beginning to taste. I feel a little different. It's not a bad feeling though; it feels like I just received a boost of energy or something. I leaned over to Toy. "Toy, I don't know if I should be feeling like this, but it feels good."

She stuck her finger in her drink stirring it around. "Girl, you alright. You're straight for real, just don't drink too much." She suggested.

I had to ask Toy because I know she's a drinker and a smoker so she knows what she's talking about. She gets lit all the time and she carry's herself well. Unlike a couple of females I've seen staggering and thangs after they get drunk. Toy says that those types of people can't handle their liquor. I noticed the guy from earlier in the impala pulling up next to Chuck's car.

"Toy, isn't that ole boy who tried to talk to you?" I asked.

She looked at him, "Yeah that's him" she replied. I knew he had to have his own car. He's in a burgundy old school cutlass with twenty fours on them with four gigantic TV's. He got out the car and started walking over to us.

"Girl, does he think he know you like that or something?" I asked.

Toy's not paying any attention to me. She's smiling so hard she could pose for a *"Crest"* commercial. Wow, he just walked right passed her.

"What up doe Chuck Deezy" he said to Chuck as he gave him a hand shake. "Oh, is this your wifey?" he asked while looking at me.

Chuck grabbed my arm, pulled me close, put his arms around my waist and pulled me back on him. "Yes sir, this is wifey right here." Chuck replied.

"Oh yeah?" He said, while smiling. "Me and my partner tried to holla at her and her girl earlier. She said she was taken and then my boy asked her once more and she told him she's faithful to her husband. So you definitely got yourself a true one by your side. That's love right there. I'm sorry, what's your name Ms. Lady?" He asked me.

"Victoria and what's yours?" I asked.

"Oh I apologize about that. My name is Juan. Well It's nice to meet you Victoria" He replied while shaking my hand.

"Are you following me? I thought you said you were going to holla at me in a few." He asked Toy.

Toy looked at him as she sipped her Grey Goose, "Following you? Not hardly and you know I can't call you right off the back, that would look desperate."

"I feel you ma." He smiled and reached for her hand. "Let's walk and talk for a minute."

As they began to walk away, Chuck and I started kissing. "Oh baby, I love you so much" I said as I wrapped my leg around his waist. I opened my eyes and noticed that my dress was rising and the sad part is in these split seconds I actually forgot that we are still outside. "Ooh, stop starting stuff. You play too much" I teased.

"Girl, it's like I am in another world when I'm with you."

"That's exactly how I feel, Chuck, seriously. Ever since you entered my life, you've changed my world completely. You have definitely changed the way I think and view a lot of things. I love you boo for real"

Um, what are you doing to me boy, I thought. Chuck grabbed the back of my neck, pulling my lips closer to his as we began passionately tongue wrestling. It's taking everything in me not to lay him back on the hood of his car, climb on top of him and ride his saddle until daylight with everybody watching. We finally let each other's tongues go.

"So did you and your girl decide what club to go to?" Chuck asked.

"I don't know for sure, Toy & I were listing to the radio and DJ Cousin was talking about St. Andrews, but I'm thinking about going to see if I can get in at the River Rock. Isn't that where you're supposed to be going?"

"Where ever you're going, I'm going. I wish I would let you go to a club looking like that without me being on your arm. Girl, don't play with me. I'm sure they're going to let you in. My homeboy is doing security at the door tonight so if anybody give you trouble let me know and I'll make sure that he gets you in." he replied.

Toy and Juan walked back over. I guess Toy's nose just got opened up that quick because she's smiling from ear to ear. Once I noticed Toy's lips appearing to be permanently glued in the form of a smile, I had to say something. "Toy, are you ok? What did he do to you? I've never seen you cheesing this hard since the first time you met Robert."

"Girl, shut up! I'm good. Are you ready?" she asked.

"I'm ready when you are. So what's the plan?"

"Well we can ride through here one more time so we can kill a little time and then we'll head to the River Rock."

"Ok that's what's up," I replied as I glanced over at Chuck. He is staring at us, *he's ear hustling whey too hard*, I thought to myself.

He noticed me smiling at him. He smiled back as he walked over to me, grabbed my thighs and then gripped my booty from the back while kissing me on my forehead. "You better make sure these clown as dude's stay out of your face and you better not be smiling at them with that gorgeous smile."

"First of all boo, don't even play me like that. You know good and well there's no other man in this world for me, but you. So stop playing." I replied while rubbing my fingers across his lips.

"I love you."

"I love you to baby" I replied before getting in Toy's car.

Chapter 10

We be clubbing ...

We're arriving at the club right now. It's only 10:30 and it's already packed. Toy's looking for a place to park. "There's a spot right there Toy!" I yelled with excitement. As she began to back into the parking spot, a guy walked up to the car. "Ladies, its ten dollars to park." He said.

"That's cool." Toy and I replied at the same time.

I hope they let me in, I thought to myself, *oh yeah I forgot Chuck said he's going to get me in if I have any problems.*

Toy and I were walking towards the line when the police flicked their lights on us. "You two ladies come here." The officers commanded on their loud speaker.

We walked over to their squad car. There is a white cop with green eyes and a black one with a ball head who resembles LL Cool J. *This is so typical, men in uniform flaunting their authority on beautiful females. They are sexy- I can't deny, but I can't entertain these guys. Besides, I'm really starting to feel the effects of that alcohol, I might mess around and say something that might get me arrested.*

"We just want to say that you both are looking beautiful. Can we go with y'all?" The bald one asked. *Apparently he's the spokesperson for the both of them*, I thought.

"Sure, you can come with us and while you're at it, you can pay our cover charge." Toy replied with a smile.

"So what are your names?" he asked.

"I'm Latoya."

"I'm Victoria."

"Ok Ms. Victoria and Ms. Latoya, we will see y'all in there."

I just smiled because I don't want any trouble. Toy and I are now in line. It's a shame how packed this club is already. We are maybe a few steps away from being around the corner. It has to be over a hundred people in this line and this is the line for ladies only. The line for the men is on the other side. The music is bumping. I hear it all the way out here. Ok, I'm feeling this right here. The line seems to be moving pretty quickly. I hope they play my song again when we get in. I can hear it out here, but I know it's got to be banging on the inside.

"♪*So don't listen to that vine of grapes they're nothing but liars hating♪ I bet they wouldn't mind trading places♪ with you by my side in my Mercedes♪*"

Ooh, I love this song right here. Every time I hear this Field Mob and Ciara song, I think about Chuck. At least 20 minutes has gone by. We finally reached the front door. Here comes security. I hope they don't trip. The big buff security guard looked at me and Toy and yelled, "ID's please!" I showed mine, he quickly glanced at it. "Ok, have fun. Next in line!" he yelled.

Toy showed hers. He gave her a yellow wrist band because her ID said twenty one, even though she won't be twenty one for another four months. I am assuming that they are looking at the years only.

Toy and I walked in the club. The music is so live. I love loud music that bumps.

"Come on Victoria, let's go upstairs" Toy directed me to follow her, since she's been here before.

"Hold on Toy, Chuck's calling me now. I feel my purse vibrating."

"Hey Baby." I answered.

"Did you get in?" he asked.

"Yes, we're going to the second floor."

"Ok, I will see you inside."

"Ok bay, hurry your sexy self-up." I said before he hung up.

Toy looked at me and asked, "Who was that, Chuck?"

"Girl, yes who else? Nobody else has this phone number, but y'all two." I replied.

Though I thought I just informed her that it was Chuck on the phone. I forgot Toy's most likely buzzing because she's been smoking and drinking all day.

This atmosphere is ok, they seem a little wild. I think me and Toy a bit over dressed cause these chic's got on baseball caps and tee shirts with busted gym shoes. But then, all eyes are on us.

Guys are offering to buy us drinks left and right. I don't want any more because I can't barely handle the way I'm feeling now. I'm already high from the drinks Chuck and I had at Belle Isle. If I do get another drink, I want to make sure Chuck is here with me. I would feel a lot safer. Toy's my girl and all, but she is buzzing. Not that I'm planning on fighting or anything, but I know how females get when they're drinking so- I have to keep my eyes open.

We sat down and watched these hood rats dancing by themselves, popping their booty all around the stage. It smells like fish. How awful. I leaned over and said, "Toy they wilding out huh?"

She looked at me and replied "Girllll" as she giggled.

So this is what the club scene is like huh, I thought to myself as I began to look around. I can't believe how overdressed Toy and I are. Toy's been here before, it seems like she would have put me up on the attire. It appears as if everybody, males and females' eyes are glued on us. I'm not sure if it's because we are trend setting or if it's our jewelry because Toy and I together is causing a shine that's glaring out from our table. The only people rocking as much ice as Toy and I are the guys. I can tell I just picked up an instant fifty plus haters.

"Toy, I have to use the bathroom."

"Oh it's down stairs. Once you go down the stairs it will be right in front of you to the right" She replied as she continued dancing in her seat.

"Aww for real Toy, walk with me down there." I suggested.

She's looking at me as if I just messed up her groove. "Ok come on, I need to check myself any way, it feels like my skirt is twisted." Toy replied as she led me down the stairs.

"♪*I can do for you what Martin did for the people*♪ *ran by the men, but the women keep the temple*♪ *it's very seldom that you're blessed to find your equal*♪.

I like the music system in this club, the DJ is playing all of my jams. I looked around as we're walking down the stairs. All eyes are still on us. I know I caught a couple of eyes glued on me. I know the majority of them are thinking I could "upgrade" them, but I'm just singing along with my girl Beyoncé. Her song is knocking in these club speakers.

We went in the bathroom. I'm glad Toy decided to come with me because she wouldn't have believed me if I explained to her how drunk this chic is right now. *Here's one of the chic's that can't hold her liquor,* I thought. I don't know why she is staring at me and Toy like that. She's standing against the wall so it could help hold her drunk ass up.

"Look at these stuck up hoes!" she slurred.

Toy and I looked at each other and at the same time we said, "What!" We looked at her and said, "Girl, please!" I was going in the stall when she jumped in front of me.

"Oh you got all your gold and diamonds on, you must be one of them bougie, stuck up Southfield hoes. Y'all got money like that ok, ok. You think you better than me?" she asked.

"I had a feeling when I came in here I was going to be receiving some new résumé's for the "hate on me" position. Try to learn how to quit hating and you might be able to get money the way we do. My suggestion to you would be to get out of my face before I show you how a stuck up lady gets down!"

"Oh ok so you hard; yeah ... un huh ... we'll see." She replied.

"Bitch, whatever!" I said as I bumped her while entering the stall. I used the restroom and came straight out. Toy was already at the sink washing her hands.

"Toy, what was that all about?" I asked.

"Girl, don't pay her any type of attention. This club is full of dusty little girls who love hating on real bossy females. Victoria, I'm serious. Please don't pay these tricks no mind. You'll be feeding into it. That's exactly what they want you to do. Let them continue to hate. When they stop hating, that means that you're not doing something right. You feel me boo." Toy replied.

"I'm not Toy, but I don't appreciate her coming on me like that. She almost got her ass kicked." I said while washing my hands.

Once we exited the restroom I noticed my fiancé over in the corner by the pool table standing with his boys. "Toy, there's Chuck and Juan, ole boy from earlier."

"Where?"

"Right over there," I pointed. "Just come on. They're right over there by the pool table."

As we were walking towards them, out of nowhere this female bumped me and spilled her drink on my dress. I looked around and realize it's the same dirty ass chic from the bathroom. I couldn't help, but to get angry. I just brought this outfit.

"You steady trying to test me right" I asked.

"Naw bitch, y'all in my way" she replied. She's staggering, can't barely hold herself up and she has the nerve to be talking smack.

"Check this out baby girl; I realize that you are obviously drunk. I really would not feel right beating the shit out of you when you are mentally impaired, so do me a favor and get out of my face before I lose this mercy I'm trying to convince myself to spare on you ok." I warned her as calmly as I could.

"You aint gone do shit, you stuck up Southfield hoes!" she continued following me while I was walking towards Chuck.

I'm not good with letting females get free licks on me so I stopped and stood still. I wish this chic would swing on me. I viewed my surroundings where I peeped that she has about five girls with her. They're all slim so I know me and Toy can take them. Even though, it's been a long time since Toy and I fought together, I know she can handle her business. She's been drinking so I hope she's able to get at these broads.

I can't believe how juvenile this girl is really acting. This is beginning to remind me of middle school. This female is obviously jealous! In my stomach, I have what seems to be a bubble. I'm ready to fight, but I always get a little nervousness because I don't know if I am going to get jumped or what. "You know what … Screw it!" I shouted as I turned around to go dry myself off when somebody pushed me. I don't know who did it, but the first female I saw got five good blows to the head. It seems like everybody is fighting from everywhere. Toy has this girl down on the ground punching her. I'm still socking this other girl when her girl has decided to jump on my back. I swung her around forcing her to fall to the ground, in the midst, I slipped on the drink she spilt. I'm back on my feet. The security guards are trying to break up the fight with Toy and that other chic, while I'm struggling to beat down both of these girls. *Hello, can y'all come and break this one up right here,* I thought to myself.

Chuck must have spotted that it's me fighting because he's running over here now. He pulled the girl that seemed like she didn't want to get off my back.

"Naw shorty, this is a one on one" Chuck said as he pushed her back.

Knowing that Chuck is standing right there has provided me with uncontrollable ammunition. The impact from the punches I applied to this females face is causing blood to leak from her mouth. *She's down,* I thought as she's appearing to no longer fight back. I never noticed my own strength. *Oh my goodness, is she dead?* Even though I'm questioning her life's existence I can't seem to stop punching her.

Thank goodness this security guard has decided to finally break it up. Even though, this chic is out for the count. I think I would not have been able to stop if this guard didn't just pull me off of her. The officers Toy and I met outside walked over to us.

"What happened here? How did this all start" the white cop asked.

"That girl came in the bathroom talking shit. She jumped in my sister's face and continued asking us if we thought we were better than everyone. So after we left the bathroom she spilt her drink on my sister's dress. We tried to walk away and then one of them pushed my sister. They got exactly what they had coming. I think my sister just beat that girl to death." Toy replied.

Ahh, Toy please do not tell them that I beat the girl to death. That's murder, I thought to myself. Oh she's not dead. As the cop began to escort her to the front she opened her eyes. She had to be carried out on a stretcher. I really feel bad about that. The black cop walked over to me and whispered "Damn baby, I didn't break it up sooner because y'all was putting those thangs on them. They deserve it because they're in here every week starting some mess."

"Hey Latoya, I didn't know that you were coming in here to fight." The white cop said.

At the same time Toy and I looked at each other, then looked at him and replied "we didn't either."

Chuck came up behind me. "Baby, you ok?" he asked.

"Yeah boo thanks. These hoes are tripping up in here." I replied.

He smiled and replied "Yeah bay, they be tripping, but they're just jealous cause y'all the finest females in here. I didn't know you can get down like that. I don't think I ever want to pick a fight with you, Mike Tyson" He said jokingly.

I smiled. "Well baby what do you think we should do now?

He grabbed my hand and replied, "Let's dance."

I looked at Toy. "Come on. Get ole boy and lets' go freak them out." I kissed Chuck on the lips "Chuck hold on, we'll be right back."

I grabbed Toy's hand hinting for her to follow me. Toy and I went in the bathroom to get ourselves together. It's a good thing I had my hair pinned up in this clip because it might have gotten me in some trouble. "Toy, did you bring your comb" I asked.

She reached in her purse and handed me the comb. I wet my hair and it's now wavy. We both put on our Bath and Body Works lip gloss and sprayed on a little Victoria Secret. I'm still pissed because I didn't feel like fighting from the very beginning. I took some paper towel and soap and washed that stain out of my dress before I let the hand dryer dry it out. Toy and I went outside and at the door, stood two sexy men. Oh they have my song playing. *What perfect timing*, I thought.

♪ *That's right- I brought all the boys to the yard*♪ *that's right- I'm the one that's tattooed on his arm, cause I'm Bossy*♪

Toy and I looked at each other "♪ I'm bossy♪" we started singing as we were walking up the stairs.

The second floor seems like this is where Toy and I should have stayed. The dance floor is packed and everyone is appearing to be having a great time. "Uh oh Toy, here goes yo song." I said once "♪shake that, make that booty bounce♪" began to play.

Chuck grabbed my hand. "Come on baby, you hear what this song is telling you to do. Make it bounce for daddy."

Once we got on the dance floor, I did just that; made it bounce. I have obviously woken up Mr. Sleepy head because he's jabbing me extra hard. He's making my midnight blue G 'string soak and wet. I also have on the matching Victoria secret bra. I'm actually impressed with this dress I brought today, even though that jealous chic spilt liquor on me.

Chuck and I slow danced for the last 30 minutes. The lights came on before we knew it; it was 1:55 am. They were getting ready to put us out in five minutes so we decided to leave. Chuck and Juan walked us to the car; he told his other boys that he would catch up with them in a few. Once we arrived at Toy's car, we noticed that we are all blocked in so we kissed our men then laughed and talked about the fight.

Chuck pulled me to the side.

"Vicky, do you want to go to Church tomorrow?" he asked.

"Yes" I replied with no hesitation. My heart feels all good and tingly.

"Ok, you ride with Toya home and I will come get you in about twenty minutes, that should give you time to get your things together." Chuck stated.

Losing my excitement I remembered and replied, "But I don't have any Church clothes."

He smiled at me, "It's come as you are and the nice skirts you be wearing would be just right, just don't wear none of your revealing shirts. I know you can't help them big girls, but just try and cover them up," as he stared at my breast.

I'm excited again. These last couple of months has been more than stressful and hectic. *Church may be just the cure that I need*, I thought to myself. Chuck kissed me on my cheek. "Ok, the parking lot is clearing out. Y'all should go ahead and leave. I'll be over in a few ok" he said as he walked over to his car where his boys are standing.

The parking lot is clearing out a great deal, but the street traffic is jammed. I got in the car. Toy's friend just walked away from the car also. She's sitting back in her seat as if she is exhausted. I looked at her and said, "Thanks Toy, for having my back."

She sat up and looked at me like I just cursed her out or something.

"Girl, you don't have to thank me. You're my sister. I wish I would see you fighting and I didn't jump in and I wish I did get in a beef and you didn't jump. That's a cause for an immediate ass whipping" she replied with laughter. "We did beat their ass though, didn't we? She asked gloating.

"Yeah Toy, I aint no punk or nothing, but I feel a little nervous before I fight."

"I think we all do that, because I feel the same way. I think that's why we beat them up so badly." She replied while pulling out of the parking lot.

"Toy, Chuck just asked me to go to Church with him. I told him that I would. Do you want to go?" I asked "Girl, the way my life has been twisting and turning, I feel like I need to go" I sighed.

"I don't know. What Church are y'all going to?"

"I'm not sure, but I'll call and ask."

"Oh, no! Please, you don't have to do that. Victoria, I'm not all into that religious mumbo jumbo. I guess you can call me an atheist, but at the same time I never needed a reason to believe in God or anything. Girl, my life's been perfectly fine without it, but don't let me discourage you. You go ahead and go; pray for me while you're at it." Toy replied.

I sat back and smiled. I'm so excited about going to Church. Toy's cell phone started ringing. Toy glanced at her phone and said "Oh girl this aint nobody, but Romeo." "What's up big head?" she answered. I over heard him say, "Toy, tell Victoria that her Uncle called. He said call him."

I called him from Toy's Cell.

"Hey sexy" Stan answered.

Oh my goodness, why does he keep doing that! I'm sure he knows Toy's number by now and he knows it's me, but why does he keep answering the phone like that? Damn, he will find a way to mess up my night. I hope Toy didn't hear him. I eased my finger on the volume button to turn it down.

"Hey what's up?" I asked. I'm sure he has to hear the irritation in my voice.

"Nothing, where are you?" he asked

"On my way to Toys house, just leaving the club. Why? What's up?"

"I thought you were coming to have a little fun tonight" Stan gestured. I realized he must have been drinking because his conversation is very reckless when he's high.

"Yeah I was, but I'm tired. I'll be there tomorrow about five, are you going to cook?" I asked, as I tried changing the subject.

"I guess, why? What do you want?"

"I don't know, maybe some barbecue and your good ole macaroni and cheese, some greens and cornbread."

"You got a whole meal planned huh?" he asked.

"Yeah, I guess I do huh?" I replied.

"Mr. Campbell, can I come get a plate!" Toy yelled.

Stan heard her. She was darn sure loud enough. *Greedy butt.* I laughed to myself. I think this liquor is what's got me craving all that food my darn self.

"Tell her I said yes." Stan replied.

"He said yes, Toy"

"Cool. A sister will be there." Toy replied.

"Alright then, I'll be home tomorrow so I'll see you then." I rushed him so I can hurry up and get off of this phone.

"Ok I miss you baby, I'm going in here to dream about you and I will see you tomorrow." He said.

I just hung up the phone. If this disgusting secret gets out, it will be because of him. What if that wasn't me calling him. I guess he figures Toy wouldn't have a reason to call him anyway.

"I forgot your Uncle be cooking like that. He can burn. Cool, so you said we going over there about five, right? Toy asked.

She's over there thinking about food. That's that weed. We both set our stomachs up for crucial conflict because the food won't be ready until tomorrow anyway.

"Yeah Toy, we can go once I get back from Church tomorrow." I replied.

Oh my goodness, look at Mama Jackson's house. Romeo and his boys have totally trashed this house. The Music is blasting, they're playing spades, about five blunts are lit and ashes are everywhere.

"Romeo, you know better than this, you nasty pig! If Mama was here you know you wouldn't do this. Clean this mess up and them Negro's got to go!" Toy yelled.

All of his boys started laughing. One of his boys said, "Dang dawg; I thought you said your Mama was out of town."

Toy is more like the older sister. Even though Romeo is 23, Toy acts much older than him. Plus he's too old to still be living at home any way. It's a good thing that Little Steven spent the weekend at his grandmother's because he would definitely spill the beans on Romeo to Mama Jackson and his dad.

Toy and I went upstairs. I took a shower and put on my t-shirt and some shorts. Laying here under Toys fan in the window is causing me to want to instantly fall asleep. I heard vibration on the dresser. I looked in my purse. It's Chuck chirping me.

"Hey baby what's up?" I chirped.

"Come on baby, I'm outside." Chuck replied.

Wow, I totally forgot Chuck said he was coming to get me. Toy walked back in the room while I was gathering my things.

"You about to go somewhere?" she asked.

"Girl, Chuck is outside. I will see you tomorrow ok."

"Oh-where y'all about to go?"

"I guess to a room, I don't know. Where ever we're going, we are going to Church from there I guess." I replied.

I grabbed my black Guess Dress; with my black guess sandals that I forgot I left over Toy's the last time I was here. Besides, I have a lot of clothes over here anyway. This is my second home. I took and extra outfit just in case. I left out and got in the car with Chuck.

Chapter 11

"Baby, I took my shower and was on my way to sleep. I totally forgot you said you were coming back."

"Oh, you're forgetting about me already?" he asked.

"Of course not; you know I have been buzzing all day. So, where are we going anyway?"

"To my house" he replied.

"What? You're taking me to the house, what about your Uncle?"

"My Uncle is spending the night over his ole' lady's house, tonight."

We pulled up in the driveway of a very beautiful house in Southfield. Many often refer to it as the *black suburb*. This is where the girl at the club assumed Toy and I were from. I do not live in Southfield; I stay in Rose Mel Park, which is considered a black successful neighborhood. We have nice houses, flowers, and nice grass at every house. Everybody on my street is semi wealthy. There are a lot of lawyers and doctors in my neighborhood who support Detroit.

However, many of our own people get a little bit of money and abandon our city by relocating to other successful cities; when they fail to realize this is where their wealth began. Many people have moved out of the City of Detroit in the last year since all of the factory and auto plants relocated down south. I often heard Stan say it's because the economy is bad. Everybody is transitioning to the south. He said this happened once before a long time ago. Everybody from the north moved to the south and then years later they moved back up north. He says it's just a money thing at this point.

Because Detroit is labeled as the "Motor City" and was built on industrialization, having all of the automotive companies such as Chrysler, GM and Ford taken away left many residents of Detroit without any experience in anything other than working on an assembly line. At least this is what my history teacher explained to our class. Many people also move because of the extremely high poverty and crime rate.

The crime is a bit high, but I don't think that we are that bad to be quite honest. Everybody I know is good. We're not struggling or anything. We do have some who are struggling, but that's because they're lazy. I know that a lot of Toy's friends in the projects don't do anything, but sit on their lazy butts and have babies so they can get a raise in their welfare instead of getting up and filling out some job applications. Without an education, it is very difficult to find employment. I admit I do want to move because of the crime and negativity but I want to help the kids out because it's not their fault. Somewhere we got lost in the sauce.

"You ok lil Mama" Chuck asked as he turned the key to the front door.

"Yes, I'm fine. I was just thinking about something that's all.

Wow, this house is so pretty. I wonder why he hasn't mentioned it to me before. "Chuck, this is a beautiful home."

"Yeah it's ok, but I want our house to be better than this." He responded as if this house is not already top notch.

I walked over to the fireplace and began to view the pictures on the mantle. I assume that this picture of two boys, a woman and a man, is his family, but I will ask just to make sure.

"Charles, is this your family?"

"Yes, that's my mom, my dad and me and my brother." He responded while pointing them out individually.

I stood here staring at this picture. "Yeah, you're right, your dad and brother look identical. Have you talked to your mom lately? I asked.

He appeared to be a little saddened when I asked him about his mom. "No, but I am going to go visit her next week. Do you want to go with me?" he asked.

Wow, he wants me to go with him. I smiled and replied, "Sure, I would love to go with you."

Chuck's mom is very pretty. This was a beautiful family; it's sad how it was destroyed.

"That's my Uncle Bud right there." Chuck said while pointing to his picture as he walked away.

Damn - he's fine. That's where Chuck must get it from. These are some nice pictures. It seems like his family is close, even though Chuck does not act as if they are.

Chuck just walked back out here stripped down to his boxers. "Are you thirsty?" he asked.

"Yes, may I have some ice water please?"

"No problem." He responded while directing me to come follow him.

I followed him into the kitchen, now this is out of sight. I wonder who did the decorating. There is a glass marble counter top all the way around this what seems to be a wraparound sink. I would really like to know why does Chuck think his Uncle is so embarrassing, because this house is all that. I thought Uncle Stan's house was the bomb, but they are running neck and neck now. The only thing is we have a pool in the backyard and Stan said he plans to get a Jacuzzi soon.

"Do you want ice?" Chuck asked.

"Yes. Just a little please"

"Crushed or cubed?"

"In that case make it crushed and you can put a little more ice. Thanks baby." I replied.

Chuck handed me my glass of water and instructed me to follow him. His room is nice. He has a big king size bed that looks like it's about 4ft high. He has a small foot ladder that is connected to his bed. I knew my baby had to lay his head nicely. It seems like you really do not know a person until you see where they lay their head. He lays his quite nicely. I glanced around at his dresser where I noticed how Chuck has all of his diamond chains laid out across the dresser. Oh my goodness, I think I am getting frostbites from all that ice. *What kind of money does*

Chuck have? I thought to myself. He must have that major doughboy money. He did state that he's been in the game for almost four years. If he's been pushing deals like the one he did today for the last four years, he's got to have more than enough to retire from the streets.

"Here bay, jump on up there, and get comfortable. I will be right back ok; I'm going to hop in the shower right quick." Chuck said as he handed me the remote.

He went in the bathroom and I climbed up in the bed after I took my shorts off. I don't like sleeping with clothes on, but I'll keep my t-shirt on since this is my first time over here. My Diva shoes are un-tying themselves and running away from my feet. This boy is really living like a royal king. I channel surfing on his 62in flat screen television with full surround sound mounted on the wall. Ooh here is one of my favorite shows, *"The Fresh Prince of Bel-Air."* Will Smith is so funny to me. This is the episode when Will and Uncle Phil's Mom sneaks out to the Heavy D concert.

"Baby, is everything ok?" Chuck asked.

I'm trying to figure out why would he just walk out here with the towel wrapped around his waist, with the water beads slowly sliding down his chest, with his six pack calling out for me, as he's holding his tooth brush. Since my Diva shoes abandoned me, I have to keep it cool on my own.

"Oh yeah I'm fine, just watching Will's crazy self. He is so silly" I replied. He smiled and continued brushing his teeth. *Oh, how I crave to be those water droplets rolling off his chest,* I thought as I watched him walk back into the bathroom.

Chuck has the central air on. It feels so good in here. Mama Jackson doesn't have central air at her house, but Toy's fan feels just as cool. I hear Chuck gargling.

Chuck came slithering under the covers. He caught me by surprise. "Ooh Chuck, you play too much!" I screamed as I gripped the sheets with all of my strength.

What in the … My body is beginning to resemble an earthquake with an 8.2 on the Richter scale."

Once I noticed how Chuck disregarded the vibrations from this earthquake he's experiencing I cannot help but to …

"*Ooooooooooooooooooh*" My strength is non-existent. "I can't take anymore Chuck, please" I begged. "You are something else, you play too much" I teased.

He looked directly into my eyes and smiled. "Come here. You know what time it is. Remember how you were making it bounce earlier at the club, show me those moves again" he requested as he gave my right cheek a smack.

"No problem!" I replied as I hummed ♪*Shake that-make that booty bounce*♪ providing myself a little hype music.

"Oh yeah, yep-yep that's the move right there Ma. Ooh you be turning me on!"

He is obviously tired, I thought as I watched him instantly fell asleep. I sat here staring at my baby sleep as if he is a baby. He is lying on my breast as if they are pillows. I rubbed his head gently as I began to replay everything that happened today.

It has been a long time since I had a fight like the one I had tonight. I wonder if that girl is ok. I would normally feel no remorse, but I feel a little different this time around. I know God seen it. *I wonder if He is mad at me*, I thought.

God, if you are mad at me, I am sorry. I hope that you do not decide not to help me out of this situation with Stan. I really want to marry this man right here. I cannot wait to go to Church in the morning. I am looking forward to seeing you there or at least having you reveal your presence. I really hope nothing that happened today has affected your opinion of me. I really hope you can hear my thoughts like Chuck said you could. Goodnight.

Chapter 12

The aroma of freshly cooked bacon has awakened me from my sleep. I put on my T-shirt and my shorts before I went in the bathroom. I brushed my teeth and washed my face. *Let me see what this boy is in here cooking,* I thought to myself.

I walked in the kitchen where Chuck has the kitchen table set up so nicely. I noticed Chuck staring at me with a towel over his arm as if we are at a fancy restaurant.

"Good morning, my beautiful Queen. Welcome to 'breakfast by your man'.

"Why thank you." I replied as he pulled out my chair.

"Enjoy. May I get you a drink madam?"

"If it's not too much trouble, maybe ice water and some orange juice please." I replied.

"No problem, my love." He responded.

He poured me a glass of orange juice and a glass of ice water. After he poured the water he sat the container down and said, "I will return to check on you" as he walked out of the kitchen.

I am trying to display proper table etiquettes, but this food is so good I cannot control myself. He made bacon, grits with cheese, scrambled eggs with cheese, and pancakes with the best syrup, Alga's. You have to be *'grown'* to know about that one. Oh my goodness, this man loves me. I ate quite a bit. It is so good. I do not want to be stuffed.

Chuck walked back in the kitchen wearing a grey suit with the matching grey gators while he is tying his grey and black tie. "Is everything okay?" he asked.

"Oh yes, it is so good thank you. You're so sweet to me." I smiled.

"Ok baby, finish up, and go get dressed. We are running late for Church. Don't worry about the dishes I will get them when I get back" He stated.

When he said Church, I almost jumped out of my seat. "Ok, I am finished." I said, as I took a small sip of my orange juice. I am so anxious to get to Church. I just have to see what is going on there.

I decided to where my black Dolce& Gabbana skirt with my turquoise and black Dolce & Gabbana button up blouse and my black Marc Jacob heels with the matching purse. I think that I am looking good, considering the fact that I am not too familiar with the attire, but Chuck did remind me that it was come as you are. I could not wear my black guess dress I was planning on wearing. I think it is a little too sexy for Church. I do wish that Chuck and I matched a little, because his grey and black with my turquoise and black is not that best color coordination. We both are sexy that is good enough for me. Besides, I already have my King so who am I trying to impress. Besides, I am going in search of God anyway.

Time for Church:

We pulled up in front of Mt. Zion Full Gospel Church. It is so many cars out here. It appears to be more cars here than it was at the club last night, nice cars on top of that. Chuck went in his trunk and grabbed his big Bible that is in a brown leather case. I hear music and singing as we are walking up to the stairs to the front entrance of the Church.

Once we entered into this place. Chuck's popularity here became evident. I lost count of how many people have walked up to Chuck and said, "Hello Brother Matthews. Good to see you again." I feel all-important. Everyone asked Chuck, "Who is this beautiful lady you're with?" I must have said, "Hi, I'm Victoria" over twenty times already.

I feel so good. I don't know what it is. I'm not sure if it's the warm welcoming hugs Chuck and I are receiving from everyone or if it's just the fact that everyone is smiling and seems to be so happy. Chuck has my hand leading us to the Ushers. These two women with salt and pepper colored hair are smiling at us.

"God bless you babies. How are you precious?" one of them asked as she hugged me.

"I'm fine, how are you" I responded. I cannot help, but smile. The persona that perceived in this Church is so amazing.

"Come on babies, follow me," she said as she led us to the front of the Church in the middle section.

"Thank you" I said as she stood there with her hand that is dressed in a white glove open. She directed Chuck and me towards the two empty seats, which seem to be directly in the middle. We finally made it to our seats, as we remained standing. I assume because everyone else is standing.

♪ *God is a worthy God and he's worthy to be praised* ♪ *He's good-* ♪ *anybody know that he's good* ♪

It is amazing how I have never heard this song before, but I am singing and clapping along with the choir as if I have been to Church every day of my life. The choir stopped singing and now we are directed to have our seats. There is a man who just walked up to the microphone.

"Praise the Lord everybody! Praise the Lord everybody!" he said.

"Praise the Lord" it seems like everyone replied.

"I don't know about y'all, but I came to praise him! Give him thanks! Give God some praise! Glory to God; he is worthy to be praised. I would like to start off by saying the Choir is doing a beautiful job this morning, Amen."

Everyone said, Amen and started clapping.

I am sitting here watching everything that is happening. The huge televisions on the walls are capturing everyone's actions. The camera just captured the woman who is sitting right next to me. *I wonder why it skipped over me, I want to see how I look on TV also,* I thought to myself.

"God has been so good, so many of us made it to see another day. Many people who did not wake up this morning, but all of us who are here in the house of the Lord did. Give God some praise!" he shouted.

Once the music began to play it seems like everyone jumped out of his or her seats, even Chuck. He is standing up clapping extra fast. I glanced up at the Television and noticed the people behind me that are dancing and clapping. This music is automatically forcing me to shake my legs. I stood up with Chuck and began clapping also. He looked at me and smiled. There is that warm tingly sensation spreading throughout my body again. It feels so good. So good, it's creating these tears that are rapidly flowing from my eyes.

The man walked back up to the microphone.

"Y'all better take your seats before some body makes a mistake and start praising God up in here. Thank you Jesus! Come on Saints hurry and take your seats. I don't want you to start losing your mind when you think about God's mercy and grace. Everybody sit down quickly before you start remembering how it could have been you lying in the hospital bed. Take your seats before you start to remember that body in the casket that should have been yours. Take your seats before you start to remember the times when you felt like you were all alone and God came and showered you with his love. Take your seats before you begin to remember that time when you had no food on your table and God came through just in time. Whoa!" He screamed before he took off running.

I cannot control these tears especially after I just noticed the tears that ran from Chucks eyes. I never knew Chuck could cry. *I guess God will bring the best out in everyone,* I thought.

"Hallelujah, come on take your seats, quickly, quickly. Continue praising him while we prepare to worship the Lord in our giving.

Chuck went in his pocket and pulled out four, one hundred dollar bills. "Here, when we go up there you can give this for offering." He said as he handed me one of them. I smiled and replied, "Ok sweetie"

We went to the front and put our money in the basket. Charles put his in an envelope and marked Tithes on it. After offering, the same man walked back up to the microphone.

"Praise God; Thanks for those who were able to give and those who were not able to give, but wished to give. I pray that you are blessed as well. Amen"

It seems like this warm quivering, tingly sensation will not leave my body. It feels so good; I don't think I want it to leave. It feels like something has come over me, entered inside of me. *God, if you are real as everyone says you are please, show me. I will be so grateful."*

I focused my attention back to the man at the microphone.

"Amen; let's give the choir a hand as they come with a B & C selection."

Everyone clapped as one of the women left the choir stand and walked up to the microphone. I assume that the woman who just stood up and waved her hands in front of the choir is the director. Once she waved her hands, the choir began to stand. I glanced at the man on the organ as he began to play music then I noticed the choir rocking back in forth. The woman at the microphone began to sing.

"♪♪♪ Lead me- guide me –ev-ery-day♪ send your anointing- father- I- pray♪"

The choir joined in. *"♪Order my steps in your word♪* ...

I was suddenly distracted when the person sitting behind me started screaming.

"Hallelujah Jesus! Hallelujah Jesus! Thank you God. Yes Lord, You're worthy."

It is funny how I would usually be upset when I am all into something and I am distracted, but I do not feel that way right now. Actually, the tingly sensation that I have been receiving all day is flowing rapidly throughout my veins. I cannot seem to get a grip on this constant flow of tears. The choirs singing along with everybody screaming and crying is overwhelming me with joy and excitement.

My joy is coming out in the form of tears. I started crying hard. *I don't know where all of this is coming from,* I thought as I came to the realization that I might as well cry and let it out, especially since the woman sitting next to me is running out of Kleenex because of me. Chuck put his arm around me and squeezed my shoulder.

"I love you baby" he whispered.

I am so overwhelmed that I cannot respond back to Chuck, but I am sure he knows that I love him. Once I lifted my head, I noticed a person walking in a white and purple robe on the television, which gave me the urged to look behind me. I noticed he was walking with three men carrying bibles as a woman who looks stunning accompanied him. I assume that she is his wife. She is beautiful in her Dolce & Gabbana Gold skirt suit with the matching shoes, purse, and hat. I know that her entire wardrobe from head to toe has got to total up to at least $4,500. That is not even counting the gigantic rock she is sporting on her finger. I am trying extremely hard to steer my focus away from fashion and listen to the choir since they have started singing a new song.

"♪ *they hung him high- stretched him wide, he hung his head, for me He died, that's love♪*

If I had a bucket sitting under my eyes to catch my tears by the time I leave this Church it would be running over. I never knew what Jesus had to go through and this song just helped me visualize it. This is my first time really hearing about anything regarding Jesus because no one around me discussed God like that especially not Stan. If Stan believed in God, I know he would not do the awful things to me that he does. I cannot believe I have not been to Church in so long. I came when I was little with my Auntie Jessie, but I was young and I do not remember much about it all. I will be nineteen June 28th and I am just now finding out about the goodness of God. I feel so left behind and so stupid.

As I am looking around it seems like everybody knows how to praise God, except me. If it was not for Chuck, I don't know if I would have found out about God as I am now. He is so precious. I know God has to see him. *His heart is so good*, I thought as I glanced at him for a second. The Pastor's wife is walking up to the microphone while everyone in the choir is leaving the choir stand.

"Hallelujah! Oh, Glory! When I think about the goodness of the Lord … I just want to praise him. Ooh lord, I know some of y'all looking at me like I am crazy. I just want to let you know that I am crazy, Crazy about Jesus! I know that he woke me up this morning. It was not my alarm clock; it was the goodness of the Lord and God's grace and mercy. It's plenty of times I could have been dead and gone, but he spared me and that makes me want to get up and praise his name. If you see me dance sometimes and you see me shout sometimes, it is because of his grace. Glory! You heard the choir! They just told you how they beat him, put nails in his hands, nails in his feet. Hung him up on the cross and he died for my sins, for your sins, for all of our sins and then, three days later he rose again. How many of you know that's love?" She asked.

Everyone began clapping and screaming "Thank you Jesus." The powerful persona that this woman gives off through her voice is awesome. She stood there, paused while she put her hands on her waist, and put her head down. Now she is walking back up to the microphone.

"Hey! Glory! I just want to say thank you! Thank you Jesus! Hey!" she yelled.

All of a sudden, she took off running up and down the Church isles. Crying and screaming "Thank you Jesus." Many are following behind her.

"Thank you Jesus!" the woman sitting next to me screamed. She started dancing and jumping around, crying and saying, "he's worthy, hallelujah"!

Find the bucket, I thought to myself because these tears are steadily flowing.

"Hallelujah" Chuck yelled.

This tingly sensation is getting stronger and stronger. As I am viewing everybody crying, screaming and clapping I cannot help, but think that God has to be real if people are praising him like this. I started thanking and praising him in my head. *Hallelujah Jesus! Thank you God, for your son Jesus.* I don't know if I am saying everything right, but I don't want to be left out. I want to praise God also. *God, I know you are going to help me get out of this situation with Stan,* I thought.

The pastor's wife is walking back up to the microphone. "I told you, you have to excuse me. Sometimes I might lose my mind when I think about everything God has done for me. I want to praise him while I can. I need all of you to stand to your feet. We are about to receive the word from this remarkable preacher. Put your hands together and help me welcome my Pastor, Our bishop, Bishop L.C. Morton Jr."

Everyone began clapping and screaming. The Bishop walked to the microphone.

"Thank you. The presence of the Lord is in the place." He said as he began singing. "♪The presence of the Lord is here♪ the presence of the Lord is here. I can feel it in the atmosphere♪ the presence of the Lord is here♪."

I have cried more today than I have ever cried in my entire life. I am beginning to fall in love with this place.

"Amen, Amen! I would like to thank all of you for coming out on this Youth Sunday to worship and praise the Lord. If you have your bibles, please turn to the book of Romans 13: 12-14."

Everyone was standing, as he read:

"'The night is far spent, the day is at hand; let us therefore cast off the works of darkness, and let us put on the armour of light. Let us walk honestly, as in the day; not in rioting and drunkenness, not in chambering and wantonness, not in strife and envying. But put ye on the Lord Jesus Christ, and make no provision for the flesh to fulfil the lust thereof. ' Every head bowed" he said as he bowed his own head.

"Dear Heavenly Father. We come to you today to ask for your mercy on us Lord. First, I just want to thank you. Lord, we thank you for waking us up this morning. We thank you for waking us up in our right minds, and in good health. We ask that you continue to keep us safe, protect us from the terrible storms, not only in the physical, but in the mental as well. We thank you for letting us make it thus far. Lord, if there is a one in this building today who does not know you we ask that you reveal your presence right now in the name of Jesus. Let them know that you are there father. You are the creator, the alpha and omega, beginning, and the end. Bless your humble servants who have come out to worship you today. I believe someone came into your place of worship to hear a word from you Lord. I ask that you let your spirit rest upon me so that I may be a messenger of your word. Please allow me to provide a clear understanding of your mercy and your everlasting humble grace. Speak through these lips of clay. Allow your word to be spoken clearly.

We ask all of this unto you in your son Jesus name, and let the people of GOD say Amen. You may have your seat." He instructed.

The Sermon:

"I am going to take my message from the thirteenth verse. *'Let us walk honestly, as in the day; not in rioting and drunkenness, not in chambering and wantonness, not in strife and envying.'*

Since today is Youth Sunday, I believe that I have a perfect example for you. Friday night after choir rehearsal, my wife and I stopped in a restaurant. A group of young teenagers entered the restaurant staggering, smelling like alcohol and marijuana. I know y'all looking at me wondering, how I know what it smells like." He said with a smile.

Everyone smile just as I did as we waited on the answer.

"Well this might be hard to believe but this old Bishop use to be a teenager many, many years ago." He said as everyone began to laugh again.

"Wait now, y'all laughing. I know you all don't think I'm old do you?" He said with a slight chuckle.

"Moving on before you all hurt my feelings. That group of teens appeared to be no more than fifteen or sixteen. I think one of them look like she could have been about eleven or twelve. I began to wonder where their parents were. What are the parents doing? Is this the work of imitation? I say this to say that you cannot let your flesh be weak and allow temptation to take a hold. You must be in control. You must understand that, just because your parents are doing it and maybe your friends are doing things that are not right does not mean you have to follow behind them. When my wife and I were leaving the restaurant one of the young men ran and opened the door for us. That right there provided me with the impression that he had someone in his life who taught him about respect. The other ones sat there laughing at him as if opening the door for his elders was wrong, or perhaps some type of joke. Young people what you have to understand is that everyone is not going to love God the way you do especially if God is not a part of their parent's lives. I understand that it's difficult trying to be a young believer when it seems like everyone around you has a completely different outlook. When you look around it seems like all of your friends are partying, staying out all night, drinking, smoking, and engaging in the activities of the world. It makes you begin to feel that maybe you should engage in those activities also. Especially when you tell your friends that, you are going to bible study or choir rehearsal or any type of positive events and they make fun of you or they try to make you feel like you are stupid for doing something positive with your life. By a show of hands, how many of you young adults have tried to introduce something positive to a group that says they're your friends and they've brushed you off?" The pastor asked.

I was a little embarrassed to raise my hand but once I looked around and seen the majority of everyone here raise their hands including Chuck I raised mine also.

"Parents take note, look around. You notice all of the hands that are raised. You better start paying attention to your children. Get engaged in their personal business. Get to know their friends. Most importantly get to know your children. The devil likes to play on children with an idol mind. Do not allow that job be so important that you forget to talk to your babies. Do not let that man be so important that you forget to love your babies. Do not let anything distract you from making sure that your children are feeling the love that they need in order to resist the temptations when their so-called friends try to influence them with drugs, alcohol, and most definitely sex. Yes, I said sex. That is the most deadly form of influence that's out there. There are more teenage pregnancies then there has ever been. The epidemic for young African American teens with HIV and Aides has shot up to nearly fifty-five percent and that's more than half. Parents we have to start taking care of home first. We have to take care of our babies. If they do not receive the love from us, trust me there is a demonic spirit just waiting to fill your shoes. How many youth in here today are being raised by a single person who is not your mother or your father?" He asked.

Now this is getting deep. It seems like he is talking directly to me. I looked around again and noticed how it is just as many raising their hands now as they did a moment ago. Chuck and I raised our hands again.

"All of you with your hands up do me a favor and stand where you are." The Bishop requested.

"Take a look around. You need to give God some praise right now. These babies are here in the house of the Lord on today when they could be out in the streets, strung out on drugs or locked up somewhere, but instead they are here praising God. Give these young men and young women a handclap. Hug your neighbor and just tell them how much you appreciate them being here." He requested.

The woman sitting next to me squeezed Chuck and me extra tight.

"I appreciate you being here suga. It is no mistake that you are in the house of GOD today, I thank you, and the Lord thanks you too. I love you suga pies," she said to the both of us.

The woman that was screaming behind me earlier grabbed me. "God Bless you baby." She said as she kissed me on my cheek.

"Now give your selves a round of applause for taking in those babies when their mother and father forsaken them, GOD used you to take them in. GOD Bless you for your obedience. Hallelujah …"

He continued preaching while I drifted off into thinking about my weekend how I was drinking and smoking. I'm basically the one who gathered everyone so we could go to the club and as soon as I went I got into a fight. I really don't know what came over me yesterday. I was never interested in going to clubs or drinking, I definitely don't like to smoke. Honestly I continue to smoke because sometimes I think that's what Chuck and Toy would prefer that I do. I didn't want to seem like a square to everyone. Toy already gets a little tired of me sharing my poetry with her, but when I smoke with her it seems like that's how we bond. Chuck said he's quitting so I know once he quits I am definitely going to stop. *I need to quit now*, I thought to myself.

Ok what did I miss? Everyone is clapping. I need to pay attention to this preacher.

"The Lord has put something on my heart. There is someone in here that is struggling with an issue of abuse, come on down and let me pray for you. There's someone here today who is going through financial stress. Someone just needs prayer to make it through the rest of the week. Is there a one who dares to step on the devil and come up and receive prayer today? You never know when God will spare your life again. He may say this is the end before you take your next breath. I know I want to be right with God. I don't know about you, but I know

God is going to comeback cracking the sky and rapture all of his people up to heaven and leave those who are not worthy left behind on the streets of hell. I dare you to step on the devil. Every one please stand right where you are. I need everyone standing. Bow your heads right now." He requested.

"Dear Heavenly Father. I am here with your babies right now Lord. My spirit is sensing a lot of pain right now. There are some of your children that are going through some very bad emotional and physical abuse and they are scared to get help. Somebody in this place right now is suffering from molestation, it's a child in here right now; I feel her pain. I feel his pain, it's so many of them Lord. The devil is abusing them in hopes of breaking their spirits, but see the devil can't have your babies. I ask you right now Lord cast out the demons in their lives who are doing all of these nasty things to them. It's not their fault Lord. It's not their fault. Lord I ask you right now to break every curse, heal every broken heart, repair all financial stress. There's somebody in here who's about to go through a foreclosure on their home Lord. Hear your babies cry. I rebuke the devil that is trying to hold these souls in their seat. They are worrying about being embarrassed. This is a home and a place of family. None of us are any better than anyone. I pray right now. Lord, free them right now. I pray this in your son Jesus name Amen."

I opened my eyes and noticed more than a hundred people walking up to the alter.

"My spirit is telling me there's one more, there's one more. Let them go Devil. Stand up on the word of the Lord. Come and receive prayer. Receive your breakthrough."

More people rose from their seats and began walking towards the alter. People are walking up there in rather large numbers. The choir began singing.

"♪ *I prayed for you, you prayed for me, I love you, I need you to survive. I won't harm you with words from my mouth* ♪"

I want to go up there so bad, but it's so many people. Bishop Morton might not be able to personally pray for me. *God, I really want to receive prayer.* I thought.

"Come on baby" Chuck said as he grabbed my hand. He walked me right through everyone. I am next in line to receive personal prayer from Bishop Morton. I looked up towards the ceiling realizing that God heard me. I didn't question Chuck because he's obviously doing what God told him to do. Bishop Morton walked over and stood in front of me. He placed his hand on my forehead.

"**Oh Glory!**" he shouted as he took a step back. "God told me to let you know that HE is real, it is so and it is so. He wants me to tell you that trouble does not last always. What you are going through can be changed just like that." He said as he snapped his finger. "Put your trust in him. Put your faith in him and leave it there. God's been there all the time. He has been protecting you."

Excuse me, can I ask you a question?" I interrupted.

"Of course you can, what is it?" Bishop Morton asked.

"I don't know if this sounds silly, but I always get this warm tingly slightly cool sensation throughout my body. I have been getting them quite frequently do you know what that could be?"

"Of course I know that feeling. That's the presence of God's spirit within you. You can often feel it when you are doing something or saying something that's pleasing to God. So God has revealed his presence to you on several occasions. Accept him, let him in and do according to his will. Now that he has revealed his presence, talk to him. He will help you with the problem you are going through at home. Stop trying to fix things that are greater than you. God will do that for you precious. You see this guy right here." He said while pointing at Chuck.

I looked at Chuck, sniffling and trying to control the tears that will not stop running from my eyes. I looked at the Bishop and replied "Yes."

"You better thank him. The Holy Spirit tells me that he led you here today. Lift your hands." He commanded.

I lift my hands.

"Heavenly Father, as you know you have your child standing here, right now. She's standing here in search of you father. Come into her life Lord and enter into her heart where she shall forever keep you. Let her know that you are on her side. You've done it for me, so I know you'll do it for her. She is your child. You sent your son Jesus to die on the cross, and you proved it to us when he rose on the third day. Heavenly Father, she is experiencing trouble at home Dear Lord. Remove her from this awful situation Lord. In the midst of her crying days; you will make them smiling days. Lord please, enter into her now Lord, so that she may accept you as her one and only personal savior. We ask this in your son Jesus name. Amen. Sweet heart, what is your name?"

I tried so hard to keep my tears from falling, but I can't. It's like everything in me is pouring out. I looked at him and replied "Victoria."

"That is a beautiful name. Victoria, it says it in your name. You have the Victory. Victoria have you accepted Jesus as your personal savior?"

"No, but I want to." I replied.

"Lift your hands and repeat after me."

"Lord, I am a sinner, I believe that the Lord Jesus Christ died for my sins on the cross and was raised for my justification, I do now receive and confess him as my personal savior"

"Lord, I am a sinner, I believe that the Lord Jesus Christ died for my sins on the cross and was raised for my justification, I do now receive and confess him as my personal savior" I repeated.

"Tell him you accept him as your personal savior. You have to mean it from your heart." Bishop said.

"I do."

"Don't tell me. Tell him."

"Lord, I accept you as my personal savior" I cried.

"Give God some glory. Give God the praise."

I started clapping because I wasn't sure of what it was that he meant.

"Hallelujah, God bless you." He hugged me and now he's standing in front of Chuck.

"How are you today young man?" He asked.

"I'm Blessed Bishop." Chuck replied.

"Lift your hands. I just want to pray for you." Bishop said.

"Heavenly Father your son is here with his arms stretched wide. He believes in you God. Create in him a new heart oh God. Renew a right spirit with in him. For I know God how hard it is for a young man to make it in these days Lord. He can't make it without you Lord. Continue to cover him Lord. Show him how to be the Strong man that he needs to be. The devils been trying to break him down, but not anymore, not anymore; I bind that demon right now through the blood of Jesus Christ.

This one you cannot have because he belongs to God. Lord, open up doors for him where he has no room enough to receive the blessings that you have for him. In Jesus name Amen. God bless you son. You take care of this young lady she needs you. My spirit tells me that God put you two together for a reason. Don't let the devil destroy what God is building. Stand on his word son. God bless you babies.

Bishop Morton walked over to the lady next to Chuck and began to pray for her. Chuck and I walked back to our seats. The pastor dismissed us. After we shook a few hands we went to the car. Chuck opened the car door for me. I reached over and opened his door.

"Victoria, do you want to go get something to eat?" Chuck asked.

"No, I have to go home. My Uncle said that he is cooking today."

"Victoria, when am I going to be able to meet him?" he asked.

"Soon, I guess. See Chuck, he looks at me like his own daughter and he is a bit over protective. I have to break it to him easily because when I told him that we were engaged he sort of freaked out, but I think everything is ok."

"Victoria, is there something going on at home?" Chuck asked.

"No, why do you ask that?"

"I was listening to the Bishop and he's usually never wrong."

"I don't know what he might have seen. I guess it could possibly be the fact that he's so strict, that's all I can think of. Honestly Chuck, everything is ok." I replied.

I really hate that I have to lie to him especially since I just left Church. I know I can't fix the situation on my own that's why I'm going to let God do it. Bishop Morton said God will protect me and he will take care of everything. I have to believe that because this situation is too big for me.

"Oh ok, so you want me to drop you off over Toy's house?" Chuck asked.

"Yes please. Thank you for taking me to Church. It made me feel really good."

"I know it makes me feel good to." Chuck replied.

"I love you" I said

"I love you too Ma, you already know that.

Chapter 13

I thought everything was supposed to get better

Chuck dropped me off at Toys house. The door is wide open. I wonder who's driving this brand new Mercedes Benz. *Toy's moving up in the game*, I thought as I walked in. What the … … *Oh my goodness! Why is Stan in this house?* Toy is walking towards me with a face full of tears.

"Toy, what's wrong?" I asked.

Stan walked over to me and said, "Victoria, I have terrible news about your mother. Come out side, let me talk to you."

I followed him outside.

"First of all, where the hell have you been?" Stan asked.

"I went to Church with Chuck."

"Chuck? Oh is this the fiancé you were telling me about? Didn't I tell you that it was over with you two?"

"Yes you did, but he is still my friend. Forget this! Stan, what happened to my mother?" I asked.

"Well the story is she was trying to run off with one of the dealer's drugs and he shot her twice. She is in the hospital listed in critical

158

condition. The doctor's said it looks like she might not make it. Come on. I will take you up there." He said.

"What hospital is she at?"

"She's at Detroit Receiving"

"Ok wait a minute."

I ran in the house. "Toy, could you please go with me to the hospital" I begged.

She dried her face and replied, "Of course, but I am going to drive my own car."

"Ok, that's cool. I'll ride with you."

I know that Stan will not cause a big scene in front of other people. So I waited on Toy to get dressed. I decided to change and put on my Apple Bottom jeans and jacket with my black on black coach tennis shoes.

"Victoria!" Stan yelled.

"Here I come" I responded.

Toy and I walked out on the porch at the same time. "Stan, I am going to ride with Toya. We are going to follow you." I said.

He looked at me as if he wanted to hit me, but he smiled and said "No problem. Just come on."

Toy and I got in the car and pulled off. What the heck is going on? I finally go to Church and then this all happens at once. *I thought things were supposed to get better.*

"Toy, why didn't you call me?" I asked.

"Victoria, believe it or not, your Uncle just came over about five minutes ago. I opened the door because I thought it might have been one of Romeo's friends driving that Mercedes. I was just about to call you right before you pulled up. When is the last time you talked to your mother anyway?"

"Toy, I haven't talk to my mom in about six or seven years. It's been a long time. When she first left she would call me once every two weeks, then once a month, to barely once a year. I wonder what she looks like. Toy, Stan said the doctors say she might not make it. I don't know if I can take this right now Toy. I can't handle that. It just doesn't seem right. How could my mom disappear and then when I finally get to see her she's on her death bed. Toy this just aint right." I said as I began shaking my legs and crying.

"Dang Vick, I am so sorry to hear that. You never know things might change. Just wait until you get up to the hospital. You can talk to the Doctors yourself. Can't no Doctor predict when you're going to die! They said that about my grandma and she lived for another five years."

"Yeah I guess you're right" I replied.

Toy turned on the radio and there was a song playing. *This Battle is not yours* by Yolanda Adams. I know this song right here because Mama Jackson played this all the time in her car. I never knew what it meant until right now, because I know about God now.

"♪ Know that you've been set up by God to be Blessed♪ Understand-that it's got to work this way♪ Understand that God knows♪ God knows what you need-before you really need it♪"

This song and the lyrics seem like it's in perfect timing. *Is this God's way of letting me know that he's here or what?* I thought as I stared into the big beautiful sky up above. *Thanks Yolanda*, I said in my mind. I'm glad she allowed God to use her to make that song. I feel a little better now.

"Toy, Stan tells me the different updates about my mom and it's never anything positive. He never bothers to take me to go see them. Right about now, I wish I had a car. I haven't seen my little sister in so long. I hope she wants to talk to me."

"Relax girl, everything is going to be fine." Toy assured.

We just arrived at the hospital. My stomach is twisting and turning in knots; nervousness is eating me alive. We are walking behind Stan. Ooh he makes me sick. He seemed like he didn't care about my mom when he told me what happened. All he thinks about is himself.

"Hello ma'am. Can we please have the room number for Tamara Campbell" Stan asked the receptionist. *I don't believe it, he has the nerves to have manners.*

"The Doctors have already admitted her. She is in room 745 ICU. The elevators are to your right. You can take it up to the seventh floor and just follow the signs." The receptionist replied.

Oh Mama … …

We located 745. Once I entered the room I noticed this girl standing in the corner with her arms folded who looks exactly like me, but she's a little younger. That has to be Jasmine.

"Jasmine, is that you?"

"Yes and who are you?" she asked with a snobby attitude.

"It's me, your big sister Victoria." I replied with a big smile. The look Jasmine has on her face looks like she really wants to say, '*and!'*

"Hey Girl" I said as I gave her a hug.

Ok, I'm feeling the vibe that no one told Jasmine about me, because Jasmine didn't really hug me back. *Don't cry Victoria, its ok, it's not her fault,* I encouraged myself.

I looked at my mother and she looks awful. "Hey Mama" I said, trying to remain cheerful because I already cried a river at Church today. *Ugh what happened to Mama?* She has a few sores on her face with a lot of tubes in her arms and one in her mouth. *This is not the lady I remembered.*

"Victoria, is that you?" she mumbled. It looks like it's very difficult for her to talk.

"Yes mom, it's me." I replied

"Oh my, y'all getting so grown and y'all look so pretty. I remember when I use to look like that." She said as if she's trying to cheer herself up.

"You can still look like this Mama" I replied.

On the inside I feel anger. The thoughts of exploding rage forcing me to scream is all I want to do, but I can't. Standing here watching this woman that I often dreamed about and craved just to get that hug from looks like she's been to hell's kitchen and back. All I can say is I am thankful Mama's here now, even though it's under these unfortunate circumstances. *God, if the words in Yolanda Adams song were correct and Mama lying here looking like this is the way it's gotta work, I'm going to ride it on out with you.*

I wish the makeup in my Coach bag could be enough to cover girl Mama's pain. I think I should stop staring at Mama like this because the tears that are falling from her eyes are triggering my eyes to water.

"I'm sorry, did I say something wrong?" I asked

"No baby, you didn't say anything wrong. I was just thinking of how I should have been able to have done better for myself and my girls. It always takes a near death experience for you to see life flashing before your eyes." Mama replied.

"Ma, I believe that you are going to make it through and when you do, can you promise to get yourself together. I will be right here supporting you Mama. It's seems like Jasmine is doing pretty good" I said as I tried to change the subject because I'm sure Mama is not in the mood for a scalding or a pep talk right now. Mama shook her head "yes" as she glanced at Jasmine.

I am trying so hard not to stare at Mama like she has screwed up because I'm sure she already knows this, but I'm just trying to understand what Mama could have possibly been going through to make her dependent on drugs. Mama looks so bad I am afraid to touch her. I want to kiss Mama on the forehead, but I think I should wait until those sores heal. Mama hair looks nice still. It's still curly like mine. It just looks a little dusty as if she was on the ground or something. I wonder why Stan hasn't said anything to my mom. Just as I was thinking this he walked over.

"Hello there, Tammy" He said.

"No! No, no, no, no, noooooo!!!!!" Mama screamed as she looked at Stan as if he was a ghost or something.

"Mama, that's Uncle Stan." I said.

"No! Please No!" Mama continued screaming and now she's crying extremely hard.

What the hell is going on here, I thought to myself. I turned around and looked at Stan and noticed he has a grin on his face. *What did you do to my Mama you evil bastard,* I screamed in my mind. It's taking everything in me not to check him about this.

"I apologize, but I am going to have to ask everyone to leave. Visiting hours are now over. Ms. Campbell needs to get some rest." The nurse said.

We all left out the room.

"Stan, what was that all about?" I asked.

"I don't know. I guess she's probably going through withdrawals and the medicine mixing with her is not doing so well."

"Oh, I see." I replied, even though I really don't believe him. He's so evil. I wish I knew why Mama was acting that way. I walked over to Jasmine.

"Hey baby sister. What's going on?"

"Nothing." Jasmine replied.

"Uncle Stan told me you had two kids. Where are they?" I asked.

"My oldest son Terrance died last year."

"I'm sorry to hear that. What happened if you don't mind me asking?"

"He was retarded. You knew that right?" Jasmine asked.

"Girl, I've been living with Uncle Stan so I don't know much. He just tells me little things." I replied.

"So I guess he hasn't told you that I have been calling either?" she asked in a sarcastic manner.

"Of course not! He hasn't told me anything. You've been calling me?"

"Yes Victoria."

"Wow, Jasmine, I really didn't know that you've been calling for me. Let him tell it, the phone barely ever rings. I have to talk to him about that.

"My other son Anthony is in a foster home."

"What happened with that?"

"I have been living with my dad's sister, Gladys and her three kids. She has two boys and a girl. Her daughter is eighteen. She's your age. I've been hanging with her. The state took Anthony because they said that I was too young, I was missing school and my Aunt has two jobs and no one could take care of him. I do get to see him every weekend though. He's doing fine. He looks just like Jared. You remember mom's old pimp right?"

"Yeah, where is he?"

"He got robbed last year and he was shot in the head. Jared is fatherless which I thought was best. My Aunt Gladys is into Church a lot; so she has been taking me with her. I got baptized last year. I've been praying for our family a lot."

"I hear that, I just went to Church today with my fiancé Chuck, and I accepted Jesus as my personal savior."

"Oh that's good."

"Jasmine, I think about you a lot you know and I been wishing that you were all right. I wanted to see you so bad. Sometimes I wish my mom was a regular mom and we grew up like a regular family, but I know wishes don't come true, besides it's too late now."

"Well Victoria, I am praying that mom is going to be ok and I am praying that the devil let loose of our family so that we will be a real family; better late than never." Jasmine said.

I can't stop these tears from falling down my face. I can't believe my little sister is giving me inspiration to be strong. She is so pretty, we look just alike. She's just thinner, but for the most- I think that we both look like mom.

"So Jasmine, where are you guys staying?"

"We are over on the Westside near telegraph and eight mile."

"Oh ok. I'm actually not too far from you. I'm over in the Schoolcraft and Evergreen area, in Rose Mel Park."

"How is Uncle Stan treating you?" Jasmine asked.

"Girl it's a long story. I will tell you sooner than later. I just got to pray on it. That's the best. So how old are you now and when is your birthday?" I asked.

"It's coming up; you know I will be fifteen May 28th."

"What's up with both of our birthday's being on the 28th? You know I will be nineteen on June 28th?

"You know mom's birthday is February 28th; how coincidental." Jasmine replied.

"Take down my Cell # and call me. I keep my phone on vibrate because Stan be tripping, I haven't told him that Chuck brought me a phone."

Jasmine pulled out her Nextel.

"Oh straight up, like that?" I asked.

"You're silly. My boyfriend Sam brought it for me."

"Sam? Oh ok. You have a boyfriend and everything. Wow my little sister is doing grown up thangs out here" I replied.

"Whatever," Jasmine said like she's doing it like that. I don't know maybe she is, after all she is ***my sister.***

"Jasmine, what school do you go to now?"

"I'm at Cass Tech."

"Oh my goodness, girl me and my best friend Toy rides past there all the time. By the way where is Toy? Oh there she is." I spotted her sitting across in the chairs of the waiting room. "Toy, come here."

"Toy, this is my little sister Jasmine. Jasmine this is my best friend Toy."

They both said "nice to meet you" at the same time. Toy looked at me and Jasmine. "Oh my goodness, y'all look just a like and I thought people said we look just a like. Yeah we all look like we could be sisters." Toy said.

Jasmine replied, "Yeah, I guess we do."

I looked at the both of them and said, "But we are in a sense because Toy is like my sister and Jasmine, you are my sister so we all are sisters, how you like that?"

Jasmine smiled. I noticed she had on a little jewelry too. "You got your gold on huh, girl what's up?" I asked.

"Sam has a job and then Aunt Gladys gets those checks for me. She lets me buy whatever I want." Jasmine said nonchalantly.

"Well I am so happy that you are taken care of."

"Ok what's your number?" Jasmine asked.

"It's 313- 525-5555."

"Oh that's easy." Jasmine said.

"Call my phone so I can have your number. Let me get your chirp number." I requested.

We switched numbers and then Jasmine informed that she has to go. She said Sam just text messaged her and said that he was outside. She has a visit with my nephew Jared today. After I hugged Jasmine before she left I felt that tingly sensation. Bishop Morton said it's the presence of God so that's what I am going to take it as.

"Toy, I'll be right back. I'm going to take a peep at my mom again

"Ok girl, take care of your business" Toy replied.

I went back to my mother's room. The nurse is still here. Good. "Excuse me nurse, I didn't catch your name."

"My name is Nurse Melanie." She replied.

"How is my mom doing?"

"Well honey, both of the gun shot wombs appear to be flesh wombs, but we will not be certain until the X-rays are in. I'm sorry honey, what's your name?" she asked.

"Victoria."

"Oh that's a pretty name. That was my grandmother's name. Bless her heart. Victoria, some of the test we have run shows that your mom has problems with her liver, but we have to take more tests to be certain of what the problem is."

"What can you do about those sores on her face?" I asked.

She walked over to the drawer, took out a small pink tub, a face cloth and then she walked back over to my mom. She started wiping her face as she replied, "We are going to clean them with this Iodine and then we have an antibiotic crème that we are going to use. They should be gone in a few days. We are going to keep her here until we get the test back for her liver and her X-ray's." Nurse Melanie replied.

"Ok thanks. When can I come back?" I asked

"We suggest that you come back in the morning."

"Nurse Melanie, I have school then."

"That's not a problem precious, just come once you get out of school."

"Ok, are you sure that she is going to be ok?"

She smiled at me. "Baby, I cannot make you any guarantees or promises. That's actually left up to God. I don't know what God wants to do with your mother. As far as I am concerned, I'm sure your mother will be just fine. This may have been God's intentions. Sometimes he shakes things up to get them in perfect order. All you have to do is pray for her and I will pray for her as well."

"Yes ma'am. So will you be here tomorrow? I asked.

"Yes, I will be here tomorrow. I'm not sure if I will have your mother as my patient because our patients rotate daily. If I'm not her nurse tomorrow I will still stop by and check on her."

"Will you please take care of my mother? Tell them that I want you to take care of my mommy" I wined.

"Yes, you just keep on praying ok. Trust in God, believe in him and have faith and everything will be fine. Come up here tomorrow and talk with your mother. Let her know that she is loved. Despite things that may have happened in the past, let it go. There is no sense in crying over spilled milk. For some reason I can sense that God just brought you two back together, is this true?"

I stood here with a face full of tears because I am so shocked that she would know this. "Yes ma'am, that's correct" I answered.

"Listen here sweetheart, ***what you got to do is, forgive*** and forget. I know that will be hard, but try. I know that you will not totally forget, but forget about the pain and what might have caused it. Remember what you can do now to fix it. I was in your mother's shoes many years before. I rested right down in the hospital bed looking just like she is now. When I came into the hospital the doctors took a look at me and said 'No, she's not going to make it'. They had given up on me. I was stabbed six times in the chest and in the back because I was trying to run off with some drugs. Honey, my daughter came up to that hospital, laid hands on me and told me that she believed that God was going to see me through. She declared that ***I shall live and not die***. She showed me that she loved me that much even though I abandoned her for cocaine. She asked me to make a promise that I would give my life to the LORD. ***I've been with God*** ever since. I'm thirty-five years clean and sober. ***I'm sixty-two years old and I feel great***. I went to school, received my degree in nursing and I've been working here at this same hospital for almost twenty-five years. I try my best to encourage you young folks today. You need to know that ***Mothers are not perfect***. We make mistakes, but that's a part of life. Every things going to be just fine. ***All you have to do is trust in God baby***; He can move mountains with faith the size of a mustard seed. You hear me?

"Yes Ma'am. Thank you so much for sharing your story" I replied as I dried the continuous tears flowing from my eyes.

"No problem precious. Go and enjoy the weather and I will see that she is ok." She stretched out her arms to me, I hugged her and I felt that tingly feeling. *The Spirit of the Lord is present,* I thought, as I continued to dry the tears from my eyes. I looked back at Mama. Although she appeared to be sleeping I noticed tears running from her eyes. I walked out of the room smiling on the inside. I left mama's room and went to the waiting room where Stan and Toy were sitting. "Toy, I'm ready to go."

As Toy stood up grabbing her keys, Stan also stood up and said, "Toya that's ok, I can take her."

"Uncle Stan, my bag is at Toy's house!" I pouted.

"Well, you can get it tomorrow." He replied.

I really don't want to be the reason for him to cause a scene, so I simply responded, "Ok Toy, I will see you later."

She looked at the both of us as if she wanted to say '*ok, y'all got issues*', but instead she said, "Ok girl be careful."

Stan, I just want it to be over!

Stan and I went back to the car. As Stan began putting on his seat belt, he looked over at me and said, "I see you done met back up with your sister huh?"

"Yeah and she told me that she has been calling. Why haven't you said anything to me about it?"

"I didn't want you to start back talking to her because I thought that you would start feeling sad and that you would be missing your family and then you would not be able to focus in school."

"News Flash Stan, I am starting to lose focus just by dealing with you alone!"

"What do you mean by that?" he asked.

"I don't want to do this anymore Stan! I just want us, this whole sick twisted thing to be over! I am tired of going through this! I want to marry Chuck and that's that! As a matter of fact, drop me off over Toys house!" I demanded.

"Who in the hell do you think you are talking to? I know you must have lost your whole damn mind!" he yelled.

"Stan, do you think that you are going to be able to manipulate me forever? Do you really think that you are going to force me to stay with you forever? It is not possible and it's damn sure not comfortable! I want to be in love and let everybody know it instead of living this secret, twisted, lie that I can no longer handle. I have been reading magazines and watching different talk shows. Oprah has different people on her show that resembles you. The psychologist says that when you sleep with a little girl if she consents or not, it's called molestation. You forcing yourself on me now is called statutory rape. Stan, I love you. I truly do, but I can't continue acting like this is not bothering me. You provided the love that I needed even though I wish I had the love from my mom and dad; you made up for it. We have tricked all the teachers, all of our family and friends, damn near everybody. I just don't feel like doing this anymore. I never felt like doing this. Please!!! I know you have to understand. Don't you arrest people at your job for things like this? It's statutory rape! Now you are being unreasonable about the whole thing, just let me move on. After I graduate I'm moving out. I am going to talk to my counselor tomorrow about an out of state college so I will be leaving anyway." I informed him.

The angry look on Stan's face is reminding me of his sporadic episode that he displayed Friday when I tried breaking it off. *God please help me*, I began silently praying to myself. I forgot this man is working with a few loose screws. The way he's driving he looks like he is trying to crash the car and kill the both of us.

"Let me explain something to you and let this be my last time! You are not going to any out-of-state colleges, you are not moving out and you definitely will not be getting married so you can get that out of your mind right now!!!" He yelled as he put his foot on the accelerator. "Statutory Rape you say. I never heard you yell out rape when I had my face buried down there between your legs. I didn't put a gun up to your head and tell you to lay there. You had all opportunity to stop me. You stop putting up a fight so I figured you liked it. Oh and for the molestation shit you started it. You came downstairs with no panties on because you said your Mama didn't wash them, you don't think I knew what you were doing."

"Stan, are you serious. I mean for real. Are you really as crazy as you look and sound right now? I was five years old, Stan. What are you talking about" I yelled.

"Oh yeah just so that you know as far as this guy Chuck goes, I guess he may be spending the rest of his life behind bars because I can make it happen."

"I will tell him to lay low or leave town! I will not let you hurt him, you sick twisted bastard!!!! I hate you!"

"Listen up little girl!!!! Matter of fact, we can talk when we get in the house" He said as he pressed the garage door opener.

I took out my keys and opened the door. I ran upstairs and locked my bedroom door. Shoot, I have to use the bathroom. *How did I get myself into this situation*, I questioned myself as I ran to the bathroom.

I went in the bathroom and locked the door. *God, is this another one of those things that's got to work this way. I can't do this. Why is this happening to me? I feel like I am living in a real life horror movie,* I said softly. Maybe God is mad at me. I am new to Him. I thought He would take care of this for me. It's nothing but bad things happening to me. Maybe Toy is right. This religious stuff is not where it's at. I have to get out of this situation on my own. I guess Stan is also right. Maybe I did start all of this. I don't know how, but I know it's happening to me for a reason.

"VICTORIA!"

Stan is yelling my name like he is really upset. I can't stop draining these fluids. I guess it's all of that orange juice and water I had at breakfast. *Hurry Victoria,* I told myself. I can't believe I have all of these liquids inside of me it seems like my bladder is working in overtime. Oh boy, he just kicked in the bathroom door and broke the lock. Now my bladder has decided to stop. "Ouch Stan! Why are you hitting me?"

"Shut up. Didn't I tell you the other day, you cannot quit me" he yelled while standing in front of me unzipping his pants. "Don't make me kill you Victoria. You are really starting to play with my emotions and I don't like that."

"Stan, No! *I hate you,*" I tried mumbling. *I can't breathe*, I thought as I am trying to inhale and exhale deeply through my nose. Why do I have to experience this pain? It seems like he is snatching my hair out of my scalp by the roots. *Why is this man so evil?* I thought as I tried squeezing my lips really tight.

"If you don't unloosen your lips **I will break your jaw!**" Stan yelled.

It seems like I had all the strength in the world last night. I am so afraid that Stan will kill me so fighting him back is definitely not an option. I closed my eyes and imagined Chuck kicking down the door and saving me. Once I opened my eyes, I'm began to realize that Chuck is not here and he has not saved me.

"Get up! Let's go!" Stan yelled while dragging me by my hair. "I'm tired of your shit. I told you about trying to play me. You probably spent the night with that nigga." He mumbled while pulling my hair and now he decided to put his hand around my neck. I guess I wasn't moving fast enough by my hair alone.

I find it rather ironic how I am a Queen in all aspects when I'm with Chuck and how I have now converted back into this helpless rose with no thorns when I am around Stan. In every room of this house I have lost a pedal. One day I might go through here and pick up every pedal I have ever lost, put them in a bag and then burry them. *I wonder if they would produce a stronger root.* I don't know how I have managed to do it but, I'm back on the outside looking in.

As I watch this helpless rose with a weak vine dragged through out this house I want to stop him. If I had at least half the strength of a strand of grass that can stand through, rain, hail, sleet and snow I would reach out and grab him. As I stand here afloat of this lifeless image being thrown on the bed as his open hand repeatedly strikes her defenseless body, I am beginning to realize that I cannot stop her pain. I couldn't stop it before; I don't know what gave me the unrealistic belief that I could stop it now. My lack of confidence has now forced me to return to the image of my existence.

The fire in his eyes strikes as a beast; the beast that he was when I was a kid and the horrific beast that he has become now is more than evident that he cannot be stopped. *I'm starting to loose trust in Chuck because he told me that God would help me if I call.* I called and it seems like no one is listening. No one cares. No matter how much I want to feel that things are going to become different in some type of way, the substantial evidence before me has changed my once self-opinionated verdict of innocent to guilty.

I am guilty for being defenseless and weak. I am guilty for not believing that I can escape this man even though he is not holding a gun to my head. The look in his eyes is enough fear to keep me bedridden. Just like all the others, *this too shall pass*. I have to realize that living a life without fear and being happy is simply not the destiny set out for me as far as I can see. I'm sure my body's full of bruises by now. I wished that I could cover girl Mama's pain earlier, but now I'm the one who need's the cover up.

"You can't leave this, can you? Huh? Can you? You can't leave me! I told you that you belong to me. Victoria, nobody is going to love you like I do. That guy Chuck does not care about you. If he cared about you, where is he now? Huh? Exactly! He's – not – here! Victoria, if we ever have to have this conversation again, I will be the only one talking and **you'll be dead because I will kill you!** You hear me? I promise. I will kill you! I kill people for a living, so killing you would be a piece of cake" He said as he squeezed my jaws. "Victoria, do you hear me! I mean it! You can forget about this guy Chuck and that's it!" He yelled before he slapped me. "Do you hear me!!!!!!?" he continued yelling.

"Yes Stan, I hear you. I am so sorry. I was wrong for trying to have a normal life" I said sarcastically. The sad part is he is looking at me as if I honestly meant that.

"So tell me, do you really love this boy Chuck?"

"Yes, I do." I replied.

"What does he do for you that I don't do? I buy you everything that you want. Everything you own is top of line. I mean what does this boy really do for you that I'm not doing?"

"It's not that you are doing everything wrong Stan. He's my age and we have fun. We don't have to sneak around and I don't feel that he takes advantage of me. It's something different that I can't explain."

"Oh I see. Well, I rather share you then lose you all together. I know you're not going to stop seeing him so I guess I have to deal with it." He replied.

Trying to change the subject "Stan, did you get a chance to cook" I asked.

"Oh yeah, I have those ribs in some vinegar water in the kitchen sink. Let me get up and start this grill. I made the macaroni last night after you requested it. You just have to put it in the oven." He replied before heading towards the kitchen.

Now I'm totally confused. Stan is now saying he is all of sudden willing to share me with Chuck. Why all this then? I feel like things will never change, no matter how badly I want them to. Since he is so willing to share me, maybe he will be willing to *just let me go all together*. I don't believe that Stan will kill me, I'm becoming numb to his continuous threats; however, I'm still going to tell Chuck to watch his back because I just don't trust Stan. I do trust his cooking though because that man can cook. Let me take a shower and heat me up some macaroni. I'm starving.

Chapter 14

I went in the backyard where Stan has the grill smoking and smelling good. I forgot all about the pool. Let me go put on my swim suit right quick. I might as well enjoy this weather while it last. I ran upstairs to look for my swimsuit. Oh here it is. My purse is vibrating. I looked at my cell and noticed that I have three missed calls, one from Toy and two from Chuck. I grabbed the cordless phone from the charger.

"Hello" Toy answered.

"Hey girl what's up?"

"Chuck said to tell you that he loves you and he needs you to call him. I am not your personal secretary or your human voice mail. You need to break the news to your Uncle so he can talk to you all the time." Toy replied.

"Thanks boo. Are you still coming over?"

"Yeah I guess. Is your Uncle cooking?"

"You know it! I just put the macaroni in the oven. He has some potato salad in there, and he just put the ribs on the grill with some hot dogs and some of those cheese sausages you like, so come on! I'm about to swim a couple of laps right quick so I'll be outside.

"Oh girl, I forgot about y'all pool."

"I did too and I live here. It's in the middle of winter though Toy, so who would have expected to have this 80 degree weather anyway?"

"Girl, I know. I'm going to enjoy it while it last. I'll be there in about twenty minutes."

"Ok see you in a few." I said before I hung up.

Stan has split personality's I swear. He is out here at this grill acting like nothing happened. "Hey Stan, you know Toya is still coming over right?"

He shook his head while putting the ribs on the grill. "Yeah that's fine" he said.

I went and jumped in the pool. After swimming about ten laps, I noticed Toy walking on the side of the house. "Hey girl, jump on in, you know how we do." I shouted.

She took off her shirt and shorts then jumped in. I looked over at Stan and noticed him *staring at Toy like she was going to be his next victim.* I think Stan knows better than to try that with Toy. Toy would probably tell everybody and have it broadcasted on the national news.

"Hey girl, what's up? Did you call Chuck yet?" Toy asked as she swam closer to me.

"No, actually I didn't. You know how my Uncle be tripping, but girl I will be graduating soon and I will be out of this house. Chuck and I will not have to worry about this anymore. I can't wait to leave this house" I replied.

"Yeah I hear you. When will the food be done?"

"It should be done any minute now" I replied. "Stan can you check and see if the Mac and Cheese is ready to come out the oven!" I yelled.

When he walked in the house I heard his Nextel chirping on the way in. I'm a little curious to know who it is. He went towards the front door and behind him as he came back are two of his friends David and Paul. Those are his buddies from work. They've been over many times before. David is the cutest white boy I have ever seen. Paul is light skinned and built like Stan. "**Damn, they fine!**" I didn't realize I was saying that out loud.

Toy apparently heard me because she said, "girl who you telling, I call the light skin one."

"Girl, that's cool with me. You know Stan would be tripping if I was to get at either one of them. Besides, I'm in love" I replied.

I heard the door bell ringing from out here. *Now I wonder who that could be,* I thought to myself. Stan walked up to the front. He came back out to the pool with a lady. I thought that was his ex-fiancé Christine, but as they're getting closer I realized that's not her. Ugh, I wonder who she is. She has to be at least 105 pounds if that. I don't know who she thinks she's fooling with all of that fake ass jewelry. I stood here pretending to swim as I stared at them.

Stan hugged her and kissed her on the cheek. He grabbed her hand and now they are heading in my direction.

"Stephanie, that's my niece Victoria, her girlfriend Latoya, and you remember David and Paul right?"

She smiled waving at all of us. "Oh, but of course nice to see you again" she said to Paul and David. I wish he could feel these sharp jabs I am trying to send him with my cut throat eyes. "Toy, I'll be right back." I said as I jumped out of the pool and stormed in the kitchen. "Uncle Stan, could you please come here for a second?" I requested soft and delicately.

I over heard him say, "Stephanie, have a seat. I will be right back."

I stood up against the refrigerator with my arms folded. He walked in the kitchen. "Oh you were tripping about me being with my man earlier, but now you're trying to play me by bringing this skinny crack head looking chic over here wearing all that fake ass jewelry! Oh so that's your style. You messing with crack heads now?" I quietly yelled.

Stan walked over to me and leaned down near my ear, "First of all, you don't check me! Second of all she is just a friend! He explained.

"So you're not messing her, but your boys already know her? Why is this my first time seeing and meeting her? Stan you are so full of it! I can't believe how you got the nerve to bring this whore in my house, but you want me to leave Chuck! It does not work like that! I want you to leave me alone and stop trying to control me. Control her please and just let me be happy"

"Wait a minute little girl! Don't get your ass beat in this kitchen! We will talk about this later"

"Little girl! Oh now you have realized that I am a little girl. Stan, I swear you are insane. I'm out of here" I said as I began to walk out the kitchen.

"Where you going?" he asked while grabbing my arm.

"I'm going with Toya to go find my fiancé" I said while snatching away from him and walking towards the door.

He grabbed my hair, threw me up against the wall and put his hand around my neck and began to choke me. "Now I hope that this conversation is over! I will talk to you later. You're lucky we have company because I would beat the shit out of you for trying to test me" he replied.

As soon as he let me know that he wasn't going to hit me since we have company I snatched away from him. "Stan, you are not going to have your cake and eat it too, so excuse me." I said as I walked out the kitchen.

I changed my frown into a smile quickly when I walked back out on the patio and jumped in the pool next to Toy. "Girl, I'm sorry about that. I had to make sure that the macaroni was done all the way. I'm hungry."

"I am too, she replied."

I noticed that David and Paul brought a 24 pack of Corona's with them. "Toy, you want a Corona?" I asked.

"Why do you insist on asking me questions that I know you already know the answers to? She asked sarcastically.

"Yeah I forgot you are a seven day a week alcoholic, what is wrong with me?" I replied while laughing.

I got out of the pool and got Toy's Corona. I grabbed one for myself as well. Stan walked out just as I was turning the bottle up to my lips. He looks like he wants to blow steam out of his ears. I continued turning the beer up. I looked a Stan and swallowed it slowly just to irritate him. I know I'm going to get it, but hopefully I can escape before then. I smiled at Stan because he is constantly staring at me. As long as I know that he will not hurt me in front of people, *I am going to have myself some fun,* I thought to myself as I hopped back in the pool next to Toy.

What's Skin Color Got to Do with It?

Paul is walking over towards Toy and I "Hey pretty lady. Can I talk to you for a minute?" he asked.

I know he is not trying to flirt with me, I'm so flattered, I thought as I smiled from ear to ear, but he put his hand out for Toy. Whoa talking about feeling stupid I played it off real good and said "you go girl."

Toy exited the pool as she held onto Paul's hand. They went over in sat down at the table located in the corner of the patio. David's staring at me. There's no harm in staring back. *Here he comes,* I thought as David appears to be walking in my direction.

"How have you been doing Victoria?" David asked.

"I'm doing well, how about you Mr. David?"

"Great, taking it day by day that's about it. Why don't you let the water go for a minute and come talk to me" he asked as he extended his hand out to me.

"Ok, I guess I can do that." I replied as I began exiting the pool.

I'm feeling that Corona. I think I'm buzzing. I feel a little bit similar to the way I felt yesterday when I sipped on that Grey Goose with Chuck. I guess it's because I drank it so fast.

David and I sat at the table near Toy and Paul. David's staring at me in this aqua blue Baby Phat two piece swimsuit drooling, so is Stan. I am not trying to attract that unwanted attention so I turned around and faced David. "David, you know you are a sexy white boy right?"

"I'm sure you know that you are definitely a very sexy Black girl right? He replied with a smile that could have lit up the entire city of Detroit.

"You are so silly" I replied while my Diva shoes remained as tight as they're going to get.

"That's you girlfriend. So what's up with you Ms. Victoria? I watched you grow into a sexy young lady. I remember that time when I came over and you had on your night gown in the kitchen and then when you noticed me staring at you, you took off running up the stairs. I was staring at you then because I thought you were already super-hot. That was what two or three years ago?" David asked.

"Yeah, I remember that incident. What would you have done if you were in your kitchen and a strange person was staring at you and you had no idea where they came from? I was sixteen then David. You were looking at me like that?" I asked as I lifted my eyebrows at him.

"Come on, don't say it like I was this old pervert standing there staring at you now. I was only twenty, myself." He replied.

"Oh ok. So you're what 23?" I asked.

"Yep. I'm a youngster; fresh meat baby girl." He smiled, obviously trying to be funny, but the jokes kind of corny. *Though he is very handsome.*

"You started out in the force early then huh?" I asked.

"Yeah, I guess you can say that. I am actually still in training. I was doing a semi internship with the FBI at that time. I was basically being tested to make sure that this is the type of work that I wanted to do. I graduated high school when I was 17. So I have been on a mission for a career ever since then"

"I hear that. So have you figured out if this is the career path that you would like to take? Is killing people every day going to make you feel like a man?" I asked a little bluntly now that I think about it. This is my third Corona. *I think I better slow down.* I really want to know what David's intentions are because Chuck did explain to me that the majority of law enforcement is crooked. Viewing Stan's action has validated Chuck's overall judgment.

"Victoria, can I be honest with you?"

"I would actually prefer that"

"Ok don't take any offense to this, but have you seen the movie Training Day?"

"Yes, I have."

"You know the role Denzel Washington played and the role that Ethan Hawke played? Let's just say me and your Uncle's relationship is similar to theirs. I'm almost positive that you know what role I play. Don't get me wrong, I respect the way your Uncle handles his business because he has at least 10 years in the field it's just, well never mind. I know you are not trying to hear about my boring life. So what's up with you girl? He asked.

I really want to tell David that he does not have to smile that hard. It's very much evident that his smile is gorgeous. I looked over at Stan and he's standing there looking furious. I simply smiled and waved at him and then I took another sip of my Corona. I swear Stan is a lunatic. He is picking Stephanie up and now she has her legs wrapped around his waist. Stan just looked at me and smiled as if he thinks I'm going to get jealous. I wish he knew how excited I am that he has someone else.

"What are you thinking about?" David asked.

"I was thinking about how I want to hug you, but I can't because I'm wet." I replied.

"That's a good thing right?" he replied while stretching his arms open.

He hugged me and his shirt got wet. I'm sure he has to feel like it is worth it. "So David, do you have a girl friend?"

"No."

"Have you ever talked to a black girl before?"

"Vicky, to be honest with you my daughter's mother is black."

"How old is you baby?"

"She's three."

"So did you and your daughter's mom get any strange looks when you were out in public?"

"Of course, that will happen anywhere. When you have a beautiful person with you of the opposite race or even the same race for that matter somebody is going to say something. Whether it is someone black or someone white, someone is going to say something or give you an awkward look. That's the messed up part about us as humans. I think we are all people and we are only different by the color of our skin tone."

"I feel you on that right there David, I can definitely respect that." I replied.

"To be honest Victoria, I really love Black females. In my eyes, they are the sexiest females of God's creation; even though you probably don't hear it often. Most of my friends are scared to admit it, but that's all we talk about. We always compliment you all on how good you all look and smell."

"That is so sweet David. Please note that we are not just beautiful outside, we are just as beautiful inside and don't forget, we have brains baby boy, you most definitely cannot forget that."

"Trust me, I know. Alicia will never let me forget it. You know something Victoria? I never understood the big race issue. We do similar things. We're all the same. I think it's just a control issue. Unfortunately, the white race chose to be dominant and start up slavery. I think that they didn't have anything else better to do so therefore they chose to dominate all races. Victoria, I really can't explain why this world is the way it is, all I know is that I try to *treat everyone equal because that's how God made us.* He just made us in different shades of color, with different languages that's all."

"Wow David, you just opened up my eyes to a wider visual, but I have always been the type of person that is open to everything. I always felt that we were the same, but you know how media does. They make a situation more than what it seems. Thanks for keeping it real David."

When I looked up I noticed that Stan is over there tongue wrestling with the bite size Mrs. T. Oh, he is so damn disrespectful. Toy and I are here. *Come on, if you are going to make out with someone at least make sure she's half decent especially when the Channel 2 news of Detroit is here,* I thought to myself. Stan being my Uncle right now is definitely not a great look while Toy is here. I can't explain this urge that has come over me directing me to grab David by his neck and plant a big succulent kiss on his lip.

"David, is it? Excuse us. Victoria let me talk to you for a minute." Toy interrupted.

"What's up girl?" I asked.

"Bitch, please don't what's up me! Are you stupid or just retarded! So I assume you don't love Chuck any more right? You remember him right? The man that would probably die for your stupid ass, while you are out here acting like- I really don't know what you're acting like right now?" Toy replied as if she's disappointed in me.

"I do. I just lost it for a minute." I laughed

"Well, you better find it and if you can't handle your alcohol consumption, I suggest that you quit immediately!"

"Wait a minute, look who's talking?"

"Victoria, I promise I really want to slap the taste out of your mouth, but I'm going to keep it cool. Besides, you do not see me with my tongue all down that dude's throat, and besides that, I'm not the one in love or in a relationship. You're the one that's engaged!" Toy replied.

"I didn't tongue kiss him though, Toy!" I wined

"So what! You still need to chill because if Chuck was out there kissing another female he doesn't know, you know you would trip so get it together and get it together now!" Toy yelled softy.

"Ok, I got this Toy!"

I know Toy is my sister and all, but dang. She's trying to act like she's my Mama. All I did was kiss David though. I guess she's right, maybe I am tripping. It's got to be this Corona because I don't even drink like that. *I know I am out of my normal character*, I thought to myself as I walked back over to David. "Sorry about that boo. Can you call my cell right quick so your number could be stored in it" I asked.

As he was calling my cell phone I said, "We most definitely have to hook up outside of my Uncle's house." I basically gave him invalid info because I know that I am not going to hook up with him. He is sexy and all, but I love Mr. Charles Matthews.

David smiled and said, "Ok that sounds good."

"Are you hungry, because I am starving? Do you want me to fix you a plate?

"Sure, what do you have?"

"We have Barbecue Ribs, chicken, hot dogs, sausages, macaroni, potato salad and some cheese cake."

"Surprise me."

"Toy, you want to help me fix plates?" I asked. I knew her greedy butt was going to break her neck to get over here. I was right. She damn near flew across this patio.

"I sure do, my stomach's been growling for the longest." Toy explained.

Toy and I went in the kitchen. "Toy, you can start fixing plates because I have to use the bathroom. I'll be right back." I informed as I walked towards the kitchen's exit. I opened the door to the bathroom. "What the!" I screamed as I stood here staring in disgust. I don't believe this! This stupid, retarded asshole is sitting on the toilet licking and snorting some type of white powder off of this chic's butt. This sick twisted dude is in here doing cocaine or heroin or whatever it is and then this chic is bent over with her finger at her nose sniffing it. I don't believe this!

"Victoria, what's wrong?" Toy asked as she ran towards me. She looked in the bathroom. "Oh my goodness! Girl what's up with your Uncle?" Toy asked.

I hear Toy, but this clown is about to make me loose it. His silly tail is still sitting there. I don't know what kind of high they're on, but that's something deeper than I can image even though I'm seeing it with my own eyes. The fact that neither one of them budged is just insane. The look in his eyes I see as he stares at me while slowly licking that white stuff from her deeply arched backside is making me want to vomit. That look is all too familiar!

"Come on Toy, let's go!!!!" I yelled.

"What about the food?" She asked.

"Girl, forget that food! We'll just buy something! I don't want anything he cooked. I just lost my appetite! Let me grab some clothes, I'll be right back" I said as I ran upstairs.

I changed my clothes, packed up a couple of outfits and the things that are important to me then I remembered *I have a bag of clothes at Toy's house.* I grabbed my books and my cell phone and ran down the stairs.

Once I arrived down stairs, I noticed Stan and Stephanie are both standing in the kitchen butt naked, looking like zombies. *Stan looks so stupid*, I thought as I viewed him standing in the kitchen doorway with a rib in his mouth. When I glanced at the front door I noticed Toy staring at Stan with a look of disgust. Despite my embarrassment and total humiliation, I yelled "Toya let's go!"

"Run trick, run! You little spoiled slut!" Stan yelled.

I can't believe this! This is so embarrassing. Why would he do that? He has jeopardized my credibility.

"Wow girl, what has gotten into your Uncle?" Toy asked

"That dope! Shoot, I don't know."

"No matter how sexy I thought your Uncle was, he is so ugly now."

I sat here looking at Toy and thinking at the same time. "Toya, I don't believe this. I really don't girl. This day has been a day to remember" I replied. I have to call my husband.

"Hey baby what's up, I been calling you." Chuck answered.

"I know baby. I was in the pool for a few.

"In the pool? Baby, it's March and just because its 80 degree's this is still Pneumonia weather baby.

"I hear you, but that's not important. I am on my way to Toy's house. I need somewhere to stay for a while because I am not moving back in with that psycho man, ever!" I shouted.

"Baby, please calm down. He didn't hurt you did he? Chuck asked.

"No, I will tell you about it. Are you coming to pick me up?"

"Yeah Ma, I'm on my way." Chuck replied before he hung up.

"Vic, are u still on the phone?" Toy asked.

"Nah, what's up?"

"Girl, was that heroine I seen your Uncle with?"

"What else could it have been, Toy? If it wasn't that, it was coke." I replied. *Nasty son of a bitch! He's always trying to run my life, but this bastard is getting high!*

Chapter 15

Chuck pulled up in front of Toy's house in a green drop top BMW, but the top is not down. *What the … Wait a minute now, what's up with this?* "Toy, what's up with Chuck in all this flashy stuff? I'll be back girl" I said as I got out of Toy's car.

I walked over to the car and opened the passenger door. Chuck sat there leaned back in his seat looking sexy and icy as ever. I looked back at Toy's car and realized that she is staring hard as hell. I continued talking to Chuck as if I did not notice. "Chuck, what's up with this car, baby?"

"Oh this? You talking about this beamer your man driving? It's another rental."

"Why baby? Why do you need all of this flashy stuff? I am beginning to get worried. You keep flashing, changing cars and expensive cars on top of that, baby why?"

"It's cool baby. I told you I got rid of that last package yesterday right? I just got this one to let me know what it will be like when I can afford to buy one. I promise you, I'm good. My Uncle's wifey signed for this one." Chuck replied.

I ran back to Toys car and grabbed my things. I am really trying extremely hard not to pay attention to Toy staring at my man. I ran back to Chuck's car with my Coach backpack. I went to get in the car and I realized that Toy is still staring. Now she is really about to piss me off. *What the hell is she looking at?* I don't know if she is looking at the car or at my man. I guess I am overreacting. Toy is materialistic; this type of stuff mesmerizes her. I hope like hell she's looking at this car. I don't want to mess up an almost fourteen-year friendship by slapping the shit out of her for staring at my man. That is my sister though, I guess I am tripping. I know Toy is not cut throat like that. I stared at her for the two minutes she stayed in a daze. I snapped her out of it when I yelled, "I'll call you later boo!"

She stuck her head out the window "Ok be careful, and Victoria, hang in there ok" she replied.

"Ok see ya." I smiled and replied as I got in the car and gave Chuck a kiss on those juicy lips that I oh so love. "Baby, you won't believe what just happened."

"What happened?" Chuck asked.

"I walked in the bathroom where my Uncle was sitting on the toilet, butt naked with a chic bent over with her booty in his face as he was licking some type of white powder off of her while Toy and I stood there staring at him. Bay, he was acting like a straight up different person. After I packed my things and began walking out the door, he started calling me sluts and everything. I can't believe him."

"Baby, it's going to be ok. Don't worry about him. Daddy's here baby, Daddy's here," Chuck repeated.

I looked at Chuck leaning back, confident and sexy. *Yeah baby, I need that father in you*, I started thinking. I was listening to Mary J Blige's Breakthrough Album. She has a song titled, "Father in you." Every time I listened to it, I think about Chuck. Being with him, letting him hold me, protect me, and love me. He makes me feel so secure and so happy when I am with him. I love him so much. I shook my head and replied, "Yeah, I know."

"So what are you going to do?" Chuck asked.

"You know what bay, I really don't know. I have not had the chance to think about it. I was so upset and embarrassed that I packed my things and left."

"Did you pray in the midst of all of that?"

"No, as a matter of fact, I didn't." I answered.

Wow, that question just blew right over my head. I was supposed to be praying for my Mama too and for some reason I forgot. I feel so bad now. Chuck really keeps talking about God. I am trying to understand why God is not helping me right now. I guess I have to get in line because a lot of people depend on Him.

Chuck turned his radio completely off and glanced over at me with what seems to be a sparkle in his eye. "See, sometimes we get so upset that we forget to call on our Heavenly Father. We want to take matters in our own hands. Don't worry about it though. We will figure something out" he replied.

"Chuck, what about your Uncle? What is he going to say?" I asked when I noticed us pulling in his garage.

"He's not going to say anything. He moved out four months ago." Chuck replied.

"What?"

"Victoria, let me go ahead and be honest with you. I am very selective and particular about bringing someone in my home. Even though I loved you at the very beginning, I needed to see if it was going to work out. I needed to know if you were really down for me. I am a drama free person and I definitely don't like all of that nonsense at my house. I cannot afford to have drama period. I feel that I can trust you and plus I love you. I apologize for not telling you, but I wanted to make sure that you were really down for me. This is my house. My Uncle gave it to me. He moved out about four months ago and I don't want to mess it up. Therefore, you know you have a home. Babe, I am really trying to grow with the Lord, slowly, but so surely. We are going to have to get married in order to continue living together."

"When are we getting married?" I asked.

"Hopefully, in a few months, if that's ok with you. I want to get some things together before I make that commitment. First, I want to make sure that I get accepted into Wayne State University. My Counselor said I should know by then. They're waiting on my grades from this current semester. I admit I was behind because I was not on my game, but when I met you; you gave me the inspiration to do what I have to do. I considered you and your life situation. I concluded that if you can do it, I could do it. Plus, I have been praying on it" he explained as he opened the door.

Chuck and I walked inside his house. He helped me with my things taking the majority of them in his room. I only have my Christian Dior suitcase and my Coach bag. I think I left my Louis Vuitton backpack at Toy's. He sat my bags on the shelf inside the walk-in closet.

"Come here, Victoria." Chuck commanded as he reached out his hand. I grabbed his hand and followed him in the living room. "***Get on your knees.***"

Chuck, you have to be kidding me, I thought. I have too much on my mind to be doing some freaky stuff right now. "Baby why?" I asked. He noticed the concerned look on my face, but that obviously does not matter.

"I said get on your knees; just do what your man tells you to do please!" Chuck replied as if he was getting frustrated.

I stared at him thinking, *I know you are not frustrated when I just told you I been through some mess with my Uncle and you have the nerve to demand me to get on my knees.*

The look that Chuck is giving me is not very friendly. *I was already beat earlier today, so I better get on my knees,* I thought. As I was getting on my knee's I noticed Chuck getting on his also. My heart is beating so fast. *I feel so stupid.*

"Close your eyes baby." he requested. "Dear Heavenly Father, I am here on my knees along with Victoria. We are here in search of your mercy, grace, blessings and protection Lord. We are going through Father. We are calling on your name Dear God to guide us in all ways possible. Dear Lord, please order our steps in your word. God, please teach me to be that humble man that I need to be, to be there for my future wife and to be there for other people in my situation. Father God, I know that you are sending me through all of the things that I am experiencing for a reason. I ask that you enter in Victoria's heart and mind. Father God, please let her know that you are real. Lord, I read it in your word that *no weapons formed against thee shall prosper*. I believe it is so and I know it is so. Thank you for keeping your angels watching over me Lord. Thank you for keeping my mother. Lord, please try to help her come into her right mind. Forgive us for our sins and Lord please help us to continue to fight temptation. However, I know that things will not change overnight. I do know that you are God and I believe that you are real. I know that all things work together for the good of those who love GOD and Lord, I love you. As I view how you have been present in my life, I am so thankful Lord. We thank you for so much. Father God, I am so humble. I want to be more humble to you Heavenly Father. You are the only one whom I shall fear. In your son Jesus name, my Heavenly Father, we pray to you as well as give you praise. Amen"

"Amen" I uttered as I sat here feeling completely embarrassed for thinking that Chuck would be that way to me. I'm beginning to feel that special feeling. I believe God is somewhere in the area. Now that we are in the midst of praying, I have to pray all by myself.

"Dear God, I hear this man saying that he is calling on you. Many people say to call on your name because you are real. I am sorry for not knowing you then, but I feel like I know you now or at least, I'm getting to know you now. I need you to help me because I see no other way. I don't know what Stan will do when he comes off his high. I do not know what is happening Lord. I prayed to you at Church earlier and I am waiting on you to show me your existence Lord. I need to know that you really had your son Jesus die for my sins. I need to know that you are going to help me get out of this situation. Lord, I want to be close with my sister. I want my mother to get well and I want us to be a family. Teach me how to love and teach me how to be loved by showing me what true love really is. I have noticed that Charles cares for me. Please teach me not to take him for granted. Lord, teach me to be good, teach me to be taught. I pray this in your name, I love you, Amen."

As tears began to fall from my eyes, I lifted my head up from my hands. I glanced over at Chuck and noticed that he has his head on the couch. My heart is beginning to tingle all over again. Leaving Chucks side would be more like torture, I would never do that to myself. I love that man, that man … Oh my, how I love him.

Chuck stood up, reached his hand out for me and pulled me up. Here we stand together face to face. He put his hand on my face and wiped my tears. He kissed me and as my tears continuously fell he licked them.

"Victoria, please listen to me and listen to me with your heart. I never want you to think that you will be unable to tell me about anything. I mean anything at all. I love you and **when you love someone you accept them for who they are without negative regards of their past or their present circumstances.** You have made my life complete. You are my better half because **you are everything that I am not.**"

"Chuck, you don't know how much joy you have brought into my life and how much pain from my past that you have already suppressed. Remember when you first proposed to me in Miami when I told you that I didn't know how to be a Queen, but I would do my best to be the best Queen ever for you, honey I meant that from the bottom of my heart. Every time I think of you, my heart begins to dance and bright lights shine in my once darkened world. You give me strength and courage. With your constant repetition of love's definition, I crave you. The love you display feels so real. When I lay asleep at night I dream of you and when I awake I chase my dream in hopes of capturing them. I know that dreams come true because here you are but, at the same time as I chase my dream I'm walking in a nightmare. I really wish my Uncle was not the way that he is."

"Baby, you never have to go to your Uncles house again. I will buy you new clothes. I will buy you any and everything that you need. If I can't get you everything you want I will try my hardest to supply you with everything you need" Chuck replied as he licked my tears again.

The concept of having butterflies is obviously applying to this tingly sensation twirling around inside my belly.

"Come with me" Chuck requested as he grabbed my hand and led me to his bedroom. He handed me the remote "Here, watch whatever you want. I'll be right back" he said as he went into the bathroom.

Everything is changing so fast. I wonder if this is all a part of God's plan. I knew that I didn't want to be at Stan's tonight and I'm not there. The way that everything is happening seems unrealistic. I want to tell Chuck everything since he has revealed that he will understand, but I think this will be too much for him. I better wait it out. Maybe God is going to work this out because these chills that I am experiencing have been given to me for a reason. There is no harm in me waiting on God so I better put all of my trust in Him because I tried escaping Stan on my own and I could not do it. *Hmm, I wonder what this Gospel Celebration on BET is all about,* I thought as I viewed the TV Guide Channel. I turned to BET.

There is a group of ladies on, by the name of the Clark Sisters. One of them began speaking into the microphone. "How many of you know that God is a way maker? How many know that prayer changes things? I'm here to testify how Good God is. Oh what an awesome blessing it is to be standing here before you today" She said before she started jumping up and down screaming "hallelujah."

I noticed the tears falling from her eyes. One of the sisters clinched her hands and leaned her head back, and then the other sister was waving her hands in the air looking up to the sky while the other continued to play the organ. Sitting here viewing these ladies praise God is creating this tingle again. "Hallelujah! Hallelujah, Oh God! Help me Lord! Help me Jesus, I love you" are the words that effortlessly began to flow from my lips. I cannot control this certain urge that has come over me. I don't want to control it because it feels so good. The rapid flow of my tears and God's Spirit being present is a powerful and uplifting combination.

It feels like the dark clouds are fading away. The sun is shining again. *How can I keep this sunlight present every day,* I thought to myself. I regained my visual strength and reality as I sat back in the chair and looked at the television. The cameras are showing everybody in the audience. Everybody is standing up with their hands in the air waving them back and forth. I know God is real. He has to be, it appears to be millions of people in attendance at this Gospel Celebration and then the hundreds of people from church earlier today. I must be crazy for thinking that HE can't be. Father *God, I apologize for continuously doubting you. I have to wait, I don't have a choice. You have been good so far. I don't know why you let Stan do that to me again today, but I guess there is a reason for everything. I will do like Chuck and Bishop Morton said and believe,* I prayed.

"You must like them huh?" Chuck asked when he walked back in the room and noticed that my eyes were glued to the TV.

"Yes, I like this song" I replied as I stared at him for a moment wondering how I could become *Blessed and Highly Favored* the way they say that they are. *Maybe my time is coming,* I thought.

"Yes, this is a great song. Justine listened to the Clark Sisters all the time. Did you know they were from Detroit?"

"Are you serious? They're from right here?" I asked.

"Yes baby. A lot of good singers come from the "D" baby. We have a lot of talent here. This is the city of Motown. We have rappers, singers, and all types of talent that come from right here in Detroit. Baby, come here for a minute." He requested as he reached for my hand.

Chapter 16

I followed him as he led me to the bathroom. "Oh my goodness Chuck" I said as I tried to close my mouth. *This is so sweet of him*, I thought to myself. He has candles burning all around the bathroom, rose pedals are scattered over the floor, falling off the tub and in the bubble bathwater. He has a bottle of Moet champagne and a champagne glass sitting in a bucket of ice. Ooh this boy has a pretty pink negligee with the matching slippers hanging behind the door. I am extremely overwhelmed right now. My heart is beating, my stomach is tingling, and my body feels numb. "Chuck, what in the name of love ... ... is this for me?" I asked.

"Who else would it be for lil Mama? Baby you deserve so much more. I wish I could be your world, I wish I could take away your pain. I pray that your mom gets better so she can be both of our mothers. I wish that everything was not the way it is, but it is what it is. All we can do is pray, trust God and deal with it. Victoria, I promise you that you do not have to be scared, nor do you have to fear your Uncle. I don't know how many times I have to tell you and what I have to do to prove to you that I have your back. I love you so much Victoria Campbell soon to be Mrs. Matthews."

I am practically speechless. My heart wants to melt from the way that Chuck is smiling at me. I see sparkles in his eyes. I am feeling the way Brian McKnight does on his song that Chuck has playing. "Is this the way love goes." *Is this the way love goes for real? Is love supposed to feel this good?* I thought to myself. I am trying to find the right words to describe the way that I am feeling. The only thing I can think of is to say exactly what my heart is telling me to.

"Charles Matthews, I have not had a good life nor have you. I wish that your child hood was not the way that it was. *I often wish that I can take your past and turn it into scribbles of pencil on a sheet of paper just so I could rubber make myself to become your eraser.* I have watched love stories on television and I always imagined what it would feel like to be loved like that. I always thought this type of love was fiction, I never knew that it was real until I met you. You have allowed me to enter into your world and I am so thankful. We have traveled to several different states and even to another country and we're both under twenty. Chuck, I know there are a lot of adults in their thirties who have not experienced half of the things that you have shown me. So many people want the type of love that we have. I often wonder how **someone like me** – is getting the chance to experience it. What makes me so special? I never knew God existed before I met you. I know with the type of love that you continuously show me that there has to be a God. Today Bishop Morton said that the chill that I have been getting lately is God's Spirit being present. I get them when I am around you and when I think about you. You took me to Church, now look at this." I said as I opened my hands towards everything Chuck has done in this bathroom. "Chuck, I think I have cried more in these last couple of days then I cried in my entire life" I said as he wiped the tears from my eyes.

"It's all good Ma; Daddy got you. You don't have to cry ok. Don't let your water get cold. Go ahead and get in the tub baby. I know you're hungry. I have a little something for you when you're finished. I want you to sit back, relax, and let your man love you. I cut the water jets on so your body can be massaged. It usually helps me ease my mind and calm my thoughts."

I glanced at the large tub with steps. "Why is your tub so large?" I asked.

"Baby, that's not a regular tub. This is a Jacuzzi ma. Go ahead and relax, I'll be back to check on you." He said as he closed the door behind him.

Ooh I am enjoying this, lying in the tub with bubbles up to my neck. It's hot and it feels so damn good. I grabbed the remote and started this song from the beginning. I am enjoying the way our love is going. Chuck wants me to let him love me and I will. I feel you Brian. *I guess this is the way love goes*, I thought as I stretched my legs and took a sip of my Champagne. This is so relaxing.

"♪ Tempo slow♪ lights down low♪ let me take you to a place where only love grooves go♪ Yes, R. Kelly sing that song boo! Tempo slow baby, take me there boo, yessss."

"You want who to take you where?" Chuck asked as he entered the bathroom door. He must have over heard me singing.

"I said I want you to take me there boo" I replied smiling.

"Yeah that's what I thought you said. Now do me a favor and – ♪tell daddy what it is you want♪ "he began singing in my ear.

"You are so good to me" I said as I sat here enjoying him washing my back. It feels so good. This is my second glass of Moet. I wonder if Chuck thinks I'm an alcoholic. I don't drink often. I had my first drink yesterday, but every time I drink, I drink it like its water. I like the way this taste though. It's so smooth. It tastes as smooth as Chucks hands rubbing my back.

"Is that good baby?"

"Yes, thank you. What are you making? It smells good."

"You'll see. You're not allergic to anything right?"

"No, not as I know of." I replied.

"Ok good. See you in a few" he said as he walked out of the bathroom.

I'm trying so hard to clear my thoughts, but it's a little feeling that has me scared about what is going to happen tomorrow. I have to go to school. What if Stan is there, what will I do? You know what; I already said that I was going to let God handle it, so that's exactly what I am going to do. I can't do this alone, I already tried, and there I was again left helpless and defenseless. Chuck is going to be there with me anyway.

Let me stop tripping for real. *Relax Victoria, just relax boo,* I thought to myself.

Ooh, this water feels so good. I feel even better especially since this bottle of Moet is darn near empty. I can't help it, it shouldn't taste this good. Uh oh, it is definitely time for me to get out of here. My skin is beginning to look wrinkled and I can't have that. It's nice to know that a person is clean, but having wrinkles as proof is not a good look. Now that I've finished cleansing my body from head to toe, it's time for me to dry off.

Hmm I wonder where Chuck keeps his cleaning supplies. Oh here they are. I hope you can clean a Jacuzzi the same way you clean a tub because I don't want to mess up anything. Ok I am not use to rose pedals besides my own and they're not recyclable so I assume these are not as well. Well I am done cleaning this bathroom. I am a little tipsy here. Oh my goodness. Did I just stagger? *Ok Victoria, you better pull it together.* Why did I just drink this entire bottle like this? I hope Chuck doesn't notice. He would probably be disappointed if he notices his fiancé just drank an entire bottle of champagne in less than an hour. I'm just going to tell him it tasted like apple juice. Yeah that's sounds good. No Victoria, you sound like a drunk. Ok, I'm tripping now. Am I talking to myself? I'll just put on this pretty pink night gown my baby brought me and get it together. I got this. Yeah, I got this.

Oh now Chuck is really outdoing himself because this negligee is a perfect fit as well as my slippers. I am up on all of the latest designers, but I'm not familiar with this I.D.Sarrieri. $340, are you serious! I shouted quietly. I am assuming he left this price tag on to really convince me that he is going to take care of me. *Ok, well that is what's up Mr. Matthews,* I thought to myself. Oh my goodness, he is so thoughtful. He brought me more Victoria Secret Love Spell; he says he loves it on me so hey-let me make sure I put some over my entire body. Damn! I look good! If I wasn't me, I would be totally jealous and definitely the first one in line for a hater application. Ok, let me stop because I am not conceited, *but this mirror cannot tell a lie,* I thought as I walked out the bathroom.

My stomach is growling. *Ooh I wonder what he is cooking because it smells so good,* I thought as I walked towards the kitchen. This man is a trip. What is up with him? *God, did you send this man to me?* I mean one thing after another. He has to be a blessing. *If this is the type of Love that you show God, I never want to leave you.* I am just to out done. I am marrying Chuck right now; at least I want to because he is spoiling me rotten.

This kitchen looks like a 5-star restaurant. Chuck has the table decorated with a white table cloth with a big candle in the middle of a bowl of water that has rose pedals floating around in it, in the center of the table. These lobsters are huge. I know he loves me because I told him that I loved seafood when we first started dating in the ninth grade and he still remembers. *I cannot wait to taste this shrimp alfredo*, I thought as I stood here viewing this beautiful feast.

"Have a seat lil Mama" Chuck insisted as he pulled my seat out. ♪Whatever you want♪ girl you know- I –can- provide♪ whatever you need- girl♪" Chuck began singing the words to Tony, Toni, Tone that's playing in his MP3 player connected to the counter. "What would you like to drink? I have orange, red, grape, and Pepsi." He asked.

"I'll have orange please."

"Orange juice or Orange Faygo"

"Orange Faygo please.

He brought our drinks and sat them on the table before he took his seat.

"Baby, you are too much." I said while trying to keep my composure and not shed anymore tears because I might become dehydrated.

"Well Victoria, I figure if I spoil you here, you don't have to look for it anywhere else and if you were to ever leave me, at least you would know what a woman is supposed to be treated like."

"Leaving you is out of the question! I know that is something that will never happen. Now my feelings are hurt."

"Trust me, that's not my intentions. I know that people change, I just told you how I feel. I want you to know that you are a Queen and you do not have to settle for anything less than what you receive from me."

"Leave you? You must be kidding me." I said as I leaned over the table and kissed him. "I'm starving, I haven't eaten since breakfast. I'm ready to dig in. Now don't laugh at me boo, but I am not used to eating Lobsters. They do look good though. I find them difficult to open so I don't eat them very often. How long have you been cooking Lobsters in the comfort of your own home?" I chuckled.

"Actually this is my first time cooking them. I have been watching this guy on T.V One. I think his name is G. Garvin. That brother can cook. I started watching his show learning some new recipes. Every day, I am trying to learn new things to make you happy." He grabbed my hands after he reached for the remote and silenced the music. "Dear God, we thank you for this food we are about to receive for the health and nourishing strength in our body's in Jesus name, we pray, Amen."

"Amen." I started with the alfredo. Oh my goodness this is awesome. I mean absolutely delicious. "Who taught you how to cook?" I asked.

"Besides the cooking shows, I have to give credit to Justine and my Aunt".

"Do you have something I can crack this big juicy looking lobster open with."

"Here, that's what this is for" he said as he handed me the lobster opener. "Here. Now squeeze it" he insisted. "Here, now use your butter to either dip it in or pour it over and enjoy."

I followed his instructions and did exactly that, I enjoyed myself. "Thank you Chuck. Everything was delicious."

He stood up and replied "That's not it."

"What? You have something else? I cannot eat another bite because I am stuffed."

"Come on baby, you can eat this, hold on." He replied as he went to the refrigerator.

He walked back over with the most perfect looking cheese cake I have ever seen in real life. As he sliced me a piece and put it on a saucer I knew I had to try a piece. It looks irresistible. I took my fork and broke off a piece. "Ooh yes, this is delicious. Boy what are you doing to me?" I asked.

"Thanks Ma, I try." He replied.

I sat here thinking of the way that Chuck and I live and the way he treats me, it sort of reminds of a movie Toy and I were watching. She said that she was going to make sure that we experienced the "*ghetto fabulous*" lifestyle one day. Now that I am thinking about it, there is absolutely nothing about this that's ghetto. It's simply fabulous and amazing. "Baby, I'll do the dishes."

"No you will not. Victoria, please relax. Let me do what I do ok. I'm the man, you don't need to do all that. Don't worry when you have our kids you will have a lot of time to help out." He said as he walked from the table smiling.

Kids huh? That would be nice one of these days, I thought as I sat here staring at the definition of a real man. "So tell me something, did you just happen to have all of this prepared?" I asked.

"Yes, I had this set up earlier. That's the reason I kept calling Toy telling her to tell you to get in contact with me. I prayed that if you were meant to be in my life for God to let it be revealed. I had the faith that you were that's why I went ahead and started cooking. I went out today after I dropped you off at Toya's and picked up your things. When you called me and told me to come and pick you up; I knew God heard my prayer."

There go those darn butterflies tickling my stomach again. "Baby let me do something please. Do you want me to get out any pajamas or anything for you? Can I run you some water in the Jacuzzi? Please what can I do to show you my gratitude" I asked.

"You really want to do something huh?" Chuck asked.

"Yes, I do"

"This is what I want you to do. I want you to continue loving me the way that you do. I need you to get to know God and love Him with all of your heart. What I want you to do most is love yourself. When you do all of those then you can have faith and stand up for what is right. You can be honest with me, but most importantly be honest with yourself. God already knows, so of course you can't be dishonest with him. That's all I want you to do. I'm going to take a quick shower once I finish this kitchen. Just go in the room and relax. You have had a long and rough day. Just this one time, enjoy yourself please." Chuck begged.

I followed his instructions. I am simply going to enjoy myself. I bet he is going to want to make love to me tonight. I feel sexy, I look sexy and I feel extremely confident. The feeling of being safe and protected is heavily upon me. I guess all I have to do is love God unconditionally. All the signs that Chuck is indicating to me is giving me a little courage.

I think I'm going to tell him tonight. I better wait. If I tell him about what Stan has been doing to me I know he will not be happy. *'God how about I just let you handle this fight huh? You have been working it out thus far. I'll leave it with you. Amen.'* I prayed silently.

This man is so sexy. *Why does he have clothes on that body*, I thought to myself. He has on his pajama pants and t-shirt. He must want me to work for it. Ok I'm ready to pull those clothes right off. "Come here baby" I requested as I began kissing on his neck.

"Victoria, now that you are living here with me we can't be intimate like that. I'm serious lil Mama" he said while pulling me back up from my knees.

I feel embarrassed right now. He's turning me down. I don't understand the meaning of this. *I know you want me*, I thought as I'm staring at him with this enticing look. *I can't believe this, he is really serious.* "Chuck, I don't understand. You don't find me attractive right now. What is it? I want to show you my love." I insisted.

"Baby girl, lying in the bed does not show me love. It helps believe me" he said with a Chuckle. "But seriously, I don't need to enter inside of you through there" he said as he pointed to my secret garden. "I want to enter inside of here and here and I want you to let God inside of here and here also" he said as he pointed to my heart and my head. "We have already explored each other's bodies. Let's do something different and explore each other mentally and spiritually. I want to make sure that my wife knows me inside and out as well as I want to know my wife. I told you once before that when someone really loves you; it doesn't mean that they have to penetrate you. Something could happen to either one of us that would prevent us from making love to each other physically God forbid, but I want to make sure that we have enough love to replace the physical affection that we have for one another. I already told you what you can do to satisfy me. Get to know God Victoria. That's what I really want you to do. Don't worry about him getting to know you because he already does."

This man really loves me. I know God is in the midst because I feel His Spirit. These chills that are flowing rapidly through my body have removed my entire thought of being embarrassed. Chuck's right. I knew that the love Stan said he had for me and the way he displayed it was strange and abnormal. I hate that type of love and at one point Stan made me despise love, but thanks to this man standing before me- I love, love and now I feel worthy of being loved. "Charles Matthews, all I can say is I love you. I thank you and I know in my heart that God is proud of you because I know I am."

"Yeah, well I hope so. I hope He understands that I am trying my best to be right and do right by Him. I still need to change my occupation, but all I can do is take it one day at a time." He replied as he snuggled under the covers next to me.

"That's all that all of us can do is take it one day at a time. Where is your alarm clock?" I asked.

"It's over there on the night stand" he pointed behind me.

"What should I set it for; I usually set mine for 6:15?"

"6:30 should be good." He replied.

"Chuck, I am so proud of you for hanging in there. Can you believe it; we are graduating in less than three months?"

"Yeah time has flown by. You know I am actually proud of myself too, and you already know that I'm proud of you" he replied.

"Chuck, can you take me to the hospital to see my Mama when we get out of school?"

"Of course I can baby. Matter of fact you didn't tell me the whole story about that. What happened?"

"When you dropped me off earlier, my Uncle was at Toy's house. He told me that my mom was shot three times by a drug dealer who she was stealing from. Chuck, when I saw my mom lying in that hospital bed, I felt like someone took a knife and stabbed me in my heart. Mama was looking so bad today. Like you said God can do anything, so I know he can fix my Mama. My little sister Jasmine was there. She's so pretty and she has gotten so grown even though she's only 15 she is very mature. You know her little tale say she has a boyfriend now and he spoils her rotten the way you spoil me?"

"That should mean that she is taken care of right? You never know who God might use to make sure that his children are taken care of."

"Yes, I suppose. She said she has been praying for God to protect us from the demons that prey on our family so we can get back together."

"I hear that baby sis, that's what's up."

"Chuck, can I ask you a question?"

"Sure, you know you can" he replied.

"Why does it seem that everything that seems so good, feels so good and what we want the most is considered to be bad for us or there is a rule behind it?"

"Baby girl, I don't know the exact answer. What I do know is God forgives us for our sins when we ask Him. We just have to try and stop making the same mistakes over and over again and at the same time having rules for living is simplistic with natural divine order. We need order in our lives so that we may disregard creating unnecessary chaos.

"Well baby, making love to you feels so good to me. My body feels good and I feel somewhat relieved. Now are you telling me that we have to stop?" I asked.

"Right now the answer is yes, but once we are married you can have daddy all you want." He smiled while turning his back to me. "We will be just fine, Victoria. Now go to sleep baby."

"Ok, goodnight Charles"

"Goodnight babe."

Chapter 17

"How many of you know that God is in the Blessing business? I know because Steve Harvey has a radio show, Steve Harvey has a radio show, Steve Harvey has a radio show!"

"What in the world!" I shouted.

"Oh baby, that's my alarm. I leave it on the radio for the alarm instead of that annoying buzz. I love his show. That's why I set my alarm to 92.3 in the mornings. He's real inspirational and funny. Sorry if it scared you. You can turn it down if you want. Wake me up in fifteen minutes. I know you women take a long time. It only takes me thirty minutes if that" Chuck said as he buried his head under the pillow.

"Well good morning to you to, Chuck and Mr. Harvey!" I replied as I walked into the bathroom. *I guess I forgot to tell you that I am a cranky person when I wake up in the morning. Sorry if I snapped,* I thought to myself being sarcastic of course. I brushed my teeth and washed my face now let me find something to wear. It's supposed to be hot again today. This Michigan weather is a trip. It was summer all weekend and now it feels like winter again this morning. It's supposed to reach the low 80's today, but I better where me some jeans. I already swam yesterday like an idiot. I hate being sick. Ok I have my notebooks, my pens, and everything in my book bag. Cool, I want to make sure that I have everything I need.

I have a meeting with my counselor to discuss which college I should go to. If Chuck gets accepted to Wayne State University, I think I am going to attend it with him. Oh my goodness, its 7:15 already. "Charles baby, wake up. Time for school! Baby wake up! It's 7:15 already. Let's Go. Move it! Move it! Move it!" I shouted as if I am a drill sergeant in the army.

"Good Morning baby, you look nice."

"Thank you. You know I try" I replied with a smile. I decided to wear red today. I have on my red Dereon blouse, my red and blue Dereon Jeans and my blue jean slide in flats, with my blue jean purse. I have on my Jennifer Lopez 'Still' perfume which is one of my favorites. I have so many different perfumes. I only brought five of them with me though. I feel like having my hair pinned up today, so I threw in my red clip. I must admit I look sexy in this red, but I better slow it down though because I almost look like a glass of Kool-aide. I have actually lost a bit of weight because I'm squeezing back into my size twelve's.

Chuck's looking good, I thought as he walked out the bathroom. He has on a black, blue, green and grey button up Roca wear shirt, his Black Roca wear jeans with his black air force one's with the dark blue swoosh. His neck and wrist look like it's on froze. My baby knows he can dress. His waves are banging and he smells extra good. "What's that you're wearing because it smells great?" I asked.

"This is Unforgivable by Sean Jean. So you like it huh?

"Yes sir. I love it on you. I love you period" I replied. I know we have to be meant for each other because we look good separately and together. It feels different with us both waking up and going to school together from his house, but it's not a bad feeling. The only bad feeling I am having is the fact that I might run into Stan today and I really don't want to.

We're finally pulling up in the school parking lot. My heart is beating extremely fast, but I'm with Chuck so I know I will be fine. People are staring at me and Chuck as if we're high school celebrities. Chuck's actions are a lot similar to mine especially when the guys walk up to him shaking his hand and speaking to him. He looks like he does not want to be bothered. *Would they give us a break, we just pulled up,* I thought to myself. I must admit, Chuck and I are the most popular people at this high school and we're pretty well known at some of the other high schools around Detroit because people talk. Everybody wants to be friends with us.

"Hey Victoria, I like your outfit. You look so nice. How was your weekend?" A few females I had spoken with before are basically bombarding me with all these questions and compliments.

"Hey" I replied with the look of not being in the mood.

"Ok see you in class" they replied obviously receiving the message.

I have very few words for these females especially since Toy graduated. I don't trust females like that because nine times out of ten, they either want what you have or their trying to get it. I trust Chuck because I know he loves me. Beside these tack heads simply don't have a thing on me. That would be more like substituting prime rib for a slice of bologna and my baby doesn't eat pork.

Prom is coming up in a few weeks. I told Stan about the Vera Wang dress I wanted. I was supposed to be getting it sometime this week, *but I guess that's not going to happen,* I thought as Chuck and I are walking past the prom posters hanging up on the walls.

"Baby, are we going to the prom?" I asked.

"I wasn't planning on it. Why, do you want to go?"

"I did." I replied feeling a bit discouraged.

"Actually, I had something else planned for us, but we can go if you want to."

"No, that's ok."

"No- we can go because you want to go. I sort of want to go too, because I want to show you off."

"Well ... ... since you want to go." I smiled in excitement.

Chuck and I hugged and gave each other kisses before we split up. We have different first hours. Actually all of our classes are different. Lunch is the only hour that we have had together for four consecutive years.

As I attempted to take my seat, I heard a voice coming through the P.A System, "Good Morning Students. Would Victoria Campbell, please report to the main office? Victoria Campbell, please report to the main office." She requested.

I have no idea why they could be calling me unless Stan is up here. If he is, I am not going in there. "Ms. Campbell they're calling you" my teacher said once she noticed that I had not budged.

Ok, this is not a good look, I thought once I arrived. There are two police officers standing in the office. That's unusual. I'm feeling a lot of negative tension especially because people are whispering and staring at me. *I'm not going in there.* I ran back around the hallway towards the cafeteria. "Chuck, please meet me by the girls bathroom in the back by the lunch room" I chirped.

"Ok, I'm on my way." He replied.

I chirped back, "Hurry!"

Once I reached the girl restroom near the cafeteria I noticed Chuck running towards me. "Baby what's up? I heard them call your name."

"Yeah they did and when I went to the office I saw two cops standing there. Chuck, please, I'm scared. I didn't do anything. Please help me. I don't know what to do. Oh God, please I don't want to go to jail. I know my Uncle Stan got something to do with this." I cried.

Chuck had an angry look on his face as he replied, "He probably does. I think he has a metal problem baby."

"I do too." I agreed while pacing back and forth.

"We can run out the side door and go back to the house." Chuck suggested.

"No baby, I don't want you to get in trouble. Please baby, If they are about to take me to jail get me out, but only through Toya because I don't want him to know who you are. Please baby, I love you."

He kissed me and replied, "I love you to."

"Ok, I am going to see what they want." I walked in the office. "Yes?" I said trembling.

"Are you Victoria Campbell?" one of the officers asked.

"Yes I am."

"Please come with us."

"What did I do?" I asked with a tear falling from my eye.

"We will explain it to you on the way to the station." The bald black cop replied.

They parked directly in front of the school door. *This is so embarrassing*, I thought to myself as I got in their squad car. Due to the fact that they didn't put handcuffs on me or anything, I figure Stan must have something to do with this. I sat in the back seat with my arms folded as they began driving off.

"Now officers, please tell me what did I do?" I begged.

The white cop who's sitting on the passenger side turned towards me and said, "You were reported missing, and even though you're eighteen because you're still in high school, Mr. Campbell still considers you a minor. Therefore, when your Uncle called and advised us to pick you up, we had to follow orders."

I leaned up in between the two cops on the arm rest. "Wait, you don't understand. The story is deeper than it is told." I explained.

The bald cop who's driving glanced back at me with a smile and said, "Yeah, well, you'll be ok."

They merged onto I-94 heading eastbound on the freeway. I sat back with my arms folded trying to figure out what is going on. I *know that Stan can't really be sending me to jail*, I pouted. I noticed that they were exiting the freeway. They came up on the "Gratiot" exit. Tears began to fall from my eyes because we are headed towards the ninth precinct. *I can't believe he's sending me to jail.*

I stared out the window and noticed that we are driving past the police station. *I wonder where we're going*, I thought as we pulled in a parking lot of what appears to be some type of warehouse. I'm beginning to notice there are hundreds of black Crown Victoria's with blue and red police lights in the back of the cars with tinted windows. *What the hell*, I thought once I noticed Stan walking towards the car.

"Thanks boys, y'all still coming to my party right?" he asked.

"You know it" both cops replied.

Stan opened the door and grabbed my hand. "Come on here girl!" He said as if I am a little kid. I got out the car and walked with him. He looked back at the cops and said, "Ok thanks boys, I don't know what has got into these kids today."

"Yeah these kids today are getting out of hand. We'll see ya later" one of them responded.

"Get in" he commanded once we approached his car. He has not given me any eye contact at all since he's been driving. *Too late*, I thought as he cleared his throat. "So how are you?" he asked.

I know he is being sarcastic. "I'm fine. Stan, what are you up to?" I asked as I sat here with my arms folded.

"Oh, nothing. I just wanted to see you since you called your self-running away last night." He replied.

"Why did you have them embarrass me like that, picking me up from school like that in front of everybody?" I asked.

Stan sat back in his seat and glanced over at me with a slight grin. "Oh that's nothing. If you ever try anymore slick stuff like that again, you will be dead and that is my word. I don't know why you insist on trying me, I really don't."

"Slick stuff! What the heck are you talking about? Stan, you were the one sniffing dope up your nose not me!"

"Yeah, well I went by Toya's house last night and you weren't there. So I was wondering where you trying to run away or something. What is it that you were trying to do? Is that your way of hurting me, spending the night at some nigga house? I promise you when I find that guy Chuck, that's his name right? Yeah that's his name, Mr. Chuck. He thinks he can still my woman away from me. I'm going to kill him."

"You're not going to do anything to him. I don't care about hurting you Stan. You sure don't care about hurting me. I'm straight for real! I am most definitely straight now that you're sniffing dope! I don't have to listen to anything you say. So if you don't mind can you please pull over and let me out of your little funky Benz! So you hot shot now; get money! Yeah you deserve it I suppose, but then what is it that you really do besides beat, molest and rape your niece and kill people at work every day? Let me out of this car or I will jump out while you are driving!" I screamed.

He looked at me with the most evil look though he was smiling and asked, "Are you done now?"

I sat up and replied, "Yeah, pull over and let me out! I appreciate everything that you have done for me, but I'm done. I will be going to college to better my life. I don't need to be caught up in this twisted affair with you. I love myself to much to continue allowing you to force yourself on me. Everybody thinks you are my Uncle, though you are my Uncle since your mom adopted my mom. So please spare me all the bull and let me out or drop me off at school please. I mean you really are tripping. You want me to be your woman, but that's not going to happen. The courts gave you custody of me so that you would take care of me, not make me your woman and your sex toy. I know it's got to be more women available. Just leave me alone! I can move out of your house, I don't need to be there. Especially, not with no damn crack head! FBI, FBI my ass. Y'all some crooked cops. Instead of y'all protecting people from criminals, y'all are the criminals. But you know what; I can't say all of y'all because the only crooked one I know right now is you; a beast that finds pleasure in molesting your own niece, a little girl who could not fight back. You are a sick pervert. I hate you Stan!! Pull this freaking car over and let me out, right now. Pull over!" I yelled.

All of a sudden he sped up. I looked at the speedometer and it read 97mphs. "Please! Are you going to kill us both? Slow down!" I begged.

He kept sniffling and fondling with his nose. "Oh, hell no! Are you high? You damn crack head! Stan, slow down!" In my head I began praying. *Dear God please if you hear me Lord, please make a way for me out of this no way situation Lord. I don't know what to do. No weapon that is formed against me shall prosper. Lord, please!"*

Wow, God you heard me instantly this time. The car is slowing down.

"Aint this bout a bitch! I done ran out of gas! Shit!" Stan yelled while beating on his steering wheel. We slowed up and pulled on the side of the freeway.

"How in the hell are you driving a brand new Benz and you let it run out of gas? You got to be the dumbest individual I know. You're an ignorant bastard. Who gave you the test to be an FBI anyway? Whoever did they're just as dumb as you. You are a stupid crack head! That crack aint no joke is it? I thought you heard that crack is wack, you wack as hell Stan. You stupid dummy."

I continued going on and on, but for some apparent reason Stan has not responded. He continued searching his pockets and under the car seats.

"Damn! I done left my cell phone at the house! Shit, this day couldn't get any worse. Stay in this car and I will be back. Don't worry, all that little shit you were talking, I'm going to handle it as soon as we get home. I have to walk up the ramp so I can get some gas and then I need to get to a phone. Stay put" He yelled while getting out the car.

"Ok hurry up boo, I don't want to be out here by myself." I said, lying to him so he would think that I would still be here.

I waited until he got closer to the exit ramp then I chirped Chuck immediately. "Baby, please come get me. Please! I think he is going to hurt me. He ran out of gas. We are on 94, right before the Connors exit westbound.

"Baby I am on my way right now." Chucked chirped in.

"We're on the freeway right now. Hurry; he just walked up the ramp to go get gas."

I could tell in Chuck's voice that he was running. "Ok baby I'm getting in my car. I've been outside waiting to hear from you. Hold on, I will be right there."

"Ok, please hurry." I sat here looking around waiting on Chuck to arrive. I started thinking about how I was just cursing Stan out. I am so stupid. What if he would of beat my head in. I should have kept my mouth closed. *Thank you God, you heard me finally.*

Wow that was fast, I thought as I noticed Chuck pulling behind me in the side view mirror. He stuck his head out the driver's side and waved his hand notifying me to come on. I don't know how fast he had to drive, but my baby got here quick. *"Thank you Jesus! Thank you God, you heard my cry."* I said as I jumped out the car. I took Stan's keys and locked the doors so he wouldn't be able to get in. I ran to the car and hugged Chuck with tears in my eyes. He put the car in gear and burnt rubber out into traffic.

"Thank you, baby. Stan was high. He said I had no business running away. The cops took me and dropped me off at Stan's car."

"What? Oh they're tripping! We're going back up to the school so you can talk to the counselor."

"No baby, he's going to come up there." I wined.

"What does that mean? I told you that I have your back! Nothing is going to stop us from graduating, and getting in these colleges. Pray baby and have faith in GOD. Didn't he make away for you a few minutes ago, don't doubt him now."

I sat back in the seat and said, "Ok, you're right."

Chapter 18

We are back at the school now. Chuck walked with me up stairs to my counselor's office. I walked up to the female at the front desk. "Hello, I'm here to see Mrs. Thomas."

"Do you have an appointment?" she asked with funk in her attitude.

"Yes I do." I replied.

"Ok, sign in and I will let her know that you are here."

Chuck grabbed me by the waist and whispered in my ear, "Baby you think I should see one too so I can check on the status of my application to Wayne State?"

"I don't think so. I think you will have to wait until you get a letter back from the University." I whispered back.

Chuck and I sat down. We sat here thinking, at least I am. The girl behind the desk walked back over to the counter smiling at Chuck.

"May I help you sir" she asked.

Without a thought, I said "no we're good, thank you."

She smiled "Oh I'm sorry, are you two together?"

"Yes," Chuck replied.

She continued smiling at him as she walked away. I have too much on my mind to get up and smack the shit out of her disrespectful ass for trying to be funny. I stayed in my Diva Shoes though, because I'm bout ready to kick them off and kick off in her ass, but she's not worth it. I have too much on my mind already. I sat here wondering what's next. I wonder what Stan's reaction will be, seeing as how I took his keys.

I was hoping by taking his keys that I would buy some time if he stays on the freeway with his car because it is a brand new Mercedes. Stan's high on that dope, I know he is. When he sees me again, I'm not exactly sure what's going to happen. Chuck stared at me shaking my legs as the tears rolled down my caramel cheeks. He wiped my tears.

"Victoria, we prayed right?"

"Yes." I replied.

"Well, if you know that we prayed, why are you worrying? If you are going to worry why even bother praying?" Chuck questioned.

I didn't understand it at first, but now it's beginning to make a great deal of sense to me. That's the whole concept of having faith. Believing and knowing that everything is going to be alright because God said it, is what I have to understand.

I glanced at Chuck as I feel Gods Spirit through these chills I am receiving. I feel so much better now. He makes me feel so secure. I don't know what I would do if I didn't have him in my life. I smiled and replied, "I understand now baby, thank you."

Mrs. Thomas walked out smiling as usual. "Ms. Campbell, how are you?" she asked.

I smiled and looked at Chuck and then looked at her, "I'm fine now.

"Great, come on back."

I looked at Chuck and in a read my lips type of way I said, "I'll be back." I read his lips and he said "I love you." I smiled and walked back with Mrs. Thomas to her office.

She opened her hands and pointed to her Italian leather chairs. "Please have a seat." She requested.

I sat down and looked up on the shelf. I read her awards and her degrees. "Mrs. Thomas, I notice your Masters of Social Work degree. I didn't know that you're a social worker?"

"Yes I have been a social worker for over ten years, but I am also certified to be a counselor and that's what I choose to do. I want to make sure young people like your self gets into college and follow up on your education. Before you leave my office today I want to make sure that you have chosen the best possible college as well as have a clear understanding of your future career endeavors. It is very important that you being a young African American have an education. You need a degree for just about anything you decide to do that's worth doing as well as a career that will provide you with your normal living standards especially now that Affirmative Action has been banned from Michigan. Before I go any further Ms. Campbell, are you familiar with the meaning of Affirmative Action?"

I sat here looking and feeling completely clueless. "No Mrs. Thomas, I'm not familiar with it." I replied.

"Victoria, Affirmative Action is a policy that was intended to provide minorities with increased social, economic, and educational opportunities. In other words, this policy was designed to redress past discrimination against women and minority groups through measures to improve their economic and educational opportunities. I guess you can say it's a way that the government gives us a hand, by making sure that minorities such as African Americans, Hispanics, and many others as a race and females as a gender to get in the schools that we want as well as be considered for different jobs that we apply for. Now that many people voted against it, it's a possibility that we as minorities may not receive fair treatment. We have a double minority standard Victoria. That's because we are black and we are women. So we have to work extra hard to prove that we deserve something more than anyone else. Though I try not to get too far in the political arena because I know that whatever God has for me, it is for me. Nobody can take that. So have you signed up for your SAT's?

"Yes, I am scheduled to take them next week. If there is some way that I am unable to take them here at the school, is it possible to schedule them elsewhere?"

"Yes, we can accommodate that for you, but you have to let me know where you want to take them. The only other site I see that is available for testing on that day is Oakland Community College."

"Good. I will take it there because I am moving in that area." I replied.

"Ok Ms. Campbell. As I am reviewing your transcripts I recognize that your grades are excellent. You have an overall of a 3.87. That's great. Good Job Victoria. Your GPA has allowed you to become available to apply for several scholarships. Tell me what do you want to be?"

"Actually, I was considering becoming a Psychologist, but my passion is focused towards being a Writer. I want to write books of inspiration and express realness in them. I don't want people to be offended or anything. I simply want them to be entertained and inspired. I love Maya Angelou she is one of the best Poets and Authors of all time. I want to receive awards and honors for my books and most importantly I want everyone who reads them to be inspired." I replied.

"Victoria, that is so wonderful. I am sure you are going to do excellent. I can tell that you really want to do that because of the passion in your voice when you speak about it. You can do anything and everything as long as you put your mind to it. So if writing is what you want to do, it's nothing wrong with going into journalism or perhaps majoring in English. Right now we want to focus on getting you in and going in with a plan. So if you really want to write go in writing for the school paper, write articles, short stories, whatever you want you can do it Victoria. Are you considering out of state or in state?"

"Mrs. Thomas, to be honest I want out of state, but I'm supposed to be getting married and my fiancé is planning to go to Wayne State so I am not sure. I guess a little of both. I wouldn't mind applying to Wayne State University, University of Detroit, Georgetown University, and Alabama State."

"Oh, ok, seems like you have done a little bit of research."

"Yes ma'am I did. I just looked up Universities on line and looked at a few classes from time to time."

"That's excellent Victoria. I have all of those applications. Can I also interest you in an opportunity for the both of you? We have Spellman for females and right across campus is Morehouse for Males, that way you guys would still be near each other just in separate schools. Plus, you will be able to focus more on your education. My husband and I took that route. We got married at a young age also. It's just a suggestion."

"Ok, that's sounds real good. Please, may I have them also?"

I wasn't thinking for that purpose, but for the fact that since I won't be able to go to classes with him he won't have any females in his face not that I don't trust him, but I just know how females are cut.

"Here are the applications. These are the self-addressed envelopes the addresses are already on them. All you have to do is purchase and apply the stamps."

"Thank you Mrs. Thomas, I really appreciate your help and your time. I will fill these out as soon as I get home."

"Thanks for stopping in Ms. Campbell. I am looking forward to purchasing one of your books and Victoria just so you know- God said everything is going to be alright precious."

I smiled at her and replied, "Thanks."

As I left the office I said "Thank you Jesus. Thank you, God." I see Chuck sitting there reading a magazine. "Come on baby lets go." He looked at me and glanced at the applications that I had in my hands.

"You must have picked up every application they had?"

"I tried. Oh, she also gave me an application for us to go to colleges out of state."

"Wait, let me guess, Moore House and Spellman?"

"How did you know?"

"Because, I know you don't want your man around females and I damn sure don't want men around you."

I kissed him as we walked out. "Do you want to leave or do you want to stay here?" Chuck asked.

"I want to leave. Can we go to the hospital to see my mom?" I asked.

"Sure." He replied.

It's almost past our lunch hour. I have been in Mrs. Thomas's office almost forty five minutes, though every minute was so worth it. We got in the car and pulled off. "Baby ride past and see if my Uncle is still on the freeway." I asked as I began rolling up the windows so that he wouldn't see me through the tint on these windows. We rode past and he was standing there with Stephanie.

"Chuck, that's ole girl who was at the house that was doing the powder with him." Chuck leaned back in his seat and looked through his rearview.

"Oh yeah?" He replied as if he wasn't interested.

I looked back as we passed and I noticed him messing with his nose. I turned back around. I wonder how long he has been doing this. How did he manage to keep it from me and was he sniffing that time when I first told him about Chuck? He had to be.

"Are you ok?" Chuck asked.

"Yes, I'm fine I was just wondering how long my uncle has been using those drugs" I replied.

"He has probably been using them for a long time because when they're on heroine they are always trying to maintain their cool without people knowing. Just like a lot of the big celebrities some of them do it just for fun, like an activity. At least, that's what I have read in a few magazines."

"You're probably right.

"Baby, everything is going to be ok." Chuck ensured.

"Yeah, I know."

He turned the radio on. Here's Yolanda Adams again. ♪no matter what♪ no matter what you're going through♪ God needs to prove to your enemies- that he is God♪ so what you got to do is♪ hold on♪ Don't give up♪ Don't give in♪ Step out on faith ♪

I sat here crying because God's trying to tell me through so many people, now he's using the radio to do it. I heard this same song yesterday when I was on my way to the hospital. I know it's going to be ok. I let my seat back and stretched out, looking up in the sky since Chuck let the top down. *Ok God, I am not going to give up. I hear you, I hear you,* I thought as His Spirit seems to caress me.

Chapter 19

We just pulled up to the hospital. We walked in and went to the receptionist desk.

"Hello, I am here to see Tamara Campbell. Is she still in room 745 ICU?" The receptionist looked on her computer and then she looked at me and replied, "No ma'am, she has been moved to the first floor."

"Can I see her?" I asked.

"What is your relationship to the patient?"

"I am her daughter Victoria Campbell."

"And sir you are" she asked while looking at Chuck.

"It's ok, Ma'am, This is my fiancé." I responded.

"Ok sign in here." She directed as she looked down the hall. "Excuse me, Nurse Betty could you please show Ms. Campbell and her fiancé to Ms. Campbell's room. She is your patient right?" the receptionist asked.

"Yes, she is." The nurse responded as she looked at me. "Ok, follow me this way. I just finished giving her a bath. I think that your mom is really brave. The doctor said that **she died last night**. Her heart stopped and she was no longer breathing. He said that he left the room and when he returned an older lady was leaving her room. But that's not the strange part, what was strange is your mom was alive when he went back in the room and she was also breathing well. The Doctor brought her down to the first floor so that she could be under 24 hour surveillance."

We followed her into the room where my mom is. I can't understand that. What do they mean she died last night? That doesn't make any since to me. Chuck and I looked at each other and twisted our faces as if we both thought that the nurse was lying and Ku-Ku for Co-Coa Puffs. We walked in the room and noticed that they had her strapped down.

"What's going on? Why is she tied down like this?" I asked.

"Ma'am, your mother has been trying to leave and she's also been refusing treatment. Your mother is going through a heroine and a crack cocaine withdrawal. We have given her something to calm her down. She will be fine."

"What about the X-rays and her liver test results?"

"Well as it relates to the gun shot wombs, it's good that the one in her leg was a flesh womb, and the one in her arm hit her bone just a little, but the Doctor removed it this morning."

"But I though yesterday you guys said that they were both flesh wombs?"

"I'm not sure who you spoke with yesterday, but I think they may have given you a roundabout opinion. They had to wait until the X-Rays returned. When the X-rays returned, they revealed that there was a bullet located right above her shoulder. The doctors removed it this morning and she's ok now, but your mom has to leave those drugs alone. It's not good for her and it is going to fail her health tremendously. She gave us quite a scare last night. Many tests were done to try and understand what happened, but we still can't make any sense of it. The only thing that was determined was that the drugs have done some damage to her liver, but the Doctor has treated it with medication. It is not to the point where she will need a liver transplant at least not yet of course. She will definitely need to quit those drugs immediately"

I looked at my mom. She's looking a little better than yesterday, but it's still hard for me to see her this way. Especially since the last time I saw her, she was so pretty. I walked over to her.

"Mom can you hear me? It's me, Victoria, your daughter."

"She can hear you," the nurse interrupted, "but it will be very difficult for her to respond. She has been highly sedated. We want to keep her blood pressure down, so if you will, try not to excite her too much ok. I will leave you all alone for a moment, but I'll be back shortly because Ms. Campbell needs to rest." Nurse Betty stated as she exited the room. I walked on the side of the bed and grabbed Mama's hand.

"Mom it's me, Victoria. I want you to get better and leave those drugs alone. I need you mommy. I need you now more than ever. Uncle Stan has been tripping lately. I mean he is really tripping Mama. I have been sane because of Charles Mama, that's my fiancé. He has introduced me to God, and God has been protecting me. God is going to protect you too. I need you to stop using those drugs. I don't want you dead Mama. I want and need you to make it to my graduation. I am graduating this year and I am going to college. I know you have to be proud of me Mama. I did this for you. I knew that when you saw me again I wanted you to be proud of me so you won't leave me again. Mom, these silly nurses say that you died last night. We all know that people don't die and come back" I laughed. "No but seriously Mama we need you. I know you seen Jasmine, she doing good Mama, she's doing so well. Please mommy you can fight this. Those drugs are not your friends. I want to talk to you about something, but I can't tell you until you get all better. Can you do this for me, Jasmine and yourself? We love you mom, for real we do. I don't care about your past. I know that mothers are not perfect. I forgive you and I understand that you did the best that you could do. It's ok. God can help us past all of that. My main concern is that you get well. God can let you live, only if you want to Mama. I know you want to. I want you to, Jasmine wants you to, and even my fiancé wants you to. I love you Mama and I never stopped."

"I'm sorry, but you need to wrap it up here. Your mom needs to sleep. You can come back at three, five, or seven since you are family." Nurse Betty said. I looked at her through the tears falling from my eyes and said "Ok, Thank you" as she walked back out of the room.

I looked back at Mama and there were tears falling from her eyes. She can't talk because of all of the tubes in her mouth. I know she is in a lot of pain. Her body looks like it is numb.

"Ok Mama, they said we have to leave and let you rest. Please let that rest on you what I've just said ok. Pray Mom, God helps everybody even me. We are going to leave now. I am going to see if it's ok to bring you a few things up here because you may be here for a while until you get better. I will be back up here to see you ok. I don't know if I will be back today because it's only one car and that's my fiancé's. I can see if he will bring me back, but if he doesn't I can ask my best friend Latoya. I love you Ma." I said as I kissed her on her forehead. I feel God's spirit again.

Chuck and I left out the room. Chuck grabbed my hand. We were walking past the nurse's station. I'm looking for Nurse Melanie. I just want to tell her Thank you.

"Hold on Chuck, I'll be right back." I let his hand go and ran over to the nurse's station. "Excuse me Miss, Is Nurse Melanie here today?" The nurse looked at me as if I have lost my mind.

"I'm sorry ma'am we don't have a Nurse Melanie on our staff." She replied.

"Ma'am, Nurse Melanie was up on the seventh floor with my mom." I explained.

The nurse glanced down at my mom's chart. "No ma'am I'm sorry, it says that your mom's nurse was John Jacobs. I can call up there and check for you."

I stood here waiting on her to check because if they are getting my mother's nurses mixed up there is no telling what else they could be doing wrong.

"Ok ma'am I was just notified that, there was a strange older woman reported leaving your mom's room last night. When security asked her to identify herself, she told them that her name was "Angel" a friend of Victoria's. Other than that, they say that John was assigned as her nurse. Do you know a Victoria?"

"I am Victoria, but I don't know any one named Angel. Thanks for your help." I replied.

I walked back over to Chuck. He grabbed my hand.

"Is everything ok?"

"Oh yeah, I'm fine."

"Baby, are you hungry?" he asked.

"Yes sir, I thought you'd never ask."

"I haven't had McDonalds in a while." Chuck implied.

"Yeah, me neither. Sounds good, plus I want one of those Mc Flurry's; them bad boys be off the chain."

We pulled up in the Drive through on Mack down the street from the hospital. It was about three cars ahead of us. Chuck looked at me.

"Man, Tamara looks so different, them drugs will mess you up. That's how my daddy was starting to become, but he let the drugs take his life. You got time to help your mom. I wasn't old enough then, but Vic you are. I will help you pray that demon of drugs off of her."

I looked at him, listening but at the same time thinking about the fact that the Nurse said that my mom died and then a strange lady left my mom's room, who calls herself Angel and she's a friend of mine. My heart is tingling just thinking about it. I guess she could have been a "real" Angel. Long as Mama is alive that's all I really care about. That's some weird shit, but I guess it's real. *Oops God, sorry for cursing again.* I glanced over at Chuck.

"Chuck, what do you think God feels about cursing?" I asked

"I am pretty sure he doesn't like it. I'm trying to stop. It's just, growing up all I heard were curse words. On my father's side that's the only language they used. It's more of a habit. I seem to do it without giving it a thought. Sometimes people make me so upset, I lose my cool. I know I can't do that. That's the language I grew up on so it's kind of stuck with me, but I have been trying to replace those words with other more suitable words."

"Yeah, I know. I was in the store the other day and these girls were cursing, calling each other bitches I felt like I was looking in the mirror. They were talking the same way Toy and I talk, but for some reason hearing them sounded so awful and it really was disgusting to my ears. Though like you said, I grew up listening to it so it's a habit, but when you hear someone else saying the same words it doesn't seem to sound the same. I keep apologizing to God for cursing. I hope he understands that it's going to take time. Oh yeah, don't forget to stop and get some stamps. I need about eight."

"We might as well go to the post office." He suggested.

I sat here thinking to myself, how I can't wait to go to college. I want my mom to be ok. *I need all types of help God. If you hear me, well I know you hear me so I guess I should say if you are listening, help me out. Guide me.* I prayed.

Hmmm, I wonder what Toy's up to. I glanced over at Chuck as I grabbed my cell from my hip. "Let me call Toy right quick baby." I dialed her number.

"Hey girl. I haven't talked to you in a while." She answered

"I know stranger, it's been almost twenty hours."

We laughed.

"Girl, why aren't you at school? Oh, you know your Uncle came by here last night? I meant to call you, but I figured you needed some rest and you weren't trying to hear all that anyway."

"Yeah I know. Stan sent the police up to the school to pick me up. They dropped me off at a warehouse. Stan was there. He was taking me home, which didn't make since. He ran out of gas so I called Chuck to come get me when he went up the ramp to get gas. I took his keys, locked the doors and left with Chuck."

"Oh my goodness, you and your Uncle be having mad issues." Toy replied.

"Yeah I know, but that's him tripping like I'm a little girl. That is exactly why I am filling out these applications tonight for some out of state schools."

"Oh, so you gone up and leave your girl like that?"

"Why don't you come with me? I think you can fill out applications on line. Ooh Toy, that would be fun if we can all go out of town together, but then again I have been thinking about my Mama. What if she gets better, I would have to stay so she won't go back to drugs then I need to look after Jasmine, girl I don't know. I really don't. Plus Chuck and I are getting married soon then he's probably going to Wayne State. I'm applying for that school also."

I looked over at Chuck because his phone rang. He started talking to whoever that is.

"Yeah Toy, I don't know girl. My life sure is moving fast and crazy these last few days."

"Welcome to maturity and adult hood. Girl, this is not new. We all got problems, just different ones that's all. Some are a little more dramatic than others. You feel me, but Rob's over here and we smoking so I will call you later. I love you."

"I love you too Toy, thanks."

I hung up just in time because we are pulling up to the speaker.

"Hi, welcome to McDonalds. How may I help you?"

"I want the spicy chicken combo with cheese." I informed Chuck.

"Let me get two spicy chicken combos with cheese and hold on." He looked at me. "Baby what kind of flurry you want?" he asked.

"Hmmm, Butterfinger … nah wait, let me get the Oreo." I replied.

"Ok, can I get an Oreo flurry and a Butterfinger flurry?"

"What type of drinks for your combos?"

"I want sprite and orange mixed." I requested.

"Can I have a sprite and orange mixed for one, and a mountain dew for the other?" Chuck said.

"Oh baby, tell her to add on an ice water too."

"Your total is $ 12.87 at the first window please."

We got our food, checked it to see if it was right and now we are heading to his cousins house. Chuck said that was his cousin that just called. He's ready to cut Chuck's hair.

Chapter 20

We pulled up to his cousin's house. It's very nice. You can tell someone puts time and effort into their yard. The flowers and grass are so neat and pretty. We walked on the porch and an older woman answered the door. "Hey honey. Come give your Auntie some sugar," she requested as she held her arms open for Chuck. They hugged. She was squeezing him real tight. She finally let him go so he could breathe. She looked at me and smiled, "Is this the one and only Victoria?" she asked.

I smiled at her as well as looked at Chuck wondering how she knows me. I replied, "Yes ma'am."

She smiled with her arms stretched open. "Come here precious, give me a hug."

I hugged her and she squeezed me just as tight. "Bless you baby. Y'all come on in."

We walked in the house. "Y'all babies go on and have a seat. Yes, Lord. My, my." She exhaled as she sat down in what looked to be his and her chairs covered in plastic. Chuck and I sat down.

"Victoria, I am so honored that you have finally graced us with your presence. We have heard so much about you. My husband and I, but right now he is at work. Sorry you couldn't meet him, but you will. Charles tells me that he loves you girl, and he wants you to be his wife." She said.

"Oh really?" I replied as I began blushing. I didn't need Diva shoes in this house because she was an older woman. I'm sure she could see right through me, so I'm going to keep it real with her. She seems like a real nice lady.

"I am honored to meet you, though Charles hasn't told me much about you." I then looked at Chuck. He picked up on the confused look that I was giving him. He then replied, "I know, I have been meaning too. Well anyhow, you all are meeting now and that's that."

"So, do you love my favorite nephew because he is a sweet heart? He has had a hard life, but the Lord has brought him through and is still bringing him through. Isn't that right Charles?" she asked.

"Yes ma'am." Chuck replied.

Wow, this is the real family deal right here. I haven't really seen real family love besides Toy and her family. I smiled as I watched them and listened to them talk.

"Yes, I know he is going to be ok. God is working with the both of us." I replied.

Chuck walked over and kissed me on my cheek. "Auntie, isn't she sweet? Well y'all excuse me while I go upstairs and get my hair cut." He said before he ran upstairs calling Roscoe.

"Come on in Victoria, I was just in the dining room eating lunch. I see you guys are eating that food that is no good for you."

"It's good sometimes, but I don't really eat fast food that much. My Uncle usually cooks for me, or Charles cooks a lot." I replied

She sat down at the table and continued talking. "Yeah, my baby can cook, can't he? I tried to teach him everything I know. That's my boy there." She said.

I was standing here looking at the pictures when I heard his Aunt's soothing voice.

"Sit down baby; let's talk." She said. Her voice was so smooth and welcoming I feel just like a little girl. This house feels welcoming and it feels so good. She gives off a motherly love type of vibe as she began speaking.

"I don't know what happened with my baby sister and Charles's father. I wish that I could have raised him at the time, but I was trying to raise the three boys I have and they were giving me the trouble. God doesn't put any more on you than you can bear. I prayed for him every day. He's doing great now. I am so proud of him. All my boys are doing well. One of my sons is a lawyer in the State of California. My oldest boy is a Judge in the State of Virginia, and my baby boy that's up stairs, cuts hair and he is in medical school. Though, he is still trying to decide if he wants to go into law. I am just a Church mother, a house wife and house mother, but my job is not that simple. I worked hard to make sure my babies had everything they needed and wanted. I made sure I was here when they left home and when they returned. I didn't really want these day cares and thangs they have now raising my babies. When they came in from school, I made sure their home work was done. I made sure I tucked my babies in at night. I wasn't alone though. I thank GOD for my husband. My husband works at Chrysler; he is a manager there in their corporate office. When he gets home he still has time to talk to us, motivate us and we discuss issues that we don't understand going on in the world today." She said before she stopped to cough.

"Excuse me precious, I think I'm coming down with a cold. That's Michigan weather for you. Now as I was saying, I raised my kids to be able to talk about everything. I grew up with my mom on drugs and prostituting. My dad was trying to be a good father, but he couldn't catch a break on getting the job he needed to provide for me and my little sister. He began to get stressed and then he started to take it out on me and my sister. My mom was running back in forth in the streets, so he was obviously looking for some type of love from a woman. He began to use drugs, and then he started molesting me and my sister. My sister is the one who kept me strong. I don't know what happened. She always told me that we were going to grow up and forget about what we were going through. I guess when her husband started to abuse her, she couldn't handle it. She killed my nephew and now she is in an s mental institution. I decided to give my life to the Lord and he carried me through. I guess my reason for sharing my story with you is because

I just want you to stay encouraged. No matter what's going on, you can make it out alright. God sent his son to die on the cross for all of our sins the least I can do is worship him and serve him to the best of my ability."

"Where is your father now?" I asked.

"He died when I was fifteen. My aunt was able to raise us and put us in Church. I knew that I wanted to serve God. My sister decided that she wanted to help children who were being abused. She said that there wasn't a God because if it was, he would not have let all of those things happened to her. I told her that God was the one in her that made her want to love kids and help kids that had been in our situation. The Lord allows us to go through certain things because it makes us stronger. Sometimes he has to let certain thangs go wrong in our life to make the correct things appear. For some reason, my sister began to stray away from me. She would get really angry and mad when I talked about God. That's when I knew that the devil had entered into my sister's spirit. I prayed for her, that's all I could do. I look at her situation now and how she didn't want to accept God and I compare it with my situation going through my life with God. My kids are successful, my husband loves me unconditionally and I try my hardest to do what I can for my nephew. Victoria, I am sharing my life with you because I believe that you are going to be a true blessing for Charles as he is for you. I feel your spirit, it is so pure and so sweet, but I also sense the fear of being hurt. Don't worry about that. Leave it in God's hands and he will be your guide. If you doubt God, you doubt everything he had his son die for."

I'm sitting here in a state of shock, wiping my tears because this lady read right through me. She has basically gone through what I'm going through accept Stan is not my dad. She is an example of what I want to be, and who I want to be. She inspired me. My heart feels like something has just been lifted. I didn't understand it, but I knew it was God trying to tell me something.

"Thank you. I'm sorry I didn't catch your name." I said.

"Oh you can call me Mrs. Lynn or Auntie, whichever one you prefer. It don't make me no never mind chile. I just think you have such an awesome spirit. I feel your spirit precious and it is so beautiful. You remind me a lot of myself when I was your age." She said.

"Mrs. Lynn, you have helped me so much. Thank you. I promised Charles that I would be there for him. I love him so much Mrs. Lynn. He is my heart. He is everything that I never imagined, but am so pleased and grateful to know. Mrs. Lynn, I appreciate you sharing your life with me. I thank you."

Chuck and his cousin came running down stairs. Ooh Chuck's hair cut is so fly. He looks so good. Chuck walked over to me.

"Sweetheart, this is my cousin Roscoe. Roscoe, this is your future cousin -in- love Victoria."

"What's up witcha cous? It's nice to meet you." His cousin said as he shook my hand.

Chuck looked at me again, "Vicky, are you crying?"

I smiled and replied. "I'm not anymore."

"Auntie, what you do to my girl?" Chuck asked jokingly.

"Nothing that I don't do with you and that's keep you encouraged. You two are some precious souls and I see that you are made for each other. Don't let the devil get in your way and don't let the devil break up your spirit. Chuck you already know how I taught you. You keep this baby strong and encourage her like you've been doing baby and you both will be ok."

Chuck hugged me and said, "My baby knows I have her back." He hugged his aunt and said "thank you." She looked at me smiling with her arms open. "Baby, you are not exempt, come give Aunt Lynn a hug."

I hugged her and it was a comforting chill that went through out my body that made me feel safe. "Thanks again Mrs. Lynn." She hugged me tight then I felt her open her hand and place it on my back. She began to whisper in my ear.

"Spirit of confusion, loose her! Spirit of doubt, loose her! Spirit of fear, loose her! Heavenly Father, hear your babies cry lord. Her heart loves you Lord. Her heart is so good. You are a precious Lord, a faithful God. Give her the strength that she needs. Lord, release all of her past. Free her Lord from the demons that prey on her. While they prey on her, I am praying for her. In Jesus name I pray- Amen."

I don't know what happened but something grabbed a hold of me. I hunched over crying as I began to yell "Thank you, Thank you, Thank you." I cannot seem to figure out what has come over me.

"That's right Lord, hug her Lord. Caress her Lord. That's right God let those demons loose. Mercy! Mercy! Thank you, Jesus." She said as her smooth, soft voice caressed my ears.

When I stood up I noticed Chuck and Roscoe wipe the tears that fell from their eyes. *This family is so full of love*, I thought as Chuck walked over to me. "God knows I love you. I love your heart, I love your soul. I love you Victoria Matthews." He said as he hugged me tight.

I cried even harder because he already added his name to mine. I wiped my face and stood here finally with a clear mind. I have this feeling that I am protected, I am now free. Mrs. Lynn walked us to the door.

"Ok babies. Y'all be safe. Trust God. I appreciate y'all stopping by. Victoria I hope this old woman haven't bored you silly." She said while laughing.

I turned around, looked at her and replied, "Absolutely not, it has been a pleasure."

"Chuck and I got in the car and pulled off. I had the feeling of being free, but a tiny gut feeling entered inside of me as soon as we pulled off. Stan popped back in my mind. I couldn't understand why. I knew that even though I was praying and everybody prayed for me, I will have to face him one day. I looked over at Chuck. Wow my baby really loves me. God, how did I get blessed with someone like him. I got into this mess with Stan by myself and I don't want anything to happen to Chuck for that. I love this man and he is ready to ride for me. The only way I think that I will truly feel safe is if I get up out of Michigan, but then Stan has his way of finding people. I can't understand how he wants me all to himself, but he wanted that other woman that he had been seeing her for a while. I know that I want Chuck; I don't really care if Stan is with someone else. I prefer that Stan finds someone else. I deserve to be happy. I love Chuck.

I know Mrs. Lynn prayed this spirit of confusion and fear off of me, but just as soon as I left her house, here it is right back again. It may just be my allowance of these thoughts to invade my mind. I am allowing this to hunt me, but I just can't leave Stan like that. I have to help him some way. I have to see him one more time and convince him not to be angry at me or Chuck. I know Chuck will be mad at me, but I have to go over there plus I have to return his keys.

"Chuck baby, I know we prayed and everything boo, but I need to talk to my Uncle one last time. I just have to see why he is going through this change. Chuck, he raised me. He was there for me when my mom and my dad were not around. I have to go and talk to him." I explained.

"Baby, if that's what you want to do. I just don't want anything to happen to you. You say he was verbally abusive to you. What if he gets physically abusive with you?"

"I don't know Chuck. I just can't leave like this. I am going to go to your house first and feel out these applications then I am going to talk to him. I don't want to live in fear Chuck. I know that you told me God is everything. I now know he is everything, but I as a person want to know why my Uncle is the way he is. Please respect me for that."

"Baby, I totally understand. I feel you. We are going to fill out these applications and then I will take you over there."

"Actually Chuck, I was hoping that Toy could take me over there because with you going it will just make it harder. Please baby, if you love me, give me that."

He rubbed his hand across my cheek and said, "Anything for you, my Queen."

"Thank you, Chuck. Oh baby stop at the post office so we can get some stamps."

We pulled up to the post office and went inside. "Baby, we can fill them out in here and mail them while we are here." I said.

"You are so right. I didn't know they would have chairs and tables, that's why I didn't think of that. Ok baby let me go get them and I will be back." He said as he headed out the door.

Let me call Toy right now.

"House of Beauty, talk to cutie" Toy answered.

"Hello."

"Yes, Cutie speaking, how may I help you?"

"Oh I'm sorry, I was looking for Toy."

"This is me you hating ass broad!"

"Toy for real, was that really called for? You said talk to cutie so I thought I had the wrong number. I didn't call to talk to myself." I laughed.

Toy laughed also. "What's up girl, with your silly ass?" She replied.

"Nothing much girl, are you going to be busy in the next thirty minutes?" I asked.

"No what's up?" she replied.

"I wanted to know if you could take me over my Uncle's house so I can get the rest of my things."

"Are you sure that you should do that? Wasn't he angry with you?"

"Girl I will be ok. He'll get over it."

"Ok, what time will you be ready? It's 5:15 now, so I guess about 6pm."

"Will you be coming over here or am I coming to you or what?"

"I will come over there. Chuck is going to drop me off."

"Ok call me."

"Ok thanks, Toy." I said as I disconnected the call.

Chuck is walking back in now. We went to the window to purchase the stamps.

"Hi, ma'am I want to purchase some stamps." I said.

"How many do you need?" The clerk asked.

"I think we have about ten applications. So I guess about ten." I replied

"Ma'am you should go ahead and get a book of stamps?" she suggested.

"Yes. I think a book would be good."

"So, are you two thinking about going to college?"

"Yes ma'am." Chuck and I responded.

"Well you make sure that you all do that because if you don't want to spend your life working for somebody else getting paid when they say you get paid you better get your education. It's hard not having a college education. I only have my GED so of course I am being paid less than my co-workers."

"You know it is not too late." I said.

"Yeah, you're right. I'm just scared because I haven't been to school in so long, I don't want to look stupid."

"Baby girl, looking stupid is when you are in a situation that you know you can get out of, but you choose not too because of that thing called pride."

She handed me the book of stamps, "Thanks that really helped me. Those were the words I was waiting on."

I smiled at her as I walked away. Chuck and I sat at the table and when I looked up I noticed him smiling at me.

"That was some good advice you just gave her. Have you ever noticed some of the advice we give often applies to ourselves. I am not calling you stupid, but that same advice you just gave her you should consider for yourself as well." Chuck suggested.

My first thought was to become defensive, but I had time to think about my response. I decided to remain silent. He is right though, but I have to do this, my mind is made up. Plus this doesn't have anything to do with my pride at all. It has to do with a person who I have watched turn into a beast with no remorse. I want to be able to walk around knowing that I am not leaving someone angry and then he would use the anger that he has against me to harm someone else. *I have to fix this; I just have too.* I thought to myself.

Trying to fill out these applications is causing me to become frustrated. I don't know the answers to more than half of these questions. My parent's names and address, my social security number, income tax what is all of this. Why do they need to know all of this information? I am the one applying for college not them.

"Chuck, what is income tax?"

"It's basically taxes you pay on the income you earn. People usually pay taxes into the city, state and federal. They usually get it back at the beginning of the year. I think that's what my Aunt explained. I'm not sure because I have not had a job." Chuck explained.

"Oh ok, so should I just leave it blank?"

"Just check the part where it says that you are a dependent because you don't have income from a job."

"I wonder if my Uncle is claiming me. See Chuck that's why I have to see him today. I need my birth certificate, my social security card and all my paper work because I don't know any of this stuff. I will fill these out when I get back from my Uncles house. Now I am the one feeling stupid. I never even asked if I had a middle name. I don't know my mom's middle name. I don't know if I was born in Detroit or not. How could I be so stupid?" I asked my self-aloud.

"Baby, you are not stupid. That is perfectly normal especially when you did not grow up with your parents. I just went and got my birth certificate last year from Herman Keifer and I didn't feel stupid. I just retrieved the information that I did not have and learned the things that I did not know. So please don't talk down on yourself like that, you will get all of the things you need. Don't worry about it." Chuck replied.

"Thanks bay, I guess you can drop me off at Toys house now. I will figure everything out today at least I will try." I said as we walked back to the car.

We are just arriving at Toys house. Toy ran straight out the house before we could park good. I got out the car after kissing Chuck, reassuring him that I would be seeing him in a few hours. I walked over to Toy's car.

"Dang, Toy you basically ran out the house. Are you in a rush or something?" I asked.

"Not exactly. I just have a date with Rob tonight. We are going to see *Welcome Home Roscoe Jenkins*. Everybody say's this movie is hilarious so I have to go see it. So as you can see it's not a major rush I just want to get back and finish my hair. I want to add me a few tracks in my hair to make it thicker. What you think?" Toy asked.

I can clearly see as well as smell that Toy has been drinking already. *This girl drinks for breakfast, lunch and dinner,* I thought to myself. "Toy your hair is already long enough you don't need to add any hair." I said as I put on my seat belt.

Chuck is still sitting there waiting on me and Toy to pull off. I stuck my head out the window and yelled "Stick around in the area so I can call you if I need you. I love you baby and pray for me ok."

Toy and I finally pulled off. She acts like we are about to go somewhere special. She sat here for about ten minutes putting on make-up and then she has to find her CD and put her cell on the charger before we leave the premises. *This girl is a trip. I don't know what I'm going to do with her,* I thought to myself.

Chapter 21

We pulled up at Stan's house. I see that his Benz is parked in the driveway. I grabbed my purse from Toy's back seat. "Ok Toy, wait out here for about ten minutes. If I am not back then everything is ok." I explained as I got out the car.

I ran up the stairs and entered the house. Stan is on the phone. "Yes, she has been missing over several hours." As I closed the door, he turned around and looked at me. "Never mind she's home" he said before he hung up the phone.

"Hello Stan." I said trying not to appear to be scared for my life because I am.

"Oh hey, come on in. I have been waiting for you." He replied looking very upset.

My heart is beating. I'm a little scared, but at this point I didn't think at all. I'm just standing here. He's standing there staring at me. "So ... I see you are into taking people's keys and locking them out of their cars. Did you know that is a federal offense?" he asked.

"Well, you been high on that stuff so I didn't want you to hurt me or yourself for that matter." I replied.

He walked over to me and slapped me and now he is continuously punching me. I wasn't expecting this. I figured he might be angry, but definitely not this. I am beginning to see stars as he grabbed my hair and dragged me across the carpet and up the stairs.

"Stan, please, please. I just came to apologize. Please Stan, I'm sorry." I cried and begged. I remembered he said that he was going to kill me, but I came back. My body is burning from the carpet. He picked me up and threw me on the bed. "Stan, please! No! I'm sorry." I continued crying. He grabbed his handcuffs and handcuffed me to the bed. One arm to one bed post and the other arm to the other bed post. "Stan, I am so sorry. Please! Why do I deserve this? I have not done anything wrong." I proclaimed.

"Shut up!" He screamed as he slapped me again. "I might as well tell you some of the things you want to know since you want to know so badly. Everything is all about Victoria! I go out of my way- for-Victoria! Victoria loves diamonds; I buy them. Victoria loves gold; I buy it. She loves designer clothes; I buy them. Now she loves another man; I can't buy that! Yes, I started back sniffing coke! You were the reason I stopped. You are everything to me. You are my only family. You are the only one I have ever loved. You are the one that I want to make mine. I want you to be the way I want you to be. But noooooo! Victoria wants to be her own person. She wants to learn all these new things! She wants friends! She wants boys her own age. What the hell is wrong with you! I have done everything for you. All I ask you to do is to let me love you. All I want is to treat you like the woman you are. Obviously that's not good enough for you. You are the reason I started back sniffing coke. You've been coming up with this molestation and statutory rape bulshit. How do you think that I'm supposed to feel about that?" He asked as he pulled out a little tiny glass bottle full of powder.

He took the stick that's in it, put it up to his nose and sniffed it. "And that little bitch Toya, I should have killed her a long time ago. I tried my best to share you with her, but I can't handle it. I pop up over there and her brother said you all went walking. I rode past the track that morning Victoria and guess what? There was no Victoria and no Toya! I figured you had gone on that little trip to Indiana."

"How did you figure that" I asked

"I have my connections. Don't interrupt me while I'm talking! You had your time to talk all day today when you disappeared with my keys. Oh yeah that was very cute by the way. You're lucky I didn't find the guy Chuck when I went to Indiana. The little fucker is smart. We traced his call and I guess he turned off his phone because we lost him. If Anthony would have kept him on the phone long enough we would have caught him. I guess he called himself looking out for this Chuck guy. That damn Anthony was destined for death. I grew up watching him trying to sell drugs like he was a big shot. He used to get his dope from me. Matter of fact, all the dope on the street comes from me. I got the whole east side of Detroit sold up! Yeah that's right. I grew up not having shit so of course I want it all. I get everything I want. If nobody lets me have it, I take it! Just like you. I've been too nice to you and you are out here running around with some two bit hustler."

This man is a lunatic, I thought as I lay here listening to him.

"All I ever wanted to do is show you the love you deserve, but that's obviously not good enough for you. I think I know what you want. Yeah, I know what you want." He continuously repeated while he's taking the clip from his gun.

"Stan, No! What are you doing? No-o-o-o-o-o-o-o-o-o-o-o-o-o-o!

"Shut up! Shut up! Shut up! Don't cry now. You were not thinking about crying when you were laid up with that nigga. I told you that nobody else is going to love you like I am. Stop all that screaming! Come on you like nine's right! I don't know what the hell is wrong with you. I MADE YOU. I created you and you're trying to leave. Why Victoria? Why can't you be happy with me?" he cried as I continued screaming at the top of my lungs.

"Bitch, stop screaming! Scream again and I'll really give you something to scream about!"

Fighting back is not an option even if I wanted to. All of my pedals have fallen off except one. My life has changed in these last few months. This is obviously my destiny. I saw a brighter light earlier today. Maybe coming over here was not a good idea. I can't help anyone like Stan. I now realize trying to save someone who does not want to be saved especially when you can't barely save yourself can be a deadly thing. I don't know what will happen to me after I leave this world that Chuck has allowed me to view. All I had to do was listen to Chuck, listen to his pastor and listen to Mrs. Lynn. They warned me. Trying to conquer something that's bigger than me is impossible. *God, I am sorry I should have left it in your hands. Can you help stop this pain? Why won't he just kill me already,* I thought to myself as I am grasping for oxygen while I lay covered in my vomit.

"Get up. I don't want you to die just yet. I'm not finished with you." Stan said as he unlocked the handcuffs.

It seems like his hand has every strand of my hair glued to it as he drags me to the bathroom. He forced my head into the toilet.

"Go ahead, let it out. You better not make another mistake like that again. You got vomit all over me. Here" he said as he handed me the face cloth. "Don't just stand there, wash it all off. Rinse your mouth out. You shouldn't look so sad. What's wrong? Are you hurt? Ahh is little Ms. Victoria hurt? Well, Welcome to my World! I hope you are feeling just as much pain as you have caused me." He said as he carried me in the room.

"Sit down" he commanded as he walked over and reached in his pants pocket and pulled out his little tube of powder. "You're a big girl, now take a sniff" he insisted.

"No!" I yelled.

"I'm sorry, you must be under the impression that I am asking you. Do it! He yelled.

I sat here shaking my head no.

"Here's the scenario, you're a smart girl so I'm sure you can figure this out. Now these are your only options. Take this bottle and sniff the coke or I can put you back in handcuffs and force it up your nose until you die. Which one will it be" he said with a big grin on his face.

"No!" I yelled before I jumped up and ran out the room. By the time I reached the first stair I heard his gun cock.

"Freeze!" He yelled.

I did just that, I froze. The uncontrollable beatings in my chest produced rapid transports of oxygen into my body as I released carbon dioxide. The fear of being shot in my back is all I can think of. As I turned back and looked at Stan in a decelerated motion I notice the red light shining off the tip of my nose.

"Why are you trying to test me? I should go ahead and kill you now because all you are doing is wasting my time. You are being very hard headed Victoria. I thought I raised you better than that. Haven't you learned by now that you cannot escape me? You don't want to anyway, that's why you came back. You love me Victoria. Why are you still standing there, get over here now!" He yelled.

"I was just playing, Stan" I said forcing myself to put a smile on my face as I walked over to him.

"Yeah, that was funny, so funny I forgot to laugh. Get in here!" He commanded as he pushed me on the bed.

He pressed the gun against my forehead. "Listen Victoria, I am not playing! If you try it again, I will kill you! Please don't try me Victoria, because I've warned you too many times."

"Yes sir" I replied.

"Hold this" he insisted as he handed me the tube. "Here, now take a sniff." He demanded.

I glanced at the gun he has in his hand realizing that I have no options available. My eyes are seeing rainbows and the room is spinning. My mind is in overdrive.

"Do you like it?"

"It's different" I replied.

"Yeah, see this is what I use to take all the pain away. Take another" he insisted.

It's mighty funny how I still feel all of my pain. It just seems like I have a splitting headache. Now it feels like my tongue is numb. My brain is still working. *As a matter of fact this gives me an idea*, I thought.

"Stan, why don't you take another sniff? Ok take another? Now one more? Yeah that's it. Ooh you look so sexy to me. What took you so long to introduce this to me? We could have been having fun. You are so right all of my pain is gone. Now I'm feeling some kind of way. Lay down baby" I said.

He sat the gun on the dresser. He got on the bed as he began to lie on his back. I took the handcuffs. "Let me put these on you. I'm going to put it on you Stan. Yeah, you're not going to be able to handle it. I'm so high Stan. I just want to rock your world. I must have been a fool for trying to leave you. I love you … … **NOT!**" I said once I was able to put the last set of handcuffs on.

"Let me ask you a couple of questions Stan. First how long does this high last?"

"About ten minutes" he replied smiling as if he's really about to get something from me.

"Yes, that's exactly what I thought. My high is gone. Actually I was never high Stan; a little spinning headache yes, but high enough to give you my body, hell no! You must really be as stupid as you look. So, my next question is when you licked that coke off that female in the bathroom is this how you got her hooked? Is this the way you got her? I wonder if you had anything to do with my mother getting addicted. Stan, I don't know about you. You tried to run my life. Create me for yourself? What do you mean by that? You thought you were going to have me hooked under your little spell. You tried convincing me that I was never good enough to be loved. See what you don't understand is, I am far from stupid and far pass intelligent. I read about people like you in some of my psychology books. You like to manipulate people and make them feel like they will never be anything without you. Stan you are a pedophile! You are attracted to children, but see Stan I'm eighteen. I'm grown! So why haven't you let me go? How many more children have you taken advantage of? When are you going to stop Stan? Answer me!" I yelled

"I don't know! Victoria, what are you doing? You know these handcuffs can't keep me down."

"They sure do look like they are doing a pretty good job of it right now. You told me how you felt so let me tell you what I feel. Yeah you're right you did raise me, but you raised me to be your woman and your lover. The times that you repeatedly used force to enter my sacred, secret garden, just thinking about it hurts me. You took that from me Stan! I did not give it to you. You stole my innocence and invaded my purity. You told me that when you love someone that you have to do what you did to me. Stan, you're wrong. I met a man that I love; this man loves me for me. He told me that if someone loves me that does not mean that they have to penetrate me. When you really love someone, you do not take advantage of them. When you really, really love someone Stan, you don't cause them pain. The love you say you have for me is ***the strangest love***. I would never love someone the way you say you love me. I would rather take a knife and stab them rather then tell them this is love. I refuse to put up with your abuse. I don't deserve it. I deserve to be loved. Its guys like you who make females like me feel unworthy of allowing someone to truly and genuinely love us. It's sad because you made me feel that I was unworthy of God's love. Chuck showed me true love. He introduced me to God. I truly believe in my heart that he will never forsake me. He will never leave me and He will always love me. **I WILL ALWAYS LOVE ME.** That's why it has always been about Victoria. I knew that I deserved better love than what you were showing me. You stole my childhood from me Stan and that's not fair. I cannot get that back. It's ok now. I realize that this had to happen. I can now tell other girls who have experienced this type of abuse that they can make it also. God will see me through. I know God sent Chuck into my life. Chuck is the man that I'm sure many women pray for. He had a very rough child hood, but he uses his life to make him stronger and to become closer to God. I don't know what happened to you as a kid and why you behave the way you do, but I do know that using drugs to coat your problems is not the answer. God is all you need. He's all that we all need. If we love people the way that God loves us, we wouldn't be sitting here having this conversation. I noticed that when you gave me those drugs, they had no effect on me because my mind is not weak. I'm too strong for it. I don't need drugs to suppress my problems. I recognize my problem and it's you! You sick twisted pervert!"

"Victoria wait, wait" he begged. "I realized that I have hurt you. I know I have a problem, but let me tell you why."

"I'm listening" I replied.

"When I was a little boy, my stepfather abused me. I don't know where my real father was because I never met him. My stepfather Jeff told me that my father left because he was a coward and he didn't love me. Jeff tried to do all the things that he felt a father was supposed to do. He sat me on his lap and explained to me that he would never leave me the way my father left me; he said that he was everything that I needed. At that time Mama was pregnant with my sister Jessie. I tried telling my mom that Jeff was beginning to touch me inappropriately and she beat me for it. She said I needed to listen to Jeff and obey him because he was her husband and the provider for our family. I hated that white man."

"So, Jeff is white" I interrupted.

"Yes. I told Mama that I hated that white man and she told me that, that white man will not run out on his family like my father did. Sometimes I would sit there and watch Jeff beat my mother down and I felt no remorse. I felt that she got exactly what she deserved for beating on me. After he would beat her he would then lock her in their bedroom and that's when he would attack me. He started doing despicable things to me. He told me that's what you do when you love someone. He said if I ever told anyone our secret he would deny it and then he would beat me and my mom. He said no one would believe me anyway because I was a nigger child and he was a white man. He used to laugh and say that average black men were lazy and they would never amount to anything. He told me that his people have been holding us down. When they see our brown skin they set off alarms and make us look like the bad guys when they are the ones doing the dirt. I don't know why, but my mom felt the same way. All of her friends were white. My mother told me that black people couldn't be trusted. She said that they always run away from their responsibilities and then blame it on the white man. That's why she used to beat me so badly. She hated for me to disrespect Jeff. I started to believe that the things that Jeff was doing to me were signs of love. When Jeff was killed in a car crash I began to realize that I love females. I didn't want to be with men. I knew that I would never do the things Jeff did to me to anyone else. When Tamara had you, I wanted to protect you and love you. I'm sorry, I don't know what happened to me, I looked at you one day and something about you caused everything in me to change.

"So let me guess, you wanted to love me the way Jeff loved you right?" I asked.

"No Vickie it's not like that. I don't know what happened. I just couldn't stop. That's the only love I knew how to display. I knew that something might have been wrong with me, but I looked past it. When I started working for the FBI, we arrested people like that all the time, but I was too addicted to stop. When you cried and begged me to stop all I could think about was the times I cried and Jeff wouldn't stop. All

I wanted to do was show you love. I wanted you to be mine and love me the way I love you. I guess I was wrong for that. I am truly sorry baby. We can still make this work. Just tell me what you want me to do. Please understand that we are meant to be together. I am your destiny. We can move far away and live happily. Come on take these handcuffs off so I can hold you"

"Ok, where are the keys?" I asked.

"They're right there in that cup on the dresser."

I grabbed the keys and then reached in my jacket pocket for my cell phone. "Oh my baby has called me twelve times. Excuse me let me make this call sweetie." I said to Stan with a smile.

"Baby, where are you" Chuck answered.

"I'm here at the house. Please come get me. This man is psycho!" I said as I smiled at Stan.

"Baby, he didn't hurt you did he?" Chuck asked with the sound of agitation in his voice.

"Baby please just hurry"

"Ok. I am on my way."

"Thanks baby, I will see you when you get here" I replied before hanging up.

Stan is lying there looking at me with a shocked look on his face. He looks so stupid. "What? Are you shocked? See, that's what you get for underestimating me Stan. I guess I am not that dumb after all huh? Oh yeah what was I supposed to be doing. Yeah that's right. You want me to release you from the handcuffs." I said as I walked over to him.

"Victoria, what are you doing?"

"Shut up! Shut up! Shut up!" I screamed while repeatedly hitting him in the face with his gun. "Stan you are such a dumb ass. Fight back! Come on hit me back. Oh you can't can you? I have another question, how did your mom adopt my mom? How old was my mom? I know that's not a tear. Are you crying! N-o-o-o-o not Mr. Big Bad Ass; Please don't cry, you know how I hate to see people cry. Now answer the damn question!" I yelled.

It's something about knowing that my fiancé is on his way that seems like it's giving me some type of power.

"Ok Victoria please don't hit me" he begged. "Tamara used to live next door to us. Your mom and Jessie became best friends. Tamara's mom was killed by her boyfriend when she was next door at our house. She didn't have any other family so my mom adopted her. I think she was about fourteen or fifteen then. Victoria, please don't be like me. This is not you."

"How do you know what's not me? You made me this way Stan. I learn from the best" I said before my cell phone rang.

"Hello" I answered.

"I'm outside lil mama" Chuck replied.

"Ok baby, here I come. I have to grab the rest of my things." I replied.

"Well, my *two bit hustler is* outside. He's come to rescue lil ole me" I said sarcastically. "I want you to lay here tonight and think about your actions. I will come back to check on you in a few days. Hopefully, you'll still be alive. If not, it was nice knowing you, you pervert! Oh, by the way. I'm going to take your nine with me." I said before I hit him in the head with it once more. "Oops, I hope that didn't hurt. See you in a few days. Chow!" I said as I grabbed my bags and headed out the door.

"Victoria, I told you I was sorry. Don't leave me here like this. Please!" he begged.

"Your apologies do nothing for me. Sorry about your childhood Stan, but you took it out on mine and that's not cool. Love you ... sike!" I yelled up the stairs before I walked out the door.

For some reason, I feel a whole lot better. I never knew I had that inside of me. *I guess that evil people will bring out the worst in you,* I thought as I looked back at the house while getting in Chuck's car.

"Baby, I got everything straight with my Uncle. I told him that those drugs were not cool and he needs help." I explained.

"Oh my God baby, look at your face. I'll kill him!" Chuck replied as he took his gun from his waist and attempted to jump out the car.

"Chuck, NO! Please! Please, let's just go! Please!

Chapter 22

It's been a week since I left Stan handcuffed to the bed. I might go and check on him today. I know that leaving him there is not right, but I'm trying to teach him a lesson. My cell's been off for about a week also, so I have not talked to Toy. I needed time to get my thoughts together. I needed a little time to get to know Mama as well. Though, I have not been up to the hospital since the day before yesterday. I have called and checked on her every day.

Mama's doing well. I am so proud of her. The doctors said that she has been improving tremendously. Chuck took me to get Stan's car about three days ago. Chuck thinks that my Uncle has changed. He does not know that I have him handcuffed in that house. Stan's a tough guy. He should still be alive. I'm on my way to the hospital now to take Mama some smell goods. I hope she likes these DKNY sweat suits I brought her. I can't have her looking like she has a bum for a daughter. I look good so Mama definitely has to.

Hmm, is that Jasmine's voice I hear? I thought to myself as I walked in Mama's room. I feel so childish for standing here eavesdropping, but their conversation sounds deep.

"Mama, why did you let daddy rape me; why did you let your pimp Henry rape me? Why would you do that to me? Why Mama?" Jasmine asked.

I looked under the bottom of the curtains that's pulled all the way around the area they are in. I saw Mama get up as she sat on the side of her bed. Mama cleared her throat and began speaking.

"Jasmine, come here and let me tell you my story."

I tip toed in the room, walked behind the curtain, and sat in the chair with my feet lifted up so they couldn't see me. Mama continued saying, "Baby girl, I love you and your sister. I'm sorry that I was a victim of rape. I thought that since my Mama let her men rape and molest me, that's what I was supposed to let happen to my kids. You have to realize that's all I knew, Jasmine. I know better now and I am so sorry. Your grandmother let her men rape me. None of that started until Mama left my daddy. She told my daddy that he didn't have what it takes to be a real man and she was leaving him for Carlos. Carlos was a big time drug dealer who traveled back and forth to his house in Atlanta and his house in Detroit. He decided to move Mama and me to his Detroit home. We left Daddy back in Atlanta. Daddy quit his job as a youth counselor and started selling drugs too. He said that Mama was telling him that the fast money is what she needed. The fast life is what she wanted and he couldn't provide it. I watched daddy turn into something he was not just because he wanted to show Mama how much he loved her. Mama didn't care. She stayed with Carlos. That's when she got hooked on drugs. When Mama started using drugs real heavy she allowed Carlos to do whatever he wanted to me just so she could support her habit. I remember asking Mama the same question you just asked me. I wanted to know why she allowed her boyfriend to do that to me. Mama said that's how we kept all of the finer things that money could buy. She said men paid good money to sleep with me. When Mama died I kind of lost myself. I didn't care about where I ended up.

"How did grandma die?" Jasmine asked.

"Mama got into a huge fight with Carlos because she wanted to stop using drugs, but he wouldn't let her. Mama was his tester. Every new drug he got he made Mama try it. She was obviously tired of being his tester so she left. She left me there with him for a few weeks. I stayed over my best friend Jessie's house most of the time. Her mom told me to call my daddy so I did. He flew me back to Atlanta. When I got there Mama was there. She was clean and sober. Daddy helped Mama get off those drugs. My mom and dad got into a huge argument because I was pregnant. After their huge fight we went back to Carlos's house in Detroit."

"Who were you pregnant with?" Jasmine interrupted.

"I never got a chance to name it or even find out if it was a boy or a girl because Mama made me get an abortion. I was only thirteen plus I was pregnant by Carlos."

Damn, Mama been through a lot; no wonder she got strung out on drugs, I thought as I continued listening.

"I called my Dad when I got back to Detroit from Jessie's house. My dad said that he had just landed in Detroit. He got the directions from Jessie's Mom and when he arrived he asked me where Mama and her boyfriend stayed. I pointed to the house next door. As soon as daddy attempted to walk off the porch we heard gun shots. After we heard the gun shots daddy ran over there. When I finally pulled away from Mama Campbell I ran over there. When I walked in the house Mama was lying in a puddle of blood and so was Carlos. Carlos killed my mom and then he pulled the gun on himself. Daddy was holding Mama. I tried to see things clearly between the tears that filled my eyes. Daddy was checking Mama's pulse. I stood there staring at daddy. He was lying over Mama crying. The police ran right past me almost pushing me to the ground. They surrounded daddy and yelled "Freeze." The police told daddy to put his hands behind his head, but he didn't listen. He continued holding Mama. All of a sudden he reached in his jacket pocket. That's when the police shot him ten times in his back. Daddy fell backwards and opened his hand. **They killed my daddy over a piece of Kleenex**" Mama said.

I sat here wiping my tears because I heard Mama break down crying, and the she continued talking.

"That's when I moved in with Mama Campbell. She adopted me and Jessie, me and Stan became brothers and sisters. Stan and I became the best of friends because Jessie got pregnant and moved in with her boyfriend. One day, I went home and no one was there, but Stan. I walked in his room without knocking and he snapped. Stan slapped me and through me up against the wall. I tried to fight him back, but I couldn't beat him. He took out a glass tube and put it up to my nose and I was forced to breathe it in. That's when I started using drugs. They helped me forget about the memory's I had about my mom and dad. I began to sniff it all the time and then I started shooting it. Stan and I began sleeping together. I met this guy name Carlos who was gay. I always thought it was interesting that my Friend Carlos was nothing like my Mom's boyfriend Carlos. Stan always accused me of sleeping with him, but I never did. He tried to forbid me from seeing Carlos, but I didn't. Carlos is still one of my very good friends.

I thought Stan said Carlos was my daddy, I thought as I continued listening to Mama.

"Stan was trying out for the FBI then. Once he made the FBI he started doing coke with me. I don't know how he was able to hide it. When he got high he would get violent and force his self on me. He told me to keep it a secret. I had no one to tell anyway because Jessie was with her boyfriend and Mama Campbell was never home. When she was home she was always drunk. Ever since her husband Jeff died she drowned herself in alcohol. So no one really cared about me anyway. Stan was the only one who showed that he really *loved me* at least that's what I thought it was …"

Stan is really psychotic, I thought to myself. He did the same thing to Mama that he done to me. I hope he is dead. I knew he started Mama on those drugs. I sat here thinking before I focused my attention back to Mama's conversation.

"I started getting sick. I thought that it was the drugs so I paid no attention to it. It seemed like every morning I vomited. Mama Campbell decided to rush me to the hospital. After the doctor ran some test he came in the room and told me I was pregnant."

"Who were you pregnant with Mama?" Jasmine asked.

"I was pregnant with your sister, Victoria" Mama replied.

For some reason everything Stan said earlier is beginning to make a great deal of sense. 'When I had you, I was so happy'. I created you for me' and all that crap.

"Mama, are you saying that Uncle Stan is really Victoria's father" Jasmine asked.

I sat here bald up in this chair hoping and wishing that Mama is not about to say what I think she is. "I can't take it anymore" I shouted as I stormed over to Mama. "Mama, are you saying that Stan is my daddy?"

Tears began to fall from her eyes while she sat there with a shocked look on her face. "Baby, how long you been out there?" She asked.

As I inhaled and exhaled deeply I shouted, "Cut the crap Mama, is Stan my daddy or not?"

The tears began pouring out from her eyes when she looked at me and shook her head, "Yes Victoria, Stan is your Father."

After I was able to stop regurgitating my insides out I took a piece of paper towel and wiped my mouth. I placed a cold towel on my head as I stood here trembling.

"You know what, I am about to kill this sick baster." I yelled before I ran out the hospital. I heard Mama and Jasmine screaming for me to come back. But fuck that. *If this sick bastard is not dead, he's damn sure about to be*, I thought as I did about a hundred to Stan's house. I reached in the glove box for Stan's gun I took the other day. *If he's dead I'm going to beat him until he wakes up.*

I ran in the house and as I was about to run up the stairs, I heard a female crying "Please don't do this."

"Oh my God" I yelled when I noticed Toy tied up naked in the dining room chair. Stan is sitting there looking like a zombie. "Stan, what are you doing? What is going on here? How did you get a loose?"

My heart feels like it is about to explode when I noticed the gun in Stan's hand. He stood up and stared at me with the scariest looking smile. "I am a man! Did you think that I was going to let you, a child keep me handcuffed to the bed!" He asked sarcastically.

I looked at Toy. She has a confused puppy dog look on her face with tears running faster by the second.

"Victoria, what's going on? You've been sleeping with your Uncle all this time? Ugh, Victoria! How could you? You are so nasty. He said that I'm coming in between you two. How could you Victoria?" Toy asked.

I stood here in a state of confusion. I can't begin to process a thought or a reply as I stared at Toy sitting in that chair crying and judging me at the same time. I feel so horrible. "Toya, I am so sorry about this.

You don't know how sorry I am. You just don't know Toy, you really just don't know. I wanted to tell you, but I couldn't. It's not my fault" I explained. The longer I stood here staring at her the faster my adrenaline began to pump. "Stan, let her go! I need to talk to you now!" I screamed.

"You don't need to talk to me about shit!" he yelled.

"Stan, I just left the hospital. Mama told me about 'your secret'."

"What did she say?" he asked as if he has something to hide.

"You know what she said, you sick motherfucker!" I yelled as I pulled out the gun from my purse. "Stan, I need to talk to you now!" I demanded.

Stan took his gun and pressed it up against Toy's temple. "I'm so sorry Victoria, it's too late now!" he said. Toya is looking so confused. I feel so bad right now. She has nothing to do with this.

"I will kill her Victoria!" Stan threatened as he put Toy in a choke hold and cocked the trigger. Don't leave me Victoria. I told you we can still make this work. Put your gun down and I will let her go."

I cocked the trigger on the gun in my hand. "Stan, I promise I will blow your head off if you don't let her go now!" I shouted. "Let her Go-o-o-o you psychotic bastard!

"Boom!"

I watched the blood pouring from Toya's head with her eyes still open looking at me. "Ahhhhhhh! You son of a biiiiiiitch … …." "Pop! Pop! Pop! Pop! Pop! Pop!" I fired six shots. I saw one hit his chest, his arm and his leg. He fell to the ground. I looked in my purse for my cell phone. I opened it up and noticed this is not my purse, its Toya's.

I grabbed my phone from her purse that I had been carrying since we last seen each other. We had the same wallet and same things in our purse, so I didn't notice the difference. I walked over to get my purse that's covered in her blood lying next to her dead body. I reached inside and grabbed my wallet with all of my Identification. I wiped my finger prints off of the gun and the door knob. I ran out the house and jumped in Stan's car.

"Chuck, where are you? I need you! Please help me!" I yelled through Chirps walkie- talkie.

"Baby, where are you?" he asked.

I explained to him that I was going to marry you and that's when he beat me and raped me. When I came back from Church he was at Toy's house waiting on me. He told me about my mom getting shot. So the first day when I went to the hospital; my mom looked at him and she was screaming "no." I asked him what that was about and he told me that it was the drugs. Though, I still don't know what that was about. I went back to the house with him and he beat me really bad then he raped me again. I played it off and acted like everything was cool. Toy came over and we chilled in the pool. I walked in the bathroom and seen him licking the powder off that lady. That's when I walked out and called you. You remember the day he sent the cops up to the school. He met me at a warehouse and he told me that he was going to kill me. That's why I told you to come get me. I decided that I would go over there and tell him that I was never coming back. He grabbed the gun and handcuffed me to the bed and forced heroine up my nose. When I vomited all over myself and him he untied me. I convinced him to let me handcuff him to the bed, that's when I called you to come get me from there. So today, I went up to the hospital to talk to my Mama and see why was this man acting crazy. I found out that he did the same thing to my mom. He was the one who got my mom strung out. I ran out the hospital and went back to the house. When I walked in the house I noticed Toya was sitting in a chair tied up butt naked and Stan was sitting at the table holding a gun. I assume that Toya came to the house looking for me because a few minutes ago on my way out the door, I noticed she had my purse and I had hers. I told Stan that Mama told me what happened. He put the gun up to Toya's head and when I demanded for him to let her go he blew her head off right in front of me. That's when I shot him. I fired six shots. He fell to the ground and I left. I am facing prison time if he's dead Chuck, but that's not the worst part. I found out that Stan is my father."

"Oh baby, I am so sorry. I am so sorry. We are going to get through this. You didn't know any better. That's exactly why I took you over my Aunt Lynn's. I knew that something like that was going on. I told my Aunt about the way you were acting and she explained to me that she was acting the same way and the day we left she called me and confirmed it. She said she knew for a fact that your uncle, well your father was molesting you. She said it's a certain way that females who have been sexually assaulted act and you fit the category perfectly. I love you Victoria. I am here for you. When I told you that I love you and I want you to be my wife that's what I meant and nothing has and or will change. He got what he deserved. I prayed that the demon that was attacking you would be destroyed."

I looked at Chuck with a face full of tears and asked, "Chuck, why do you want me so badly, why do you love me the way you do? What is it in me that makes you still want to love me? My best friend is dead because of me and I am facing life in prison. Chuck, I don't understand what happened. I prayed that God would help me out. I just don't understand it seems like everything has gotten worse since I decided to trust in God.

"Watch your mouth little Mama. Don't say that. Trusting in God is the best thing you could have ever done. Just because things don't work out the way we think they should doesn't mean that God is not working them out. You have to understand that when we decide to give our lives to God, the devil hates that. He is going to attack you at your weaknesses. The devil knew that Toya was your best friend; he knew that you wanted to escape Stan. He made that man do those evil things to you. That's why you shot him. God seen everything before it happened. Sometimes God will shake things up to put them in perfect order and to provide you with perfect peace. Did you call on God in the mist of all that?"

I looked at him feeling so bad. I kept remembering *God will shake things up a bit in order to put them in perfect order.* I heard that before. Oh the lady at the hospital Ms. Melanie, My Angel. I continued to stare at him with tears running down my face. I shook my head and replied, "No Chuck, I didn't remember to call on God."

"See that's what happens, we don't remember to call on his name in the midst of our troubles. I can pray for you only of so much. If you don't ask God to protect you then me asking is obsolete. Do you understand what I am saying?" He asked.

"Yes, I think I do."

"Now when one or more comes in agreement then he is in our presence. That's why I always ask you to pray with me. If I was praying for you and you were not praying for yourself then my prayers don't work as good. I can pray for you all I want, but if the person that I am praying for is not calling on his name then the prayers are faded. God hears all of them, it's just he needs that soul that is being prayed for to want prayer and pray to him also."

"Well Chuck, let's pray now. Please help me pray." I begged.

Chapter 23

We pulled up in Chuck's garage. We walked in the house. He locked his door and walked in the living room. "Victoria, come on get on your knees." He insisted.

We kneeled down in the same spot that we were in before. He grabbed his bible and began reading.

"He that dwell in the secret place of the most high shall abide under the shadow of the Almighty. I will say unto the Lord, He is my refugee and my fortress: my God; in him I will trust. Surely he shall deliver thee from the snare of the fowler, and from the noisome pestilence. He shall cover thee with his feathers, and under his wings shall thou trust. His truth should be thy shield and buckler. Thou shall not be afraid for the terror by night, nor for the arrow that flee by day, Nor for the pestilence that walk in darkness, nor for the destruction that waste at noon day."

He paused, and then he turned the page and continued,

"For he shall give his angels charge over us, to keep us in all thy ways. I have just read *Psalms 91:1-6 & 11.* Lord, please add your blessings unto this reading."

He reached over and grabbed my hand.

"Dear Lord, it is I, Charles Mathews and Victoria Campbell coming before you once again, in search of you father. I know that you say when one or more comes in agreement to worship your name, you are in our presence. I am here Lord because one of your souls is in need. I am always in need, but right now we have a special request Lord."

Chuck opened his eyes and looked at me. "Victoria talk to our father, tell him what is on your heart" he said.

I sat here quiet in shock, not knowing what to say. Chuck noticed my hesitation. He then said, "Victoria, speak from your heart. God already knows, but he wants you to confess it with your mouth."

Heart pounding, crying, I took a deep breath.

"God I am so sorry for what just happened. I know that you saw the whole thing. I know that you've seen everything. I feel that I am not worthy of your grace, but I know that you are a forgiving God. I feel so lost. I don't know if I killed Stan, only you know. My best friend is now dead because of me. She was at the wrong place at the wrong time. I did not mean for her to get in the middle of it. I did not know that she would have been there. Lord, please let her go to heaven. I will vouch for her even though I know that's not much. I have been told and I have noticed how you moved in so many people's lives. I know that I may be punished for my actions. I am scared for my life. God, I don't want to die. Lord, please I don't want to die. I know that people say what goes around comes around, if you live by the gun you die by the gun, but I don't live by it. I used one towards who I just found out was my father. I don't want my life to be shortened because of that. I did not know that he was my father until today. Lord, I am so scared and I don't know what to do. I want you to protect me, please. If you would let your angels surround me. I am grateful. Lord, if it is your will that I have to go to jail, can you please make it so that my judge will hear my case and see that it is not entirely my fault. Please don't let my mother go back to drugs because of this. Please don't let my little sister Jasmine be influenced by my actions. God, I am so, so, so, scared right now. I don't know what to do, I need you. Thank you for allowing Chuck to stay by my side Lord, Thank you. Amen"

Chuck squeezed my hand and continued praying. "Heavenly Father, I pray that you hear our prayer. I know that you will not put more on us than we can bear. No weapons formed against us shall prosper. We pray this in your son Jesus name Amen."

I replied "Amen" as I stayed on my knees, crying, pouring out my tears. Chuck kept rubbing my back telling me to let it out. Charles is so strong, he is holding it together for the both of us and I am so thankful. I stood up, without knowing what to do. Chuck grabbed my arm and walked me back to his room.

"Baby, you know we have to watch the news and see what's happening." Chuck stated.

Chuck and I sat on his bed. He grabbed the remote and turned on the news. There it was "Breaking News on Detroit's west side." Chuck raised the volume.

"It appears to be a double shooting. One of the victims is described as a young African American female in her early twenties, who authorities have pronounced as dead on arrival. The other victim is an Ex- FBI agent by the name of Stanley Campbell. He was fired several months ago due to child molestation, sexual assault and attempted murder charges pending against him."

Chuck and I looked at each other and then continued listening to the news reporter.

"Mr. Campbell has been air lifted to the hospital by local officials. We are in search of his niece, Victoria Campbell for questioning. If anybody is aware of her where about please Contact Channel 8 action News at 1-800- Speak- Up. Police are on the scene now trying to locate evidence as well as any witnesses who may have seen anything. Once again you can call the number on the bottom of your television screen, back to you Dan."

I sat here staring at the Television screen. I don't know how they got that picture of me. I can't believe how embarrassing this is. I feel so bad. Chuck obviously felt my pain because he put his arms around me and squeezed me tight.

"A dog aint that yo girl on the news" the guy said as he burst through Chuck's chirp. Chuck didn't respond. He pressed the power button and turned his phone off.

I sat here in Chuck arms crying. I lifted my head out of his chest and looked at him. "Chuck, I just want to say thank you. Thank you for loving me." I laid my head back on his chest as he held me tighter.

"Baby, we are going to get through this." When he said that, I felt that tingle sensation throughout my body.

"Chuck, God must not be mad at me because I just felt his spirit. It's still tingling" I said in excitement.

Chuck squeezed me tighter and replied, "God is not mad at you. He loves you."

Chuck's right. I know God saw everything that happened to me in my whole entire life. *He can't be mad at me at least I hope He isn't*, I thought. I know God is going to help me through this either way. "Chuck, I am going to call the number and turn myself in."

"Victoria, are you sure?" Chuck asked.

"Yes, I'm sure." I replied as I grabbed the phone and called the number. I paused as I listened to the woman on the other side of the phone.

"Hello 1-800- Speak Up, how may I help you?"

I took a deep breath. "Hi, my name is Victoria Campbell and I just seen the news."

"Hold one moment while I connect you with the police department."

I heard a little music then, "Special Crimes Unit, this is Lieutenant Braxton, Ms. Campbell is this you?"

"Yes it is."

"Ok Ms. Campbell we need you to come down to the 7th precinct right away"

"Ok sir, I'm on my way." I said before I hung up the phone.

Chuck didn't say anything. He just grabbed the keys and my jacket and we went to the car. We pulled up at the police station. I am so nervous at this point, but I trust God in this situation. Chuck and I went in. I walked up to the desk.

"Hi, my name is Victoria Campbell. I need to see officer Braxton."

"Have a seat, he will be with you shortly." The officer behind the desk said.

Chuck sat down with me and held my hand. There's a tall, black older looking cop in a suit walking over to us.

"Ms. Campbell, I'm Lieutenant Braxton" he said as he stretched out his hand. I shook it even though my hand is trembling.

"Please, come with me." He requested

"Can my fiancé come with me?" I asked.

He smiled. "No, he cannot, but he can have a seat you won't be long."

I followed Officer Braxton thinking all types of things. *That is so nice of him being friendly, shaking my hand and all before he takes me to jail,* I thought. I wonder does he want Chuck to wait here so he can take my jewelry home with him. I don't know what's going on. I took several deep breaths on my way to his office.

I walked in his office.

"You may have a seat." he said.

As I went to sit down, I noticed Mama sitting there.

"Mama, what are you doing here?" I asked as I am beginning to notice how pretty she looks.

She looked so much better, she was looking better earlier, but after I heard the news about Stan I didn't pay any attention to her. Mama looked at me with a tear rolling down her cheeks and a smile on her face. She patted her hand on the seat next to her. "Baby, have a seat" She said.

I sat down and looked at her.

"Sweet heart, I knew that Stan was molesting you. I've been seeing Stan every week since I left you. First let me tell you that was not by choice. I will explain that story to you later. As I was saying, Stan told me that he was molesting you. I was too high to hear it. At least I forced myself not to hear it because there was nothing I could do about it at the time. He told me how he was going to make you fall in love with him so that you could replace me. I didn't want to hear it at the time. Ever since I had gotten pregnant with you, I explained to Stan that he was your father. He continuously denied it. Though, I know Stan knew that you were his. You look just like me and your Aunt Jessie. Jessie and I are not blood as I'm sure you heard me explain to your sister earlier. Well baby, Last Sunday I seen Stan at the store. I told him that I had been working on getting myself together, so that I could get my kids back. I threatened Stan by telling him that if he didn't let me talk to you that when I did talk to you, I was going to reveal to you that he was your father. He said that he didn't want that so he told me to get in the car and ride with him. He said that he was taking me to you." Mama said as she was squeezing my hand trying to hold back her tears.

"I thought that he was taking me to go and see you, but he pulled into this alley and forced me to get out of his car. When I got out of his car he shot me twice. His last words to me that I heard before I fell to the ground were, 'since you want to see your daughter so bad, I'm going to make sure that the last time she sees you is going to be on your death bed.' I fell to the ground. Apparently Stan thought that I was dead because he called the ambulance, disguised his voice and said that he wanted to report a dead body in the alley. He told them exactly where I was. When I came to I was in the ambulance and Stan was nowhere to be found. I thought I was dreaming because it didn't seem real. I filed a police report against Stan about three years ago. I told them that he was molesting our child and of course they weren't going to believe a female who was a drug addict. Though, they said after their investigation my accusations were proven to be invalid. I filed a new report about two months ago that's when Paul and David were assigned to watch him. Sunday after Stan shot me, Officer Braxton here," Mama said as she smiled at him and he smiled back, "came up to the hospital and told me that he would send David and Paul over to his house to keep an eye on him. About a month ago, my good friend Charlene agreed that she would try to occupy Stan's time so that he would not bother you as much. That girl you seen in the bathroom with him was my friend Charlene, but you might know her as Stephanie." Mama said as she smiled.

"I had her come over there to distract him so that you would get away. I knew that if you were anything like your Mama, you would have noticed that opportunity to leave. Charlene told me that you did leave. Then she told me that he called her at the phone booth telling her that you had taken the keys and left his car on the freeway with the doors locked. I smiled because I knew my baby girl was stronger than her Mother. Charlene had just left me that day that you came up to the hospital with your fiancé. Remember baby" Mama asked as she wiped the tears from my eyes.

"Remember baby, you came up there with that fine fiancé of yours, you stood by my bed side and said 'Mama, you have to leave them drugs alone. We need you Mama. I am graduating and I did this all for you. I hope you are proud of me.' You said. I sat there crying because I knew that my baby was just like me. I saw in you what I had in myself, but never had the courage to do, or be and that's being my own person. Victoria, I love you so much and I just want to say, you make me want to live again. Both of my babies make me want to live again. You two are so strong."

I sat here crying, and I cried even harder when I watched Mama cry.

"Mama, Thank you. I love you and I missed you. I need you. I have Chuck and I have God. I know that God is enough but I want you, Jasmine and Chuck in my life. I need y'all. I know that without a doubt none of this would be possible without God, so He is never left out. Mama we should all go to Church and get saved. I'm saved Mama. I have accepted Jesus Christ as my personal savior. Do you Mama?" I asked smiling inside and out. Mama smiled, squeezed my hand and replied, "You know I do precious."

"Excuse me Ladies, I hate to break up this touching moment here, but we have a dead body here and an Ex- FBI agent listed in critical condition." Lieutenant Braxton said commanding me and Mamas attention.

"Victoria, I have voicemails on both of the victim's phones that I think that you should hear. The first voicemail you should hear is the one from Mr. Campbell that was left on Latoya's voice mail."

He pressed the speaker phone, I heard Stan's voice.

"Hey Toya I need you. Victoria dumb ass done locked me up on the bed with handcuffs. She came over here going crazy. I don't know what has gotten into her. I broke away from the bed, but I need you to bring me the keys to get these damn bed rails off of my wrist. I think I left a set in your car the other day, look under the front seat and bring them boo. A, hurry up, big daddy misses you. Don't ask any questions just hurry and I will beat it up when you get here."

"Ok we have a voicemail from a few days ago." Officer Braxton said.

"Hey Toya this is your chocolate bear, make sure you come over because I am still barbecuing. I'm glad Victoria didn't pick up on me, when she called and I answered the phone, 'hey sexy'. Damn she could have caught us. Also I need you to stop looking at me like that. You were staring at me hard when you came out the house Saturday. I'm glad my niece didn't pick up on it. I love you girl. Call me back.

I do not believe this, I thought to myself. I acted as if I was not bothered by the voicemails, yet I was interested in hearing what Toy had to say. "Let me hear his voicemail please." I insisted.

"Ok this is the one that was left a few days ago." He said.

"Hey Chocolate Bear, Victoria just called me she wants me to drop her off over there, so I'm waiting on Chuck to drop her off. I miss you baby, I love you. You lucky I forgive your ass for being with that crack head looking whore. I understand you had to have her over there to keep our affair secret. Don't do that shit no more. I mean it. Oh and you should go ahead and let Victoria go to an out of state college so we can be together. I love you. Call me right back"

"Here is one another one."

"Hey baby, Victoria is long gone with Chuck to Indiana. I guess he went to drop off another package. I will be over there tonight. Make sure you tell her that you are going to Indiana, but it doesn't matter, I don't think she thinks anything is happening any way. She's too busy stuck in Chuck's ass. Don't forget that I need some money. Just drop off about $800, I will tell her that you only dropped off $500. I know that she's going to tell me that I can have some anyway, I'm her best friend."

Then there is one more on here that was left today.

"Hey Stan it's me. You know who it is. You know I am not fucking anybody, but you. I know you know that this is your baby. Why are you dodging my calls? If I don't hear from you today I am going to have my cousin come over there and put a couple of hot one's in your ass. We've been together for the last two and a half years, now all of a sudden when I get pregnant you don't want anything to do with me. This is bulshit Stan! I love you. I need you to come and pick me up daddy I am so horny, I need you. I don't want to be with anybody else, but you Stan. Please call me back. We can raise our family together. Let Victoria go to college and marry Chuck. You act like you want her for yourself. Ok, sorry maybe I shouldn't of said that, but seriously. You did this to me. I'm in love with you Stan. Me and your baby needs you. Call me back, I love you, Bye."

Lieutenant Braxton deleted all of the messages on Toy's phone. He saved the last message from Toy that was left on Stan's phone. "We're going to save this one as evidence" he said as he put the cell phones back in the clear plastic bag and looked at my mom smiling and then he looked at me. "Victoria did you have any idea that this was going on?" he asked.

"No sir, I didn't." I replied as I continued to sit here thinking. Oh that's how Stan knew that I was in Indiana, he just made all that up. Damn he's a good liar. Toy was a good one too. All those little comments talking about 'damn your Uncle sexy and all that crap. I was wondering why he was answering his phone, Hey sexy and hey baby. *He's a trip with luggage*, I thought. I guess Stan realized the people he could take advantage of. He could have fooled me about Toy though because I would have never suspected Toy to even get down with him like that. Did Stan know our weak points? I am his daughter for crying out loud. That's what he meant when he kept saying that he created me. At first I didn't understand why he killed her. I knew that it had to be more to the story. He was sleeping with her and she had gotten pregnant. If she would have had the baby, he or she would have been my little brother or sister. Yeah that would have been weird.

"It's scum like him that makes good cops like me appear to be the bad guys. That man has major issues." Lieutenant Braxton said. "Victoria we advise you not to leave the state until the pending investigation is over."

"Ok, no problem," I replied.

"Officer Braxton, I think you should take a look at this." The officer who walked in his office said.

I sat her shaking, nervous and ready to break down. Did somebody see what I had done? What's going on? I sat here thinking to myself as I watched Lieutenant Braxton reading. He kept sucking his teeth mumbling "um, um, um" He looked at me.

"Victoria, this is a statement from your next door neighbor."

Tears began to fall from my eyes. *Oh my God I'm going to jail*, I thought to myself. Officer Braxton looked at me with a strange look. "Victoria, what's wrong? I know things could get a bit overwhelming, but is everything ok?" He asked.

I wiped my tears and replied, "Oh no Lieutenant Braxton everything is fine. I just had visions of Stan that's all, it startled me. I'm fine though. God is good." I sat here trying to convince myself the same thing that I just told him.

"Oh ok, I understand" he replied. "Now back to the statement I was reading, your neighbor by the name of Mrs. Angel Love, says that she witnessed a guy dressed in all black with a face mask on leaving Stan's house. I guess he's who's responsible for the gun shot wombs that Stan received. At first we could not figure out who fired the shots. That's what we were investigating. She said he drove off in Stan's car. This guy was very smart because there are no finger prints on the door or in the car anywhere. I guess that settles it. This case is closed. It's simply a case of Domestic Violence. You are free to go. Thanks for coming in. We appreciate it." He stood up and shook my hand. "Have a good night" he said.

I smiled and said, "Ok thank you Lieutenant Braxton. You have a goodnight as well. As I began walking out the door I turned around and looked at Mama. "Come on Mama, are you going with me?"

She smiled, "Oh yeah baby, I will be out there in a minute. I have to talk to the Lieutenant for a minute. Gone on out front, I'll be out there in a second." She said showing her pretty white teeth.

I walked out into the lobby thinking, *Yep, that's my Mama because Lieutenant Braxton is fine. Mama in there flirting with that man"* I laughed to myself. I noticed Chuck pacing back and forth. I snuck up behind him, "oh I know your feet must be tired because you've been running through my mind all day."

He turned around hugged me in excitement. "What happened?" he asked.

"I will tell you in a few. I think we have to drop my Mom off."

Chuck smiled. "Your mother's back there?" he asked.

"Yes she is" I said as I smiled from ear to ear. I started thinking *Mama must have brushed her teeth while she was on drugs because they are so pretty and white.* I like the way she looks in that baby blue DKNY outfit I brought her.

"Here Mama come now" I said to Chuck. She's walking over here with a smile wider than mine. "Did you get his number" I teased.

She held up a card and smiled.

"Hi Tamara, How are you?" Chuck asked appearing to be just as happy as I am. She walked up to him and looked at him real close. "Chuck baby, is that you?" she asked.

"Yes ma'am" he replied. She hugged him. "I knew that I kind of seen a fine guy up in my hospital room, but I didn't know it was you. You take care of my baby now, you hear me." Mama said actually sounding like a mother, though she is my mother; it's just new to me.

"Mama, we are going to take care of each other." I said. She smiled and kissed me on my cheek.

"So mom, where are you staying?" I asked.

"Well your Aunt Jessie is going to let me stay there with her and all those kids of hers. I am going to baby sit for her and she said I can get them babysitting checks instead of her paying the day care. I will only be watching Joseph, and James, the other ones are in school. I'm going to get back on my feet again. I may start back doing hair. You know your Mama can do hair right?" She said, smiling while putting her hand on her hip. *Of course I didn't know that mom; I haven't seen you in almost twelve years.* Of course I didn't say that to her. I just smiled at her and replied, "No, I didn't know that.

"Yeah, I think I may go and get my license, and start back doing hair again." She said.

"That's good. So you can hook me up at graduation, because I graduate in two weeks."

"Oh that's right, I am watching my baby graduate. My friends are going to be so jealous." She said as she snapped her neck as if she was one of the young girls.

Chuck interrupted, "Excuse me, I don't mean to disturb you, but how about we all go to Church on Sunday and then to dinner all on me."

"Yeah Mama and we can get Jasmine to go. Cool. So Mama you need a ride to Aunt Jessie's?"

She picked up her Detroit Receiving Hospital bag and replied, "Yeah, why not."

We got in the car. Mama said "ooh we Chuck this is a bad car, you done had this for a while now?" Even though she wasn't talking to me

I replied, "Yeah ma, he had it when I first met him when I was in the ninth grade."

"Oh that's how long you two been together." She asked.

"Yeah it's been about four years now. We are graduating together, and hopefully we will be graduating college together." I replied. Chuck grabbed my hand and smiled.

We pulled up at Aunt Jessie's house on the eastside. You can tell a lot of older people live here. *Mama is going to be ok*, I thought as we got out the car. I hugged Mama and then I walked her to the door. Aunt Jessie opened the door, and screamed. She grabbed my Mama hugging her and crying, she kept saying "Thank You Jesus." I was crying too because I know how she feels. I am so happy to see my mom, and she's getting better. I know she is going to be ok.

Aunt Jessie looked at me and said "Come here and hug my neck honey" I hugged her. "You look so much like your Mama chile." I was looking at her because I didn't know if she knew what happened to Stan. I knew she knew though, because Mama had to have told her. Just as I was thinking this, Aunt Jessie looked me in my eyes and said, "God is going to take care of it. Don't worry about it. God knows trust me suga he knows" and then she grabbed my mom and they walked in the house.

Chapter 24

I walked back down to the car crying because I'm happy, but then again I'm a little sad because Toy was my girl. I am going to miss her.

Chuck hugged me. "So baby, tell me what happened." He said as if he was anxious to know.

"Well baby, basically Toya and Stan had been sleeping together for three years. They called it a case of Domestic Violence. Mama said that Stan was the one who shot her. He shot her because she was going to tell me that he was my daddy. I reached in my purse, "hold on baby, I need to make a call."

"Hello, May I speak to Mama Jackson?"

"Yes. This is she."

"Hey Ma, this is Victoria."

"Hey baby, the police just leaving they say it was Domestic Violence. I didn't know that she was sleeping with your Uncle Victoria."

"I didn't know either. I am so sorry, do you need anything." I asked.

"No honey, I just need you to come by and see me. That was my only baby girl and now she's gone. She was only twenty one. My baby had a whole life a head of her. I just don't know where I went wrong. I thought if I brought her everything she wanted, kept her in nice clothes and let her do what she wanted that she would be ok. After me and her dad split, we always competed on who would buy her the most things instead of providing her with the things she needed and that was love. Instead, she searched for it in a man, twice her age; someone who was more of a father figure. I don't know how I can forgive myself."

"Mama, Latoya was grown. She was aware of what she wanted. You didn't do anything wrong. You basically helped raised me and I think you have done an excellent job. Please don't be mad at yourself God just needed another angel on duty. Now you know who your angel is." I said.

I listened to her screaming and crying, my heart couldn't bear it. I began to think about the days we hung out, riding around Belle Isle, getting high, going shopping, oh yeah that time we had to fight those girls in the club. Yeah we had some fun. Sharing clothes, playing cards at Kettering, talking about what we wanted to do with our lives. I don't know how she felt about God though. I asked her and she said that the Church thing wasn't for her. I can't judge her for that; I can't judge her at all. I am going to miss her so much. I sat here crying too. "Ma, I will come over and help you tomorrow, ok. Be strong please. I will call you tomorrow. I love you."

"Ok, I love you to baby." She replied before she burst out crying again before hanging up the phone.

I hung up the phone sitting here thinking about the fun times Toy and I had and how she's gone now. That was my best friend. She was my sister. Chuck stopped at the red light and reached over and hugged me with tears falling from his eyes. I know that he had good memories about her too. She was just in love with the wrong man. And the same man was in love with me, his own daughter.

Charles pulled up in the garage. We went in the house, sad but thankful that God heard our prayers. Chuck went in the bathroom and turned on the shower while I fell to my knees.

Dear God, you already had it in your plan, you had already seen my situation and you worked it out. I thank you. I am sad that I had to lose a best friend and a sister in the process, but I am thankful that you brought my mom to me. I hope that I can be a good big sister to Jasmine and a good Aunt to my nephew. Lord Thank you for keeping your eye on

Chuck. Thank you for sending him to me. Thank you God for everything. I love you Amen. Oh yeah God, Thank you for Ms. Angel. Amen"

I got up and noticed Chuck standing here smiling with tears falling from his eyes. I don't know about anyone else, but he is a true definition of a real man. I would love for my kids to be blessed with a father like him. I walked over to him and said "Thank you," then I kissed him on the lips. "Baby I'm going to get me a glass of Kool Aid, do you want a glass? I asked.

He said "yes." I went in the kitchen, got the Kool Aid from the refrigerator, got the glasses from the dish rack and sat them on the table next to the unopened mail. I looked and noticed there was a letter that said Wayne State University.

"Chuck! Chuck! Baby, did you know you had a letter from Wayne State in here." I yelled.

He ran in here with his towel around his waist. "Oh yeah, I threw the mail on the table today when I came in. I forgot about it after I called you about ten times and you didn't answer. I was a little worried."

"Well open it." I replied in excitement.

"Nah baby, you do it for me."

I opened the letter and began to read it.

"Dear Mr. Matthews,

We are pleased to tell you that you have been accepted in our University. You will need to call and schedule an appointment with one of the Academic Advisors to schedule classes for this upcoming fall semester. Again, we would like to welcome you to Wayne State University."

I looked up at my baby and he's standing there happy, smiling from ear to ear. All of a sudden he jumped up and yelled, "Yeah! Yeah! I told you your man is going to take care of you. It's only the beginning but it's all good. Thank you God, once again."

I love a man that shows emotion. He is happy about something and he's not afraid to express it. Yep, I want to marry this man in the morning. I thought to myself as I stood here smiling at him.

"Congratulations baby. I am so very proud and happy for you. That reminds me, I'm calling my mom in the morning so I can get my information so I can apply too."

"Yeah you make sure you do that. Victoria I love you. I will never leave you and I will never forsake you. You are my better half. Without you I don't feel complete. I knew from the day I met you in the lunch room when you were playing cards with your girls that I wanted you to be my wife. I knew from that moment I wanted to spend the rest of my life with you."

I am not going to cry, I thought as I laid my head on his shoulder while he squeezed me hugging me extra tight.

♪It's a brand new day♪. Chuck has Patti Labelle's song blasting and the aroma of something delicious woke me up. I here Patti telling me it's a brand new day, but all the drama from yesterday is still weighing kind of heavy on me.

Oh my God, I am so sick. I can't believe it seemed like I just regurgitated everything inside of me up which was not much at all. After I washed my face and brushed my teeth I walked in the kitchen. This food looks so good. My baby cooked some bacon, sausage patties, French toast, scramble eggs with cheese, and grits with cheese, with milk and cranberry juice. I walked over to him and kissed him. "Good morning baby. You have to teach me how to cook." He kissed me back and replied, "Good Morning to you to and I most definitely will." I grabbed Chuck's house phone from the charger so I can call over to Aunt Jessie's.

Someone picked up the phone. I heard music blasting. "Good Morning" Aunt Jessie answered.

"Hello, is there a party going on over there? I asked.

Aunt Jessie laughed. "Oh baby no; me and your Mama just catching up on our teenage years since we really didn't get a chance to catch up on them."

"This early" I asked sarcastically.

"Baby we didn't go to sleep. You know Stan died at 5:53 this morning."

"Oh. Sorry to hear that. Can you put my mom on the phone real quick?"

"Hey my little Angel" Mama said.

"Good morning Mama, how are you?"

"Baby I am so blessed. I'm too blessed to be stressed cup cake. What's up?"

I tried to keep my composure because chills are running all through my body. God's Spirit is here. "Mom, do you know my social security number, and what should I mark on my application for college when it asks about you and my dad's information."

"Just bring them over and I will fill them out for you. Your Mama was a straight A student before. I filled out a few applications to different colleges myself, back in the day."

"Is that right? Ok mom I will be over there later I have to go to Latoya's mom house and help her out with whatever she needs.

"Ok baby, you tell her, I said to be strong ok"

"Ok bye" As I was hanging up I heard her say "wait a minute, girl."

I put the phone back up against my ear. "What is it?" I asked.

"I love you precious and I am so proud of you. Mommy is going to do better now."

"I know Mama and I love you too."

I hung up the phone and started eating. Oh this man can cook. I am still nauseated. *I hope my stomach doesn't throw this food back up,* I thought as I rubbed my stomach. After I finished my food, I got dressed and Chuck took me over to Mama Jackson's house. We pulled up in front of the house. There are cars up and down the street and its only 10:30 a.m.

"Chuck baby, please stay with me for a minute, just until I see if she needs me to help with something."

We walked to the door and Romeo looked at me, he shook his head and walked away. I kind of figured that he would be mad at me because I am the reason that Toya met Stan anyway. I saw Mama. Jackson.

"Hey Ma"

She grabbed me and hugged me real tight. She held on to me without saying a word for about ten minutes. *I know losing a child has got to be tough,* I thought to myself when Mama Jackson finally released me from her arms.

"Thank you for coming Victoria. Every time I look at you, I see my baby girl. You two look so much alike." She said as she reached for Chuck's hand.

"This is my other baby girl. You make sure you love her. If you ever feel that you have to put your hands on her, just leave please. This has got to stop. Cowards kill their wives, and girlfriends. Men today get frustrated with everyday life issues, some are victims of a traumatized child hood and they take it out on the person who shows them the most love. Baby, y'all have to be careful. I know it was my daughter today, but it can be someone else's daughter tomorrow, or someone's son. We just have to pray a little harder for our children. Lord knows I try to raise my babies to the best of my abilities despite the child hood I had. My Mama was a drug addict, but before then she was a child that suffered abuse. I know what I wanted and I knew how I wanted to be treated so that's how I treat my children. I give the best that I can. Sometimes I forget to give them that companionship that they need so badly. They need that love at home so they won't go out in the street looking for it in others that could really care less about them. It's been hard, having to be a good mom, plus provide the income because the cost of living is increasing and the value of our dollar is decreasing daily. I divorced my first husband because he wanted to run around in the streets. He financially provided for Romeo and Latoya, but he wasn't there. I have realized that it is not the amount of money we give our kids or how much we spend on their wardrobe, it's the time and compassion that they need. I am so sorry that I had to learn it from losing my baby girl." She said before she paused and took a deep breath as she wiped her tears.

"All I can do now is be here for my two boys. Steven has been so good to them, taking them to play basketball, going to games. I appreciate that because it is only so much that a mother can do. God created Man and wife. Men are who gives us our strength and God gives the strength to men, but they don't know how to use it sometimes. So God gives the strength to us. Victoria, you keep your strength. Charles you be that strength that Victoria needs. God places people together because he knows what we need. You two have to be there for each other. Get married like you plan to do and live righteously. God will be so pleased and you will forever be blessed. Well babies, God put that on my heart to share with you. I hope you receive it as well as understand it. I have to go and talk to all my relatives from out of town. Victoria, I don't need anything baby. We can handle it all over here; just absorb what I just told you. Charles you absorb it too because you are the strength. Trust God babies. I'll see you. I have to go down to the morgue today and get the autopsy report on my baby. Take care. I will call you baby, y'all gone ahead and do what you have to do today. I'll be ok.

Wow, Mama Jackson is so strong and her words are so heartwarming. I had chills in my body because everything she said made sense to me. The feeling of strength from a man is so powerful.

Chuck and I walked out of the house, sat in the car both looking and feeling different. I could tell that Chuck was thinking real hard. He reached over and hugged me. "Everything Mrs. Jackson just said is so true and so helpful. Baby I appear strong in front of you because I know that I need to, especially since you are going through right now. I went through early in my life and it has affected me now, but it has affected me in a very positive way. I know that I will be there for you as well as my own mother as a matter of fact I am going to see her today. Are you still going with me?"

"Yes boo, you know I am." I replied.

"But like I was saying baby, I could have let the beatings that I witnessed my Father display towards my Mama influence me to be violent towards women as well, but my Mama was the best mother to me. She held me every night and told me that everything was going to be ok. She always told me not to let the way that my father behaved-influence me to act like him. She always said he was just having a rough time in his life at that time. Mama told me that life wasn't perfect and never will be, but I have to remember that I am the only one who can change it. Mama never talked about God that much, but when I visited my Aunt Lynn she never let me forget. When I went to stay with my foster mom Justine, she told me to keep my faith as well. I am thankful for the women that were in my life and I am most definitely thankful for the woman I have in my life right now. That's why I do what I have to do. I knew that you didn't need a drop out for a man. You had your head on and you weren't one of those give me give me girls, like a lot of the females that I dated were. You remember when I said, you would look like a winner on my arm. You replied with oops boo I am already that, so maybe I will add a little finesse to your style. I never forgot that. I smiled on my way back to the table because for the first time I felt that a female did not need me to make her whole. You were already your own person and I liked that. I am going to be the best man I can be, for myself as well as for you and hopefully one day for our children.

As I sat here listening to Chuck I began to think about everything that he just said. I actually remember that day, that's the day that I was blushing and I was so happy that he talked to me … *Bluh,* ugh I had to open the car door because I had to vomit. Chuck is rubbing my back, "Baby you ok" he asked.

"Yes, I'm fine. I think that I am just over whelmed at all the things that are going on. I probably ate too much. I'm ok." I said. He reached in the glove box and handed me some napkins. He opened my hand and gave me an altoid.

"Baby let me tell you in response to what you just said. When I just listened to you I remember all of that. When you walked away from the table, I looked at my girls and said oh my Goodness; I can't believe that he would be interested in someone like me. I felt honored and privileged to be in your presence. It was something about you, and it's still something about you that gives me butterflies every time I look at you. Every time I am near you. I knew from the beginning that I would do any and everything in my power to be the perfect woman for you. I loved you then and love you even more now. I was going home to Stan and even when he would do his do with me, I imagined that it was you. I always thought about you. I always cared and still care about what your thoughts are towards me and about me. I want you in my life forever. I love your soul; your spirit around me makes me feel protected. I feel like nothing else matters when I am with you. I am so happy that God sent you in my life. Charles Matthews, I love you so much and I love you even more just knowing that you love me back."

He looked at me and said "Victoria we were meant to be together, you are my rib."

I smiled and replied, "Chuck, you are the skin and flesh that protects my ribs."

"Baby, we sound like a soap opera" Chuck chuckled.

"No, we sound like love." I replied. We hugged again. Chuck started up the car and put it in gear. "Where to first?" he asked.

"We can go to my Aunt Jessie's house so my mom can help me with my College Applications. I am going to apply to colleges here in the city, since you already got accepted to Wayne State, and then we can always move when we finish school" I suggested.

Chapter 25

We arrived at Aunt Jessie's house. We went in and witnessed Mama and Aunt Jessie doing the hustle.

"Now y'all just have been partying like crazy." I said while smiling.

Mama looked at me and replied, "Baby, I'm so happy that's all. We are all happy. You're happy too, right" she asked.

"Yes Mama, I am."

Mama smiled as she walked over and hugged me squeezing me really tight. After letting me go, she walked over to Chuck and squeezed him just as tight. "Hey son- in- law, what's going on" Mama asked while continuing to squeeze and hug him.

I felt a tap on my shoulder I looked around and Jasmine hugged me. *Ahh, she is so pretty,* I thought to myself. "Hey little Mama, what's going on" I asked while hugging her and smiling from ear to ear.

"Nothing much, just been over here chilling with the old heads, watching them party." She smiled.

I put my hand on my hip, "Now wait just one minute, look at them," as I pointed to Mama and Aunt Jessie, "do they look old to you?" I asked.

We all smiled. Chuck walked over to me and pulled me close to him, "Baby, come here for a minute." He requested.

I followed him onto the porch. "Baby, I have to shoot a move. I need to go check with my boy and pick up my money ok. I'll be back shortly." He said.

I hugged him and kissed him. "Be careful and hurry back baby."

"You know I will." He replied as he got into his car.

I stood here and watched him pull off. I walked back in the house. Everyone is doing the old school hustle to "My eyes don't cry no more" by Stevie Wonder. I jumped in and began hustling with them. I learned this hustle when I was younger from Aunt Jessie. We did this same hustle at my 12th birthday party that was over here. I assumed Aunt Jessie taught Jasmine too. My little cousins were doing it with us also. This is fun; it's like a dream come true. Mamas happy, my little sister is happy, everybody is happy.

You wouldn't believe we are celebrating and I just lost my father, Aunt Jessie lost her brother and Mama lost her child's father. I guess that he was so full of the devil that God had taken him away. Now we are all rejoicing. I am finally happy. This is all the work of God I know.

God, I am sorry that I didn't tell you this earlier, but Thank You. Thank you for everything, Thanks for waking me up this morning. Thanks for the talk with Mama. Jackson. Thanks for bringing my family together. Thanks for sending Charles to me. Thank you for making everything Ok. God, please watch over Charles while he is out there in the streets. God, he is so humble to you and he doesn't want to continue living in that life style. Lord, you know that he has a plan. I have a plan and it is only by your will, please let it be done. I thank you so much and I love you unconditionally in your son Jesus name I pray. Amen."

"Vicky! Victoria! Do you hear us calling you? You're messing up girl, and you throwing us off. Turn! Now dip baby, dip." Mama said while grabbing my arms spinning me around trying to help me get back on track.

I got right back in beat and kept up on speed. The song went off and everybody is out of breath. This is some good exercise. *Bluh*, oops I vomited all over Aunt Jessie's carpet. I know she's pissed; I thought as

I ran to the bathroom and stuck my head in the toilet bowl. I can't wait until this funeral is over. I think that's why I keep throwing up.

Mama walked in the bathroom and sat on the tub with a towel, "Hey precious you ok." She asked while rubbing my back.

I lifted my head from the toilet bowl, "Yeah Mama, I just been sick a lot lately because of all this drama. But I'm ok."

Mama continued rubbing my back while saying "Well baby, I don't know. You have a glow about you. You remind me of me when I was pregnant with you."

"Huh? Mama I'm not pregnant. I had my period last month. I am not pregnant mom, seriously. I am just a little tired and I ate a lot earlier. I'm cool."

She wiped my face with the warm towel and said "ok baby, get on up then and come back out here. Wash your face and get that mouth wash and gargle a bit because oh wee your breath is kicking," as she giggled and fanned her nose.

"Mama, stop it," I said as she walked out the bathroom. I stood up, rinsed my mouth out and continued staring in this mirror trying to see this glow Mama said I have, but I don't see it. *Oh well*, I said to myself as I walked back out into the living room.

I glanced over at the table and noticed that Mama had already taken out the applications and began filling them out. I walked over by her, stood over her and noticed she was almost done with the one for Wayne State. "Oh my goodness, you finished fast."

Mama looked up at me, "I told you I filled out a lot of them before" she smiled.

"Oh ok, that's what's up." I replied as I looked at the pile of Applications. I noticed that Oakland Community College was written on. I picked it up, "oh ma, somebody wrote on this one" I said as I read the applicants name. It read Tamara Campbell.

She took the application from my hands, "oh baby, I wanted to keep this one for myself."

"Ok no problem." I stared at her smiling. On the inside I felt that tingle again. I knew that God was busy up there working in our lives. I am so thankful.

"Can somebody open the door?" Chuck asked bursting through my Nextel.

I jumped up and ran to the door in excitement. I opened the door. He has three big boxes of pizza, cheese bread, and three big bags of Better Made potato chips. He has all the good kind; barbecue, sour cream and plain, with three 2 litter Faygo soda pops. He also has a bag full of candy for the kids. "Ah boo, you are so sweet" I said as I helped him with some of the bags.

The kids ran out from their rooms. My little sister and my little cousin's faces are lit up expressing excitement. Aunt Jessie came out the kitchen smiling. "Oh baby, you are so sweet thank you" she said as she walked over to him and hugged him. "I guess we can eat this chicken I took out, later on for dinner. Lord knows I sure didn't feel like cooking, thank you."

Mama sat at the table continuing to fill out my applications when she looked up and said "my son in law is something else. Don't we all wish we had a man like this one right here?"

"Yeah, y'all keep wishing because this one is mine." I said jokingly. Mama took the stack of applications and smacked me across my butt with them.

We sat around the house after Mama showed me what I need to know and if I had thought about filling out a job application what I should do. She told me that it was so important that I remember my social security number. "You know we ain't nothing, but a number to the government anyway" as Mama said.

"Son -in -law come here for a minute," Mama requested. She told him to kneel down so she can tell him something. I couldn't make it out, but she whispered something to him. He's smiling. "Yeah I kind of figured that too." He said while staring at me smiling. He stood up and walked over to me and hugged me.

"Baby you're still going with me to see my mom right?" he asked.

"Of course I am" I replied.

"He glanced at his Kenneth Cole watch that I brought him, "Ok, baby we need to get going cause I don't want it to get too late."

Chuck's ready to go and see his mom. I'm a bit anxious to meet her. "Ok Chuck and I have to go. I guess we will see y'all later. I love you all."

"We love you too," everyone said as they smiled at me. "We love the both of you be careful out there." Aunt Jessie said while everyone agreed.

I ran and hugged Mama again. "Mama, I'm going to put this application in the mail for you along with mine. I am so proud of you."

She hugged me back and replied, "Thank you baby, now you two be careful ok."

"Yes ma'am." I replied as Chuck and I walked out the door.

Chuck and I got in the car. "Chuck look at this" I said while holding up Mama's application.

"Get out of here!" He replied as he smiled in excitement.

"Yes, Mama is applying to college. She filled out all of my applications and she showed me how to fill them out for myself as well. God is so good Chuck." I said as I let my seat back and began to look up in the sky.

Chapter 26

We pulled up to the Detroit Mental Health Rehabilitation Residential. We walked in. Chuck walked up to the receptionist." Hello, I am Charles Matthews here to see Andrea Matthews."

The receptionist smiled and replied, "Ok come on back."

We followed her back to the room. When Chuck and I walked in her room I noticed that she had baby dolls, balloons, flowers and stuffed animals decorating her room.

"Hi mom. How are you?" Chuck asked as he walked over to her.

She is a beautiful woman. Just by looking at her you wouldn't believe that she is supposed to be here. She opened her mouth and said, "Chucky, how are you sweetie. Mama sorry baby, Mama's real sorry. Daddy mean, Daddy real mean! He beat mommy. Mommy beat Detrick, and mommy killed Detrick. Mommy didn't mean to kill Detrick. Mommy wishes she could have killed Granddaddy. Mommy sorry baby, Mama is so sorry."

Chuck has tears falling from his eyes; I couldn't help the tears that were falling from mine because I am witnessing a child of pain that is in an adult occupying a woman's body. She talked as if she was still in her child hood years.

I remembered Mrs. Lynn said that she chose God and Chucks Mom chose to take matters in her own hands. I do see the difference, but I think that Chuck will help her see the light or at least pray for her. The incident with his brother happened over eight years ago. Detrick would be 24 now. I stood here staring at her. I can feel her pain. I know God has forgiven me for what I've done so I know he will most definitely forgive Chucks mom. I know that he's forgiven her. Besides, God is the only one who matters anyway. I thought about the shots that I fired that ended up killing Stan. I said that I was going to kill him before I got there, but I didn't really know I was going to kill him. He forced me too. The whole situation is so messed up, but at the same time I figured it out. It's just like Yolanda Adams said in her song. God just needed a chance to prove to my enemy that he is God and I had to understand that everything had to work this way. God fixed it and I know if Mrs. Matthews decides to let God in, he'll fix hers too. I am living proof.

Chuck went over to his mom and laid his head upon her chest. "Mama, I love you. Mama God forgives you. You have to talk to God and tell him that you are sorry. He already knows, but you have to confess it with your mouth and it has to come from your heart." He sat up and hugged his mom. "Dear God, I am here asking for a blessing once again."

I walked over to Chuck and grabbed his hand so that more than one would come in agreement.

"I am asking that you enter into my mother's heart so that she knows that everything will be ok. It is not her fault that she was a victim of molestation from her father. It's not her fault that she was a victim of abuse from my father. Heavenly father it is never our fault when things that we have no knowledge of- happens to us, but it is our fault when we don't put it in your hands so that you can fight our battles. God, I am here asking that you bless us, bless my mother Lord. I know that she is forgiven once she asks to be. I have forgiven her, but it is not up to my forgiveness, it's yours. God, I thank you for what you have done thus far in my life. Thank you father; I notice that I often come asking you for so many things, but I forget to thank you as well, so I thank you Lord.

I thank you father, please help us Lord. Thank you for hearing Victoria and I last night. Thank you for hearing me right now. Lord I thank you and all blessings I ask in your son Jesus name. Amen"

"Amen"

"Amen"

Chuck and I both looked up shocked after the third "Amen" was said. It was Mrs. Matthews. A few tears fell from Chuck's eyes as he stared at his mom. Mrs. Matthews sat on the bed hugging her self then she began speaking.

"God, I am so sorry, I am so sorry. Please forgive me God. Give me the strength Lord. I am so proud of my boy, so proud. Lord please; give me the ability to show him. Give me the ability to show myself. I am so sorry" Mrs. Matthews said as she stood up and walked over to the window.

Chuck and I watched her as she began looking up in the sky. "Detrick mommy is so sorry. I know it doesn't mean much now, but mommy is so sorry. I know that you are an Angel now." She walked back over to us. She looked at me, "Chucky, who is this?" she asked.

I smiled and replied, "Hi Mrs. Matthews, my name is Victoria."

"Mama, this is going to be your daughter-in- law." Chuck said.

She smiled and then took her soft caramel hand and rubbed it across my face. "You are so pretty." She said softly. She hugged me, "everything is ok now."

I hugged her back and said, "It sure is." She let me go and walked over to Chuck. She embraced him with so much love. She hugged him, holding on to him real tight. "You take care of my Grand Baby ok." I looked at her because my mom just said that a few hours ago. Chuck smiled, looked at me and said, "Mama, you know I am."

My heart was tingling because I couldn't understand what everybody was talking about, if anything I think that I would be the one who would know first. She sat down on the bed and held her teddy bear.

"Ok Mama, we are going to leave now and I am going to come and check on you soon ok. You have to get well Mama so you can see your Grand baby." Chuck said.

I stood here staring at Chuck thinking, *oh now he's tripping too.* I wonder what has gotten into these people. What are they seeing that I don't see? Chuck and I were walking out. Mrs. Matthews looked at me as she held on to her Teddy.

"Bye Victoria, it was very nice to meet you." She waved.

"The pleasure was all mines. You will be seeing me very soon." I replied.

Five months later … … …

Five months have passed by so rapidly. Chuck and I finally walked the stage, even though I threw up all over the stage. We received our High School Diplomas. For my birthday, Chuck threw me a surprise birthday party. All of my family and his were there. Mama is working at Beauty by Us, hair salon. She started Melanie's hair school for Natural's and received her license. Jasmine, transferred from Cass Tech to Renaissance High school. She's in the 10th grade now. Mama has been going to court to try and get custody of my nephew Anthony. We went out to the grave yard to pay respects to Terrance, Jasmine's other son. Chuck and I married three months ago. Bishop Morton gave us a wedding for free.

Guess who was my maid of honor? Yep, my mother did me the honors. Mama Jackson was one of my bride's maids, as well as Jasmine, my little cousin Chandra, and a very special bride's maid, my mother-in-law.

Our wedding was so beautiful. Chuck's Aunt Lynn did the majority of the decorating. Chuck and I both started classes the beginning of September. The only thing is I think I might have to take a few semesters off, because **I'm going to be a mommy.** Yeah I'm young, but I'm married and God is on our side. I will have both Grannies' to help me out, a blessing of a husband; my baby will have an aunt, and a grandfather I think.

Mama and Lieutenant Braxton (well he insist that we call him Simon) has fallen head over heels in love with one another. He has a very big four bedroom house so Mama and Jasmine lives there with him. I can't rush it, but Mama and Simon set the date for December 19th. That's going to be both of their Christmas gift.

Mama is now an Usher at Mt. Zion Full Gospel. Jasmine, my aunt Jessie, my mother- in- law, Mama and Simon, myself and Chuck walked up to the alter and rededicated our lives back to Christ as a family.

I am so happy and nervous because I know that if I get pregnant again I won't need a pregnancy test because I have two Moms who will tell me before I will ever know.

Well I have to go because I am spilling mayonnaise and Cheetos all over my shirt. Oh yeah I am having twins, the ultrasound revealed that they are both girls. I'm thinking of naming them Angel and Miracle. I'll stay in touch to let you know how everything works out. Though now that I have God, I am sure that everything will be fine and I know that it won't be more than Chuck and I can handle. See ya!

Oh~ one last thing, well maybe a few more things I have to tell you. Chuck was hired at a Youth Home as a Youth mentor, and he decide to get his degree in Social Work. He visit's different homes and motivates the men of today to be all they can be and that doesn't mean joining the army. He's doing it in style because I brought him the green drop top BMW he wanted so badly with the money that Stan left me.

He took out a $ 1,000,000 life insurance policy on himself and put it in my name and he also left $100,000 of his own money, plus the house. Stan wrote me a letter before he died. After the funeral his attorney delivered it to me.

The letter basically was apologizing for what he had done to me because he knew that his day was coming soon. Of course I sold the house, because I wanted no part of the nightmares and tragedies that occurred in it. I thought about the time when I said I was going to go through the house and pick up all of my fallen pedals, but I realized my pedals had shed for a reason. I let them die out in that house because my root is stronger than ever and I am blossoming with better and stronger pedals every year.

I went next door to check and see if there was actually a Mrs. Angel living there. They said there was a lady there by the name of Angel Love, but she had died about five years ago. I don't know how everything worked out like that, but all I can say is ever since I turned my life over to God my life has done a 360 degree turn around.

I admit, when I first gave my life to God, the devil tried to attack me in so many different ways, but my faith and Chuck's faith in me helped me through. I know that Life's not going to be perfect and it's not meant to be, but working to perfection is always a goal.

Well, the construction workers are disturbing me. They are building Chuck's new office since he is the co- owner of Latoya's beauty supply and salon. I thought I'd surprise him with it for his birthday. I figured since Toy did have the idea for her dream, I might as well keep her dream alive.

I never gave up my dream either. I decided to write my own autobiography which you're reading now and Mama wants me to write hers. She said that she has a story to tell that will help Mom's who've felt bad about abandoning their children for drugs and men.

So stay tuned. I've already started on it. I try to hold back my tears but it's so deep I can't help it. Hopefully, I can finish it before I drop this double load. These twins aint no joke y'all. Pray for me, while I pray for you. I love you.

Yours Truly,

Mrs. Victoria Mathews
I'za married now. ☺ God Bless!

To my readers:

I pray that The Strangest Love has provided you with knowledge and insight on the everyday lives of our neglected and abused youth. We're just like everyone else, it just might seem to take us a little longer to get there, but trust me, WE WILL GET THERE.

I hope that this story has blessed you and provided some bright lights into your life because it has brought some into mine. God is so good and so worthy to be praised.

Can I share something with you? I don't know if you know this or not, but YOU ARE SPECIAL. You deserve to be loved and you deserve to be blessed, but you have to put yourself in that position. Nothing worth having comes easy except the love of GOD and his son Jesus Christ who died for our sins. His love is automatic. As soon as you were formed in your mother's womb, GOD ALREADY LOVED YOU. Nothing's changed.

He will never turn his back on us. People may fail us every single time, but God will never fail us. Get to know him and you'll find out once you get to know God, you will get to know yourself.

No matter what dream you decide to pursue in life, just make sure you pursue one. Just like Mama Jackson told Victoria and Toy, *"It's better to wake up and chase a dream instead of sleeping your entire life away."*

Don't spend your entire life asleep! Wake up and explore this beautiful world that God has created. Despite the worldly circumstance, God is still good and you can still be happy.

Thank you for reading my novel The Strangest Love. I hope that you have enjoyed it. Please feel free to email me with your comments at authormelaniecalhoun@yahoo.com I check my emails personally and will respond as soon as time permits.

Remember your only competition is Y.O.U! And sometimes, we have to learn how to get out of our own way!

Love Always,

Melanie "GODmadeQueen" Calhoun

Dedications/ Acknowledgments:

First and foremost, I would like to acknowledge My Father in Heaven. God, you are so worthy and I Thank You. If it wasn't for God, I would not be able to share with you the talent that he has given me.

I also would like to acknowledge those family and friends who believed in me and who has continuously supported me, you know who you are. I love you very much and humbly thank you from the depth of my soul and from the bottom of my heart.

I would like to dedicate this book to the "Victoria's" that's out there. You can make it too. It's a lot of "Stan's" out there at this very moment. I pray that the demon's that lies within you are cast out. The Chuck's that are out there trying to rise above the street life, I feel your pain. I pray that more Chuck's would stand up every day because <u>we need you!</u>

God Bless,

With Love,

Melanie "GODmadeQueen" Calhoun

Plot Summary

Set in the City of <u>Detroit, Michigan</u>, The Strangest Love is the story of Victoria Campbell, a *eighteen* year old daughter of a drug addicted, prostitute mother, and unknown father. Stan, Victoria's Uncle, an FBI Agent, becomes her legal guardian after she was left at his doorstep. After being abandoned by her mother, separated from her baby sister, and having no ties to her father, she begins to believe in the idea that Stan is all she has and the "Love" he shows her, is the only love she'll ever know and need.

Victoria maintains a sense of balance of being a girl and the woman she's forced to become, by maintaining her relationship with her best friend Toy. Though, she shares everything with Toy, Victoria refuses to share her secret. Unknown to her Uncle, Victoria meets and falls in love with Charles "Chuck" Matthews and they become High School sweethearts. Chuck begins to sense something is wrong with Victoria and suggest her to believe in GOD and trust HIM with her secrets.

Her life changes after she confesses that she does believe GOD exists. It seems like the bright lights and weight that was lifted from Victoria, darkened and piled up heavier than before when she is reunited with her mother in a hospital bed, after being found shot twice in an ally, left for dead. Noticing Victoria is facing more trials than ever, Chuck continues to pray with Victoria, helping her find her Spiritual strength.

As she continues to strengthen her Faith, Victoria discovers she's not the only one with secrets. Victoria overhears her mother revealing a horribly shocking secret to her baby sister. After Victoria learns that she was not the only one manipulated and abused, she sets out for revenge. When she arrives to confront her abuser, in the heat of the argument, shots are fired. Victoria flees the scene and is now wanted for a possible double homicide.

Despite the unfortunate tragedies, the story ends with a surprisingly very happy ending. There are triumphs over tragedies.

Printed in the United States
By Bookmasters